It
Takes
Two

Natalie Cox is a lifelong fan of both romantic comedy and dogs, and the sometimes-proud owner of a mantle Great Dane, Grace, who makes up in brawn what she lacks in brains, and Billie, a Merle Great Dane puppy whose life's ambition is to annoy her elder sister. Natalie's first book, *Not Just for Christmas*, won the RNA's Romantic Comedy Award in 2019 and was published in ten countries. When not being pestered by dogs, Natalie divides her time between writing and bookselling. She co-owns one of London's leading independent bookshops, Ink@84 Books, in Highbury.

Find out more: www.nataliecox.me or follow Grace and Billie's antics on Instagram @natcoxwrites

It
Takes
Two

Natalie Cox

ORION

First published in Great Britain in 2021 by Orion Fiction,
an imprint of The Orion Publishing Group Ltd,
Carmelite House, 50 Victoria Embankment
London EC4Y 0DZ

An Hachette UK Company

1 3 5 7 9 10 8 6 4 2

A CIP catalogue record for this book is
available from the British Library.

ISBN (Paperback) 978 1 4091 8331 0
ISBN (eBook) 978 1 4091 8332 7

Typeset by Input Data Services Ltd, Somerset

Printed in Great Britain by Clays Ltd, Elcograf S.p.A.

MIX
Paper from
responsible sources
FSC® C104740

www.orionbooks.co.uk

To all those we've lost this turbulent year,
but most especially M.

And for Schrödinger's cat, who lives and dies in parallel
worlds, and giant dog breeds everywhere, who bring their
own bit of magic to our universe.

Prologue

You know those people you see flying down the road on tiny wheels, bobbing their heads to music, weaving effortlessly in and out of traffic, like they're somehow immune to both the laws of physics and the consequences of a sudden impact? Well, I'm one of them.

Which is totally annoying, I know.

In my defence, roller-skating is the only thing I'm really good at. I wish it could have been something more noteworthy, or of greater value to society. Like quantum physics or classical violin or brain surgery. Even cooking would have amounted to a higher contribution. But we don't get to choose our talents in life, do we? They choose us.

The upside is that no matter how bad things get (*quite* bad of late, to be perfectly frank), skating is the one thing that never lets me down. When I'm out on my quads, sailing through the streets of London, the world seems to glow that little bit more brightly, like it's been colour-washed. And with the city rushing past and the wind kissing my cheeks, I barely even notice all the bad stuff. Run-down housing estates, overflowing bins, traffic jams, dirty pigeons, scraggly parks, even the train wreck that is my life – it all looks more palatable at high speed. Everything is improved with acceleration. Any racing enthusiast will tell you that velocity alone is worth the effort.

I bought my first pair of roller skates when I was eleven,

with money earned from delousing my own hair. My primary school was perpetually infested, and my feckless parents simply weren't up to the task. When my older sister (who was usually drafted in for the more rigorous jobs in our household) point-blank refused, I was offered 10p per nit. I combed my wet hair assiduously every Sunday evening for half an hour, and after thirteen weeks, I'd saved enough to buy my first pair of rainbow quads. I've been a big fan of skating ever since; because unlike most things in life, skating is as much fun as it looks.

Which doesn't say much about life, does it?

I studied psychology at university. And while I think hobbies are important, there's a reason they don't really feature in Maslow's hierarchy of needs. The things he singled out in his pyramid – food, security, love, esteem, success in one's endeavours – I don't really think he was talking about ten-pin bowling there. Or skating. So, as much as my hobby pleases me, at the end of the day it's not something I can point to proudly and say: this is me. This is who I am.

So who am I, then? Today is New Year's Eve, and maybe it's because it's been an especially crap year that I'm asking myself that question. Because as the year draws to a close, I realise that my life falls short in every single one of Maslow's categories. That's right – all five of them.

At the tender age of thirty, I'm already a failure.

Chapter One

Happy new year to me. This morning when I wake, my head feels like it's been stapled to my pillow, and my tongue feels like it's done a few laps around the salt pans. Charlie Bucket, who is under strict instructions to remain on his side of the bed at all times, has ignored the golden rule and is splayed across my left leg, cutting off my circulation entirely. I try to wiggle my toes but can feel nothing. I am effectively an amputee.

Though he is not a purebred, Charlie Bucket looks exactly like one of those dogs that has a wooden barrel tied beneath its neck, though why anyone would want to extend the body mass of a dog like Charlie Bucket by tying *anything* to him is beyond me. He is quite enough dog as it is, with or without a barrel. His head is the size of a large inflatable beach ball, his coat is a mottled brown and white and extremely shaggy, and his feet are like large, hairy dumbbells. On rainy days, I have to dip each one in a bucket of warm water just to get the mud off. Drying them requires a blanket-sized towel and Olympic levels of patience.

With some effort, I manage to extract my leg from beneath his sleeping form. My phone pings and Charlie Bucket does that canine thing of moving from unconsciousness to high alert in a split second, raising his head to stare at me accusingly, as if to say: *Surely that phone should be on silent at this time of day?* His enormous jowls wobble slightly with the effort of condemnation.

I reach for the phone, even though I already know who the text is from. Today is Sunday, the day when my lovelorn ex-boyfriend Marcus most acutely feels his singledom, as if the day is some sort of personal affliction that he alone must bear. Perhaps many single people feel this way, but because I work Saturdays in the shop, Sunday for me signals the start of my weekend, and is the day when I totally indulge myself. It is most definitely *not* a Marcus day.

Happy new year! What you up to today?

Hmm. How best to reply to his opening salvo? Over the past several weeks I have already enlisted some of the more obvious excuses: illness, period pain, toothache, piles. Perhaps I should tell the truth this week, instead.

Nursing a hangover.

Big night last night?

Ah. Another dilemma. I know from experience that if Marcus thinks my own social life is better than his, it will plunge him into a deep pit of despair, one which I will ultimately have to dig him out of. Equally, if he thinks my social life is crap (which it is) he will come at me with renewed urgency, bombarding me with all the reasons why my life is better with him than without. So it's a finely judged line I need to draw here.

Middling, but turned out better than expected.

Anything I should know?

What Marcus means by this is: *Anyone I should know about?* He keeps close tabs on my dating life, ranking the guys I see on his own personal scale of 1 (far too close for comfort) to 10 (the last guy on earth I would settle for). He does this based on a) his extensive knowledge of me and b) the tiny snippets of information I drip-feed him about who I've gone out with. Any sane person might well wonder why I share details of my love life with my ex. I do so because he insists;

4

because, according to Marcus, *mates do that sort of thing*.

The day I broke up with him, Marcus had looked at me with mournful eyes and asked tremulously if we could still be friends. *Of course, we'll still be friends,* I reassured him, unwittingly. I'm not heartless, and everyone has room in their life for more friends, don't they? Without missing a beat, Marcus promptly moved me like a statuette from the girlfriend shelf to that of best mate, where I remain trapped to this day, seemingly for all eternity. Right now, I type a carefully considered response.

Nah. Just out with Bianca.

OK, it's a teeny-weeny lie, but a necessary one, as I know this will stop his interrogation cold. My best friend Bianca and Marcus are like chalk and cheese. Actually, it's worse than that; whenever they are in close proximity, they physically repel each other, like the positive and negative ions in magnets. The truth is Charlie Bucket and I spent New Year's Eve on our respective sofas, me nursing a good bottle of Sancerre and re-watching old black and white musicals, and him masticating an old Birkenstock he'd taken a shine to. All told, it was a jolly evening, better than most.

During the eighteen months I was seeing Marcus, Bianca basically refused to hang out with me if he was around. *Clem, I need all of you when we're together, not just your left ear lobe,* Bianca used to say. Her contention was that Marcus sapped 98 per cent of my being, and at times, I couldn't disagree with her. It was like I mislaid myself during the time I was with him and became someone else entirely; I wasn't his partner, I was more like his sidekick, enabling him to wreak devastation on both our lives. I was Gromit to his Wallace. Rocky to his Bullwinkle. Which is why I broke up with him, in the end. Or at least, one of the many reasons why.

My phone pings again with his reply: *Oh.*

Two letters that contain so much more: jealousy, frustration, longing. Sometimes I think Marcus would change gender for me if he thought it would bolster our friendship. I stare at the phone screen and am suddenly walloped by a wave of remorse. Charlie Bucket, with his unlimited capacity for canine empathy, chooses this moment to stretch out fully, pushing his enormous paws deep into my side, prodding me to do the right thing. He raises his head then and looks at me with his big, soulful eyes. As usual, the damn dog can see right through me. I take a deep breath and type into the phone.

Hey. What you up to Thursday night?

Marcus replies at the speed of light, just as I'd known he would.

Nothing! At your disposal!

There's a comedy thing on. I'll text you the details.

Cool! See you then.

I chuck the phone to one side and lie back against the pillows. It will not kill me to spend an evening at a comedy club with Marcus. And in the meantime, I have just bought myself four days of Marcus-free time. Barely a moment later, my phone pings again. This time from Bianca.

Come for brunch at Dolly's.

Bianca's approach to communication is entirely different. She not only speaks, but thinks, in the imperative.

I thought you'd be post-coital, I reply.

My cup runneth over. Need sustenance.

Quit bragging.

That was more of a complaint.

Some of us have not drunk from that particular cup in months.

Your cup will filleth again.

Shut up about my damn cup.

*

An hour later Bianca and I are slouched on a battered black sofa made of not-quite-leather at the back of our favourite bar, eating buffalo chicken wings and sipping Bloody Marys. Dolly's is more like a down-at-heel pub with modest aspirations to more: the food is edible but not gastro, the décor is dominated by cheap chrome and amber lighting, and the cocktails are both affordable and refreshingly ordinary. No woodland bitters or chestnut puree Bellini served here. Plus, it's owned by the eponymous Dolly, a big-chested woman with a hearty laugh and a broad halo of bleached blonde hair, who styles herself after Dolly Parton (a woman who has just about achieved sainthood in my book). I only wish I'd thought of this concept first, and all my problems would be solved.

'I need a new life,' I tell Bianca.

'Don't be ridiculous,' says Bianca. 'You just haven't mastered the remote on the old one yet.'

'I can't even *find* the remote. And if I did, it would be out of batteries,' I grumble.

'Down the back of the sofa,' she says authoritatively. 'That's where it always is.'

'No,' I shake my head. 'I'm telling you. It's more than that. I need a factory reset. A total overhaul.'

'Listen to me. There is *nothing* wrong with your life. It just needs . . . tweaking,' she says, flourishing a long stalk of celery at me like a wand, before taking an enormous bite from it.

'Paragraphs and nipples get tweaked,' I say. 'Not lives.'

'You have everything going for you.'

'Such as . . .'

'You're self-sufficient and gainfully employed,' she says. I shake my head.

'I'm perpetually broke. And my boss hates me,' I reply

7

sullenly. She points the stub of celery at me.

'Your boss doesn't hate you. He just doesn't *trust* you. There's a difference.'

'He thinks I'm a thief.'

'Because you stole from him.'

'Because I *borrowed* from him.'

'Without his knowledge. Which is pretty much the same as stealing,' she says. 'Anyway, you have fabulous friends.' She smiles at me smugly.

'Apart from my stalker ex-boyfriend.'

'Apart from him,' she agrees. 'And you own your own home, which is not trivial in this city,' she reminds me.

'The bank owns my home. And the tax office. I'm like a passing pigeon who's temporarily roosting there. Until I default on my mortgage and some squatters kick me out.'

'And you love your job.'

'No,' I say emphatically, shaking my head. 'I like my job. Sometimes.' But not much lately, if I'm being completely honest, something I am loath to admit even to Bianca. Managing a cheese shop has not proven to be as nourishing to the soul as I'd hoped when I left my previous role in marketing three years ago.

'But you love cheese,' she says.

'And is that really a good thing?'

'On top of that, you have a family who . . .' Bianca stops short and frowns, suddenly at a loss for words. She knows that I'm decidedly ambivalent about all things familial: my parents, while nice enough people, are barely worthy of the label; and my older sister Julia, though well-meaning, can only be described as charmless. I wait patiently for her to continue.

'A family who what?' I ask, genuinely curious.

'Well,' Bianca says, popping the celery in her mouth. 'At

least, you've *got* a family. Which is more than some people have.'

'So, I'm better off than an orphan?'

'Technically, yes.'

'Thanks. I'll remind you of that the next time my parents hit me up for cash,' I say. 'At least you have the common decency not to mention my love life,' I add grudgingly. Bianca blinks at me.

'What love life?'

'Very funny.'

She kicks off her tall boots and folds her impossibly long legs beneath her like an origami swan. Beneath us, Charlie Bucket sprawls across the floor like a living rug. At full stretch, his body is slightly longer than the three-seat sofa we are sitting on. Not every pub in the neighbourhood will tolerate him, but Dolly is his biggest fan – yet another reason why we come here.

A bald guy in a cheap pale grey suit who is *clearly* too old for us has planted himself at the table a few feet away and has been giving Bianca the eye ever since we sat down. *Yawn.* Bianca is tall and thin and preternaturally blonde, and she has a keen sense of style, which means she's a man-magnet. I once asked her what her real hair colour was. '*Dreary,*' she'd said. '*Trust me. I've done humanity an enormous favour by never letting it see the light of day.*'

In the game of life, Bianca takes no prisoners. She works in advertising and has been fired more times than I can count, not because she is incompetent, but because she is constitutionally incapable of towing the line. Bosses are terrified of her, and Bianca delights in tormenting them, but she is bloody good at her job in an industry that recognises talent and rewards it amply. Which is why I generally let her pick up the tab.

9

This is in stark contrast to my own looks, which are more of the short, dark and sturdy variety. I'm five foot two-and-a-half inches tall, something I resigned myself to years ago; it has forever consigned me to the front row in group photographs, the middle seat on road trips, and platform heels when I want to be taken seriously. It also means that at the age of thirty, I still occasionally get asked for proof of age when ordering drinks. At least twice weekly, when I am out walking Charlie Bucket, someone makes a joke about me riding him instead, and while I'm not overweight for my size, I'm what my mother likes to call 'solidly built' and my father 'Rubenesque'. My hair is dark brown and shoulder-length; years ago, a stylist advised me that long hair would make me appear even shorter, advice I have heeded faithfully ever since.

In truth, I don't begrudge my height. There are definite advantages: apparently, I'm at less risk of cancer and I will probably live longer, provided I do not get swept up by a street cleaner who fails to see me on the side of the road. Being short also means my centre of gravity is low; I have better balance than most people, which is why I'm good at skating. On the flip side, statistically I am less likely to find a mate, something my experience has borne out. Since my first boyfriend at the age of fifteen, I've dated only three other guys, and all of them have been vertically challenged; the pool of availability is definitely smaller for those of us swimming in the shallow end.

Unlike Bianca, who is currently seeing three guys *simultaneously*, all of whom are called Will. Don't even ask how this came about; I have a strong suspicion that the last one only got the job because of his name, though Bianca insists it was merely a coincidence. Will #1 is a charming, urbane art historian who works for Christie's. He is half Algerian, half British and 100 per cent eye candy, and for a while I thought that Bianca had met her perfect match. But over time it has emerged that he is also a hypochondriac, or at the very least, a germ magnet, who is forever cancelling dates at the last minute due to some sort of trivial affliction (man flu, inflamed bunions, palpitations, whatever). Lately, I've taken to calling him Ill Will.

Will #2 is a self-proclaimed fan of 'ethical non-monogamy' (what my parents would have called *swinging* but I just call *skanky*). 'If he's a skank, then so am I,' says Bianca proudly. 'No need to crow about it,' I say defensively. 'Not all of us can be skanks. Even when we want to be.' Which I don't, by the way. Dating multiple partners strikes me as the romantic equivalent of one of those expensive gastronomic tasting menus: the first two courses are amazing, but after that you just start to feel bloated and regretful. Will #2 does something vague (and possibly shady) in real-estate finance and drives a souped-up, soft-top wannabe sports car. He knows all about the other two Wills, apparently, and is fine about it. '*You do you*,' he told Bianca on their third date when she confessed she was seeing other men.

'What? And he'll do everyone else,' I'd asked her. Since then, I've taken to calling him Free Willy. A moniker he apparently loves.

Bianca's final paramour is a strapping Dutch guy called Willem with a hearty manner and a fetching gap-toothed smile. He is so tall that on the one occasion we met, my line of sight fell just above his navel, which means that (somewhat inevitably) I've dubbed him Sheer Will. Sheer Will works in advertising for a rival firm, and he and Bianca met when they were both pitching to the same client and she got the meeting time wrong. Bianca lost the pitch but won an eye-wateringly expensive French meal with Willem, who insisted on taking her out to one of the best restaurants in Soho as a consolation prize. (And then taking her to bed, which apparently was even more of a prize, according to Bianca.)

Unsurprisingly, she frequently gets confused and sends the wrong text to the wrong Will. Last weekend, she accidentally double-booked Ill Will and Free Willy and when both turned up at the wine bar where she was waiting, she had to do a runner out the back door, cackling down the phone to me from the taxi.

'Maybe I should go abroad,' I say with a sigh, emptying my drink. 'Then I could reinvent myself completely.'

She frowns. 'Abroad where?'

'Dunno. I've always fancied Bora Bora.' I grin at her.

'That's not a real place,' she says, waving a dismissive hand.

'Tell that to the Tahitians.'

'How do you know you'd even like it there?'

'What's not to like? Turquoise seas, palm trees, bungalows on stilts.' Bianca frowns at me.

'You've been watching *South Pacific* again, haven't you,' she says in a reproachful tone, as if I've relapsed on an old cocaine habit. Bianca knows I have an escapist's predilection for old musicals, especially those of Rogers and Hammerstein, a taste she patently does not share. And it may or may not be true that Charlie Bucket and I spent a large chunk of last night watching *South Pacific* for the hundredth time. Though I would never admit it to her.

'Plus, it happens to be the farthest point away on the globe from London,' I add.

'I thought that was somewhere in New Zealand,' she says sceptically.

'OK, it's a few thousand miles *away* from the farthest

point away on the globe. But Bora Bora sounds better.'

'You do realise they speak French there,' she says.

'Not in the musical,' I reply.

'But you can't carry a tune to save your life. So it definitely wouldn't work.'

'Honestly, I need a hiatus from my life,' I say, a bit desperately.

Bianca narrows her gaze at me. 'If it comes to fight or flight, I'd have pegged you as a fighter,' she says.

I shrug. 'You'd have been wrong.'

Just then, the bartender comes over to us, clearing our empty plates and glasses. This one is new and looks about fourteen. We've always suspected that Dolly is a bit of a taskmaster because her staff turnover is faster than those revolving toast makers you see in luxury hotels. When he's finished, the bartender turns to me and cocks his head to one side. 'Need anything else here?' he asks with a cheeky grin. He's wearing a black T-shirt and skin-tight black jeans and, for once, his attention is fixed squarely on *me,* rather than Bianca. I can't help feeling a tiny bit chuffed, even though I'm old enough to be his . . . auntie.

'No thanks, we're all set,' I reply.

'Good to see you,' he says quietly, in a slightly too familiar tone. I freeze and glance up at him, while Bianca throws me a look. He's actually blushing!

'Um . . . you too,' I say, a little embarrassed. *Poor kid!*

'I've got your IOU. From the other night,' he adds. 'Should I put it on this tab?' Bianca and I frown at each other. We've not been here since before Christmas, so I have no idea what he's talking about.

'Which IOU?' I ask.

'You wrote it out. Last Wednesday. When you forgot

your card?' He brandishes a small white paper cocktail napkin with some faint pen scratchings. Bianca turns to me with an accusatory look.

'Have you been two-timing me?' she asks.

'Pot. Kettle. Black,' I reply staunchly. I turn back to him. 'I'm sorry, I wasn't in here last Wednesday,' I inform him politely. I know this with certainty: on Wednesday nights I'm to be found jockeying around an indoor roller derby track with two dozen other brawny women on wheels.

'Oh,' he says uneasily, his eyes darting from me to Bianca. 'But . . . your name's Clem, right?'

'Yeah,' I say cautiously.

He holds out the napkin towards me. 'So . . . who wrote this?'

He seems well and truly confused at this point, and not a little disappointed. I lean forward, squinting at the napkin, where I can just make out:

I owe you £12.75. See you soon. Love Clem xx

'This isn't my writing,' I say with a frown. 'For one thing,' I point out, 'I never sign my name with those little xx's, as a matter of principle.'

'I can vouch for that,' says Bianca, nodding authoritatively.

'But she looked just like you,' the waiter says doubtfully.

'Honestly. It wasn't me,' I say. This guy is really starting to irritate me now. He gives me a wounded look, like I have somehow just betrayed him.

'OK,' he says half-heartedly. We watch as he makes his way back to the bar.

'I don't think it *is* OK,' says Bianca in a whisper. 'I think you may have just broken him.'

'What the hell?' I whisper back.

'Maybe we should have just paid it,' she admonishes.

'Why should we pay someone else's tab? Someone who's deliberately posing as me!'

'Because he'll get into trouble!'

'It's not my fault that he extended credit to someone who looks like me!'

'No one is blaming you.'

'*He* was blaming me! Honestly, sometimes I feel like the entire universe is conspiring against me!'

'Clem. It's not that bad.'

'Anyway, why would *anyone* in their right mind want to be me?' I grumble. 'My life is a mess.'

Bianca raises her glass in a toast. 'Maybe theirs is even worse.'

Chapter Two

How exactly is my life a mess? Let me count the ways.

First, my boss thinks I'm a thief. Maybe this is overstating things, but it's not without basis. I did siphon a few hundred pounds from the shop's coffers a few months ago in a desperate moment of financial need, but at the time I genuinely thought of it as a short-term loan. I had every intention of repaying it before he noticed. And I had *no* idea he got text notifications of the shop's bank transactions, which strikes me as a little sneaky, even if he *is* the owner. In that respect at least, my actions were completely innocuous; in other respects, they were completely amoral. Suffice to say my boss was not best pleased. It was a miracle he didn't sack me on the spot, but at the time he was in the middle of a big case, and frankly he had bigger fish to fry. Six weeks later I am still officially 'on probation', struggling to redeem myself in his eyes.

Second, my upstairs neighbour has taken out a restraining order against my dog. It is still strange for me to write the words 'my dog', having never intended to acquire a flatmate, much less one who sheds, but life takes unexpected turns, and Charlie Bucket was most definitely an unexpected turn. Even with all his hygiene and behavioural issues, I still prefer my hairy, oversized flatmate to my odious, opera-singing neighbour, so either I need to broker an armistice between them, or one of them has got to go. Preferably the one without a tail.

Third, my ex-boyfriend refuses to accept that I am no longer his best friend. I fully accept that this is as much my fault as his, because in breaking up with him, I somehow enabled his long-term dependency, like some sort of co-conspirator. Nearly three years on we are both stuck in a permanent groove of singledom, like broken LPs. Marcus clearly needs to enroll in a twelve-step programme to wean himself off me, or failing that, he needs to find a new girl-friend. Either way, I need to be free to move on with my not-so-great life.

Fourth, my parents have fled the country, leaving me to deal with their shambolic tax affairs. One does not expect one's parents, even mine, to mismanage their own finances. What kind of crap role model is that? Admittedly, I con-tributed to their financial problems when they loaned me the deposit on my flat, money that technically belonged to HMRC, as it turns out, but how was I to know? I have now struck a deal with the tax office to pay off their arrears in monthly installments, an amount that, when coupled with my mortgage and other outgoings, only very *slightly* exceeds my income, which partly accounts for the first item on my list. It will take a mere four years to pay off HMRC, which is approximately one-fifth the length of the remaining term on my mortgage. Meanwhile, my parents are gleefully eking out the remainder of their meagre pension on the beaches of Kerala, a destination they chose after consulting the global cost-of-living index, where the bottom five countries were: Uzbekistan, Syria, Pakistan, Afghanistan and India.

Namaste, Mum and Dad.

Last but not least, I'm addicted to cheese. Which inad-vertently led to all of the above.

*

According to my mother, my first love was cheese – and looking back, I reckon cheese has proved my undoing. If I were not addicted to cheese (and more specifically, to aged farmhouse Cheddar, which is to say *real* Cheddar, not the plastic version that masquerades in its place on most supermarket shelves) then I never would have met Marcus, my extremely needy, highly excitable, cheese-loving ex-boyfriend. And if I had not met Marcus, I would not have been persuaded to chuck in my well-paid job as a marketing analyst with Allegra Solutions to 'follow my passion' into the world of cheese, a passion which has reduced me to near-penury and has also turned my infatuation with cheese into a bitchy love–hate affair.

If you're in any doubt that cheese is addictive, ask a biochemist to explain how the proteins inside dairy products, especially solid ones, act as mild opiates in the brain, producing tiny hits of dopamine with every bite. Cheddar has the highest concentration of these proteins, so it really is the crack cocaine of cheeses. According to my mother, by the time I was four years old I could gnaw my way through an entire block of Cheddar in far less time than it took her to whip up a more balanced meal: cauliflower cheese, for example, or lasagne. So being the practical sort, she filled the fridge and left me to it. (Recently, when I registered online to access my digital records from the NHS, I saw that the health visitor had actually written the words *benign neglect* in my case notes.)

It was Marcus who first spotted the sign in the window of Say Cheese, a small artisan cheese shop around the corner from his offices in Bermondsey, advertising for a shop manager. Marcus harangued me for days to apply, convincing me that I deserved to be in a job I felt truly passionate about, rather than one I was merely good at. And once I'd secured the job at Say Cheese (by tinkering only *slightly* with my CV, inventing retail experience I needed but did not have), it was Marcus who persuaded me to invest in the one-bedroom flat directly above the shop, which came onto the market almost as soon as I'd taken the job. *It was kismet!* Marcus said. Paying rent was a mug's game if one could possibly afford to buy, he argued, plus I'd save zillions on commuting costs.

So I took the job, bought the flat (with money borrowed from my parents), and not two months after I'd moved in, I discovered a three-month-old puppy tied up outside the shop's door, with a hastily scrawled note tucked into its collar apologising for the inconvenience. Why the puppy's owner chose Say Cheese only became apparent later that morning, when I discovered that dogs, too, can be addicted to cheese. Who knew?

I did think about calling a rescue society that first day – of course I did. But once he'd had his fill of old Cheddar rinds, Charlie Bucket curled up on the shop floor and went to sleep, and truthfully, I was a little bit smitten. I did not know that, at that stage, the puppy was only a tiny fraction of his eventual size and body weight. Eight months and nearly 200 pounds later, I discovered through genetic testing that he is three-quarters St Bernard and one-quarter Irish Wolfhound; in dog terms, that's like crossing Jonny Wilkinson with LeBron James. Marcus played a pivotal role in this, too; he was all for me keeping the puppy (conveniently, his lease was strictly no pets), but once again he pressed me enthusiastically. *I owned my own home now, didn't I?* There was nothing to stop Charlie Bucket from moving in. So really, cheese is to blame.

And Marcus.

*

I met Marcus on an introductory cheese-making course three years after I'd moved to London. The course was a birthday gift from my parents (back in the days when they bought *me* things, rather than the other way around). I went along excited, hoping to learn the secrets of rennet and whey and bacteria, but instead I got Marcus, together with the discovery that cheese is far better to buy than to make. It took sixty-five pounds and a rather dreary afternoon's discussion of skimmers, thermometers and muslin to find out what I probably should have known in the first place: that my cheesy talents lay in consumption rather than production.

Amazingly, Marcus *did* get inspired by the course, and managed to produce two batches of rather gluey ricotta and another batch of something he optimistically called mozzarella in the weeks that followed. Having traded phone numbers, a few Sunday afternoons later he texted me out of the blue to ask if I wanted to sample his latest effort, inviting me for homemade pizza at his flat in Deptford. I went along with mixed feelings, weighing up the pros and cons en route. Pros: He seemed likeable enough, and relatively normal. Also, he wasn't bad-looking: neat and lean and angular, with a long, thin face and a nose that was well made for the job. I'm not averse to strong features, but I'd noticed at the workshop that from the side, Marcus's nose extended like a banner out in front of his face. Cons: I suspected he might be boring. *Ha!* If only I'd been a better judge of character. Marcus is many, many things. But boring is not one of them.

We were the only participants under thirty that day, so naturally we'd ended up standing next to each other and shared a series of knowing smiles and raised eyebrows at our overzealous instructor, a bald, chunky fellow with startled eyes who introduced himself as Zinger. (That was our first moment of sceptical exchange: *What sort of person calls himself*

Zinger?) Zinger was like a children's TV presenter on speed: all snappy elastic smiles, over-the-top hyperbole and frantic gesticulation. It goes without saying he was fanatical about cheese.

During the break, Marcus told me he worked in the law (in fact he's a paralegal, so technically this was not a falsehood, but it was still a trifle misleading) and in a moment of premature candour, said that he'd recently broken things off with his university girlfriend. (This was more than a trifle, it was a giant *pavlova* of a lie; in fact, she'd dumped him for a distant cousin, whom she'd met at a family wedding the previous summer, though I did not discover this until we'd been dating for several months.) But that day he seemed easy to talk to, and relatively harmless, so when he asked for my number at the end of the workshop, I surrendered it willingly enough.

Actually, our first date went much better than expected. Apart from cheese (in the end, his homemade mozzarella had to be *poured* onto the pizza, like dairy sludge), I discovered we had two other things in common: we were both prevaricators (which is to say, we both have a talent for ducking and dodging), and we both hated to spend time with our respective families. *Kismet!* Don't get me wrong – I love my family. I just don't like to hang out with them, and Marcus is the same, which is why he still insists that I attend his extended family gatherings as his plus one, like I'm some sort of human shield.

We lapsed into a relationship, the way you do when you're young and don't know any better. And truthfully, we had some good moments, mostly early on, before I discovered that Marcus was impulsive and needy and well-meaning and a little bit hapless. Things always took a turn for the worse when Marcus got involved, but he had a way of carrying me along in a great swirling current of misguided enthusiasm. Like female flotsam.

In all, Marcus and I were officially 'dating' for eighteen months; we have now been apart for nearly twice that length of time, though it often feels like much longer. Decades. Centuries, even. Because being Marcus's mate is even more exhausting than being his girlfriend. If anything, I am now privy to even more of the permutations of his daily existence: the ongoing row with his therapist, the weird rash he gets on the soles of his feet when he's nervous, his obsession with winter sun to combat his moods (followed by the inevitable angst over his carbon footprint whenever he flies abroad), whether he should sleep with the strange woman in his fencing class who keeps giving him the eye (*really? through insulated mesh?*).

Now he drops round to my flat without warning whenever he's at a loose end (*frequently*), insists we organise post-work drinks at least once a week (*cause mates do that, don't they?*), rings me late at night when a tinder date has gone disastrously wrong (*to relate all the mortifying details*), and insists I attend all his family functions (*you split from me, not my family, he argues, and besides, they prefer you*). As far as I can see, the only thing that has changed is that I no longer have someone to take out the rubbish or snake the drain when it gets clogged.

But the worst thing is – there's no breaking up with friends.

Chapter Three

On Monday mornings I always drop Charlie Bucket off at the shop before going for a long skate. True to his breed, Charlie Bucket is not really an exercise enthusiast. Indeed, anything beyond walking he regards as excessive, and even that he prefers in small doses, as the effort of movement appears taxing for him. Unless, of course, cats are involved.

I belong to the South London women's roller derby league, and my coach insists I put in at least one day per week of cardio training. If you've never seen it, roller derby is a little bit like rugby on wheels, except there's no ball, and it's played on a circular track instead of a pitch. Plus, there's no goal. So actually, apart from being really violent, it's not really like rugby at all. It does involve teams, however, who skate anticlockwise around the track: each team has a jammer who scores points by lapping members of the opposing team, breaking through their defensive line by any means possible.

I didn't even know roller derby existed until I got to university, when someone saw me skating one day and invited me to come along. Because of my size, I quickly got recruited as a jammer. We're basically like sprinters who evade the opposition, while blockers are defensive and more confrontational: blockers are basically brawlers, while jammers are more like artful dodgers.

I train twice a week with the league. Jammers need to be

fast and nimble and a little bit squirrelly. We're identified by a star on our helmets, which means we're like a rolling target for all the players on the opposing team. Being a jammer isn't for the faint of heart, but when you break through the other team's line and are free and clear, the rush of adrenaline is amazing – at high speeds it feels like flying. Or in the words of my skating pal Sadie, it's like an orgasm on wheels.

As soon as I joined roller derby, I quickly became addicted, though my mother remained mystified. She couldn't seem to grasp the point of the sport; when I tried to describe it, she kept asking where the puck was. Finally, I resorted to showing her a video one of my teammates had made on my phone. It showed a gaggle of women thrashing around an indoor track slamming into each other at every opportunity. I could tell she was alarmed. 'It looks violent,' she'd said, shrinking back from the phone. My parents are ageing hippies, and like any good peaceniks, they are staunchly opposed to conflict in any form.

'It's fun,' I said.

'Is there a uniform?' She frowned down at the phone. This was her polite way of asking whether I dressed like the women in the video. My particular league tends towards the more glamorous end of the fashion spectrum: fishnet stockings, leather hot pants and peroxide blonde hair are the norm, rather than the exception.

'Not really. I just wear sports leggings,' I said. Though the irony of my mother questioning another tribe's apparel was not lost on me; she has a wardrobe full of peasant blouses and colourful ponchos, circa 1972.

'These people look terrifying,' she said. I smile. It's true that roller derby players tend to be physically imposing, especially when you get them up on skates.

'They're just women, Mum,' I said. 'Besides, I wear

protective gear. And there are rules, like any other sport.'

She nodded, unconvinced. To be fair, sport was never really her thing. My mother likes her leisure activities to be quiet and reflective: gardening, meditation, t'ai chi. On a particularly active day, she might knead bread.

When Charlie Bucket and I enter the shop, my *aide-de-camp* June is tidying up from the weekend, flattening delivery boxes at the back. June is a little introverted for a job that's customer-facing, but she's a walking encyclopaedia when it comes to cheese, so we make allowances for her. Right now she pulls a mock face of pique when Charlie Bucket comes barrelling through the front door. He wags his way to the back of the shop and lavishes her with snout-nuzzles while she tuts disapprovingly, turning away. June is small and prim and bespectacled, and next to her, Charlie Bucket looks like a shaggy mammoth. He is extremely fond of her, even though she is patently *not*, in her own words, 'an animal person'. She feigns indifference towards him, but in reality he has wormed his way into her affections over time, and she is consequently overgenerous with scraps.

All this in spite of being a Virgo, which according to June, is the only star sign that is more closely aligned to animals than people. June's a committed practitioner of astrology, and her daily movements are influenced by the stars in a way that the rest of us are guided by the weather or our bowels. She is shy, meticulous and reliable, all traits associated with Virgos, and inexplicably thin for someone who eats so much cheese. Like Bianca, she's a committed singleton, but in June's case this means quiet evenings at home in front of the telly or with her tarot cards. I don't think she's had a date in five years, but she doesn't appear to mind. She really ought to be working in accountancy, as she is far too exacting for our modest little retail operation, but the pace and rhythm of shop life appeals to her, and the forced interactions with customers are, in fact, just the right amount of socialisation for someone with so reserved a nature.

When I first mooted leaving June alone with Charlie Bucket on Mondays, she baulked, but I offered to pay her for an extra hour each day and she eventually relented. Charlie Bucket hates being alone, so it was the obvious solution, freeing me up on my days off. Besides, I told her, the shop dog is part of the allure of Say Cheese. Our customers would be sorely disappointed if Charlie Bucket wasn't there to greet them, even if he insists on doing so while asleep.

'Has he been walked?' she asks me sternly now. June knows that I am capable of cutting corners in this respect.

'Absolutely,' I say. 'All relevant business attended to.'

'And has he breakfasted?' she asks. June's a great one for using nouns as verbs. Ribbons need scissoring and bottles need corking in her small universe.

'Done.'

'Fine. What time are you back?'

Next year, I think? When the rainy season in Bora Bora comes?

'Mid-afternoon,' I say instead.

'I'll clock that,' she says with a crisp nod, before turning away.

I leave the shop and head off through the back streets towards Southwark Park. Bermondsey used to be an industrial slum, full of burnt-out factories and disused docklands, but over the past century it has undergone massive change; the Blitz, deindustrialisation and gentrification all played a part, with the result that it is now a veritable smorgasbord of design, age and function. Victorian shopping parades nestle between ancient ruins and Georgian terraces, with council

26

flats, modern eighties developments and brand-new luxury housing sandwiched in between. Last year, one of the broadsheets voted it the best place to live in London: with its Friday antiques market, trendy Borough food market, and scores of restaurants, bars and shops, it's supposedly a paradise for well-heeled millennials. Of which I am definitely not one.

When I reach the park, I do a few fast laps around the outer path, then head north along tree-lined avenues towards the Thames. The tide is at its low point and a few folks are mudlarking on the banks, ferreting around in the exposed river bed with tools in the sand. They're wind-bashed hearty souls, kitted out in knee-high wellington boots and dark mackintoshes and carrying plastic buckets to collect their spoils: Elizabethan clay pipes, roman coins, the odd tiny animal skull. This part of London thrived in Shakespeare's day. Before Bermondsey and Rotherhithe were consumed by urban sprawl, they were bustling villages where all sorts rubbed alongside each other.

I split off from the Thames just before Surrey Quays and loop back through the tiny inner-city woodlands at Russia Dock before heading back towards the trendier bit of the borough in the hope of a late breakfast. Woman cannot live on cheese and wine alone, and an hour's vigorous skating burns more than 600 calories, so I always feel a certain entitlement when I finish. I head straight for one of my favourite sandwich shops and casually duck inside, walking as normally as I can so as not to draw attention to my skates. The place is heaving and I grab a couple of sandwiches (one for now and one for later) and a bottle of lemon water and join one of two long queues several people deep, quelling a wave of mild irritation. A few people clock my skates, but most don't seem to mind. There are two serving staff, and annoyingly, I realise within the first minute that I have chosen the wrong queue, as the thin-faced young man serving mine seems to be moving like an underpowered robot. I sigh.

My life is a series of tiny decisions gone wrong.

The queue crawls forward. When I reach position number four, a young Spanish woman at the front begins to read out a fiendishly complicated order from a ragged piece of scrap paper. Her accent is so thick, it is almost impenetrable: two *care-meel* lattes, one *vaneella* made with soya, one *treeple* venti, one flat white made with *oath* milk, she enunciates carefully. For a moment, the thin-faced man simply stares at her uncomprehendingly. Everyone around me is straining to hear, and we all collectively swell with frustration. Part of me is sympathetic and wants to leap across the counter, grab a stainless-steel jug and make the damn coffees for him. And the other part of me wants to shout: *For God's sake man, get a grip!*

On top of that I am famished, so I quietly, ever so discretely, take a small bite of one of the sandwiches. Warm halloumi, chorizo and red pepper. *Divine.* I sneak another bite and by the time the Italian woman has been sent off clutching her overloaded cardboard cup holder, I have eaten nearly half. It takes the remaining two customers ahead of me to almost polish off the other. Now desperately thirsty, I crack open the lemon water and quickly guzzle a bit, then stuff the last bite of the sandwich into my mouth just as I reach the counter.

The young man's face instantly darkens – he has clearly seen me chewing. I swallow, giving my best closed-mouth smile and gaily wave the wrapper like a banner, to let him know that a) I have every intention of paying and b) I am not a thief.

'Sorry,' I say, shoving the empty package across for him to scan. 'Afraid I was a bit peckish.' I pass the second sandwich and half bottle of lemon water over to him. 'Plus, halloumi really needs to be eaten warm,' I add authoritatively. 'Trust me, I'm a bit of an expert.'

The young man inhales, and as he does, his thin nostrils flare slightly.

'Anything else?' he asks in a clipped tone.

I have to stop myself from saying, *Yes please, a half-caf cinnamon dolce latte with whipped cream topping.* 'No, that's it,' I say instead, quickly flourishing my debit card, poised to pay. I turn and flash a smile to the nice-looking man behind me, as if to say, *this will only take a second!* He raises one appraising eyebrow very slightly in response. Hang on! Is he judging me? Because he has absolutely no right! Even if he is a hotty. I turn back around and that is when I hear the tell-tale signal from the card machine: the ominous double beep that indicates a void transaction, and instantly brands me as a shirker.

'Oh!' I say with surprise. 'Perhaps I just need to pop my pin in,' I quickly tap the four-digit pin into the machine and it gives the warning beep again. I make a face. 'Oh dear. That was a very disapproving sound. My card must be broken. Or maybe it's your machine that's gone wrong?' I suggest with a nervous laugh.

'Would you like to pay in cash?' the young man asks, fixing me with a hard look. I glance down at my tracksuit bottoms. I have only my phone and my debit card on me. I don't even have my keys, as I typically leave them in the shop when I go for a skate. I certainly have no cash, though now I make a brief pretence of checking all my pockets.

'Um . . . that would not be possible,' I say after a moment. 'Another card perhaps?'

'I *do* have another card,' I say slowly. 'But not on me, I'm afraid,' I add sheepishly. 'I'm so sorry.'

'I see.'

'Well, obviously we can put this one back,' I start to reach for the uneaten sandwich and he quickly snaps it away behind the counter, out of my reach. *As if I am a common thief!* I can't help but feel a little affronted. Instead, I hold up the water. 'I've only had a sip of this,' I say half-heartedly, an assertion that is patently untrue, and anyway is irrelevant, as clearly it cannot be resold.

He shakes his head. Just once.

'Could I possibly owe you?' I ask. 'Or maybe we could do a trade? Except I don't really have much on me,' I pat down my running clothes and feel the only other things of value I am carrying: my earphones, and a tiny compact plastic carrier that holds two regular-size tampons. I never leave home without it, not since that one, truly memorable, time. Every woman has had that one, truly memorable, time. *Maybe he has a lady friend?*

'I'm sorry madam, but I'll have to call my manager.'

Whoa. 'OK,' I say hesitantly. 'The thing is . . . I'm actually a shop manager myself. And what I would do in this situation . . . is to let it go. You know, buy a little customer loyalty?' I am leaning forward over the counter and speaking as quietly as possible. The young man moves back a few inches. He is actually recoiling from me.

'Could you please stand over there?' He motions to one side.

'Excuse me,' says a voice behind me. 'I'll pay for her.'

The voice is smooth and dark and lush as a chocolate fountain. I turn around and the handsome raised-eyebrow man is brandishing his debit card. For the first time I take him in properly: medium height, early thirties, with curly

30

dark brown hair and three-day old facial hair, the sort of guy who might occasionally shave but knows he looks better without it. My eyes dip to a tiny dimple just above his chin, then slide up to his mouth. Nice lips, I think. *And that voice! That voice could unlock fortresses; it could tumble citadels.*

'Really? You'd do that?' I ask incredulously, because in truth, I'd quite like to hear that voice again.

'Yes. I'm in a bit of a rush. So if you don't mind, I'd just as soon pay.' He steps forward past me and hands across a sandwich and a drink to the young man. 'Could you just add these onto hers?' he asks the thin-faced young man. I am now effectively sidelined in this transaction. Neither man looks at me.

'Oh wow,' I say. 'That's incredibly kind. Thank you so much. If you give me your details, I'll send you the money right away. I promise.'

'It's OK. Really. It's only a few quid,' he says, reaching past me for his items.

'No honestly, I insist.' He turns and fixes me with a look.

'Why don't you just pay it forward,' he says. It feels more like an order than a question. He meets my eyes directly for the first time, and I nod, abruptly silenced.

Then he and his chocolate voice disappear.

Chapter Four

As I skate slowly home, I try to remember when I last checked my bank balance. I'm not hugely surprised that my accounts are in arrears; making ends meet in London has always been a Sisyphean struggle, but the situation appears to have worsened of late. These days my money seems to disappear in a constant trickle, like a leaky radiator. In recent months, I'd cut down on various luxuries: switched from Uber to Uber Pool, went twice as long between haircuts, bought only generic chocolate at the supermarket. Really, I was doing my best, but it never seemed to be enough – my account balance is always lower than I imagine it to be.

When the genes were divided up between my sister and I, the practical ones all went to her. Particularly those that deal with finances. In this respect at least, I take after my parents, who have always been the sort who skirted round their financial obligations. To their credit, they always knew how to find gratification, whatever their circumstances. Long before the term *mindfulness* was invented, my parents had perfected the art of living in the moment. Which is to say that if they had a ten-pound note, they spent it, and if they didn't, they spent it anyway, on credit. As a result, both my sister and I have made it a point *not* to emulate their spendthrift ways.

Unfortunately, only one of us has succeeded. Ever the pragmatist, Julia weighs the pros and cons of even the most minute financial decisions and can tell you which brand of loo roll has the lowest cost per sheet, or which hairspray lasts the longest. When I moved to London to start my adult life, she advised me to sign up for one of those online bank accounts that allow you to track all your spending and budget accordingly. Six months later I decided it was a killjoy and turned off all the notifications, deciding that it was too much like Scrooge looking over my shoulder.

How Julia developed any financial acumen growing up in our household remains a mystery to me. My parents were children of the sixties. Even though they were born just a shade too late to experience the excesses of the decade, I'm convinced that growing up in its long shadow somehow stunted their development because they embraced the spirit of the times and never really let go. I once caught my mother reminiscing fondly about the Summer of Love while we were watching a TV documentary. 'Hang on,' I'd said, doing the maths in my head. 'Weren't you only twelve in 1967?'

She shrugged. 'Times were different then,' she said.

'In what way?' I asked, alarmed at the thought of my mother engaging in free love as a pre-adolescent.

Both my parents grew up in the West Country. They lived a few towns apart and met at Glastonbury when they were sixteen. Back then, Glastonbury was a very different affair. For one thing it was free; otherwise, they never would have been able to afford it. The line-up in 1971 included David Bowie, Traffic and Joan Baez. Mum was a huge fan of the latter, and when I was growing up, still styled herself after a series of women artists from the seventies: Joan and Joni, Janis and Cher. She was the only mother in my primary school whose long hair fell nearly to her waist. She used to turn up at the school gates wearing clogs and kaftans,

33

even though by then it was the nineties and everyone else's fashion had long since moved on.

Our household was largely vegetarian, partly out of a vague moral stance, but mostly because we couldn't afford meat. Neither of my parents ever had a proper 'career' to speak of, though they cobbled together a subsistence livelihood from a variety of occupations. We lived in a small, terraced house on the outskirts of Guildford that my father had inherited from a childless aunt shortly after I was born. Without it, I suspect we would have been modern-day nomads, so I was supremely grateful to Great Aunt Rita, whom I never had the chance to meet. Throughout my childhood, my father had a chequered employment history, trying his hand at a series of jobs that never really stuck, including telesales (magazines, timeshares), long-distance lorry driving, children's party entertainment and gravedigging.

Oddly, the last suited him best and he ended up managing a cemetery. He liked being out-of-doors and didn't mind being surrounded by the dead, whom he said were less demanding than the living, and often more congenial. While my father communed with the soil and its occupants, my mother tried her hand at a series of cottage industries conducted around our kitchen table: scented candles, macraméplant holders, essential oils, découpage ornaments, pickled chutneys. These she flogged with varying success at local craft fairs and markets. In this manner, we managed to scrape by.

My parents officially 'retired' a few years ago, the same year one of my father's more dubious associates lured him into a 'sure-fire' investment scheme that was guaranteed to yield a high return. Without telling my mother (much less Julia and I), he remortgaged Great Aunt Rita's house and ended up losing everything, bar his meagre pension and an even more modest annuity that Julia had persuaded him to invest in before his finances went south. A few years earlier they'd loaned me the down payment on my flat, and when HMRC came knocking at their door, my bewildered parents came to me, cap in hand.

I was surprised to discover they were penniless, though I probably shouldn't have been. I promised to dig them out of their position with HMRC, in spite of the fact that my own finances weren't brilliant. I negotiated with the tax authorities on their behalf, and agreed a careful repayment schedule, which I reckoned I could just about keep up with, even though I'd taken a small cut in salary to move to Say Cheese. The money for the flat had been a loan, but somewhat naively, I hadn't expected to ever have to make good on it.

More fool me.

When I arrive back at the shop, I see with relief that I have just avoided one of my least favourite customers – Feckin' Frank is leaving just as I enter, and even though I'm not officially working, I heave a sigh of relief. Just to be within his orbit is enough to sap me of the will to live. Most of our customers are absolutely lovely, but Feckin' Frank is a classic cheese bore, who insists on asking detailed questions about the provenance and ageing of every single purchase, and delights in tripping you up if you are wrong. June has far more patience and expertise to deal with him than either me or Declan.

'Everything all right?' I ask June. Truthfully, I don't really want to know, but as she's done me a favour by dog-sitting, I feel obliged to at least enquire. Charlie Bucket is lying sprawled across the floor in front of me. He raises his head and wags his tail in greeting – too much effort to actually stand.

'Yes, all good,' says June with 100 per cent competency. Feckin' Frank has not even ruffled her feathers. I nudge Charlie Bucket with my foot.

'Come on big fella, time to go upstairs.' Charlie Bucket opens one eye to look at me, then closes it again, feigning sleep. June materialises at my side, brandishing a small piece of cheddar, and Charlie Bucket instantly pops up, sitting obediently in front of her. I roll my eyes as he gobbles up the treat.

'There was one slight issue while you were out,' says June, turning to me. I raise a querying eyebrow. 'Your upstairs neighbour stopped by,' she says.

'Carl?'

'Well, he didn't actually come in. In fact, he shouted to me from the doorway. He told me to inform you that Charlie Bucket is no longer allowed in the common area between the flats.'

'You mean the stairwell?' I ask with incredulity.

June shrugs. 'I wasn't sure,' she says. 'It was all a bit difficult. I had another customer here and Charlie Bucket was a little . . . disruptive.' Her voice trails off.

'Oh June, I'm so sorry,' I say.

'It was fine. I managed to restrain him. In the end,' she says, patting Charlie Bucket's head. 'Afraid I lost the sale, though,' she adds apologetically.

Christ. Leave it to Carl to communicate his offensive messages when I'm not around. What a coward. Relations with my upstairs neighbour have deteriorated at a dizzying pace these past few months. Carl is a professional opera singer, one whom I suspect is destined to remain forever out of the limelight. He often practises his voice exercises at home, trilling scales in a curiously high tenor that sounds more like a distress call than a melody. Miraculously, when Charlie

Bucket first landed on my doorstep, we did not meet Carl for the first several weeks after his arrival. By the time we *did* encounter each other on the stairs one evening, Charlie Bucket had doubled from his original size and was already an imposing two feet tall, with paws like massive shaggy dumplings.

I was surprised to see that Carl had grown a bushy moustache during the interim. The sight stopped me in my tracks. It was patently *not* a good look. I've got nothing against moustaches personally, but Carl's really didn't suit. Hair isn't his best physical attribute; the hair atop his head is stiff and a strange shoe polish brown, and his newly acquired moustache was similarly dense and coarse, straddling his lip like an oversized caterpillar marching across his face.

At the sight of him, Charlie Bucket began to snarl and strain against his lead. Carl flattened himself against the wall in terror and I dragged Charlie Bucket past him, shielding him with my body. Later that night, I received an angry note from Carl shoved under my door, to the effect that he intended to check our ground lease for any restrictive clauses regarding dangerous pets (there are none, thank heavens) but he would expect me to control my dog at all times, irrespective of the lease.

Carl also has a pet, a grey female cat called Luca, who delights in sitting on the fire escape just outside my kitchen window and tormenting Charlie Bucket through the glass. Luca is more than partly to blame for the unfortunate incident that occurred two weeks ago, when Carl left the front door of his flat open for a moment and Luca decided to seize the day. She was busily raking her claws across my doormat when I opened my door to see what the noise was.

Charlie Bucket had been lounging on his sofa, his enormous nose resting on his paws, when he and Luca spotted each other. With no glass in between, it was like the air between them suddenly became charged with thousands of excitable protons. Charlie Bucket's eyes widened, as if he couldn't quite believe his luck, and Luca arched her back, her grey hair literally standing on end. Both remained frozen for an instant before Charlie Bucket hurled himself past me like an obese panther, sending Luca skittering back up the wooden stairs. I think Charlie Bucket took the entire staircase in one flying leap, and before I knew it, he was through Carl's front door.

I hesitated only for an instant, then followed, and by the time I got through his front door, Luca was on top of the fridge, spitting venom, and Charlie Bucket was standing on his hind legs, his paws atop the fridge, barking at her. 'Charlie Bucket, get *down*!' I shouted, grabbing his collar and yanking all six feet of him away.

'Get your monstrous animal out of my kitchen!' shouted Carl from behind me. 'How the hell did he get in here, anyway?' he demanded.

'Your front door was open,' I informed him over my shoulder, dragging Charlie Bucket past him.

'Get him out *now*,' Carl snapped. 'And if I ever find him inside my flat again, I'll have him put down!' I pulled Charlie Bucket out of the door and heard it slam behind me.

Ten days later I received an official-looking missive from the council in the post. It appeared that in response to complaints from my upstairs neighbour, Charlie Bucket had been given an ASBO! Or at least, the animal equivalent of one. According to the letter, my dog was not to pass within one hundred yards of my neighbour or I could be fined, or even taken to court. How this was meant to work in practice, I had no idea. Carl *must* realise there is no way Charlie Bucket can access my flat without passing through the common areas, so his message today is especially irritating.

We head up the stairs, and as I unlock the door, I think about how small, seemingly random, events can produce seismic shifts in one's existence. If Marcus hadn't spotted the ad in the window for Say Cheese, for example, I wouldn't have either a dog *or* an annoying upstairs neighbour. Where would I be right now? And would I be any happier? Last week, I heard about a new app on the radio called Universe Splitter. It lets you input a life decision and the app will generate two parallel paths. Should you eat a piece of cake? Or forgo it? You input both actions, then click 'split', and the app sends a signal to a lab in Switzerland where a single photon gets hurtled toward a splitter. The photon can go left or right: in one direction you eat the cake and in the other you don't. But the lab splits the photon and both versions of your life get played out in parallel universes, and the app tells you which one you are living in: a world with or without cake.

The only hitch is that the two worlds can never, ever, intersect, which seems a bit of a shame, but I guess quantum mechanics can only take you so far. Right now, I look down at Charlie Bucket, who has clambered happily onto his sofa, and now looks utterly content.

'I think that means you're stuck with me,' I say with a sigh.

My other self might be out there somewhere, but I'll never get to meet her.

Chapter Five

I thought managing a cheese shop would bring me job satisfaction in a way that my previous marketing role did not. Like a lot of people, I wanted to feel a sense of purpose and meaning in my work; this was difficult when I was being asked to crunch data about which colour washing-up liquid sells best, or whether people prefer roll-on or stick deodorant (the latter, in case you're wondering). I'd taken the job with Allegra Solutions because I was desperate to escape Guildford and it was the only job offer I received out of university. I moved to London and stepped into adulthood like climbing into a well-worn pair of boots. For a few years, it felt amazing to be on my own and self-sufficient. But over time I realised that the boots weren't quite the right style or size. And eventually, I had to admit that I'd never have chosen them new.

The problem was I didn't know which boots I wanted, much less where to find them. And when the job at Say Cheese appeared, it felt as if swerving into a completely new career might be the best option. After all, cheese was food. And food was a basic human need. If I took the job at Say Cheese, I'd be connecting with humanity in a vital and elemental way, by *feeding* people. But the day-to-day reality of running an upmarket cheese shop has proved disappointing. It certainly doesn't feel vital or elemental, and some days, it can be difficult to remember why selling luxury dairy products is even necessary.

The truth is: it may not be. At least, not for me.

I'm not the first person on the planet to stumble through a series of ill-fitting jobs. Worryingly, my father comes to mind. He came to visit me in the shop last year to sign some papers shortly before they went abroad, taking the train up from Guildford to Waterloo one morning. When he arrived, he seemed totally out of place in Say Cheese. I remember him glancing around at all the carefully wrapped parcels of cheese. As always, I was painfully aware that he could never afford to buy them.

'How goes it in the world of cheese?' he'd asked.

'OK. Business is good,' I'd said, nodding.

He'd peered at me. 'But is it good for you?' he asked.

I blinked and stared at him, uncertain how to answer. *Was it?*

It was only after he'd gone that I realised how much satisfaction he'd got from looking after the dead throughout the last twenty years of his life. For my father, death was the final leg of a much longer journey, and he was proud to be its overseer; it was important work and he was happy to be doing it.

Could I say the same?

In spite of the unfortunate hiccup with my boss over the loan, I do take my job seriously. Philip, the shop's owner, has nothing to do with the day-to-day running of the place. I handle everything: from hiring and firing staff (OK apart from me, there are only two other part-timers, but still) to ordering stock and balancing the books. I pay all our suppliers, make weekly cash deposits at the bank, do the payroll and file our quarterly VAT returns. I also curate our monthly cheese club and programme occasional events and speakers – anything to bring more customers into the shop. In fact, Philip's ambitions for Say Cheese appear to be modest at best; provided the shop does not actually *lose* money, he's happy to leave me to it.

When he first hired me, I asked whether he wanted to be kept abreast of day-to-day issues, and he flashed me a pained smile. 'Preferably not. That's why I've hired a manager. To *manage* things,' he said. Philip is in his early sixties and unlike Marcus, he *genuinely* works in the law: he's a barrister specialising in human rights. Like me, he is small of stature (I've long suspected my height was a key factor in his decision to employ me) but at five foot six, he still manages to cut an imposing figure. It's something about his bearing: his piercing gaze perhaps, or his ferociously intelligent manner; he reminds me of a greying, scholarly ferret. I got the sense early on that owning a cheese shop was little more than a hobby for him. Something to dabble in, or perhaps the sheer simplicity of cheese gave him a respite from the complexities of his more demanding day job. Who knows? But he is not one to suffer fools gladly, nor to tolerate incompetence, much less indolence among staff. That much was clear from the outset.

'What sort of things would you *like* to be informed of?' I enquired cautiously that first day.

'Are you familiar with the concept of *force majeure*?' he asked.

'Isn't that like . . . acts of God?'

'If one were that way inclined,' he said a little cryptically. 'But yes, that's the basic idea. It's an insurance proviso. It refers to unavoidable catastrophes that interrupt the expected course of events. And prevent people from fulfilling their obligations,' he added pointedly.

I gulped. *OK*, I thought. *Would an attack by terrorists qualify? Or a flood? Maybe the sudden appearance of Bigfoot?* Clearly, not the time a well-dressed middle-aged man came in, asked to sample the smoked manchego, and while my back was turned, stripped down to nothing but a shirt and tartan plaid woolly scarf. Would that it had been wrapped around his lower appendage, which waggled at me like a bobbing head toy when I turned back round to face him. I yelped and dropped the cheese, and the man continued to stare at me in disapproving expectation. Without really thinking, I cut another slice of cheese and handed it to him almost apologetically. When he'd finished sampling the manchego, he simply turned and left, walking out of the shop. Once he'd gone, I telephoned the police, who politely informed me that although public displays of nudity were not illegal in England, indecent exposure was. *Had the man exposed himself to me deliberately to elicit a reaction, they'd asked?* I couldn't help wondering if this was a trick question. The answer seemed fairly obvious.

Apart from Philip (who rarely appears) and June, there's only me and Declan, a mid-twenties musician from Northern Ireland who is struggling to launch his music career. I hired Declan out of sheer desperation one afternoon when June had phoned in sick and I had fifteen people booked in for a tasting that evening. When Declan poked his head in at half past five to ask if the shop was hiring, I looked him over for about a nanosecond. He was clean-shaven, with a slim build, an appealing face and wiry ginger hair pulled tightly back in a fetching man-bun. 'How do you feel about cheese?' I asked cautiously.

'Generally pro,' he said, nodding. 'Except for yak cheese,' he added. 'Not a fan. Texture's all wrong. Like cheesy chewing gum.' This was not the answer I was expecting; I was used to prospective applicants waxing lyrical about Vacherin or Shropshire Blue, their eyes glowing fervently with excessive sentiment.

'Where'd you eat yak cheese?' I asked, mainly out of curiosity, having never come across it myself.

'Nepal,' he replied.

Fair enough, I thought. 'Can you start now?' I asked. Declan's eyes widened.

'Really?' He seemed a little surprised.

'Yep.'

Declan beamed. 'That'd be grand,' he said.

So that was it. No interview, no references, no demonstrable knowledge of the product. If his teeth and hair were clean, and he could string a sentence together, that was good enough for me. Which just goes to show: timing is everything. In fact, Declan has turned out to be a surprisingly good salesman. Customers like his breezy, unaffected manner, and the fact that he doesn't talk bollocks about cheese. I once came into the shop when he was serving an American customer. 'Is this made from raw milk?' the well-dressed woman asked uneasily. She was frowning down at an unpasteurised goat cheese he'd offered up. Declan cocked his man-bun thoughtfully to one side, in a manner that was designed to both reassure and assuage.

'I'm afraid it is,' he said, fixing his bright blue eyes directly onto hers. 'But real cheese isn't for the faint of heart,' he said in his lilting Irish accent. The woman smiled back at him.

'I'll take it,' she said. And the next day she came back for more.

The fourth member of the team is Charlie Bucket, who has a habit of splaying full length on his side across the shop floor whilst napping, like living décor. The shop is tiny and square and attractively kitted out in rustic wood, with a specially designed walk-in cheese area at the rear on the right. (June likes to call it the 'cheese room' but it's more of a cheese privy.) At the front of the shop, wooden shelves on the left are filled with upmarket biscuits, crackers and condiments, and on the right a waist-high refrigerated glass case holds a small selection of pastries and dairy products. The till counter is squeezed into the left-hand corner at the back, which leaves Charlie Bucket to take up approximately two-thirds of the remaining available floor space. Our regular customers are remarkably tolerant of this, stepping gingerly over his enormous shaggy form on their way to the cheese privy.

For his part, Charlie Bucket is generally a model employee, enduring strokes and pats and the occasional poke from toddlers in prams, all with equanimity. The one thing he cannot abide is moustaches (on men, at least; on women he seems absolutely fine with facial hair.) This we must be quite vigilant about, running interference when necessary, which is pretty much any time a moustache owned by a man walks into the shop. Charlie Bucket has yet to meet one he finds tolerable. Thank goodness he is fine with beards, which are far more fashionable these days.

It was Declan who decided that all our shop regulars needed monikers. Roller derby players all adopt skate names, and when I explained this convention to him, he got very excited and proceeded to nickname them all. One of his favourites is Miriam (Mammy Goat), a sweet pensioner who loves chevre, especially the sort with herby bits on the outside, though she has trouble remembering which are her favourites, so Declan puts them to one side and reprimands us if we sell them to anyone else. And there's a middle-aged guy called Gordon who only ever buys Gorgonzola or Cambazola (Gordonzola, somewhat predictably), and Busy Lizzie, who only buys bog-standard Brie, no matter what else we try to entice her with, ostensibly because she's always in a terrific rush, though Declan maintains that she is simply lacking in gastronomic imagination.

One of our favourite customers is the Faltering Cheese, who is constitutionally incapable of making up his mind, but comes in every day for one modest portion, weighing up the pros and cons of a hundred different varieties before finally, *finally,* settling on a small slice to take away. It sounds maddening, but in fact it's sort of endearing. And then there's Chuck E, a fashionable thirty-something guy whose real name is Charles. For a long time I thought Chuck E might have motives that went beyond cheese, though I genuinely couldn't tell which of us he fancied (me, June, Declan or Charlie Bucket). The fact that he came in almost daily and was always willing to take our suggestions, no matter how bizarre (we literally tested this theory out last summer, when the three of us ran a competition over the course of several weeks to see how many different types of cheeses we could persuade him to buy. We actually kept a spreadsheet of his purchases and June won.)

I guess I should also mention Ethan, early thirties, who works in film distribution and lives around the corner. Ethan is charming and affable and wears trendy clothes that practically scream *men's style magazine* at you. And yes, somewhat predictably, he's quite good-looking: medium height, square-jawed, dirty blond hair worn longish but not shaggy, big blue eyes, perfect white teeth. He always comes in on Friday afternoons to buy cheese for the weekend, and occasionally mentions that he's off somewhere glamorous: a house party in the Scottish Highlands or skiing in France.

Full disclosure: for a long time, I had a massive crush on Ethan. We flirted over the cheese counter for the best part of a year until I finally worked up the courage to ask him out for a drink one evening last summer. It was over a bottle of Sauvignon Blanc outside a Thameside pub that he finally (finally!) revealed that he was married. (Wedding bands don't form part of his style book, apparently.) His wife is French, which may partially account for his tastes (he prefers regional French cheeses like *tomme* or *Beaufort*) and she works in finance. He explained that she was based mainly in Paris (which is why I've never seen her) but commutes back and forth to London at weekends via Eurostar. He also said she was scarily good at her job, which is presumably why he can afford to shop at Say Cheese. In my mind, Ethan's wife is slim, blonde, impeccably dressed and utterly efficient; the sort of woman who can achieve mind-blowing orgasms in record time.

For some reason, Declan took against Ethan from the start, nicknaming him Ether. When I asked him why, he shrugged and said, 'Pleasant, colourless and anaesthetising', which I thought was a bit harsh. Though I did think it was offside for Ethan to flirt with me for so long without informing me of his relationship status. And when he finally did tell me, it was in a meandering and oddly melancholic way.

The night of our drink it was a glorious late summer evening. As luck would have it, we'd bagged the best table right by the water. The tide was up and the Thames was in full swing, with tourist boats and commuter ferries ploughing up and down the river. I was wearing a white and navy blue striped halter dress that I knew set off my tan nicely, and Ethan looked almost edible in a faded orange expensive-looking T-shirt. As the sun dipped lower, the light turned everything around us radiant, bathing us in a warm golden syrup. I remember Ethan holding up his wine glass and looking straight into it. 'Sometimes time slips sideways, doesn't it,' he said a little nostalgically. 'We could be anywhere right now. At any time.' He looked up at me and smiled.

I nodded, because I knew exactly what he meant. There was a déjà vu quality to the evening, of summers past and forgotten moments that rose up like bubbles that burst upon your consciousness, forming effervescent memories. Personally, I was more than happy to be in the present, and was about to say as much, when he surprised me with his next comment.

'I fell in love on a night like this,' he said with a wistful smile.

'With who?' I asked, expecting him to tell me about a girl he'd met on a camping holiday when he was fifteen. Or the first person he'd slept with at university. Ethan took a deep breath then and let it out slowly, as if he was exhaling the truth.

'My wife,' he said simply.

And that was how I learned that he was married.

Wanker.

Chapter Six

'Pay it forward? So he wouldn't even give you his phone number? Clem, you need coaching.' Bianca looks at me side-eyed from a downward dog position. Even upside down, she looks amazing. Tuesday evenings she insists I accompany her to yoga, though by roller derby standards, it doesn't really qualify as exercise. Still, the stretching is useful, and keeps me supple for jamming.

'I was in trackies!' I whisper defensively. 'And I hadn't washed my hair in two days. So I wasn't at my best.' Eyeing the instructor, we both move into a sitting position and cross our legs.

'Clearly,' she says, pulling her feet tightly into position.

Bianca would have lassoed him, demanded his number, and before he'd even finished typing it into her phone, nailed him down with a date for drinks – she knows how to close a deal. 'Well, anyway,' I say with a sigh, 'I gave the old guy who panhandles outside the shop some change this morning. So at least I've held up my end of the bargain.'

'How so?'

'I paid it forward, of course.'

Bianca shakes her head with dismay. 'You are such a quitter,' she mumbles.

'I never even got started!'

'Exactly. And whose fault was that?'

*

In the changing room half an hour later, we swap our sweats for street clothes. Bianca slips into a gorgeous burgundy wool sheath dress while I wrestle myself into light brown wide wale corduroys that appear to have shrunk during the hour I had them off. 'Isn't yoga meant to be slimming?' I say, tugging at them uncomfortably. Bianca pauses, appraising the dungarees, then looks me in the eye.

'You want my honest opinion?' she asks.

'No,' I say emphatically.

'You're channelling Tweedle Dee,' she says, closing her locker, and turning away.

'Which bit of *no* did you not understand?'

She tells me she'll wait for me outside, and just as I'm finishing getting dressed, a pale young woman using the locker next to mine returns from the sink and gives a little cry of dismay.

'What's wrong?' I turn to her with concern. She's in her early twenties, with perfectly straight, white-blonde hair pulled back in a taut ponytail and flawless skin. *Youthful* skin, the sort that doesn't last past the age of thirty, though I'm sure she doesn't know it yet. Her pale blue eyes flash at me with alarm.

'My necklace! It's not here. I put it right here on this shelf!'

'Are you sure?' I lean over and crane my neck to see inside the locker. The shelf is clearly empty.

'Yes, I'm sure!' she says a little defensively. 'I *definitely* left it right here.'

'Oh,' I frown. 'Well, I guess you'd better notify the management.'

'I only walked away for an instant,' she cries with dismay. 'Less than twenty seconds! How could it happen so quickly?' She is staring at me with an odd look. Suddenly I glance

50

around and see that we are all alone – everyone else has changed and gone. *Uh oh.*

'I have no idea,' I say quickly. 'I never saw a thing.'

'Are you *sure*?' she asks, her blonde eyebrows knit together with suspicion.

'Positive,' I say, nodding emphatically. 'I'm really sorry, but I have to go. My friend is waiting for me outside.' I gather up my handbag and gym bag and scurry out of the locker room, leaving the young woman glaring at my back with distrust. *How dare she suspect me?*

A minute later, when I tell Bianca what's happened, she shrugs. 'She probably left it at home.'

'Exactly. Why is everyone so quick to point the finger of blame? It's like we've lost all faith in humankind.'

'Either that or she's a scammer,' says Bianca. 'She'll file a police report, then collect the money on her insurance.'

'See? Even you're doing it! We're a nation rife with suspicion!'

'Clem, sometimes I think working in a cheese shop has warped your sense of reality. It's a tough old world out there. People are struggling. Not everyone can afford aged Camembert at nine pounds for a hundred grams.'

'That young woman is *definitely* not struggling,' I say. 'No one with real blonde hair that colour needs to struggle,' I add grudgingly.

'People commit crimes for all kinds of reasons. Sometimes it's just for the thrill of it.'

I glance over at her. 'Have *you* done that?'

'Have I done what?'

'Committed a crime for the thrill of it?'

'Certainly not,' she says dismissively. 'My thrills are far more corporeal.'

'Sex and alcohol, you mean.'

'Precisely.'

'And don't forget chocolate,' I remind her.

Bianca rolls her eyes. 'Sweetie, I *never* forget chocolate.'

Charlie Bucket greets me like a long-lost relative when I get home – as if we have been separated for years rather than a matter of hours. Indeed, such is his enthusiasm that it really ought to be classified as assault: he batters me repeatedly with his paws, which as they are attached to his legs, are more like enormous hairy truncheons. 'Yes, yes, I missed you too,' I say, depositing my bags on the hall floor and fending him off with both hands. He reminds me that he has not been fed and I cross to the kitchen, scooping two massive cups of generic dry dog food into a large bowl, then topping it off with half a tin of posh wet stuff. I know he's only a dog, but I can't help thinking that if I ever got reincarnated as a pet, I'd want someone like me for an owner – in other words, a pushover.

The flat buzzer rings and I go to the intercom and ask who it is. 'Met Police,' says a woman's voice.

Really? I press the button, then cross to my front door, opening it and peering into the hallway, where I can see a male and female police officer trudging up the stairs. The woman leads: she is broad-shouldered and stout-limbed, her oatmeal-coloured hair swept tightly back in a fierce ponytail. If she had a tattoo, she could definitely play roller derby, I think. The mixed-race officer following her is tall, thin and athletic-looking, and looks as if he could easily outrun most criminals, if the situation warranted. I glance back at Charlie Bucket. As usual he is lounging on his sofa, but when he hears footsteps he immediately rises up into a sitting position. '*Lie down*,' I say sternly. For once he obeys, easing himself back down with a groan. When the pair reach my threshold, I open the door a little wider, so as to seem welcoming, and smile.

'Good evening, officers!' I say heartily. 'What can I do for you?'

'Are you Clemency Frye?' says the woman abruptly. Not even a pretence of a greeting or small talk! Perhaps they're in a hurry.

'Yes,' I nod and she withdraws an envelope from a folder, handing it to me.

'We have a warrant for your arrest.'

'What?' I stare at her in disbelief for an instant. She nods at the envelope and I slowly open it, unfolding a single sheet of paper inside. There's an official-looking coat of arms in the left-hand corner, together with the words: *Her Majesty's Courts & Tribunals Service*, and to the right, written in blood-red ink and block capitals, as if I might somehow miss it: *ARREST WARRANT*. My eyes drift down to the black box below and sure enough, my name is written clearly inside. I glance back up at them.

'Is this about Charlie Bucket?' I ask, incredulous. The odious Carl must be to blame! 'Because if it is, then I've got a few issues of my own to raise,' I continue quickly. 'In fact, I was just about to file a noise complaint with the council's environmental services. I know it's meant to be entertaining, but I can promise you that opera can be *extremely* challenging to live beneath.'

The woman frowns and lobs a quick glance at her male companion, who raises an eyebrow. She turns back to me. 'Who's Charlie Bucket?' she asks.

I step aside and motion towards the sofa, where at the sound of his name, Charlie Bucket has lifted his head and is watching us intently.

'That's Charlie Bucket,' I say. Next to her I see the flicker of a smile pass the male officer's face. Clearly, he's amused. The woman shakes her head.

'No, ma'am. This has nothing to do with your dog.'

'Oh,' I say, somewhat deflated. 'I don't understand. It isn't about that thing yesterday, is it? Was there like . . . CCTV or something? Because the guy behind me paid for my sandwich in full. I swear it.'

'You were due in court yesterday.'

'I was? For what? I hadn't even eaten that sandwich then!'

'Four counts of credit card theft. Three counts of identity fraud. One count of impersonation.'

I stare at her for a moment, then burst out laughing. 'I'm sorry. I don't mean to laugh. But I think you must have the wrong person.'

The woman throws her companion another glance.

'That's pretty much what we expected you to say. I'm afraid you'll have to come with us.'

'To where?'

'The station. You're under arrest.' I look from one to the other, speechless. Surely this isn't happening? Then I spin round to look at Charlie Bucket, who has lost all interest and is now feigning sleep. I'm under threat! Isn't he supposed to defend me?

'We're also going to need to search your flat,' says the male officer.

'Seriously?' I ask. 'For what?'

They shoot a glance at each other.

'Evidence of criminality,' says the female officer in a voice that suggests I am an idiot for even asking. 'Could you take a seat please?'

I sink down onto the sofa beside Charlie Bucket and watch while they frisk the contents of my life: peering into my wardrobes, pawing through my drawers and even rummaging through my kitchen cupboards. After ten minutes, they look at each other and nod, silently agreeing to call a halt. The female officer turns to me.

'Right. Time to go.'

'Find anything incriminating?' I ask pointedly.

She flashes me a pat smile. 'You're out of bog roll.'

The male officer laughs outright.

Damn. She's right. I meant to buy some on the way home.

So now I am a *bonafide* criminal. Or at least, the police think I am. They arrest me, and in the process of doing so, even read me my rights, just like on TV. They insist on my accompanying them back to the station, though they decline to use handcuffs, which I am secretly a little disappointed by. As I grab my coat, phone and handbag, I give Charlie Bucket a perfunctory pat on the head and tell him I'll be back later. He sighs in a resigned sort of way and lowers his head onto his paws, watching us depart – as if me being carted away by two strangers is a perfectly normal occurrence on a Tuesday evening. *Ho hum.*

We drive to Bermondsey Police Station, which apparently has been relocated in recent years to an enormous leisure complex in Rotherhithe. (I get that fitness is a priority for the police, but this does seem a little excessive.) We park in a vast car park and they escort me inside, where I am booked in by an ageing, lumpy duty sergeant who looks like he has forgotten to avail himself of the nearby facilities. Indeed, he looks ready for retirement – all loose jowls and latticed lines around the eyes. Clearly he's seen one too many *real* criminals in his time. I flash him my most winning smile: *Not all of us are bad guys!*

He takes down my details and photographs me for posterity, in spite of the fact that I have *still* not washed my hair, though I resist the urge to tell him so, and confiscates my handbag and phone, informing me that both will be held securely.

'Don't I get a phone call?' I ask him as I hand it over.

'You have the right to notify someone you're here,' he says in a bored tone. 'And the right to free and independent legal advice, should you desire it.' He looks at me expectantly.

I hesitate. Honestly, who would I call? The closest thing I have to a lawyer is my boss, and I am hardly going to call him, am I? I rifle mentally through the list of alternatives: Bianca, Marcus, my mum, my sister, and quickly decide that there's not much point until I know what's going on.

'No, thank you,' I say, a little petulantly. 'Besides, I'm innocent,' I add.

'Funnily enough, I've heard that before,' he says in a bored tone. 'This way, please.' He escorts me down a long corridor to a holding cell, but when I see where we're headed, I stop short in the doorway.

'Hang on,' I say. 'You're *literally* locking me up?'

'Yes, ma'am. That's what we do here.' He nods towards the inside of the cell and I reluctantly step inside, before turning round to face him.

'But . . . don't I even get a chance to explain?'

'Absolutely,' he says, shutting the door and addressing me through a small window at eye level. 'We'll look forward to it.' Then he slams the window shut too.

I sigh, turning to look around the room. It's tiny and windowless. Somewhat worryingly, there's a fold-down bed attached to the wall with a thin plastic mattress and a dark grey blanket folded on top. In the far corner, opposite the bed, is a metal rimless toilet and tiny wash basin. *Ensuite facilities!*

I suppose I should be grateful. There's even toilet paper, unlike at mine.

Twenty minutes later someone unlocks the door, and a young PC appears, holding it open and standing to one side. His pale brown hair has been shorn so closely I can see his scalp peeking through beneath, and his cheeks are unusually pink, as if he's in a permanent state of embarrassment. He nods at me to go, refusing to meet my eyes, and stares silently at the floor as I pass, as if my criminal female gaze will taint him somehow. He escorts me down the hall to a series of interview rooms and parks me in one, nodding towards a white Formica table with two straight-backed chairs at opposite ends. 'Either or,' he says, his voice cracking nervously as he speaks.

He retreats to the doorway, facing away from me, and it is only after a moment that I realise he's standing guard. *Christ. Where on earth would I go?* I take a moment to look around the room: dim white walls, rather unfortunate overhead strip lighting that will definitely not flatter, and a large rectangular mirror on the far wall, presumably so that I can check my make-up. I see that my hair has now entered that late phase of grime where it almost looks good.

But not quite.

A tape recorder and microphone sit off to one side on the table in front of me.

Just at that moment I hear footsteps in the corridor outside and the sound of two men talking as they approach. As the voices draw near, I experience an odd moment of déjà vu: I definitely know one of those voices. In fact, it seems eerily familiar. My mind scrambles to claw back the memory. *Good grief. It's Pay-It-Forward!* I know it is! In the next moment, a sandy-haired man with beefy features in his late forties pokes his head into the room, then indicates to the young PC that he can go. 'I've still got this one to process,' I hear him say. 'But I'll come along after.'

'OK,' says Pay-It-Forward. 'See you later.'

No! Don't go! I realise he and I didn't meet under the best of circumstances, but surely he'll be able to vouch for me? I leap out of the chair and rush to the doorway just in time to collide with the sandy-haired man who is coming back in. His clipboard clatters to the ground and over his shoulder I catch a glimpse of Pay-It-Forward's back as he disappears down the hallway. Suddenly he stops and spins round to see what all the fuss is about. Our eyes meet and he regards me uncertainly for an instant.

'You,' he says, almost a little accusingly.

I knew he'd remember! I smile and give a little wave. 'Hello,' I say. The sandy-haired man turns back to him with a questioning look.

'You know her?'

Pay-It-Forward nods. 'We've met.'

We have! Only yesterday!

'She steals sandwiches,' he adds.

'Fine,' says the sandy-haired man grimly. 'I'll add it to the list.'

Chapter Seven

'Is this you?' DC Hill asks, opening up a folder and turning it towards me. Pay-It-Forward has disappeared and DC Hill has just introduced himself as the officer in charge of my case, after pressing the record button on the tape recorder and reciting the time and date. He has also repeated a litany of cautions and rights, just like his predecessors did, as if I'm a toddler who needs to be told several times that there are consequences if I'm naughty. Disappointingly, his voice is not a patch on his colleague's. I peer down at the mugshot of the young woman laid out in front of me: shoulder-length dark brown hair, blue eyes, prominent dark eyebrows, long-ish nose, thin lips.

Good Lord. She looks just like me!

There are subtle differences. Her chin is a bit more pro-nounced and her nose is perhaps a little longer, and she is probably younger than me by five years, but the resemblance is uncanny. There are two photos, one taken face on and one in profile, shot against a black and white wall chart that shows height in inches, and I see that she is almost exactly my height: five foot two. She's even wearing the sort of top I might wear: a straight-neck, slinky long-sleeve T-shirt in maroon with tiny white stripes. *Where did she get that? And who knew criminals could be so fashionable?* Weirdly, it's like she's me, but not me. Or at least she *could* be me, in bad lighting, or if you were short-sighted. I look up at him.

'No,' I say emphatically, shaking my head. He frowns and pulls the photo back towards him, studying it for a moment, then looks back up at me. 'Looks like you,' he says in a challenging tone. 'In fact, I'd say she's a dead ringer.'

'Look here,' I say, indicating the photo. 'Her nose is a teeny tiny bit longer, and her chin is more . . . pointy.' He looks down at the photo.

'Pointy?' He raises a sceptical eyebrow.

'I know! I've got a scar!' I say, lifting my chin and pointing to a spot directly underneath. 'I fell off the swings when I was five. I'll bet she doesn't have that!' We both look down at the woman in the photo; clearly, there is no way we can see beneath her chin.

'Well, if she was here, we could ask her,' he says in a sarcastic tone. He shakes his head and sighs, then stands and crosses to the door, where he pauses and looks back at me. 'Stay,' he orders, using exactly the same tone of voice I use with Charlie Bucket. I look around the room. What option do I have? It's not as if I'm going to attempt a jailbreak. After a minute he returns, tossing two sets of fingerprints onto the table in front of me. He is also carrying my handbag and phone, which he hands to me.

'Right,' he says with a sigh. 'The prints don't match.'

Phew. I exhale with relief and beam at him. I'm not a criminal, after all! He crosses his arms and fixes me with an accusatory stare.

'Why would she impersonate you?' he asks.

As if I would know!

'I have no idea.'

'She was arrested, charged and bailed three weeks ago on multiple counts of fraud. Then failed to show for her court date yesterday. Have you ever seen her before?' Every morning in the mirror, I think. But apart from that, no.

'Never. At least, I don't think so. I mean, I work in a shop. So I see a lot of people.' I shrug. 'But I'd definitely remember if someone looking like me walked in.'

'What sort of shop?'

'A cheese shop – Say Cheese. On the high street in Bermondsey.' He raises an eyebrow.

'I'm guessing she's not your typical customer,' he says, nodding at the photo. I shake my head.

'Not really. Millennials don't buy cheese,' I say. 'Or at least, not our sort of cheese. Too pricey.'

'She's behind a series of credit card frauds. We think she's part of a more organised gang or possibly a team of fraudsters operating out of south-east London. Clearly you've been targeted and your details have been compromised. When she was arrested, she gave your address and showed us a valid driver's licence with your name on it.'

'She showed you *my* driver's licence?' I ask, incredulous.

'Apparently. Have you lost one lately?'

'No. I don't think so.' *Have I?*

'You might want to double-check,' he says, nodding at my handbag. 'Anyway, there are plenty of places on the dark web where you can obtain a fake driver's licence,' he adds, as I pull out my wallet. I open it and leaf through the cards. Bank card, gym membership, loyalty cards. *Whoops.* My eyes slide up to his.

'It's missing.'

'There you go,' he says. 'Have you had any fraud on your bank account recently?'

I frown. 'Not that I'm aware of. How would I know?' I ask.

He looks at me askance. 'Surely you'd know if someone was stealing from you?'

'I guess so,' I reply uneasily. *Would I?*

'Do you check your bank statements regularly?'

'Um . . . not as often as I should,' I admit.

'How about recently?'

I hesitate. *Not. As. Such.* In fact, I meant to ring the bank yesterday after the fiasco over the sandwiches. But I forgot. So much to do and so little time! I shake my head no.

'You might want to check it now,' he suggests, nodding towards my phone.

I frown and pick up my phone, trying to remember my login details. I punch in my username and password while he watches, then bring up my statement and see at once that I am overdrawn by £62! No wonder my card was rejected!

'What's wrong?' he asks.

'I'm overdrawn,' I say with dismay.

'What a surprise,' he says flatly. I scroll down through the payments over the past thirty days and while I recognise some of them, others look strange.

'Not all of these transactions are mine,' I say eventually. 'But some of them are. It's confusing.' I rack my brains trying to remember where I've been and what I've bought of late. There is a purchase almost two weeks ago from a small clothing boutique not far from where I live. I love to shop there, but I can't really afford it at the moment, so for the past few months I've given it a miss. But *she* hasn't! She spent £49 of my money there! I scroll through and see that she has also dined at restaurants I've eaten in, and gone to bars I use, including Dolly's! Clearly, she and I have scarily similar tastes. I look up at him uneasily. 'We shop at the same places,' I say. 'And eat in the same restaurants.'

He nods. 'That's so you wouldn't notice and cancel your card. Clever, but risky. How far back do the bad transactions go?'

'It's difficult to say. A few months, maybe?'

'You really need to check your statements more often,' he says, his tone barely a notch below head teacher. 'So how did she get hold of the password on this account?'

'I don't know.'

'Did you disclose it to anyone?'

'No,' I say emphatically. *Did I?*

'When was the last time you changed it?'

I hesitate. 'I'm not sure,' I say. *Never?*

'Are your passwords written down anywhere?'

I nod. 'In a file. On my computer.' *Organised!*

'And would that file, by any chance, be called *passwords*?' he asks in a withering tone. I wince.

'Maybe?'

He gives a weary sigh. 'You do realise that's the cyber equivalent of walking around carrying a bloody great sign that says: *ROB ME*.'

'How do they get access to my computer?'

'Specially trained ants,' he says. When I give him a confused look, he rolls his eyes. 'They use bots. Software applications that allow an attacker to remotely take control of your computer and perform malicious tasks. Have you downloaded any free software lately?'

'I don't think so, why?'

'Well, don't. That's another tool they use to install spyware.'

'Oh wait,' I say, frowning. 'Maybe there *was* one.'

He raises a querying eyebrow.

'*Re-In-Canine*,' I explain. 'You feed it all your information and it tells you which dog breed you are. In another life,' I say, a bit sheepishly. 'Then it superimposes your features onto that breed so you can see what you'd look like. As a dog,' I add.

'Yeah, I got that.' DC Hill is clearly unimpressed.

'It was a bit rubbish,' I admit.

'Which breed were you?'

'Pug.'

He laughs out loud at this, which is the jolliest I've seen him yet, even if it is at my expense. 'Listen, these people will try all sorts,' he says now. 'Phishing, Vishing, Smishing, it's all fair game to them.'

'Smishing?'

'Uses SMS text,' he says. 'Same fraud. Different medium.'

'So what should I do now?' I ask.

'Call your bank and notify them of the security breach – with luck they'll refund your money. Then change all your passwords and destroy that file.'

'OK. But why did they target me?'

'Why *not* you? Look, if it's any consolation, you're not the only one. Scammers fleeced ten million pounds out of people like you in this country last year.'

'Oh.'

'Though most of those people were more than twice your age,' he adds under his breath. He picks up the folder and stands up.

'So now what?' I ask.

He looks down at me. 'Now we need to find her,' he nods towards the photo.

I frown. 'How do we do that?'

'*We* meaning us. The police. Not *you*. You're free to go.' He nods and turns away and I leap up to follow.

'But surely there's something I can do to help?' I ask.

He turns and flashes me a Cheshire cat smile. 'You've done enough.'

As if it's *me* who's the criminal, rather than the woman who scammed me!

*

I make my way out of the station on my own. Good thing I'm *not* a criminal, as no one seems to pay much attention to me as I wind my way back down the corridor towards the front entrance. I glance around as casually as possible for Pay-It-Forward, but disappointingly he is nowhere to be seen. What a pity that I am unlikely ever to hear his velvet tones again.

As I'm walking out of the station, my phone rings. I glance down and see that it's my mum ringing on FaceTime, which she does whenever her internet in India is good enough. Reluctantly, I push the button. 'Hi Mum.'

The screen wavers and suddenly my mother appears wearing a dark red and orange sweep of cloth. 'Clemency, are you there?' she asks with alarm, as if she has suddenly gone blind.

'Press the camera symbol, Mum.'

'Ah . . . right.' Suddenly my mum is beaming up at me. 'There you are.'

'What's that you're wearing?' I ask.

'A sari. Isn't it lovely,' she says. 'I wish I'd discovered them sooner,' she adds.

I doubt if my mother has even heard the term *cultural appropriation*, but if she had, I suspect the concept would be lost on her. 'We should have come here years ago,' she says. 'India is our spiritual home,' she says earnestly.

'Where's Dad?'

'Right here.' She swings the phone around and for a moment all I see is a blank concrete wall.

'Hi Clem,' my father says. The picture dips and suddenly I am staring at his legs, encased in a sheath of pale plaid purple cloth. He, too, appears to have gone native.

'Hi Dad, what have you got on?'

'It's surprisingly comfortable,' he says. 'To think I've

been wearing trousers all this time. And it keeps my bits cool, too,' he adds, flapping the cloth dangerously with one hand.

'I'll take your word for it,' I answer. 'No need to demonstrate.'

'When are you coming to visit?' my mum asks. The camera swings around the room wildly until she is smiling down at me. Now I can see straight up her nostrils.

'I can't right now, Mum. Too busy at work.' This is my standard excuse. Honestly, FaceTime constitutes plenty of family time for me. *Enough* family time. Sometimes it amounts to too much.

'We're dying to show you India!'

This is something I truly hope I never see: my parents' version of India. Who knows what it involves? Presumably it would be unrecognisable to an Indian. 'Anyway, I'm a bit skint now, Mum. Foreign holidays aren't on the cards.'

'Oh,' she says. Instinctively, I can tell she's been thwarted somehow.

'What's wrong?' I ask.

She sighs. 'Your father insisted on hiring a motorbike the other day.'

'It went badly,' he says off screen.

'How badly?' I ask with mounting alarm. The camera swings to his face.

'Quite badly,' he admits.

Oh dear Lord, please do not let there be casualties.

'Peter Fonda made it look so effortless,' my mum says, returning to the camera.

What is she talking about?

'*Easy Rider*,' says my dad, reading my mind. 'I've wanted to try one ever since.' He shrugs.

'Dad, what happened? No one *died*, did they?'

'Goats,' says my mum, nodding. 'Bless their little animal souls.'

'You hit a goat?'

'Two goats,' says my dad with dismay. 'And now the farmer—'

'Goatherd,' interjects my mum, nodding meaningfully at him.

'The *goatherd* is demanding compensation,' explains Dad. 'They were very expensive cashmere goats, apparently. And the law says we have to compensate him for two years' lost income.'

'We were hoping you might be able to help us out with a small loan,' says Mum. 'We've got an annuity payment coming in any day now, but we just need a few hundred quid to tide us over.'

'I'm broke, Mum. Genuinely. Someone scammed my bank account and spent all my cash.'

'You mean strangers?' asks my mother, genuinely shocked.

'Well, it wasn't friends,' I reply. 'Cybercrime, Mum. It's all the rage. The bots trawl through your computer and steal all your passwords. You two had better be careful,' I warn her authoritatively.

'Oh, don't worry, we change our passwords every fortnight,' says my dad.

'You do?' I ask.

My mum nods emphatically. 'Julia made us promise before we left the UK.'

Ah. Of course she did. Where was I at the time?

'Have you asked Julia for a loan, Mum?'

'I did try. But she seems a little preoccupied right now,' says my mother tentatively. This is, if anything, an understatement. I don't even know why I suggested it. Actually, I *do* know why: because lately it's been left to me to sort out

67

my parents' affairs, rather than my older sister Julia, who lives in the Midlands and is in the middle of an all-consuming divorce from her husband, Robby.

Or as Julia insists on referring to it now: a *conscious uncoupling*. Because apparently these days one doesn't just split from one's partner, one releases negative energy, reclaims one's power and finds emotional freedom in the process, like one of those meal deals at a fast-food place where you get burger, fries *and* an extra-large soft drink, all for one price.

True to her nature, Julia has fixated on the minutiae of the process. The last time I spoke to her, she was obsessively cataloguing and splitting up the marital assets: spice jars, ice trays, half-used shampoo bottles, leftover Christmas wrapping paper, even mismatched gloves were to be evenly divided between them. When they could not agree who should get their favourite sofa, apparently Robby had offered to take a chainsaw to it. All of this might be understandable if Julia did not work as the practice manager at a mindfulness counselling centre, whose stated aims, she had told me when she first took the job, were to 'strengthen one's inner qualities of presence and connectedness'. Over the past few months, Julia had somehow managed to take disconnecting to its most mindful level.

'Sorry, Mum,' I say now.

She shrugs. 'We'll muddle through. We always do, don't we, Pepper?'

'Oh yes. One way or another,' my father calls out cheerily. Which is true.

The next morning I ring my bank. It takes considerable time and patience before I can speak to a human being, but when I finally do, the woman on the other end of the line asks me a long series of questions, then calmly informs me that because I did not safeguard my passwords, the bank would only be prepared to reimburse half of what I am claiming for. 'But what about the other half?' I ask.

'We believe both sides should bear equal responsibility for the losses that occurred.'

'But you're an enormous company with huge assets. And I'm just a lowly individual with tiny means!'

'One of many lowly individuals that we serve,' she says. I cannot help but bristle at her use of the word 'lowly'; it was fine for *me* to use it to describe myself, but for the bank to use it now strikes me as almost offensive. 'We send regular advice via email about how to safeguard your accounts,' she continues.

Do they? I must check my inbox. Certainly, it was not advice I ever noticed, much less heeded.

'It's your responsibility to adhere to our guidelines. Otherwise, we can't guarantee the safety of your funds,' she informs me now. Evidently, she is used to saying this. There is a bored, almost indifferent, quality to her voice, as if theft of one's savings is no more unusual than a hangnail, or a ladder in one's tights. *Heigh ho.* Just another day of bog-standard fraud. As I hang up the phone, it strikes me that criminality is no longer considered deviant; somehow it has become the norm. When did this happen? And how did I miss it?

After the call, I begin the laborious process of changing all my passwords. The woman on the phone said I should never keep them stored on my laptop, never write them down, and never, ever, disclose them to anyone. How on earth am I meant to remember them, I wonder? My brain is already clogged with too much information, including the lyrics to several dozen hit musicals, the tasting characteristics of endless varieties of cheese, and the names of all *The*

Great British Bake Off finalists going back several years, not to mention their finale showstoppers. I will definitely need a system to codify the passwords, especially if I am meant to be changing them all the time: star signs? Disney princesses? Crisp flavours? A complex combination of all three?

As usual, Charlie Bucket has the answer. He is fast asleep on his side and his legs now begin to tremble with dreamlike urgency. He draws a sharp intake of breath, then a moment later exhales with a long, meandering whimper. Just as the Inuit People are rumoured to have fifty words to describe snow, I reckon that dogs have just as many sounds in their vocal repertoire, which humans have tried ineffectively to characterise: woof, yelp, bark, ruff, growl, whine, howl. Charlie Bucket has been known to use them all, at one time or another, and often simultaneously. In that instant I decide that my new passwords will be a nod to my flatmate and his unerring ability to make himself heard. I smile as I type in *CharlieBucketBarks1!* I will simply change the last word every few weeks. It is a genius system, one I am bound to remember. As Charlie Bucket is impossible to forget.

Chapter Eight

June handles the shop floor on Wednesday mornings, which leaves me free to focus on bookkeeping, stock ordering and other tasks without the constant interruptions of customers. Sometimes I do this upstairs in my flat, because the shop is too small to have an office, but mostly I perch on a stool with my laptop on the tiny counter behind the till, because June likes it when I'm there, and it's good to keep an eye on things. In between customers, while she unpacks stock and tidies up, we gossip about the regulars and discuss the news of the day, while Charlie Bucket has a snooze on the shop floor.

This morning she is concerned about a report on the radio saying that 325 % more people in the UK will be vegan by the end of the year. 'The overall number is still very small,' I tell her. 'Three hundred and twenty-five per cent of tiny is still tiny − it's only a bit *less* tiny than before.' Perhaps understandably, she's worried about job security. June unwraps a large log of goat cheese and lays out cling film and a small digital scale on the counter, preparing to slice it into portions.

'I definitely understand going meat-free,' she says, picking up a knife. 'But giving up dairy strikes me as unnatural. For mammals, milk is about as natural as it gets.' She carefully slices a portion of goat cheese and wraps it in cling film, before weighing it on a small digital scale.

'I think it's the thing of one species exploiting another for its milk,' I suggest carefully. Truthfully, I'm not really of a mind to defend veganism; Lord knows we'd both be out of a job if it really took off. And as far as I'm concerned, vegan cheddar more closely resembles windscreen wipers than it does cheese.

'But what about exploitation across genders? Men have exploited women's milk for millennia. No one complains about *that*.'

'True.' I smile. June often lobs such offbeat observations into our conversation, but they usually land with a resounding ping of accuracy.

'Apparently there's a restaurant in Knightsbridge that serves a really delicious steak made from watermelon,' she says. 'I'm quite tempted. Though I wouldn't want to misrepresent myself.' She finishes wrapping the last piece of goat cheese, and I throw her a puzzled look.

'How?'

'By posing as a vegan.'

'You don't have to be Chinese to eat Chinese food,' I point out.

'No, but it's perfectly obvious I'm not Chinese. And it's *not* obvious that I'm not a vegan.'

True again, I think. Though in this instance, her logic eludes me. 'Someone's been posing as me lately,' I say.

June looks up at me, surprised. 'Really? Who?'

'A woman who looks like me. I'm pretty sure she lives locally, too. She definitely shops around here.'

'That is so creepy! How did you find out?'

'She stole my driver's licence. And my bank details.'

June's eyes widen. 'Did she steal any money?'

'Um . . . yes. And she impersonated me when she was arrested,' I add, though I'm starting to feel a little uneasy about divulging all this to someone who works for me. It makes me look foolish. Or stupid. Or both. Which would not be wide of the mark. But June's next comment veers sharply off this track.

'I impersonated someone once,' she admits. I look over at her, amazed.

'Really?'

'Well, it was a few years ago. And it all started pretty innocently. But one thing led to another and . . .' June shrugs. 'It was sort of a needs-must situation,' she declares finally, bundling up all the newly wrapped portions of goat cheese and carrying them into the cheese room. 'I think the technical word for what I did is called *sock puppetry*,' she says over her shoulder.

I stare after her, slightly aghast. June is the last person on earth I would suspect of deception or wrongdoing of any kind. And while I've never actually set eyes on it, I suspect that June has more integrity in her sock *drawer* than the rest of us have in our entire messy lives. As for honesty, June is definitely *not* the person whose opinion you ask when you've made a dodgy impulse purchase in the sales over the weekend, as she will definitely tell it like it is. In fact, I have always thought she was constitutionally incapable of dissembling.

Just then the bell on the shop door tinkles and a well-dressed older man enters. For a moment he frowns down at Charlie Bucket, who raises his head appraisingly, judges him to be a low threat level, and then goes back to sleep. The man blinks a few times, then cautiously steps around him, following June into the cheese privy, where I can hear him enquiring about *ricotta salata*. After he has paid and left, I corner her behind the till. 'I'm struggling with the notion of you as a sock puppet,' I say.

73

June laughs. 'I invented a false identity in order to persuade my great aunt Mimi to move out of her bungalow into assisted housing. I knew it was absolutely the best thing for her, but I didn't have the authority to make her do it, so in the end I invented someone who did. It was as simple as that.'

'So who did you invent?'

'A local builder called Derek. Who told her the bungalow needed so much work, that she was better off selling it.'

'Why didn't you just get a real builder in?'

'Because, in fact, the bungalow was in quite good shape. She'd looked after it really well.'

'So how did you persuade her?'

'I told her I'd taken him round the bungalow when she was out at the hairdresser and that he'd found evidence of subsidence. Then I sent a really high estimate in the post on fake letterhead,' she adds sheepishly.

'June, that is shocking!' I exclaim. She shakes her head defiantly.

'She loves the assisted housing! And she's made loads of new friends. Plus, she got a really good price for the bungalow. The best part is: a year after she moved out, the bungalow *did* develop subsidence, and in the end it needed underpinning. So I was right.' June picks up a broom and begins to sweep up some sawdust from the packaging.

'Right as in morally right? Or right as in correct to act as you did?'

June stops sweeping to consider this. 'Both,' she says finally, then carries on sweeping.

Huh.

That evening I close the shop up quickly and go to roller derby practice. I'm on the B team and on Wednesdays we do drills while on Sunday we scrimmage, but I look forward to both for different reasons. Drill nights don't usually require as much energy or adrenaline and are far less likely to end in sprains or bruises, but they aren't half as exhilarating as scrimmages. On Wednesdays we work mainly on skills and speed, but there's still a competitive edge, as we're all keen to be rostered for the scrimmage the following Sunday, and the line-up isn't revealed until the end of the session.

Tonight when I enter the locker room I see at once that it's a busy session, as there's barely any space to change. I shoulder my way through the group, greeting some of my teammates, the ones I've got to know, as I only got promoted from C to B team in early December, so I'm still learning who's who. Derby can be confusing because the persona we adopt on skates isn't necessarily the one we wear all the time. When we go to the pub afterwards, I can barely recognise some of my teammates without their helmets, body pads and mouth guards. Right now, my friend Sadie spies me from across the room and grins, her eyes widening to indicate the crowd. Sadie has only been skating for a year but has progressed amazingly fast; she and I moved up from the C team together, and both of us are still trying to establish our place in the squad.

Everyone who skates has a number, a derby name and a skating persona to match. Your skate name is usually a pun on your real name, or on some aspect of your personality, and is meant to suggest how tough you are: I guess it's meant to be part funny, part threatening. On my team we have names like Bloody Nora, Raving Ruby, Tequila Sheila or my favourite, Eleanor Bruisevelt. Clemency was a difficult one, but in the end I decided on Calamity Lane, and chose my lucky number, 22, to go with it. Sadie's derby name is Screaming Sadie, which is sort of ironic, because off the track she's quite soft-spoken.

I change and pull on my gear as quickly as I can, eager to get out on the track. We always start with ten minutes of free skating to warm up and loosen our joints. This is always one of my favourite bits of the night, when you can let go and push yourself hard and fast without worrying about your position with respect to everyone else. Also, it's a chance to literally skate off what's bothering you, because when skating is fast and furious, it's better than therapy.

Or even sex. Well, it's certainly better than mediocre sex.

The only issue tonight is that the track is overcrowded, so I have to check myself more than I would like. After the first few minutes, I drop back behind a cluster of blockers who are flying round the track like a tight formation of geese and slip further to the outside so that I can really lengthen my stride. But just as I do, a skater I vaguely recognise arrives late and steps right out in front of me, nearly cutting me off and forcing me to do a toe-stop. In derby this is called clipping and it's definitely not on. I turn and glare at her: she's mixed race, about my height and wearing red and white sweet-striped leggings, a black spandex tank top and a white helmet with a visor. For an instant I see her eyes flare with aggression, then just as suddenly the anger dissolves and she gives a quick apologetic nod before pushing off, disappearing into the passing throng of skaters. I follow a little more slowly, but not before I clock the number on her arm: 44. I don't know her name but I have definitely skated with her before. Maybe she, too, has just moved up?

We go through a long series of drills, including several requiring us to weave around cones, and a few that involve jumping small obstacles like noisy, ungainly hurdlers. During the course of the evening it becomes clear that 44 is also a jammer. So far I've identified six jammers here tonight, which means I might not get rostered for the scrimmage this weekend, as they generally only choose four, so I push myself a little harder than normal.

It's during the final drill of the night, which is more like a mini-scrimmage, when the accident happens. I'm not sure whose fault it is, but as I make a move to smash through a gaggle of blockers, suddenly something slams into me from behind and I go down like an overstuffed sack of grain, taking Bloody Nora and Screamin' Sadie with me. The three of us end up sprawled across the floor in a heap. On the way down, Sadie's knee smacks hard into my eye and for an instant I literally see stars (which I genuinely thought was a myth) and then my vision goes scarily dark for a long moment, before slowly coming back into focus. *Ouch.*

I clap a hand over my eye and roll over onto my hands and knees, struggling to get my breath. To my right I hear Sadie wince a little. She is holding her ankle, while Nora is struggling a little shakily back onto her skates. The referee has stopped play and all the other skaters are slowly circling us like vultures. A few pause now to lend a hand, and I see a pair of black skates with lime green wheels come to a halt just in front of me, and a gloved hand appears in front of my face. I look up, trying to focus my vision in the bright lights of the gym. For a moment I'm not sure whose hand I am staring at, but then I see that it's 44. I hesitate, then reach out and take her hand and she yanks me upright with a grunt, but before I can say thanks, she spins round and skates off. I still don't even know her name.

Someone produces icepacks for us and I sit down against the wall and watch as Sadie limps off to a bench at the side, grinning at me. I might have a shiner in the morning, but it looks like she may have properly messed up her ankle, which I feel bad about. Bloody Nora has fared better than either of us and has joined the rest of the squad to finish the drill, but Sadie and I are definitely done for the night. I suspect my chances of being rostered this weekend are well and truly scuppered now. While the accident wasn't exactly my fault, I was certainly at the epicentre, which never looks good.

After practice, most of us head to the pub across the road. Sadie is limping but still keen to go and urges me to come along. She has a new girlfriend she is dying for me to meet: another derby player from a different team, apparently, who has promised to join us, but Sadie's been so secretive that I don't know who it is. The pub is pretty crowded, but once we've elbowed our way to the bar and got drinks, we join a big table of skaters. There are at least fifteen women and together we make up a pretty raucous crew.

'Is your mystery friend here yet?' I ask Sadie.

'She's due any minute,' says Sadie, craning her neck towards the door.

'So spill. Who is she?'

'You'll see.'

'Why the secrecy?'

'Because I don't want a fuss.'

'Why would there be a fuss?'

All of a sudden, the tenor at the table shifts slightly as an attractive young woman with closely cropped bleached blonde hair appears and makes her way towards us. She's wearing dark red lipstick and a knee-length banana yellow faux fur coat. As she sidles over to us, Sadie's eyes flash with delight. The blonde woman bends down to give Sadie a quick kiss on the lips, her movements casual but definite, as if she's staking her claim. 'Hey babe,' she says quietly.

All the other women at the table are surreptitiously watching us as Sadie's new girlfriend shrugs off her coat and heads to the bar, but it takes a few moments for me to work out why. She's wearing slim-cut cream-coloured jeans and a tight black T-shirt with a skating logo on the back, but then my eyes land on the tattoo on her bicep: the number 001 with a serpent wound around the digits. I may not have recognised her without her derby gear on, but I'd know that tattoo anywhere, because Sadie's new girlfriend is Abby Noxious – one of the top jammers in the UK. This woman is not just a rising star in British roller derby, she's a world-class player. I turn to Sadie and her lips are puckered in a knowing smile.

'Oh my God,' I say quietly. 'Is that who I think it is?'

'It might be,' she says coyly.

'Why didn't you tell me?'

'Because I wanted to make sure it was a *thing*.'

'It is most definitely a thing. A big thing. How the hell did you meet her?'

'Sat next to her on a train.'

'A train where?'

'My last trip home at Christmas. Turns out she's from Cardiff, too.'

'Santa was certainly good to *you* this year,' I say.

Sadie smiles a little coquettishly. 'Maybe it was *me* who was good,' she replies.

'On top of being one hell of a skater, she's utterly gorgeous,' I say quietly, as we both watch her cross the room carrying a pint.

'She is, isn't she?' murmurs Sadie, looking very pleased indeed. Who wouldn't be?

Abby Noxious squeezes in next to us, and nods to me easily. 'I'm Abby, by the way. Sadie's crap at introductions.' Like I don't already know who she is. Which makes me instantly warm to her.

'I'm Clem.'

79

'Ah right,' she says knowingly. 'Good to meet you. How was practice?'

Sadie darts me a quick glance. 'Bit of a pile-up at the end. Think I may have done my ankle in,' she says sheepishly. Abby rolls her eyes.

'Let's have a look.' She reaches down and gingerly lifts Sadie's ankle higher to examine it, frowning. 'Swelling isn't too bad, but you need to elevate it,' pulling the ankle onto her lap. 'Keep icing it at twenty-minute intervals. And no skating for a few days.'

Sadie pulls a face. 'Yeah I know.'

'All part of the fun,' says Abby with a grin. 'Drink up. It'll kill the pain,' she adds. 'Looks like your face got it, too,' she says, nodding towards my bad eye, which I can tell is already swelling.

'Think I caught Sadie's knee,' I say.

She smiles. 'There are worse knees,' she says suggestively.

'How many black eyes have *you* had in your skating career?' I ask.

Abby shrugs. 'A few dozen. No lasting damage. And you know what they say: no pain, no fame.' She grins at us. In spite of her easy manner, I've seen this woman skate before, and on track she's as gritty as they come. Somehow I don't think I'll ever achieve even a tenth of her status, but funnily enough, Sadie might. Like Abby, Sadie has the perfect physique for roller derby: she's medium height with a wiry, muscular build. Her short black hair is cut in a stylish Louise Brooks bob, and sitting next to each other, the two of them look like yin and yang. Now Abby murmurs something quietly in Sadie's ear and I can't help but feel a little flare of envy. It is perfectly obvious the pair are in the hot flush of . . . *something*.

Something I haven't felt for ages.

Chapter Nine

Later that night my sister rings me up, ostensibly to complain about our parents and how irresponsible they are, but in reality to make sure I've filled out a form from her solicitor that she emailed me last week, something I haven't quite got round to. The form is all about proving that she and Robby are genuinely separated, even though they are still living under the same roof. They continue to live together because they are both too stingy to live apart. Ironically, parsimony is one of the main things they have in common – though clearly it's not enough to base a marriage on. According to Julia's lawyer, the court will give more weight to *my* evidence than theirs when I attest that they do not sleep in the same bed, share the same dessert spoon, brush their teeth from the same tube of toothpaste or watch Netflix together. How I am meant to know these things remains a mystery to me; it is not as if I cohabit with them.

Julia makes a modest effort at small talk before getting down to the real reason for the call. 'Clem, you haven't sent the lawyer's form back,' she says accusingly.

'Sorry, I've had a really busy week. I promise to look at it soon.'

'You don't seem to appreciate how stressful this is. I'm having to *completely* reinvent myself.'

'Julia, you're still you.'

'You wouldn't understand. Marriage *changed* me, Clem.

The person I became inside my marriage wasn't really me. It was some strange hybrid version of me, and the real me got swallowed along the way. Now it's not just Robby I'm divorcing, it's the *married me*.'

I frown. Did Julia really change once she'd married Robby? And if so, why hadn't I noticed? Marriage isn't like some sort of outer skin you can shed like a snake. If it changed you, wouldn't that be permanent? For my own part, I've never been so deep inside a relationship that I've lost sight of myself. Though wasn't that partly what Bianca had complained about when I was with Marcus?

'I need to work out who I'm going to be,' she continues.

That part, at least, I can sympathise with.

'I really need your support, Clem,' she says earnestly. 'All the literature says I'm meant to lean on my extended family during this time.' She sounds as if she is reading directly from a pamphlet. Which she may well be. Julia conducts all aspects of her life strictly by the book and divorce is no different.

I sigh. 'I'm here for you, Jules.'

In truth, I'm struggling to muster the appropriate level of sympathy for her situation. A part of me thinks that Julia might actually be enjoying her divorce. At the very least, she seems to be wallowing in it. She has thrown herself headlong into the process; indeed, I haven't seen her this galvanised in ages. My own suspicion was that after several years, she and Robby had slid into a classic couples' rut: they'd woken up one day to find themselves mired in the monotony of day-to-day married life. It probably didn't help that they'd opted out of kids, something Julia has always been trenchantly opposed to. (Last year, when the nation was transfixed by the television adaptation of *The Handmaid's Tale*, she totally identified with the infertile wives and Marthas, rather than the breeding handmaids, even preferring the wives' blue dresses to the handmaidens' red.)

I have a theory about why Julia doesn't want kids: I think it's because she never really *was* one. Growing up, my sister never mastered the art of childhood. It was like she emerged from the womb pre-propagated with a sensible, middle-aged mindset, complete with habits and values to match, instead of acquiring them along the way like the rest of us. From the earliest age, she eschewed most of the things that made childhood fun: mud pies, toothpick swordfights, spaghetti faces, disgusting potions, naughtiness. This trend continued into adolescence, where she drank only in moderation (who *does* that?), shunned anything illegal (ditto) and guarded her chastity until she found true love (I rest my case). Which turned out to be Robby, at least, for a time. So it was no surprise to me that she didn't want to spawn offspring – they were alien to her.

My parents didn't help. While Julia was busy being far too sensible, organised and tidy for her own good, I was the polar opposite: rash, messy and chaotic. From a young age she was happy to boss me about, and as soon as my parents realised how competent she was, they were quick to jettison their responsibilities and leave her to do their job for them. And while she was fiercely loyal to the family, defending me at school or finishing my homework so I wouldn't get into trouble, she was never very affectionate or demonstrative. Nurturing did not come naturally to my sister, even if orchestrating did.

The funny thing is, I always thought that when it came to Robby, Julia made the right choice. Temperamentally, Julia and Robby are very well suited. They were always one of those couples who seemed to know each other inside out. When you went out to dinner with them to a restaurant, they always knew what the other would order without even asking, and never needed to confer when it was time to go. But maybe that was part of the problem. Maybe marriage needs a little mystery to feed on, or at least a few surprises. At any rate, it seems a shame that it has taken divorce to give my sister a new lease of life.

'Robby and I are on *exactly* the same page,' she says now. 'In fact, we're communicating better now than we ever have.'

'Great,' I say half-heartedly. To my mind, they communicated perfectly well before. Besides, if they really *are* on the same page, why are they getting divorced?

'He's off to see his brother in Edinburgh next weekend, so I've booked myself into a spa for a few days, where I plan to rebalance and rejuvenate,' she says a little triumphantly.

'Good for you,' I reply. But what I'm really thinking is: Robby is off for the weekend, so you're leaving too? Isn't that what married couples do?

'I need to look after myself. Did you know that divorce can compromise your immune system?'

'No, I didn't.'

So can brownies, apparently, but it doesn't stop me eating them. 'Maybe you should get a dog,' I suggest, shovelling my feet under Charlie Bucket's immense hind quarters for warmth. He groans and shifts slightly to accommodate me. 'Apparently, dogs can boost your immune system.'

'That's because they're filthy and breed bacteria,' she says flatly.

True.

I do not mention my arrest, the theft of my identity, nor the fraud on my bank account, as my sister would no doubt chastise me for failing to look after myself properly. Maybe Charlie Bucket and I also need a spa weekend to rebalance and rejuvenate? Though at this rate it is unlikely we will ever be able to afford more than a trip to the pond at Southwark Park. Charlie Bucket likes to snaffle up all the fallen breadcrumbs people toss to the pigeons there, though once or twice he has fallen foul of the swans, who clearly don't like the cut of his jib. Each time they rush at him with wings menacingly raised and chests puffed out, Charlie Bucket responds with characteristic aplomb by lifting his leg against them.

The next day when I wake, my eye is swollen and a lurid shade of purple. I apply make-up as best I can to cover it up, but the bruise is surprisingly stubborn, bleeding through three different types of foundation in succession. In the end I am forced to give up; my eye now looks like an overstuffed blueberry muffin. When Bianca pops by the shop at lunch-time on her way to a client meeting near Tower Bridge, she looks at me aghast. 'What happened to you?' she asks.

I shrug. 'Roller derby accident.'

'Death by gliding,' she says shaking her head. When it comes to roller derby, Bianca is firmly on my mother's team. 'Any news about your creepy identity thief?' she asks, reaching into the refrigerated cabinet and helping herself to a macaroon. She pops it into her mouth before I can stop her.

'Oi! You can't just come in here and steal stock! You have to pay for that!'

'Fine. *I* can afford to shop here,' she says pertly, taking out a credit card and wafting it about. Unlike *me,* she means. I scowl and wave it away.

'Nothing's happened,' I say with a sigh. 'The police haven't been in touch.' I've heard nothing from DC Hill in the last few days to suggest that they've made any progress on my case, so I expect that it's dropped to the bottom of the in-tray by now. Bianca pulls a face.

'Feeble,' she pronounces.

'I suspect they have bigger fish to fry,' I say.

'What *I* suspect is that if you want something done properly, you have to do it yourself,' she replies.

'Like *what* exactly?'

She shrugs. 'Like track her down.'

'How?'

'You know what she looks like. And she left a trail of clues on your account.'

'So?'

'Well, it's not rocket science, is it? Work it out. Who *is* this woman? What does she do for a living? Where does she hang out? What does she do for fun?'

'I can answer most of those questions already: she's a thief who likes to spend my money.'

'But that's not *all* she is.'

'OK, Sherlock,' I say, opening my laptop and logging into my bank account. I turn the screen round towards Bianca. 'Here are all my bank transactions for the past three months,' I say. '*You* work it out.'

'Fine,' says Bianca. 'Show me which ones are hers.'

I scroll down, ticking all the transactions I don't recognise. Bianca frowns at the screen for several seconds, biting her lip. 'I'll tell you one thing,' she says. 'She's had more fun in the last few months than *you* have.'

'You don't know that,' I say, a little defensively.

'Yes, I do. Hang on. What about this one? And this?' She points to two transactions I haven't marked.

'That's *us*, brainbox. It's yoga,' I say. Bianca shakes her head.

'We don't do yoga on a Friday, Clem,' she says. Then she turns to me, her lips curling into a sly smile. 'But we do *now*.'

Before she leaves, Bianca extracts a promise from me to accompany her to yoga the next day after work. The week has slid by and it is already D-Day, the date of my comedy gig with Marcus. I've arranged to meet him at the club that evening, and when I arrive it's already crowded. Somehow, he's managed to bag a table right at the front (*when did he get here – yesterday?*) and has ordered drinks: a large white wine for me and a Drambuie for him. Marcus only ever drinks Drambuie, another one of his many 'quirks', and it is frankly a relief to no longer encounter the bemused stares of bartenders when he insists on ordering it neat. It took at least six months of us dating for him to realise that I was never, *ever* going to order one for myself.

Even though the club is dark, Marcus still notices my black eye as soon as I sit down. 'What happened?' he asks.

'It's nothing. Just a bruise. Roller derby.'

He frowns. 'Maybe you should take up curling instead,' he offers.

'No thanks.'

I am no longer his girlfriend, so I do not even have to feign interest in his suggestions for how to improve my life.

'It would be safer.'

'It would be duller.'

We make small talk for a bit before the main act comes on, during which time Marcus digs around for intelligence relating to my non-existent love life. I answer a little evasively, just to wind him up, until he finally blurts out the question he's been desperate to ask. 'So,' he asks, 'are you sharing your cheese plate with anyone these days?'

I wince. *Cheese plate* is a Marcus euphemism for sex, one I truly hope I never have to hear again in this lifetime. As he speaks, he leans back with a leer on his face that is probably meant to be a grin, but somehow goes horribly wrong *en route*. Marcus doesn't really *do* casual; everything about him is premeditated.

I shake my head. 'The only guys I've met lately are cops,' I say, and tell him about my arrest and the discovery of the identity thief instead. When I do, his eyes widen with interest.

'So she looks just like you?'

Uh oh. Red flags begin to unfurl in my brain.

'Well, she looks *quite* like me,' I say, back-pedalling. 'A bit younger.'

Marcus's large nostrils flare with excitement at the suggestion of a younger, unbruised version of me. Oh God, why did I not realise that talking about my doppelgänger to my lovelorn ex-boyfriend was a really crap idea?

'Anyway, I'm sure she's legged it by now,' I say. 'Whoever she was.'

'We have to find her!' he cries eagerly.

'No, we don't, Marcus,' I say flatly. 'I've notified the police and the bank and changed all my passwords. It's finished.'

'But she has your ID! And she looks just like you! She's still out there! She could be posing as you right now!' He looks around the room for a moment, as if he expects to see her ordering at the bar, then leans forward, a fiery look in his eye. Vigilante Marcus is a version I've not met before, and I shrink back almost instinctively. I know what he's like once he gets an idea into his head, and my heart sinks at the prospect of having to rein him in.

'I think we should leave the police to do their job,' I say firmly.

'Clemency, trust me. The police will never, ever follow this up. They don't have the time or the resources, or even the inclination. We need to get hold of that mugshot.'

'No, Marcus, we don't,' I say, in my most authoritative voice. But I needn't have bothered because Marcus is no longer listening. He has already pulled out his phone and begun tapping frantically into it. I take a large swig of my wine and watch as he pings off a series of texts. Finally, he looks up at me, beaming.

'Sorted,' he says smugly.

Good grief. He does, after all, work in the law.

The next day, when I get a text from Bianca saying she'll collect me from the shop rather than meeting me at yoga, I am instantly suspicious. 'Why?' I text back.

'Because we have to prepare,' she replies ominously. Once again, red flags begin to flutter in my head. What sort of preparation does she have in mind? Isn't it a bit late in the day for martial arts training?

When she eventually turns up, she's carrying a shopping bag, which she plonks down on the counter in front of me. 'I think I've finally found my *métier*,' she says with satisfaction, reaching into the bag. I watch as she pulls out two ladies' wigs (one blonde, one ginger), two long, flowery scarves and two pairs of oversized sunglasses. 'Subterfuge,' she says with satisfaction. 'I've been wasted in advertising all these years! Plus, I've always wanted to try life as a ginger. And this was much cheaper than a salon.' She pulls on the redheaded wig and positions it, then plucks up one of the scarves and throws it extravagantly around her neck before selecting the larger pair of sunglasses and putting them on. When she's finished, she turns to me. 'How do I look?' she asks, pursing her lips in a self-conscious pout.

'Like Miss Marple crossed with Florence Welch.'

'Good.' Bianca nods with satisfaction, even though I

hadn't really meant it as a compliment. Clearly, she is loving her reincarnation as ace lady detective. She hands me the platinum blonde wig and I hold it up a little doubtfully.

'So, I'll be channelling . . . you?'

'We need to throw her off the scent. She mustn't recognise you.'

'Fine.' I sigh and pull on the wig, scarf and sunglasses, then cross to the back of the shop to look in the mirror, where I see that I look just as ridiculous as I expected to. No one in their right mind would think this was my real hair. And who wears sunglasses in the dead of winter?

Meanwhile, Bianca is scrutinising me like I'm some sort of heifer at the county fair. 'Interesting,' she says, narrowing her eyes. 'Blonde isn't really your vibe, is it?'

'Let's just get this over with,' I reply.

It seems neither of us anticipated the problems of doing yoga with a cheap wig on. Half an hour later I am clutching my newly acquired hairpiece to keep it from falling off, while simultaneously bent sideways doing the triangle pose. To make matters worse, the damn thing is itchy, and my doppelgänger is nowhere to be seen. Bianca is beside me having similar difficulties; I can tell she is annoyed because she is breathing excessively through her nose, like an irate stallion. The male instructor keeps glancing back at us suspiciously. Fortunately, we have never taken this particular class before, so he doesn't recognise us. After only a few minutes I am half expecting Bianca to stalk out. We've positioned ourselves at the back deliberately, so we can keep an eye on everyone else, though I can see now that, handily, it would also make for an easy exit.

Suddenly we hear the gentle click of the door just behind us as someone enters and slides into place on my other side.

Although I am still bent over, I angle my head to get a look and see that it's her!

Good Lord! She really *does* look just like me.

No wonder she stole my identity! It would be so easy! I look back down at the floor and my heart begins to pound like a jackhammer. Surely she'll recognise me? I sneak another sideways glance, but she appears to be 100 per cent focused on yoga, bent far over in an extreme version of the triangle position, her legs extended in a wide V, her arm pointing ramrod straight towards the ceiling. I see the instructor nod hello to her with more than a little interest; clearly, she's one of his favourites. After another moment he changes positions, sitting down on the floor and moving into a tight seated forward fold, his legs stretched out in front of him. I do the same, struggling to grab my toes, and when I glance sideways, I see that my doppelgänger's torso is *completely* flat against her legs. The woman is a bloody pretzel! Who knew criminals could be so limber? I push myself further down, but my hamstrings scream so loud that I'm afraid she'll hear them.

On the other side of me, Bianca gives a tiny, not-very-discreet grunt. I turn my head towards her and she is bent over, clutching her toes, her head tilted a little awkwardly so as to look at me. Her eyebrows shoot up to form a question. *Is that her?* she mouths silently. I give the tiniest of nods and Bianca emits a sort of half-gasp. I glare at her fiercely. Clearly, she needs to work on her subterfuge!

We both carry on with the lesson, trying hard not to look at the woman next to me, while my mind races ahead. Now that we are actually in the same room with her, what comes next? I don't think either of us thought this through, and as the class continues, dread slowly seeps across my insides like an oil slick. Should we confront her when the class ends?

And if so, could she be dangerous? I'm not sure I trust Bianca *not* to do something rash, so am now kicking myself that we did not formulate a plan.

On top of that, the yoga is bloody impossible. This class is far more advanced than the one we do on Tuesdays (which I now realise is yoga for people who just want to be able to *say* they do yoga). After half an hour, I am sweating like an aubergine and have discovered muscles I didn't even know existed. The final pose is something called the 'firefly', which requires us to squat down, place our hands on the ground in front of us and lift our entire body off the floor with our legs extended *over* our shoulders, like contortionists. I watch in horror as the instructor demonstrates, concluding that 'firefly' is beyond any normal human capability. This is comic book yoga, designed for people made of stretchy elastic, rather than bones and ligaments, and there is no way I will even attempt it. But beside me, my doppelgänger places her hands squarely on the ground, takes a deep breath, then rocks forward and lifts her pelvis up, flinging her thighs over her shoulders. She balances for an instant, then exhales, and as she does, her legs shoot out like two bayonets either side of her head, while I watch in open-mouthed amazement.

Of course she can do firefly! She can probably scale buildings as well.

The instructor finishes the class and thanks us all for coming, giving a quick nod to her, as if to say *nice job!* Clearly, Firefly is some sort of teacher's pet. In spite of myself, I feel envy rise up inside me like bile, and I have to stop myself crying out: 'Hang on! Firefly may be super flexible, but she's still a criminal!' I hang back as the class files out and see her vanish into the changing rooms. Bianca is waiting impatiently off to one side, her ginger wig slightly askew and a frenzied look in her eye. 'Hurry up!' she hisses under her breath, nodding towards the exit.

'What do we do *now*?' I whisper.

'We follow her,' she whispers back, disappearing into the changing rooms.

So we do.

Chapter Ten

Finding Firefly was surprisingly easy; hanging onto her proves more difficult. By the time we reach our lockers, she has already put on her coat and is hastily gathering up her things. No time for a shower, or even to relieve my full bladder. Instead, we grab our clothes and stuff them into our bags and hurry to follow her out of the building. Outside it's rush hour and she nearly vanishes in the crowded sea of commuters, darting around people and heading towards the Tube entrance across the road. She's wearing a dark blue pea coat (*nice! Did she buy it with my money?*) and a violet wool beanie hat that I have to admit looks rather good on her. (*Maybe I should get one? Or maybe I could borrow hers, seeing as how we share everything else?*)

We follow her onto the Jubilee line at London Bridge, jumping into the carriage just behind. The tube is packed but we manage to squeeze right down to the end of the carriage so we can watch through the small window that separates the two cars, but not before we draw irate glares from all the other passengers we have to push past, whose feet and handbags and briefcases we stumble over on the way. Once there, Bianca crouches down to watch through the window, and a bald man with turquoise blue designer glasses seated just beside us hisses in an icy undertone: 'Pardon me, but those are my dahlias you've just trodden on.' We both look down to see a large bunch of bright orange flowers peeking out of a pale pink wrapper at his feet. The bouquet is bent halfway down the stem at an odd angle. As if it has been trodden on.

'So sorry,' I murmur, shoving further up against Bianca, who at this point is pretty well flattened against the door, her ginger wig slightly askew. The man reaches down and snatches the bouquet up to his chest, his eyes snapping at us from behind his glasses. The train comes to a halt at the next station, and Bianca peers through the window, struggling to keep an eye on Firefly, while a load more people squeeze onto our car. The train is completely rammed, and after the exertions of our workout, I am now really desperate for a wee.

We set off again and for the first time, I wonder where Firefly is going? What if her destination is miles away, in Barking or Upminster or Epping Forest? How far exactly are we prepared to go? And how long *exactly* will my bladder hold? The train pulls into Canada Water and Bianca gives a little squeak as she sees Firefly step off the carriage ahead. 'Quick!' she says. We hurl ourselves across the crowded car, shouldering other passengers aside like rugby players, emerging from the train just before the doors close. We tumble onto the platform and see Firefly disappear down a tunnel at the far end of the station leading to another branch line.

We set off after her, our wigs flying in the wind as the tube pulls away from the platform with a whoosh, and two minutes later we emerge onto another platform just as a train heading towards New Cross pulls in. Firefly is a little way down the platform towards the front end of the train and steps into a carriage, while once again Bianca and I dash onto the one directly behind. The doors close and the train pulls away, and we both slump down into empty seats. My bladder feels like a bloated puffer fish. I turn to Bianca.

'I need a wee,' I confess. She rolls her eyes.

'That is *so* not helpful!'

'Maybe we should try again next Friday?'

'You are literally the *worst* detective ever.'

'Besides,' I say, 'who knows where she's headed? We could end up somewhere really dodgy.'

Bianca gives a derisive snort. 'This is East London, not Angola.'

After a minute the train pulls into New Cross Station and we realise that it's the end of the line. We gather up our things and as we do, we see Firefly walk briskly past our carriage heading towards the stairs. We follow at a distance and a minute later we emerge out onto the street. Firefly is hurrying away and we watch as she turns off down a side road. My eyes dart to a nearby pub, and Bianca reads my mind instantly. 'Absolutely not,' she says, shaking her head.

'I promise I'll be super-fast,' I say in a pleading voice.

'Forget it,' she says, grabbing my arm and pulling me after her.

We follow at a distance, but even so, I am convinced that Firefly will see us. If she does, she is bound to recognise my platinum blonde wig from yoga class, which glows like a beacon in the dark, but she appears to be in a hurry and never once turns around. After two more blocks we enter a housing estate and Firefly crosses to a long, low building, suddenly disappearing through a ground-floor door. The door slams shut before we can reach it, and when Bianca tries the handle, it's locked. 'Damn!' she mutters with a sigh. We step back from the building and look up. It is four storeys high with outside walkways on each floor leading to separate flats. After another moment we see Firefly emerge from a doorway onto the second-floor walkway and cross to the third flat from the end, taking out keys from her bag.

She fumbles with the lock for a moment, then disappears inside. Bianca quickly takes out her phone and photographs the flat's exterior. Then she turns to me with a smug grin.

'Easy peasy,' she says.

First thing the next morning, Charlie Bucket and I swagger along to the police station in Bermondsey to report our findings. I am looking forward to seeing the look on DC Hill's face when I tell him that we've managed to track down my identity thief. When we arrive, the station reception buzzes with activity and Charlie Bucket draws a few raised eyebrows, but no one stops us from entering. Police officers come and go and half a dozen people wait on plastic chairs lined up against the wall in the reception area. The duty sergeant is on the phone, so Charlie Bucket and I wait patiently for him to finish, taking our time to glance casually around. Even though it's only half past nine in the morning, there's a strong smell of cannabis in the air.

Are the people waiting here victims or criminals, I wonder? An elderly black couple wearing matching grey cardigans sit side by side, clutching each other's hand rather tenderly. They look much too frail and affectionate to be felons, but the teenage boy sitting next to them looks positively sheepish! He's wearing black jeans and a dark grey hoodie and is leaning forward with his head in his hands. The lad has definitely been up to no good, I decide. He looks full of regret or despair, or possibly both. The thirty-something woman sitting a few seats away is more difficult to pinpoint: she has shoulder-length dirty blonde hair and dark rings under her eyes, so has obviously had a long night. When she catches my eye, she scowls a little and shifts her body away from us – obviously guilty.

The duty sergeant hangs up the phone and looks us over,

first taking in my now-yellowing black eye, and then Charlie Bucket, who although he is sitting patiently and quietly by my side (the very model of canine obedience), admittedly has not been bathed in some time, and quite possibly smells. Though no worse than the overpowering stench of cannabis.

'Can I help you?' he asks.

'We're here to see DC Hill,' I say.

The officer shakes his head. 'Sorry, he's on leave.'

'Really? As of when?'

'As of . . .' He pauses to check his watch, in a move that is obviously facetious. 'Yesterday,' he says then, flashing me a glib smile.

I frown. Seriously? How annoying that he's gone on holiday when I am out fighting crime! 'Is there someone else I could speak to?' I ask. 'Someone who's covering in his absence?'

He sighs and picks up the phone and pushes a few buttons, then turns away. He murmurs a few mostly unintelligible words into the phone, though I distinctly hear the words *colossal* and *dog*, and after another pause, he hangs up, turning back to us. 'Someone's coming,' he says, indicating that we should wait with the others.

I sigh and wander over to a rack of educational pamphlets on the wall, pulling Charlie Bucket along with me. The pamphlets cover a range of topics, from blindingly obvious crime prevention advice (e.g. lock your doors) to rather terrifying terrorism alerts. Charlie Bucket eventually grows tired of standing and deposits himself on the ground with a loud sigh, then stretches out rather languorously on his side, as if the floor of a bustling police station is the most natural place in the world for a kip. I give him a little nudge with my foot to try to rouse him, and the woman with circles under her eyes glares at me, clearly of the view that we are taking up more than our fair share of space.

Which we patently are.

'Excuse me, can I help you?' says a familiar male voice behind me.

Good grief. I'd know that voice anywhere! I turn around and sure enough, it's Pay-It-Forward. He's wearing navy blue corduroy trousers and a green and blue checked shirt, and his short brown hair stands up a little messily, as if he only just rolled out of bed. I reckon he's wearing four days' worth of stubble, which I decide in that instant is optimal, because he looks seriously hench. I draw a breath and catch a faint smell of deodorant soap. I wonder what he looks like in uniform?

His eyes widen when he recognises me and, like his colleague, I see his gaze drift to my fading black eye.

'Hello,' I say, giving a little wave. 'It's me again.'

'So it is,' he replies, nodding. 'And now there are two of you.' His eyes drop to Charlie Bucket, then back up to me. 'Does he steal sandwiches, too?'

My face reddens instantly, and I am aware that everyone around us is now staring. In point of fact, Charlie Bucket *has* been known to steal sandwiches on occasion. But I am scarcely going to admit this to Pay-It-Forward, even if he does have an amazingly sexy voice. 'Absolutely not,' I say, shaking my head emphatically. He raises an eyebrow.

'What happened to your eye?' he asks. His tone is just this side of indifferent, as if he is somehow obligated to enquire, rather than genuinely concerned.

'Just a small . . . incident,' I say, mustering my dignity. 'Unrelated to . . . anything.' Really, my sports injuries are none of his business! He nods.

'You wanted to see DC Hill?' he asks. I glance sideways and see that the elderly couple, the teenage boy and the sleep-deprived woman are now all unabashedly staring at me, like I'm the criminal rather than the victim. Which I think is very disloyal.

'Could we go somewhere more private?' I ask.

He leads me to the far side of the reception area and down a long corridor. We appear to be on the opposite side of the building to where I was held before, though the tiny interrogation room we reach a minute later could be a carbon copy of the one in which DC Hill interviewed me. Once inside, Charlie Bucket looks around for a moment, sizing up the available floor space, then sinks down beside the table with a soft groan, lowering his muzzle onto his paws. Pay-It-Forward indicates the chair. 'Make yourselves at home,' he says with more than a trace of sarcasm. I take out my phone and bring up the photo of Firefly's flat. I have circled the door in bright yellow, and written the address below, helpfully, in bright red font.

'We found my identity thief,' I say.

'We?' he asks, looking down at Charlie Bucket with scepticism.

'My friend Bianca and I. We followed her home from yoga. And this is where she lives.'

I hold out the phone and he takes it, eyeing it dubiously. He stares down at the photo, enlarges the screen for a moment, then hands it back to me. 'The police don't really encourage DIY justice,' he says.

'We were doing *your* job!' I say defensively.

He crosses his arms. Far from looking angry, he looks vaguely amused.

'OK, fair. Let's say you're right about this,' he says, nodding towards the photo. 'What do you expect to happen now?'

'I expect you to arrest her,' I say. *Simple!*

'It's not that simple,' he says, shaking his head, as if he knows exactly what I'm thinking.

'Why not?'

'Because we don't have enough evidence.'

'But we know she lives there.'

'Do we? We know she was in possession of a key to this flat on this particular occasion. She may or may not reside there,' he points out.

'So you're not going to do anything?' I look at him aghast.

He takes a deep breath and exhales, running a hand through his hair.

'Look, I only just got handed this case half an hour ago. And to be honest, I've got others that are far more pressing.'

I stare at him in open-mouthed amazement.

'Did you recover your money?' he asks.

'Not all of it,' I say. 'And she's still got my ID! She could be out there right now. Impersonating me.'

He frowns, nodding. 'OK,' he says in a placating tone. 'We'll send a pair of officers round to investigate.' He stands up then, indicating that the interview is over.

'And you'll let me know?' I ask.

He looks down at me. 'Police investigations are generally confidential.'

'But I'm the victim! Don't I have a right to know?'

'Fine.' He takes a small notebook and pen out of his breast pocket and hands it to me. 'Write down your phone number. I'll give you a ring to let you know what we find.'

'OK,' I say, somewhat mollified. I write my number down and hand it back to him. 'It would probably be good to have a contact number for you, too,' I suggest then. 'A mobile preferably. Just in case something happens and I need to reach you quickly.' He raises an eyebrow, then jots down his number on a separate page, tears it out and hands it to me. Bianca would be so proud!

'What's your name?' he asks, pen poised to write it down beside my number.

'Clemency,' I say.

He looks up at me with surprise. 'Seriously?'

I nod, a little affronted.

He gives the tiniest snort of derision, then writes it down, and I stiffen with anger. Isn't it against some sort of professional code of conduct to make fun of a victim's name?

'Actually, it's just Clem,' I inform him coldly. 'And you haven't told me yours,' I say.

He hesitates for a split second. 'DC Angus Meadows,' he says.

'Like the beef?' I ask.

'It's Gus, actually,' he says. I hold my hand out for the pen and he gives it to me, watching while I carefully write the word ANGUS in large block capitals beside his number. I underline it twice, then hand it back to him with a pert smile.

'And this is Charlie Bucket,' I say, hauling the dog up sharply to his feet. Not that he asked. We sashay past him out of the interview room, while DC Angus Meadows watches us go.

Chapter Eleven

On Sunday afternoon I head off to roller derby, where in spite of the pile-up I caused on Wednesday, I discover that I've been rostered for today's scrimmage. Bloody Nora walks past as I am studying the list and clocks my surprise. 'Haven't you heard?' she asks.

'What?'

'Half the team have gone down with some sort of gastric bug.'

'Unlucky,' I say. *But not for me*, I refrain from adding gleefully. Sadie is also on the list, though she isn't really meant to be skating so soon after her injury (*what will Abby Noxious say?*) and so is 44, whose roller derby name I now discover is Tart Attack. Cute.

I change into my gear and head down the long corridor that leads to the gym, my skates slung over my shoulder by their laces, but when I pass the shower rooms off to one side, I hear the low murmur of an angry female voice inside one of the stalls, the plastic curtain half drawn. Whoever it is has clearly ducked into the showers to make a private phone call, and without thinking I instantly skid to a halt. I pause to listen and at once I feel a tiny illicit thrill – accompanied by an even tinier flare of guilt.

What is it about spying on someone else's life that is so titillating? I remember Marcus and I debating whether eavesdropping was a crime over breakfast one morning.

According to Marcus, it's OK to listen in on a private conversation, but it's against the law to disclose what you overhear to a third party. So technically, I decide as I edge closer towards the showers, I haven't done anything wrong.

Yet.

I hold my breath and strain to make out what's being said. 'Don't be such a plank,' hisses the female voice. 'You know it'll backfire. And he'll chuck you to the wolves when it does!' The speaker pauses for a moment to listen, then continues. 'But it only takes once! You'll end up in the shit like Mum!'

Family eh, I think?

She pauses again, then I hear her sigh. 'Look, it's your life. If you wanna screw it up, go ahead. I gotta go. I'll see you later,' she says and suddenly I hear the phone snap shut. Instantly, I spin round to head back towards the changing rooms, as if I've forgotten something, and in the next moment I nearly collide with 44 as she emerges from the shower cubicle, her head down.

'Sorry, mate,' she says, pushing past me, and apparently completely unaware that I have just massively assaulted her privacy. I stop and stare after her, my mind pondering what I've overheard.

It makes me warm to her, actually; the fact that she's looking out for someone close to her, a sibling perhaps, and the idea that her mum is in some sort of trouble. I sigh, thinking instantly of my own mother, who one way or another, always manages to sidestep her difficulties, and then of Julia, who would literally have to *take lessons* in order to knowingly commit a wrongdoing; both could still unwittingly land themselves in trouble if fate went against them. So much of life is down to luck and timing, I decide. I wait for just long enough to make it seem plausible, then head back towards the gym.

*

It's a banging night at roller derby! I play my best scrimmage in ages, and Sadie manages to skate a few jams during the first half until her ankle starts to complain and she is forced to sit out for the remainder. But the top player of the evening by far is Tart Attack. Because of her, our side wins a decisive 15–4. I knew 44 was a good skater, but tonight she's an even better jammer – fearless, fast and wily, and constantly surprising in her tactics. Time and again, she outwits the expectations of everyone skating around her, including me. *Damn!* How I wish I had even half her guts and instinct on the track! At the end of the night, as we leave the rink, she tosses me a nod. 'Good match,' she says.

'You were on fire,' I say.

'Thanks,' she says. 'Got a bit cranked up just before,' she adds. She looks at me and something passes between us like an invisible thread. I realise that she's referring to the phone call. Instantly, my face colours. Did she know I was listening?

'Well, whatever it was, it worked,' I say, a little awkwardly. She nods at me, just once, and heads off down the corridor to the changing rooms.

We're all in a jolly mood when we pile into the pub afterwards. I spy Abby Noxious and her shock of blonde hair at the bar chatting to some other skaters, and when 44 enters the room, there's a small spontaneous cheer from everyone. She grins and Abby turns round to see what all the commotion is about. For the briefest instant, her face clouds over, but just as quickly, it clears. I glance behind me at Sadie who is laughing with Ruby over some private joke. Fortunately, she wasn't paying attention. Now Sadie looks up and sees Abby at the bar and waves. We get our drinks and Sadie hooks her elbow in mine and pulls me along towards Abby, as if she needs me to bear witness on the wonders of her budding romance. *Cheers for that, mate.*

'How was the bout?' asks Abby as we approach.

'Awesome. We won!'

'That's my girl,' says Abby, and Sadie shimmers, as if someone's flicked a light switch on inside her.

'No thanks to me,' she adds with a laugh. 'I only played two jams in the first half. But Tart Attack was unbelievable! She scored three grand slams!' Abby's eyes slide over to where 44 is standing at the other end of the bar, her back to us.

'Top skater,' she remarks.

'You know her?' asks Sadie.

Abby nods. 'We were fresh meat together. Back in the day. But I haven't seen her in ages. Everyone said she'd quit.'

'Hardly. She was ace out there tonight,' says Sadie.

Abby nods thoughtfully. 'Was she,' she says. It isn't really a question, and she doesn't seem to expect an answer. She takes a drink from her pint.

'Were you two skating partners?' asks Sadie.

'For a bit. We had each other's back,' says Abby with a shrug. 'Until she quit. I didn't see much of her after that.' Something about her delivery alerts us both, and I see Sadie's eyebrow raise.

'So . . . you hung out with her off the track?' asks Sadie. It's an innocent enough question, but laced with an undertone of something I can't quite identify. Jealousy? Suspicion?

Abby hesitates, looking into her glass. 'A little. She had kind of a tough time,' she finally pronounces. Sadie's eyebrows shoot up, and I can't help but think of the phone conversation I overheard earlier. Abby knocks back the rest of her pint, then slams it onto the counter and signals to the bartender. 'Who's ready for a celebratory shot?' she says, turning to us both with a smile. 'I'm buying.'

*

I leave three shots and forty-five minutes later, by which time the pair of them have consumed enough alcohol they no longer require my presence to amuse them. Sadie is well on her way to being tipsy, and is practically draped across Abby, who still seems remarkably lucid; maybe it's her athlete's metabolism, or maybe she's just more adept at faking sobriety then either Sadie or me, but you would scarcely know that she was more than twice the legal limit. On my way out, I glance around to see if 44 is still down at the end of the bar, but she must have left earlier. I push my way out into the freezing cold night, drawing up the hood of my parka and burrowing inside like a tortoise. Whoever said alcohol keeps you warm is a liar.

I dash across the road and enter the Tube. As I step onto the top of the escalator, I see 44 nearing the bottom; she must have left the pub only moments before me. She's on her phone, her voice raised, speaking animatedly into it. I can't exactly hear but I can see her, head juddering with agitation and body coiled tightly with suppressed energy. Watching her I can't help but wonder what, or who, made her play so fiercely tonight. *My* life is complicated, but that doesn't translate into triple grand slams. I see 44 reach the bottom and disappear down the right-hand tunnel. She is still on the phone. And a moment later when I reach the bottom, instead of turning left as I'm meant to, I follow her.

Now that I've tried it, I quite like subterfuge.

When I reach the end of the tunnel I pause and peer out onto the platform – 44 is no longer on the phone but waiting for the train some distance down. I hang back in the shadows until the tube arrives, then jump into the carriage in front of me just before the doors close, but not before I see 44 step into the next carriage down. Once on board I sink into a seat, where I instantly realise three things: first,

I'm a lot drunker than I thought I was. *Whoops.* Second, I have no idea why I'm following 44. (And is doing so better or worse than eavesdropping, morally speaking?) And third, I need a wee. Again. It appears that three shots and a pint of lager on an empty stomach are all it takes to well and truly cloud my judgement. On top of that, I should definitely be wearing my wig if I'm going to make a habit of this.

After three stops, 44 gets off the train and hurries past my carriage towards the exit. I wait until she's further down the platform before I disembark, then jump off and follow behind with what I imagine to be drunken stealth, hugging the walls, hood up, my head hunched over furtively. She heads for the exit, racing up the escalator two steps at a time. Damn, woman! We've just done two hours of gruelling sport, but she is powering up the escalator like the Duracell bunny. I struggle to follow at the same pace, my skate bag slapping against my thigh like a bloated udder, but when I reach the top of the escalator, 44 has gone.

I turn and scan both sides of the high street, frowning. Across the road is a shabby terrace of shops: a newsagent, a scruffy café, a grim-looking pub, and a brightly lit betting shop. A few people scurry along in the darkness, but not her. I stare into the night. I was only moments behind her! How the hell did she disappear so fast? A bus pulls up across the road now and blocks my view for a minute, disgorging half a dozen people, before slowly pulling away. I turn back towards the Tube entrance, feeling foolish. Perhaps subterfuge isn't my calling, after all.

And that is when I see her – disappearing down a side alley, her arm linked with someone else, their heads bent tight together. And Oh-My-God I'd recognise that dark blue pea coat and violet beanie anywhere.

Because 44 is with my doppelgänger.

Chapter Twelve

When Charlie Bucket and I turn up at the police station the next morning and ask to see DC Meadows, it is the same officer on duty at reception. He looks us over again a little dubiously, as if by our very presence we are wasting valuable public resources, then tells us to take a seat. At first, Charlie Bucket lies down next to me, but after a quarter of an hour, he begins to grow restless, snuffling around on the floor on his belly like a commando, poking his head beneath the chairs in search of crumbs, and stretching the lead to breaking point. In the end, I decide to undo him and let him have a little wander. What harm could he do?

Once free, he moves about the room with casual aimlessness, like an airline pilot greeting passengers, sniffing shoes and coat pockets, and nosing in the bins. At one point, the duty sergeant looks up to see Charlie Bucket standing right beside him staring over his shoulder. He looks over at me. 'Do you mind?' he asks with irritation.

I call Charlie Bucket over to my side and order him to lie down, and fortunately, he obeys. But then a young woman with a nose ring and day-glo pink hair sitting a few seats away pulls out a peanut-flavoured granola bar from her pocket and opens it, crinkling the wrapper loudly. Charlie Bucket sits bolt upright, sniffing at the air, his nostrils twitching.

Uh oh. Peanut butter is one of Charlie Bucket's favourites. He stares straight at her, and the young woman meets his eye cheekily, slowly eating the granola bar bite by bite, as if deliberately tormenting him. Charlie Bucket's eyes expand with saucer-like yearning, and I see his jowls begin to quiver.

Oh dear God, please do not let it happen.

But in the next instant a thin line of drool spontaneously forms like a long icicle dangling from his lip. I scramble around in my pockets for a tissue and leap forward just in time, catching the spittle as it falls, then wipe his muzzle off like I am washing a toddler's face.

'Nice,' says a familiar voice just behind me. 'Must have taken years of practice to get the timing right.'

I turn round and DC Angus Meadows is standing there holding a sheaf of papers under one arm and a coffee mug in the other, looking pleased with himself. He's wearing the same navy blue trousers but today's shirt is purple and white plaid, and he *still* hasn't shaved. Quickly I crumple the tissue and stuff it in my pocket. It's difficult to maintain one's dignity when disposing of canine effluent but I do my best, throwing my shoulders back and lifting my chin.

'It's an involuntary response,' I inform him.

'No kidding.'

'Plus, we've been here nearly half an hour,' I say, a little accusingly.

'I'm afraid we've been hard at work safeguarding your identity,' he replies, jerking a thumb back to the offices.

'Well then, you'll be pleased to know I've got more information for you,' I say. He shakes his head, looking at me with false wonder.

'I don't know how we ever managed without you.'

Once again, he escorts me down the hall to the interview room, and this time Charlie Bucket wastes no time in sequestering a large patch of floor, as if he's in charge of the place. 'Did you send officers to investigate that address?' I ask, sitting down.

'Not yet,' he says, flopping down in the chair opposite. I note that he hasn't offered me anything to drink. So I guess this doesn't really count as a date.

I roll my eyes. 'Why not?'

'Believe it or not, *Clemency*, we're a bit busy here. Perhaps you've heard that our resources have been cut?'

It's not the first time I've heard my name wielded like a weapon, but I'm secretly pleased that he remembered it. Does that mean we're on a first-name basis now?

'In fact, a pair of officers are scheduled to visit later today,' he informs me evenly.

'Fine. And you'll let me know what happens?'

'And I will let you know what happens,' he says in a placating tone.

'In the meantime, I think I found out how she got my ID,' I say. 'I think it was stolen by one of my teammates.'

He frowns. '*Which* teammates?'

'My roller derby team.'

'Roller . . . *derby*?' He pauses. 'I can't even begin to imagine what that is,' he says then.

'It's a little like rugby. On skates. Except there's no ball,' I explain.

'So the aim is to . . . *what* exactly?'

'Break through the opposing team's line.'

He nods. 'That is fascinating. Genuinely. But how is it relevant to this case?'

'I think her friend stole my driver's licence from me at practice. And possibly a bank card. Last night after our scrimmage, I saw her on the tube and when she left the station, they met up.'

'So you *followed* your teammate?' he asks, his voice laced with disapproval.

'No!' *Not really. Well, sort of. But he doesn't need to know the details.* 'We just *happened* to be going the same way, and we both *happened* to get out at the same stop, and I just *happened* to see her meet the other woman outside the station.'

'The other woman being . . .?'

'My identity thief.'

He takes a deep breath and leans back in his chair, eyeing me. 'A lot of stuff seems to just *happen* to you,' he says pointedly. As if it's some sort of offence!'

'Doesn't a lot of stuff happen to everyone?' I ask.

He shakes his head. 'Not the way it does to you.'

'I can't help that,' I say.

'Clearly. So do you have the name of this person whom you believe stole your ID?'

Ah, I think. *Bit tricky.*

'No,' I say. 'But her roller derby name is Tart Attack.'

'Tart Attack,' he repeats. I see the corner of his mouth twitch with a bemused smile.

I nod. 'Yes.'

'Catchy,' he says.

'We all have names. It's a . . . roller derby thing,' I say, a little embarrassed.

'I see.'

I hold my breath, hoping he won't ask.

'So what's yours?'

Damn. I hesitate for an instant. He cocks his head to one side and crosses his arms, and I feel my face redden.

'Calamity Lane,' I say.

'Figures,' he says.

*

After my meeting with DC Meadows, Charlie Bucket and I head back to work. It's Saturday, always the busiest day in the retail week, and Declan has opened up the shop this morning so I could go to the police station first thing. When I arrive, he is putting away today's delivery of perishables in the fridge, and the Faltering Cheese is standing in front of the cheese privy surveying the selection. I say hello to Declan, who winks at me, then I turn to the Faltering Cheese. 'Good morning! Looking for anything in particular today?' I ask, as I take off my coat. This is like offering a cold stein of beer to a recovering alcoholic – it will instantly paralyse him. But after my trip to the police station, I'm feeling a little mischievous.

'I haven't decided yet,' he says ruefully, shaking his head.

'OK,' I say, putting on my apron and tying it behind my back. 'Perhaps I can help. Let's start with hard or soft?'

'Hard,' he says decisively. 'I think,' he adds, a moment later.

'Right. And what about the animal – cow, goat, sheep or moose?' I hear Declan snort with laughter in the background, then cover it up with a cough. The Faltering Cheese looks up at me, his face blurry with confusion.

'Moose?' he asks.

I smile. 'From Sweden,' I tell him. Which really is a thing, apparently, though I've yet to try it. To my surprise, the Faltering Cheese's eyes light up with sudden interest, as if I had hit upon the one thing he truly wanted. *Seriously?*

'Actually, I think we're out of stock on that one,' I add hastily. 'Apologies.'

'Too bad,' he says, with what appears to be genuine regret. 'So, I guess maybe cow?' He raises an enquiring eyebrow.

'Good choice,' I say.

'OK,' he says, nodding with evident relief.

'Aged or fresh?' I ask. He frowns.

'Tricky,' he says.

'Good time of year for aged,' I suggest. He sucks in a deep breath, then nods.

'Right. Aged it is, then.'

'Cheddar?' I ask. He hesitates.

'Cheddar could be good . . .' he replies cautiously, his voice rising an octave.

'I've got just the thing,' I say firmly, reaching for a large wheel. Because as much as I like the Faltering Cheese, I am now running low on patience.

Once he has gone, Declan turns to me with a cheeky smile. 'That was grand salesmanship.'

'Thank you. But I believe the word you wanted was *salespersonship*.'

'Could we order in some moose cheese, please? For the crack?'

'No.'

'But he'll be wanting it next time.'

'Too bad.'

'Hey. Do you have a sister?' he asks suddenly.

'Yes. Why?' I eye him dubiously, wondering where the conversation is now headed.

'Older or younger?'

'Older.'

'Oh. She definitely looked younger. Though women's ages can be an unfathomable thing,' he says, pronouncing the last word *ting*.

'Who looked younger?'

'Your sister. She came in this morning.' I stare at him.

'My sister's on a spa retreat in the Midlands,' I say slowly.

'Well, then it must have been your double,' he says

cheerfully, walking to the back door to throw away some cartons. I stare after him, aghast.

Why in the world would she come here? I hurry after him.

'Did you speak to her?'

'I did.'

'About what?'

'Let me *tink*,' he says, frowning. 'Ah yes, I believe it was cheese we spoke of. On account of the fact that we're a cheese shop,' he adds. He flattens a cardboard box and stuffs it into our recycling bin, then turns to go back inside.

'Did she buy anything?'

'Aged parmesan,' he says over his shoulder. 'And very nice it was, too. Even if I was the one to flog it to her.'

'How did she pay?'

He stops and turns to face me, frowning. 'Let me *tink*. I believe it was cowrie shells. Or was it glass beads?'

'Declan!'

He rolls his eyes. 'She paid with contactless, like everyone else,' he says. 'Why? Who is she then, if she's not your sister?' I shake my head and sigh.

'I wish I knew.'

Chapter Thirteen

It's a busy Saturday in the shop with mostly normal, cheese-loving customers. Inevitably, there are a few random types through the door, including a pair of Japanese tourists wanting directions to the London Eye (we are not even remotely close to what is one of London's most visible landmarks), a confused elderly man wanting to buy stamps (who sweetly offered a tip when Declan took him by the arm and escorted him across the road to the nearest newsagent), and a middle-aged woman accompanied by a pair of Shih-Tzus that sorely tested the limits of Charlie Bucket's patience by sniffing every inch of him from head to tail.

Late in the afternoon, my phone buzzes inside my pocket with an unknown number. I signal to Declan and step outside the back door. 'I'm just ringing to follow up,' says DC Meadows when I answer. 'As promised,' he adds pointedly. He makes no effort to identify himself, as if he knows I will recognise his voice instantly. Which I do, *obviously*.

If anything, his telephone voice is even more glorious than his real one. Honestly, I would buy *anything* from this man. Vacuum cleaners, timeshares, hair removal products. I wonder if he has ever considered telesales?

'And?' I ask.

'And she wasn't there,' he continues. 'The officers spoke to an old woman who lives alone in that flat, and she had no idea what they were talking about. Are you sure you got the address right?'

'Positive! Are you sure *they* got the address right?' I ask instead.

'Positive,' he says flatly. 'I'm afraid that's what we call a dead lead.'

'But I saw her go in! She had a key!'

'Sorry.' He does not sound even remotely sorry. In fact, he sounds a little bit smug.

'You need to do a stakeout,' I say urgently.

'A stakeout,' he repeats. As if I've ordered the most expensive item on a fancy à la carte menu. Then he laughs outright. I redden, even though he cannot see me.

'Yes! It's the obvious solution,' I say.

'I'm afraid we don't have the resources for that sort of thing.'

'Why not? We're so close to catching her!'

'Look, we're quite busy at the moment,' he informs me. 'We've been dealing with an incident, in case you haven't heard.' I *had* heard. When Declan came back from his lunch break, he'd reported that a masked man wearing a bright red cape had launched himself abseiling down the side of the Shard, the 1000-foot tower not far from here. The police had cordoned off the entire area; apparently, they were worried it might be a terrorist incident, but they eventually discovered it was some sort of protest.

'So what you're saying is that Peter Parker takes precedence over my identity thief?' I ask.

'Who's Peter Parker?' he asks in a bewildered tone.

'Spiderman.'

'Clemency, it was potentially a very serious incident. People could have been hurt.'

'What was he protesting about?'

'The weather.'

'Well, it *has* been a bit shit,' I say.

'Climate change,' he says.

Ah right.

'Fine. If you don't have time, I'll deal with it,' I say.

'What do you mean?' he asks, his voice now laced with suspicion.

'Nothing.'

'Do *not* deal with it! Please leave policing to us,' he admonishes. I hesitate and there is a brief pause while we both consider our options.

'She was *here*, you know,' I say then.

'Who was where?'

'My identity thief came to the shop this morning. When I was at the police station. One of my staff served her.'

There is a momentary pause before he replies. 'Are you sure?' His tone has shifted, and for the first time, he sounds genuinely concerned. 'Why would she come to your place of work?' He sounds as if he's thinking aloud.

'You tell me.'

'I wish I could.'

'So what do you intend to do now?' I ask. I hear him take a deep breath and exhale.

'I'll let you know,' he says finally. And then he hangs up. Without even a *fare-thee-well*.

I ignore his instructions and ring Bianca. 'What's up?' she says.

'We have to find her again,' I say.

'Who?'

'My identity thief. The police went to that address and she wasn't there.'

'Maybe she was out.'

'No, the old woman who lived there said she'd never heard of her.'

'She was lying. Obviously.'

'Exactly. What are you up to later?'

'Date with Will.'

'Which one?'

'Why?'

'Because if it's Wee Willy Wanker, then you're cancelling.'

'It's with Sheer Will, if you must know. And I have no intention of cancelling.'

I sigh. Asking Bianca to cancel a date is like asking swallows not to return home.

'Can't it wait until tomorrow?'

'Maybe,' I say.

Or maybe not, I think, after I hang up the phone. If Bianca isn't free to stake out my identity thief, then I'll have to do it myself. I can take Charlie Bucket with me. For warmth, if nothing else.

I close up the shop, dig out my wig, then buy a gyro from the nice Turkish man who runs the kebab shop down the road, asking for some extra offcuts for Charlie Bucket. If my flatmate and I are going to spend Saturday night staking out my identity thief, we can at least be well fed. Also, I suspect I will need an inducement to lure Charlie Bucket onto the Tube, as he's not overly fond of public transportation.

When we reach the top of the escalator, I dangle a few bits in front of his nose and he clambers tentatively on. But instead of sitting, he stands facing downwards, his front paws on one step, his hind paws four steps behind, like he's snowboarding down a mountain. He stares straight ahead with intense concentration, his eyes fixed on the bottom, as if he (and not the stairs beneath him) are moving. When we finally disembark, he turns to me with a tail wag of relief and pride. I pat him on the head. 'Brave boy,' I say. In spite of his size, Charlie Bucket can be such a wimp.

I use a few more bits to lure him down the tunnel and onto the platform, where momentarily all is peaceful. But a minute later when the train approaches, with its blinding white light and hideous screeching noise, Charlie Bucket stiffens, his tail curled right between his hind legs like a giant hairy apostrophe. The tube comes to a halt and its doors open. Charlie Bucket plants himself forcibly opposite the open doors, his legs braced, refusing to budge. 'Please Charlie Bucket,' I say in desperation, pulling on the lead with no success. Then I position myself behind his giant arse and with my entire body behind, I rugby-shove him onto the train. We tumble inside and the doors shut behind us.

Fortunately there are only a few other passengers. I drag him over to the end of a row and sit down, and Charlie Bucket nervously tries to climb onto the seat next to mine. I push him off and an older man sitting opposite, wearing a narrow tie and a bowler hat, like something straight out of *Jeeves,* frowns with disapproval. Thank God he does not have a moustache. I order Charlie Bucket to lie down on the floor, and I only have to repeat the command six times before he finally obeys, collapsing in a heap at my feet with a grunt. I look up and Jeeves has pinpointed us with beady black eyes. 'He's a service animal,' I say. Which could almost be true. Jeeves raises a dubious eyebrow in reply.

When we reach our stop Charlie Bucket leaps up, only too pleased to disembark, but not as relieved, it would appear, as Jeeves, who exhales audibly as we get off. Charlie Bucket doesn't need any encouragement on the up escalator, slinking up the stairs like an oversized panther stepping on hot coals, and once out on the street I quickly pull on the wig and we head towards the housing estate. It's fully dark now and cold enough to see our breath, though Charlie Bucket seems to have got his mojo back, trotting along happily in front of me, content to have his feet back on the pavement where they belong.

When we reach the entrance to the housing estate, we pause. A man and his wife are just loading a pushchair into a red hatchback in the car park, but once they have finished and driven away, the area is deserted. We cross the car park towards my doppelgänger's building and scan the vicinity to see where the best vantage point is – somewhere we can see but not be seen, ideally. There is a refuse and recycling area off to one side that looks perfect. I pull Charlie Bucket over behind the bins and he needs little encouragement – skips are his favourite form of street furniture. I duck behind the largest one, and handily there is an old plastic milk crate someone has discarded. I turn it upside down, sit down and pull Charlie Bucket in tight between my knees for warmth, like a monstrous furry hot water bottle.

Now all we have to do is wait.

From where I am sitting, I have a clear view of my doppelgänger's flat. Someone on the top floor has their windows open, and Bon Jovi are singing 'It's My Life', the music drifting across to us. Charlie Bucket nuzzles my coat pocket, where the still-warm gyro nestles in its wrapping, and I can't help but smile at the irony of the situation: it is half past seven on a Saturday night and instead of dinner and a movie with my non-existent boyfriend, I am sitting by a skip in a freezing car park with a soggy sandwich in my pocket and Charlie Bucket between my knees. But far from despairing, I'm buzzing with excitement.

Something is going to happen. I can feel it.

At that instant a battered black Volvo saloon pulls up and

parks a little distance from where we're sitting. It's so old it looks almost retro. The engine switches off and I hunch down low so as not to be seen by the driver when they emerge, but the car remains silent. I wait a minute, my face squashed into Charlie Bucket's fur, thinking that he really does reek of *eau-de-dog* at such close proximity. I make a mental note to schedule him for a bath and keep my eyes trained on the black Volvo.

How annoying! We were just starting to enjoy our little stakeout!

What's taking the driver so long?

Five more excruciating minutes pass. I can no longer endure the stench of dog in my nostrils, so I slowly straighten, hoping I am not visible in the darkness. Perhaps the driver has fallen asleep, though it is more likely he or she is on the phone. Or maybe there are two passengers, and they are engaging in some sort of furtive sexual activity? I peer at the car – I can discern no movement inside, and the windows appear completely opaque, as if they have been artificially darkened. Just then, I feel Charlie Bucket stiffen. His head swivels in the opposite direction, towards the block of flats. My eyes follow his gaze and I see a flash of white and black scurry along the balcony wall outside my doppelgänger's flat. Suddenly Charlie Bucket hurls himself forward, the lead stripping through my hands as he races across the car park towards the block of flats.

A cat!

Charlie Bucket vanishes in a hairy blur around the side of the building just as a slightly stooped elderly Indian man emerges from the door at the bottom of the outside stairs. Before I can shout a warning, Charlie Bucket has hurled past him and disappeared up the stairwell woofing loudly, his deep bass thundering off the concrete. I sprint across the car park where the elderly Indian man stands holding the door ajar, looking slightly bewildered.

'Thank you so much,' I call, as I dash past him through the doorway and up the stairs. Behind me I hear a car door slam and a man call out, 'Hold that door for a sec, will you?' right behind me. And oh-my-God, I do not even need to glance behind me to know *exactly* who is chasing me up the stairs. Because I'd know that voice anywhere.

When I emerge out onto the first-floor walkway, I'm just in time to see Charlie Bucket disappear up the stairs at the opposite end of the balcony. I sprint right past my doppelgänger's door and when I reach the stairway I half-shout-half-whisper: *Charlie Bucket, get back here!*

I bolt up the stairs two at a time, and behind me I can hear Pay-It-Forward's footsteps smacking the concrete, hard on my heels. *What is he doing here, anyway?!* Charlie Bucket is now flying across the second-floor balcony to the next set of stairs, and I obediently follow, running as if my life depended on it. He vanishes again and I stumble up to the third and final set of stairs leading to the top of the block (*thank God!*) and when I eventually reach the walkway, I see that he has cornered the cat atop a large green wheelie bin at the far end. Charlie Bucket is still woofing heroically (like he's the first dog in the universe to discover how to bark: *note to Charlie: you missed it by 10,000 years, mate*) and I see that the enormous white and brown tabby he has cornered has practically doubled in size, owing to the fact that every hair on its body is standing on end. The cat is hissing like a maniacal radiator, its teeth menacingly bared; if the two of them got into an arena, my money would definitely be on the tabby.

I reach Charlie Bucket and grab hold of his collar just as DC Angus Meadows catches me up, and in the next instant we are both doubled over, panting loudly, struggling to catch our breath. 'What the hell . . .' he starts to say, ' . . . are you doing here?' he finishes after a second. 'And why are you wearing that stupid wig?' His eyes alight on my wig and I quickly tear it off, stuffing it in my pocket.

'I could ask you the same,' I exhale back, even though I am practically hyperventilating – black dots gyrate in front of my eyes. Just then Charlie Bucket lunges towards the cat again and I yank hard on his lead to restrain him, leaning down to snarl into his ear, 'You are in *such* trouble! I am *never* bringing you on a stakeout again!' When I straighten up, I see that DC Angus Meadows is regarding me stonily, his arms folded across his chest like an angry matron.

'That makes two of you,' he says in a low voice. How dare he! This was *my* stakeout!

'Can I remind you that I was here first?' I hiss back.

Both of us turn as we hear a flat door close below. We peer cautiously over the balcony just in time to see a man and a woman slip into the stairwell from the first floor. She's wearing the dark blue pea coat and violet beanie hat and the guy she's with is tall, lean and mixed race, dressed in an expensive-looking dark grey down jacket. I turn back to DC Meadows with a pointed look.

'See? I *told* you she lived here,' I whisper.

He nods once, raising a finger to his lips just as the pair emerge from the stairwell into the car park. They cross to the far end and climb into a dark green Audi. DC Meadows pulls out his phone and quickly takes a few photos as the car backs out of the car park and drives off at speed.

'Come on,' I say excitedly. 'Let's follow them!' I start to pull Charlie Bucket down the corridor.

'Whoa,' he says, reaching out to grab my coat.

'What?'

'We're not following anyone.'

'Why not?'

'Because I'm off duty, for one thing. And we've established that she uses this address, which is what we came for.'

'If you're off duty, then what are you doing here?' I ask in a challenging tone.

'Just happened to be passing. On my way home,' he says a little warily.

I hesitate, eyeing him. 'You were worried about me, weren't you? After I told you she came to the cheese shop.'

'I was just checking,' he says slowly.

'Right,' I smile. Pay-It-Forward was worried about me! I don't know whether this is good or bad. But it makes me feel a teeny-weeny bit happy.

Now he frowns down at the photograph on his phone, enlarging it. I lean forward to get a closer look and see at once that the image is too blurry to read the number plate. 'Damn,' he mutters under his breath.

'KY62 PJX,' I say. He looks up at me with surprise.

'I have excellent night vision,' I add.

'Of course you do.'

'No need to thank me,' I say blithely.

'Thank you,' he says, a little reluctantly.

'You can buy me and Charlie Bucket a beer instead,' I say.

Much to my surprise, he agrees. The three of us clamber into his old Volvo, Charlie Bucket sprawling across the entire back seat like he was born to be chauffeured. 'What's that smell?' says Pay-It-Forward as I fasten my seat belt. I suddenly remember the gyro and pull the brown paper bag out of my coat pocket, unwrapping it. Inside, the sandwich is still vaguely warm and the smell of lightly charred lamb fills the car.

'Best gyros in South London,' I say. He eyes the sandwich, one eyebrow raised with interest.

'That's a tall claim.'

'I'll stand by it.' With a swift motion I break the gyro in half and hand one to him. He shrugs, then accepts it.

'Thanks.'

In the back seat Charlie Bucket suddenly sits up with interest, hitting his head on the ceiling of the car. 'Lie down,' I order sternly over my shoulder, and Charlie Bucket obeys with a disgruntled sigh. I feed him a few scraps from the bottom of the bag and he gobbles them down. I suddenly realise that I'm famished. On principle, I never let a man come between me and my food, and this time is no different: I launch into my half, already regretting my generosity. We both tuck into our sandwiches as if we haven't eaten in days, chewing in companionable silence, and the gyros are gone in less time than it takes for the windows to steam up. When I've finished, I hand him a paper napkin from the bottom of the bag. 'Well?' I ask.

He nods, wiping his mouth. 'You may be right,' he concedes. I smile.

'I'm never wrong about food.'

Pay-It-Forward says he knows a decent pub nearby and we drive out of the car park, heading towards the high street. 'So do you live in this area?' I ask him.

He looks over at me with a sceptical raise of an eyebrow. 'I live in Walthamstow.'

'Right,' I say. So not *exactly* on the way home, I think. But I do not belabour this point.

'And you live above the cheese shop,' he says. It's not a question. I turn to him with surprise.

'How'd you know that?' *Has he been stalking me?*

'It's on your file.'

'Oh.' Of course it is.

'So I guess you like cheese,' he adds.

I feel my face colour. 'I guess so.' I do not want to explain my complicated history with dairy products to DC Angus Meadows. 'And *you* like . . . crime and punishment?' I ask instead.

He laughs. 'I guess so,' he admits. 'My dad was a cop. And his dad before him. I swore I'd never follow in their footsteps.' He shakes his head. 'And now here I am – nine years later.'

'What happened?'

He shrugs. 'I tried a few other things. But nothing quite . . . stuck. I guess it was the safe option in the end. It was certainly what I knew.'

'Except it's not safe. As jobs go. I mean, you could have gone into sales. Or accountancy.' He sucks in a breath.

'Risky.'

I look over at him with a quizzical expression.

'Might have died of boredom,' he adds.

I laugh. 'So is it the danger you like?'

He rolls his eyes. 'No one actually *likes* placing themselves in harm's way. But I don't *dislike* it either. I like the adrenaline. And the sense of urgency and value. I guess I like making a difference, at the end of the day.'

'Fighting the bad guys,' I say. He nods, then raises an eyebrow.

'It's not only men who commit crime, you know. Women are surprisingly good at it,' he says. I look at him askance, mildly offended on behalf of my doppelgänger.

'Why wouldn't they be?'

He smiles. 'No reason.'

After another minute he pulls over outside a slightly

shabby traditional pub. He turns the car off and nods towards it. 'This is it,' he says. I survey the outside. The pub is old and decidedly run-down. Nothing exceptional.

'The Scattered Hare,' I read aloud.

'Don't be fooled by appearances. They brew their own ale in the cellar,' he says, climbing out. I follow and open the back door for Charlie Bucket.

'Come on, Charlie.' DC Meadows turns back to me with a quizzical expression.

'You're taking him in?' I look up at him, again mildly affronted.

'Charlie Bucket loves pubs,' I say.

DC Angus Meadows pauses and looks at us for a long moment, and I lift my chin a little defiantly – Charlie Bucket and I are definitely a package deal. If he's not on board with that, I'd rather know now.

'Fine,' he says amicably, turning back towards the pub.

And my insides do a little flip.

Chapter Fourteen

'Only one drink? What is *wrong* with you?' says Bianca the next day.

'He was driving! And he's a cop! So he's hardly going to go over the limit, is he!'

'Still.'

'I thought you'd be proud of me.'

'I am, sweetie. Anyway, baby steps,' she says, patting my knee. 'You don't want to mess this up.'

I frown. 'Why would I mess it up?'

'Because you're you. And you have a propensity for doing exactly the wrong thing.'

She's talking about the time she set me up on a blind date with her newly divorced dentist. Things were going OK until I asked him whether he went into dentistry because he enjoyed causing pain. He took offence at the suggestion that he was some sort of sadist, so to try to lighten the mood, I asked him if he ever administered laughing gas for fun. I was only joking (sort of) but five minutes later (we hadn't even got to pudding!), he signalled to the waiter, abruptly curtailing the evening.

I hadn't held out great hopes for the date in the first place, and had only been goaded into accepting by Bianca (who knows exactly how to push my buttons). I'd warned her that dentists weren't exactly high on my list. Not since the time I was fourteen and our family dentist used my chest as a tray to lay his instruments upon, picking them up and depositing them casually, chatting to me all the while, while I lay passively beneath him, practically combusting with mortification.

Why anyone would ever choose to become a dentist remains one of the great unsolved mysteries of our time. To consign oneself to a lifetime of prowling around the sewage in the back of other people's mouths, ferreting out decay and battling halitosis – this is pretty much my idea of hell. The honest truth is that I don't have the patience to maintain my *own* teeth properly, much less anyone else's.

'Anyway, I don't know what you're talking about,' I say now. 'There's nothing to mess up. He's just a cop I happened to run into a few times.' Four times, I think. *Or was it five?* A cop with an exceptionally nice voice.

'Hot cop,' says Bianca. 'Just think of it. Uniforms. Billy clubs. Handcuffs,' she says, eyebrow arched.

'Stop it.'

'If you don't go for him, I will,' she says. I narrow my eyes at her.

'Keep your hands off my hot cop.'

'That's my girl,' says Bianca with a twisted smile.

I have to stop myself from texting him on Monday morning when he's back at work to find out what progress he's made on the case. He was quite explicit with me when we parted outside the pub on Saturday. 'No more Sherlock stuff,' he'd said sternly.

'Got it,' I'd replied, nodding emphatically. (Was that a tacit agreement, or just confirmation that I'd heard his message loud and clear? To my way of thinking, it was the latter.)

'And yes, I'll let you know how we get on,' he duly added. 'As long as you promise not to interfere.'

He paused then, awaiting my answer.

'Thank you,' I said instead, and his eyes narrowed at me.

'Clemency.'

'Yes, Gus?' We'd finally progressed to first names at the pub; in truth, I was already feeling a little bit nostalgic for Pay-It-Forward. It suited him.

'I need your word,' he said.

'Do you though? *Really?*' I asked.

'I really do.'

'Because it seems to me that I've already helped you quite a lot on this case.'

'For which I'm very grateful.'

'Are you though? *Really?*'

He'd laughed then and patted Charlie Bucket on the head, before turning away and climbing into his car. 'Good night, Clemency,' he'd said over his shoulder. 'Stay out of trouble.'

'We'll try,' I said cheerily.

Just not very hard, I thought, as he drove off.

On Monday morning I finally get round to filling out the form for Julia's divorce lawyer. I cycle through a series of questions about her and Robby's co-habitation, ticking a long line of negative boxes. No, they do not share a bedroom. No, they do not socialise outside the home together. No, their laundry does not co-habitate either. (Does this mean that his darks do not mix with her lights, and vice-versa?) No, they do not take meals together. (What if she's about to put on some spaghetti when he walks in from work, famished? Does she look away while he trawls through the fridge?) But there is one question that stops me dead: *Have the parties in question engaged in sexual relations at any time during their period of separation?*

Gosh. I have no idea. They've been separated for more than a year. But have they actually been *separate* that entire time? And what exactly constitutes sexual relations – does that mean intercourse? Or is the definition broader somehow? I mean these days quite a lot of things constitute sexual activity. I read recently about a man who only became aroused when clad entirely in woollen knits; he even has a specially made sock for his willie. For him, knitting might constitute a sexual activity, mightn't it?

I'm not sure how to respond to the sex question, so in the end, I put a very faint X in the negative box, but feel a small prick of remorse doing so, as if there is a tiny jury perched upon my shoulder waggling their index fingers sternly at me. What if I'm wrong? When it comes to the official bit at the bottom, asking me to certify that I've answered all the questions truthfully, I suddenly baulk. In spite of recent mishaps on the wrong side of the law, I am basically a rule-abiding person: I would strongly prefer not to lie on a legal affidavit. Instead I decide to ring Julia to see if I can clarify the situation. Though I cannot simply ask my older sister outright if she has shagged her estranged husband over the last year, so I shall have to resort to subterfuge.

'Hiya,' I say cheerily. 'Just ringing to see how your spa weekend went!'

'Oh my God. It was fabulous! I feel totally recentered! You *have* to go there!'

Hmm. Unlikely. At least in my present incarnation. Perhaps in a future life.

'Definitely,' I say instead. 'Really pleased for you.'

'Everything was perfect. The room was cosy. The treatments were amazing. The staff were super welcoming.'

But how were the puddings? I want to ask.

'Did you meet anyone?' I say instead.

'Oh, I met loads of people. A bunch of us decided we'd rebook for Easter, so we're already planning a reunion weekend in three months' time.'

'Wow.' That's Julia. A reunion. With strangers.

'One of the trainers even asked for my phone number,' she says with a titter.

'Really? Did you give it to him?'

'Nah. I didn't fancy him, to be honest. In spite of his abs. Anyway, I don't think I'm ready. It's too soon.'

'OK, fair,' I say. 'How long has it been anyway? Since you and Robby . . .' I allow my voice to trail off suggestively.

'Since we what?' Julia sounds perplexed.

'You know . . . since you stopped . . .'

'Since we *uncoupled*?'

'Yes.' Sort of. I hesitate. Are we talking about the same thing here? I have no idea.

'Eleven months.'

'Oh. Wow,' I say. Time flies when you're getting divorced. 'So you two haven't even . . .in eleven months?'

'Haven't *what*?'

'You know . . . relapsed?'

'You mean had sex?' she asks, sounding appalled.

'Well . . . or something,' I stammer. Who knows what I mean? Certainly not me.

'God, no! We're *uncoupled*, Clem!' she says, now truly shocked.

'I know, I get that. But you're human. And you do live in the same house.'

'He's on another floor!' She says this like he's on another planet.

'I just thought, *maybe*, there might have been a time when you two may have had a glass or two of wine, and . . . let your guard down a bit.'

'Clemency, conscious uncoupling is a *process*. I don't think you understand. I wouldn't do anything to destabilise it. And neither would he. We are both *totally* committed to the process.'

'Right,' I say, making a big black X in the NO box on the sex question. My sister and her soon-to-be ex-husband are definitely not getting any.

And I am not a perjurer.

After I drop Charlie Bucket off with June in the shop, I retrace my skating route of the previous fortnight. It's not that I think I'll run into Pay-It-Forward again. I am fully aware that people do not, generally, frequent the same sandwich shop at the same time each week. (*Or do they?*) But this time, I have the exact amount of money he loaned me for the sandwich nestled in the tiny pocket of my tracksuit bottoms, as I intend to fully repay my debt to society. Since I've already paid it forward to the panhandler, in karmic terms, it will be like having a little extra money in the bank of destiny.

Fate must approve of my plan, because when I finish my skate and arrive at the sandwich shop, the same thin-faced guy is serving, looking just as disaffected as he did on my earlier visit. How sad for him, I think benevolently, as I take my place in the queue. Even though the young man appears to be unfulfilled in his chosen form of employment, perhaps I can brighten his day. I forgo any form of refreshment and wait patiently as the queue inches forward: my visit today is not about gratification; it's about putting past wrongs to right. I stare straight ahead, resisting the urge to glance over my shoulder to see if Pay-It-Forward is behind me in the line – he seems to find me everywhere else these days, so it is not inconceivable that he will do so today.

But alas, not this time. Soon I am at the front of the queue and I beam at the young man behind the counter. 'Hello,' I say with a cheery smile. He nods at me a little suspiciously.

'Did you forget something?'

'I'm here to repay you.' I pull out £5.75 in exact change from my pocket and hold it out to him. The thin-faced young man frowns at it. Admittedly, the fiver has been folded into a tiny square no bigger than a celebratory postage stamp, and the other coins have been rammed inside. I suddenly feel like a nine-year-old handing over several weeks of hoarded pocket money.

'I'm sorry. What is this for?' He is clearly confused.

'Don't you remember? I bought a sandwich and a drink and then my card wouldn't work? So the man behind me paid?'

His nostrils flare ever so slightly. 'And?' He asks.

'And now I'm paying him back. Or paying *you* back, rather.'

'But he already paid. So what *exactly* is this for?' He asks suspiciously.

'It's for you. Or the shop. Or . . . whatever.' I wave my hand, indicating the universe. The young man eyes the money.

'Yes but . . . why now?' He seems genuinely perplexed.

'Because I want to repay my debts.'

'Why didn't you give it to me the other day?'

'I'm sorry?'

'You were here like . . . two days ago,' he says with irritation. 'Why didn't you give it to me then?'

I stare at him, speechless. *What the hell?*

'Look . . . whatever,' he says, pocketing the money. 'There are customers waiting. So if you don't mind . . .' He nods towards the queue of people behind me, indicating that I should go.

I turn and walk slowly out to the street. Once outside, I can't help looking around, as if she'll be there somewhere, waiting for me. She's no longer stealing from me, so what exactly does she want? Was her visit to the café just a coincidence? Or is she playing with me somehow?

When I go to retrieve Charlie Bucket from the shop, June is on the phone placing an order and the dog is nowhere to be seen. 'June, where's Charlie Bucket?' I ask in a puzzled voice once she hangs up. She nods behind the counter.

'Occupied,' she says. I peer over the counter where Charlie Bucket is deeply nestled in a pile of shredded and partially masticated cardboard boxes. He is busily devouring the crate from a Camembert delivery, his two massive paws clamped tightly on it, as if the box might leap up and escape at any moment. As I watch, he tears at the sides with his enormous teeth, splitting the box in two.

'Charlie Bucket, what are you doing?' I ask in a stern voice. Charlie Bucket pauses briefly in his labours to look up at me. He stares at me, perplexed for a long moment, as if to say: *Isn't it perfectly obvious?* Then returns earnestly to the task at hand.

'I'm not sure this activity is up to code,' I say uneasily to June.

'Why not? It's just another form of recycling,' she says philosophically. Charlie Bucket has just regurgitated a large wad of wax paper wrap with a gagging sound. He burrows into it for a moment, plumbing its depths, before casting it aside with his nose.

'I think the environmental health department might take a dim view,' I reply.

'If they could be bothered to *have* a view. Which they can't,' she adds, turning away.

It is true that the environmental health department rarely, if ever, visits the shop. But it would be just my luck if they dropped in now. On the one occasion they *did* appear, they informed me that the cheese privy should be kept cooler (wrong!) and the water in the toilet tap hotter. Both of which I ignored.

'Oh, by the way, Ether came by this morning looking for you,' June says over her shoulder now. I look up at her with surprise.

'Ethan?'

She nods.

'What'd he want?'

'No idea, but he said he'd stop by again tomorrow.'

Why would Ethan come looking for me, I wonder? Apart from the obvious: to buy cheese. But June is a cheese impresario: she can flog cheese with the best of them, so it must have been something else. I hadn't seen Ethan around much lately and wondered if he'd been away for an extended period over the holidays. I knew that he often spent the new year with his wife's family in France. His in-laws owned a fabulous chalet in Megève, apparently.

After our Thameside drink that evening, we'd called a halt to the flirting. Or at least I'd curtailed it, and Ethan followed my lead. (As a rule, I don't do married folk, even if some others do – Bianca, for example, though I'm not naming names.) Ethan still frequented the cheese shop and he and I reverted to being not-quite-mates who made small talk over the counter about work and the weather and the council's failure to keep the high street tidy and that odd new vegan café that sells lumpen baked goods you'd have to pay us to eat. And if all else failed conversationally, we could always talk cheese. Over time I came to see through the shiny veneer of his breezy manner and his oh-so-glamorous life, and often wondered if maybe Ethan wasn't a little bit lonely inside his commuter marriage. But I wasn't about to ask.

Charlie Bucket and I head up the stairs to the flat. He has insisted on bringing with him a portion of the Camembert box, carrying it in his mouth like a prize from the county fair. Further up the stairwell I can hear Carl trilling his scales with what seems like joyless determination. The music Carl makes always sounds vaguely angry to me, as if he is remonstrating with someone, or maybe arguing with the notes themselves. Wasn't singing supposed to make you feel happy? I thought it was a cure for depression. As I unlock the door to the flat, Charlie Bucket shakes his withers with dismay, as if he can shed the noise from upstairs like a wet overcoat. Suddenly the trilling stops and I hear the door to Carl's flat open. A disembodied voice calls out from above.

'Clemency, your sister came by to collect her stuff,' he shouts down. 'Your phone wasn't picking up, so I let her in.' I glance down at my phone and see two missed calls from Carl, who is saved on my phone under the moniker *Snarl*.

'Carl, what are you talking about? My sister isn't in London right now,' I call up the stairwell. Suddenly his face pops over the banister, peering down at me, his bushy eyebrows knit together with concern.

'Are you sure?' he asks uneasily. His tone has shifted up an octave, and his moustache twitches slightly.

'Yes. She's in the Midlands. I just spoke to her a few hours ago,' I reply.

Carl blinks several times, his thin lips pursed in a tight line.

'But she looked just like you.'

Chapter Fifteen

Carl follows me inside, seemingly reluctant to accept responsibility for letting a complete stranger into my flat, even though he eventually confesses that he left her unattended for several minutes and told her to let herself out. 'I was right in the middle of an oratorio,' he says defensively. 'And I did try to ring you. More than once, in fact! How was I to know you weren't related?'

After we establish that the most obvious targets of theft aren't missing – my handbag, laptop, spare keys and the television are all sitting right where I left them – he visibly relaxes. 'Well, someone is clearly having fun at your expense,' he says, a little peevishly.

'She's a criminal, Carl. Who's been impersonating me. So I'm not sure you can categorise that as fun. More like breaking and entering. Except there was no need for the breaking bit, was there.' The question is rhetorical. I look around the flat, puzzled. She is definitely playing with me. But if this is a game, it's starting to feel pretty creepy. Carl shrugs.

'Then you'd best call the police,' he says.

My thoughts exactly.

Once Charlie Bucket and I rid ourselves of Carl's presence, I phone Gus. It takes me four tries before I finally reach him, and when he eventually answers he sounds a little exasperated. 'Clemency, when someone doesn't pick up the first time, they maybe didn't hear,' he admonishes. 'When they don't pick up the second time, it's usually for a good reason. And when they don't pick up the *third* time, it's because they don't *actually* want to speak to you.'

Mmm. Even when he's telling me off, his voice is delicious. 'She broke into my flat,' I tell him. I hear him draw a breath.

'When?'

'Earlier this afternoon. When I went out. My upstairs neighbour let her in. She told him she was my sister.'

'Ah. So technically she didn't *break* in.'

'No, but she was here. Alone in my flat. For like . . . ten minutes, apparently.'

'Did she take anything?'

'I'm not sure. I don't think so. Nothing obvious, at any rate.'

He sighs. 'Right. Well, keep looking. And make sure you lock your doors from the inside.'

'Don't you want to send someone round to dust for fingerprints or something?'

'Why?'

'To prove she was here!'

'But we *know* she was there. What we don't know is why. And contrary to what you may think, impersonating someone isn't actually illegal unless they commit a crime.'

'It isn't? Why not?'

'Because no one gets hurt.'

Huh.

'Look, if it makes you feel any better, I'll be done here soon. I'll swing by on my way home and take a look round. You may have missed something.'

My insides do a little happy dance. Yes, it makes me feel better!

Soooo much better!

'Fine,' I say pertly. As cool as a cucumber.

Pay-It-Forward is coming over! And even though his visit is work-related, I have to make myself presentable. Or maybe a bit more than presentable. I don't want to get ahead of myself, but maybe I should aim for attractive. Or even alluring. And then I might end up with appealing. And oh gosh, the flat! I glance around quickly. It looks quite . . . lived in. Well, maybe a bit more than lived in. Maybe a bit dishevelled. Or even untidy. OK, it's a mess.

At the speed of light, I strip off my running gear, jump in the shower, speed-shave my legs and underarms (only two cuts!) then blow-dry my hair and my body at the same time. (Multi-tasking! Clever!) But when faced with the wardrobe, I am suddenly paralysed. What should I wear? It's my day off, so I'd normally be in trackies. But Pay-It-Forward doesn't know this. I might have been out to lunch with a friend! So I choose a very casual dark green swingy A-line cotton dress (that happens to have a very flattering cut) and do my make-up with admirable restraint, so that it looks as if I put it on first thing this morning and haven't touched it all day. (Tactical!)

I scurry around the flat tidying away all the detritus of my life that is normally invisible to me: yesterday's discarded bra, my skate gear, various bits of old post that Charlie Bucket has helpfully shredded, a few old marrow bones and filthy dog towels, a pair of fluffy cat slippers that I really should have donated to charity years ago, no less than *four* hairbrushes stuffed behind cushions (because you can never find a hairbrush when you need one, then suddenly they're *everywhere*, like breeding rodents) and an empty bag of cheese straws peeping out from under the sofa. Crap! The more I look, the more I see. Do I really live like this?

Charlie Bucket is languishing upside down on his back on the sofa, one amused eye trained on me. I could swear he was grinning; either way, he is obviously relishing my panic. His four enormous paws are spatchcocked in the air, his great wide belly splayed, his genitalia proudly exhibited like the crown jewels. I step closer to him and sniff the air. I suspect he smells, though I couldn't say for certain, having permanently lost the ability to discern his odour ages ago. There isn't time to bathe him, and anyway there are few things less conducive to romance than a wet dog. For about a nanosecond I consider grooming him, then discard the idea. Grooming Charlie Bucket is like disappearing down a hairy black hole. I might not emerge for months.

I do a final whip-round of the flat. The sitting room could use a quick hoover but there isn't time. Instead, I lower the lighting, turn off all the overheads (really quite unflattering, both to me and my flat) and put on a few atmospheric low-lying lamps. Then I rush to see if there's any white wine in the fridge. Hurrah! Bachus must be smiling down on me because at the back of the fridge lurks a perfectly chilled Chablis, one of my favourites. I grab two glasses and place them together with a corkscrew and the wine bottle on the coffee table by the sofa.

I don't want to seem presumptuous; just . . . prepared. Finally, I search frantically on my phone for some background music – something understated but interesting. Jazz? Blues? Vintage French? Or maybe he's into new stuff. Would Billie Eilish be trying too hard?

The buzzer goes. He's here! There's no time to choose, so I randomly jab at my favourites playlist, then cross to the intercom and tell him to come up in as casual a tone as I can muster (though I can't help wondering if my voice is even *half* as appealing as his – can one actually cultivate a sexy voice or is one simply born with it?) I don't want to open the door too quickly, even though I hear footsteps running up the stairs. He's eager! A good sign, surely. I hastily fold Charlie Bucket's legs closed like he's some sort of gigantic, shaggy storybook, glance one last time in the mirror, moisten my lips, take a deep breath and throw open the door. And there, perched on my threshold, is Marcus.

My heart sinks at the sight of him.

'Marcus. What are you doing here?' He grins and waves a slip of paper triumphantly.

'You are going to be *so* happy with me,' he says, in a worryingly self-satisfied tone.

'Am I?' I ask weakly.

He sashays into the room and deposits himself on the sofa opposite Charlie Bucket. 'And I've had quite a time laying my hands on it,' he says, rattling the paper. 'But not only have I managed to get hold of the mugshot, I've got her fingerprints, and the transcript notes from her police interview. She knows everything about you!'

I frown. 'She does?'

'Yes! She knows you work at Say Cheese, and that your parents live in India and that you play roller derby twice a week.'

'Really?' I stick my hand out for the paper and he hangs onto it a little coyly. 'Marcus!' I say. He hands it over to me and I quickly scan the transcript. How could a complete stranger know this much about me?

'See what I mean?' says Marcus. 'You're an open book.'

He's right. I feel almost violated. Or belittled. Or reduced to a template version of myself. How come Gus hadn't shown me this transcript? Did he even see it? Maybe he didn't want to alarm me.

And why oh why did Marcus have to stop by right *now*? How could I be so unlucky? His eyes alight on the Chablis and pair of glasses and he crosses over to them. 'Nice,' he says picking up the bottle and examining the label. Marcus knows next to nothing about wine, but it would never stop him feigning expertise. And without another word, as if we have suddenly been pitched back in time to coupledom, he picks up the corkscrew and begins to open the bottle.

'Marcus,' I start to say, and then the buzzer goes. *Damn*. Slowly, almost unwillingly, I cross to the intercom.

'Hello?'

'It's DC Meadows.' *Great*. Pay-It-Forward has reverted to formalities. I glance over at Marcus, who has deftly inserted the corkscrew and now pops the cork with a flourish. He looks up at me.

'Coppers!' he says with delight. 'Great timing!'

'Come on up,' I hear myself say into the intercom.

Twenty minutes earlier, if you'd asked me to imagine my absolute worst-case scenario in the world, this would be it: me, Charlie Bucket, Marcus and Pay-It-Forward all in my tiny sitting room together. A jolly evening at home with just me and the lads. I am almost tempted to scamper out of the kitchen window and down the fire escape and leave them to it.

Instead, I cross to the door and open it to see Pay-It-Forward standing there, looking positively edible. He's wearing plaid again: this time in brown and magenta, and I instantly decide that magenta is my new favourite colour.

'Hey,' he says, his eyes devouring me. I can tell that the swingy green dress was just the right choice, as there is something meltingly intimate about his tone of voice. But then his eyes sweep past me to take in Charlie Bucket, splayed wide on the sofa, and Marcus at the far end of the room holding a glass of white wine. Pay-It-Forward stiffens. 'Sorry, I didn't know you had company,' he adds awkwardly. His tone has shifted; he's all business now. I step back to let him in, while at the same time Marcus steps forward, eagerly extending one hand.

'Good evening, officer,' says Marcus in his most sycophantic voice. Pay-It-Forward hesitates for an instant, then gives the world's briefest handshake to Marcus, before turning to me with an expectant look.

'DC Meadows, this is my friend Marcus,' I say awkwardly. 'He just . . . happened to stop by.' My voice trails off.

'Right,' says Pay-It-Forward, casting his eyes quickly around the flat. 'I just wanted to make sure you were OK,' he adds. 'But it looks like you're fine. Did you find anything missing?'

'Not yet.'

'Keys, wallet, passport?'

I stare at him for a moment. *Whoops*. I completely forgot to look for my passport. 'Um, I just need to check one more thing,' I say quickly, turning on my heel. I cross to my bedroom and start to ransack it. I have no idea where my passport is, but it is normally somewhere obvious – in the top drawer of my dresser or in the pocket of my wheelie bag or on the small bookshelf beside my bed. As I search, I can hear Marcus bombarding DC Meadows with questions the latter clearly does not want to answer, and I become increasingly frantic as it becomes obvious that my passport isn't here. Finally, I return to the room and Gus raises a querying eyebrow.

'All good?'

'Um, I think my passport might be missing,' I say sheepishly.

'Might?' Gus asks sceptically.

'*Is*. Missing,' I admit.

He sighs and nods. 'Right. I'll file a report and send a pair of officers back to the flat.'

'Which flat is that?' asks Marcus eagerly, like an overly keen pupil.

Please do not tell him, I think. Pay-It-Forward's eyes slide up to mine and for once we're on the same page.

'Just one of several leads we're pursuing,' he says dismissively. 'I'll leave you to your evening.' He turns to go.

'No, don't—' I blurt out, then stop short. He pauses and tilts his head at me quizzically.

'Don't what?'

'Um.' I hesitate. Pay-It-Forward is staring at me and I feel like such an idiot: dressed for a casual date, my hapless ex-boyfriend in tow. As if on cue, Charlie Bucket sits up and begins to lick his genitals. 'Don't forget to let me know what happens,' I stammer.

He nods. 'Right.'

'And thanks so much. For stopping by,' I add, a shade too desperately.

'My pleasure,' he says grimly.

When it so obviously wasn't.

Once he has gone, I turn to Marcus, who steps forward to hand me a glass of wine, as if he has been hosting the entire evening like an MC.

'Wow,' he says admiringly. 'Top-notch service from the Met Police.'

I nod and take a huge gulp of wine in an effort to drown my disappointment. I now have an entire evening to kill with Marcus. One bottle of wine will definitely not suffice.

'What say you to a game of *Parcheesi*?' he asks with a grin.

Chapter Sixteen

Each morning we breakfast together, my doppelgänger and I. The photocopy of her mugshot is now pinned to my bulletin board, which is mounted on the kitchen wall just to the right of the tiny two-person wooden table that butts up against the window. As I eat my porridge laced with apples and cinnamon, I stare at her photo and ponder what *she's* having to start the day? Is she a tea and toast person? Or more of a fry-up fan? I reckon criminals must have hearty appetites, even white-collar ones. It can't be easy breaking the law.

I peer more closely at her face – it definitely looks thinner than mine. Thinness suits her. Maybe she skips breakfast? I look guiltily down at my bowl and decide to forego the last few bites, even though the irony of wanting to emulate my identity thief is not lost on me. (Julia would be apoplectic if she knew; she has long insisted that skimping on breakfast merely leads to binge-eating later in the day.) When I set the bowl down on the floor, Charlie Bucket is only too happy to finish the job. Afterwards, he gives an approving wag of his tail, as if to say: *Wise move. You'll feel more sprightly as a consequence.*

And just like that, my doppelgänger has transformed me into a better version of myself. I should probably thank her. Even though I still don't know her name, which feels wrong somehow. After everything that's transpired between us, and everything she knows about me, I reckon we should be on more familiar terms by now. I am thinking that her name must lean towards the exotic. Like Luna. Or Nikita. Or maybe Tyra. She needs a warrior's name, because you have to be a little bit badass to break the law, don't you? Not that I am romanticising or justifying her criminality. But she is pushing the boundaries of her world in a way that would never occur to me in mine, which just makes me more curious about her. How did she end up on the wrong side of the law?

It's been three days since she stole my passport, and I've heard nothing of consequence from Gus (or DC Meadows as he has now reverted to calling himself in our communications, much to my dismay) apart from a text message yesterday to say that the flat was empty when they went round. Apparently, the theft of my passport has now been logged with both the National Crime Agency and Interpol's Stolen and Lost Travel Document database.

Interpol! How glamorous! Just the word conjures up furtive men in dark trench coats with walkie-talkies hidden in their wristwatches, or well-coiffed women with mysterious accents wielding stylish cigarette lighters that double as cameras. Once again, my doppelgänger has opened doors to another universe that seems light years away from dog poo bags and Cheddar.

I really must find her.

Fortunately, I have a plan. Tonight is roller derby practice and I resolve to corner 44 this evening and get some answers, one way or another. I head downstairs to work excited, like I'm an agent finally taking control of my destiny. But I'm also a bit nervous. As the morning progresses, I keep making stupid mistakes on the shop's computer, which June then has to rectify. 'Sorry,' I tell her just before lunch. 'Clearly I'm not fit for purpose today,' I joke.

'That'll be the lunar eclipse,' she says nonchalantly. 'Happening at the end of the week,' she adds. 'But already having an impact. Time to buckle up.' Though I don't believe a word of it, June's astrological predictions never fail to reel me in.

'Why? What could happen?' I ask.

She shrugs. 'It's just a very dynamic period. Kind of like a sliding doors moment in the universe. Eclipses speed things up; they can make things happen.'

She turns away and I ponder this information, but before I can dwell too long a message pops up on my phone. Bizarrely, it's from Ethan.

Hey. Free for a quick lunch?

I stare down at my phone. Ethan and I have never, *ever* had lunch together. We very occasionally text, but normally it's about whether his Beaufort has come in. I wonder what's up. I type back cautiously. One word that is guardedly agreeable. But not overkeen.

OK.

Great. There's a new Italian place just off Shad Thames I want to try.

I reply, careful not to use any emojis or exclamation points.

Sounds good.

What's he up to?

June graciously offers to cover while I slip away for an hour to my 'lunch meeting', though I refrain from telling her who it's with. As I walk along the river towards Shad Thames, I ponder her comments about a sliding doors moment in the universe. Is that what's happening here? And if so, do I want it to? When I reach the restaurant, Ethan is already seated at a table for two by the window. He's wearing a crisp white

149

linen shirt with a Nehru collar and rinse-wash black jeans – uber trendy, even for him. He's obviously made an effort, and a part of me can't help but feel a flutter of excitement.

As I approach the table he's frowning down at his phone, a little distracted. But when he sees me, he jumps to his feet eagerly, running his hands through his hair. We air kiss: not skin to skin, but close enough for me to smell his aftershave, which is of the shoe-leather-meets-wood-mulch variety. Not a scent that instantly chimes with me (carnally speaking), but not overtly unpleasant either. As we sit down, I'm reminded of how unbelievably buff he is, a thought I struggle to banish.

'So,' I say, once we've dispensed with greetings and the business of ordering food (roasted squash and chive ravioli for me, wild boar ragu for him).

'This is . . . nice,' I say, letting my voice rise quizzically. It's a leading question, but Ethan doesn't take the hint.

'It is, isn't it?' He looks around the restaurant, as if I'm making a comment on the décor, rather than the fact that we are eating our first meal together tête-à-tête.

'But unexpected,' I add pointedly. Ethan shifts uneasily in his chair, his gaze flitting moth-like from his water glass to the cutlery to the windows, and finally settling on me.

'Yes. I imagined you might see it that way,' he admits.

'How's Cecile?' I ask. No time like the present for a bit of honesty, I decide. Ethan nods.

'Good. Fine.' He sucks in a deep breath, holding onto it for a moment, then eventually exhales, his shoulders drooping like a deflated balloon 'Actually, we've been on a bit of a break,' he confesses. 'A time out, I guess you'd call it.'

From marriage? Is that even a thing, I wonder? And if so, does it mean that someone's on the naughty step?

'I'm sorry,' I say, invoking a voice that is cautiously sympathetic.

'Well, it's been a bit up and down for a while,' he admits, looking around the room. 'Different priorities, I guess.'

'I didn't realise,' I say. *Though maybe I did?*

'Well. It happens. Often, apparently. If one believes the self-help books.' He gives a joyless laugh.

Once again, I can't help thinking of Julia. Maybe she and Ethan have been reading the same books. Why is marriage so difficult for people to stay in? Don't they realise how lucky they are – that all the fraught business of finding and choosing a mate is over and done with.

'Cecile says I'm not the man she married,' he says.

'Really?' I ask, a little surprised. 'Who did she marry?' He takes a deep breath and exhales.

'An earlier version of me, I guess. When I left university, I had this idea in my head of who I wanted to become. And then I went hell for leather making it happen. I worked hard through my twenties, had a bit of luck along the way, and in the end, I got everything I'd dreamed of. Or, at least, everything I thought I wanted.'

'And then?' I nudge him gently.

He shrugs. 'It didn't feel the way it should. It didn't make me happy. I started to crave something . . . else. Something simpler.'

'So maybe it was your vision that changed. Rather than you.'

'Yeah. Maybe.'

'So what does it look like now? This new dream life?'

He smiles and shakes his head. 'I suppose what I want . . . is a life together,' he says slowly. 'I mean *really* together. Which is to say: the two of us in the same place, seven days a week. Coffee in bed every morning, log fires in the evening, pottering in the garden on weekends. Maybe a couple of kids. Isn't that what most people want? To share life with someone else?' He looks up at me and gives an embarrassed smile, which is rather sweet, but also a bit sad.

'I guess so,' I say. I can't help thinking of Marcus and his cheese plate metaphor. Although I joke about it, I know that for Marcus, the idea goes far beyond sex; what he's really referring to is a proper union, exactly the same as what Ethan has just described.

'Do you even *have* a garden?' I ask after a moment. Ethan shakes his head forlornly.

'Penthouse flat,' he says.

'Ah. Right. I see.'

'*Do* you?' he asks solemnly, his gaze probing me. 'Do you really?'

I hesitate. What exactly is he asking? Whether I understand? Or whether I share his vision for the future? The answer to both is yes, but it won't help Ethan. Or me. Because Ethan is still very much married to Cecile.

'Ethan, why did you ask me here?'

'I'm not sure,' he says, sounding genuinely confused. 'I just thought . . . you and me . . . we have a connection. Don't we?'

I look at him and think: *do we*? Yes, we're friends, of a sort. And yes, he's almost lethally attractive. And had we met at another time and place, maybe something might have happened between us. But right now, I feel no more tethered to Ethan than I do to the Faltering Cheese.

'Do you remember what you said to me that night we had a drink on the river?' I ask him. 'About time slipping sideways?' His eyes cloud for a moment, groping for the memory.

'Maybe,' he says uncertainly.

'You said: *We could be anywhere right now. At any time,*' I remind him. Ethan's eyes light up and he smiles.

'Yes, I believe that,' he says, leaning forward. His hand inches hopefully across the table towards mine, then halts uncertainly.

'But it's not true,' I say gently. 'There are no sliding doors in the universe. There may well be a parallel world out there, but we have to live within the one we've created.' He listens, taking in my words, and as he does, his spirit seems to sag. He slowly retracts his hand and it falls to his lap.

'I guess you're right,' he says finally.

'Go to Paris. And *talk* to Cecile. Tell her what you want. Find out what *she* wants. Maybe she'll surprise you.' He nods.

'Maybe,' he says half-heartedly.

I say a little silent apology to both June and the Babylonians.

Because just like that, I've dispensed with more than three thousand years of ancient astrological beliefs.

Lunch is not entirely wasted, however. The ravioli is utterly delicious and I resolve to hit this restaurant again. Ethan's mood remains preoccupied for the rest of the meal. He eats only half his ragu, so I take the liberty of finishing it for him, telling myself that I can work it off later at roller derby.

When we part outside the restaurant, I give him a hug. It's been a woefully long time since I've had any real physical contact with Y chromosomes. As my arms circle his shoulders, I feel the breadth and tautness of him underneath, and my muscle memory snaps to attention like an overeager cadet. I can't resist sniffing his neck a little wistfully, thinking that in another life, old shoe leather might have been my destiny.

Heigh ho.

*

The lunar eclipse continues to conspire against me, no doubt out of spite. Later that evening, my plans to confront 44 go awry immediately. I'm a little late to arrive at practice and when I step onto the track, I discover with one quick scan that she hasn't turned up. Where is she? Did she somehow know I was going to interrogate her? It's like she and my identity thief anticipate my every move!

Disappointed, I spend the whole night watching the door, with the result that I skate worse than I have in months, missing three opportunities in a row to score during the scrimmage. By the end of the night, the coach is throwing me pained looks of dismay and even Sadie flashes me a pity smile over her shoulder as she sails past. Afterwards, as we shuck off our gear in the locker room, Sadie nudges my shoulder and says, 'Everybody has off days.'

'In my case, it's an off year. Actually, it's more like an off life,' I say grudgingly.

'Come for a drink with me and Abby.'

'Nah,' I shake my head.

Sadie mock pouts. 'Please? We promise not to make out in front of you,' she adds with a naughty smile.

'Generous of you.'

'Unless I get drunk,' she adds. 'In which case, I can't be held responsible for my actions. But we'll let you watch,' she adds, slamming her locker.

'Sadly, that's the best offer I've had in a while,' I admit.

We head across the road to the pub, where Abby Noxious is already seated at a stool at the end of the bar. When she spies us, her face splits into a broad grin beamed straight at Sadie, like a gigantic gamma ray of love-lust.

God, they're so irritating!

Once we've settled ourselves with pints next to her, Sadie

throws an arm around my shoulder and turns to Abby. 'Clem needs cheering up,' she tells her. Abby raises an eyebrow.

'What's wrong?' she asks.

'Bad day,' I shrug. I don't really want to go into details about my identity thief. More and more, our relationship feels weirdly private. She nods at my drink.

'Looks like you're gonna need a bigger glass.'

'Gonna need at least a bucket,' I agree.

She smiles. 'Seriously,' she says, tilting her head to regard me. 'What *is* wrong? You seem totally together. Sadie says you have a good job and a nice flat. And I *know* you have good friends,' she says, winking at Sadie.

'Not to mention a stupidly large dog,' adds Sadie. I smile. Sadie has only met Charlie Bucket once, but he made a lasting impression on her. I hesitate before answering. *What exactly is wrong?*

'I don't know,' I shrug. 'Some days you wake up inside your life. And you realise that . . . it's not the one you wanted,' I say, echoing Ethan's words. Over the course of the afternoon, I must have been mulling them over, consciously or sub-consciously.

'So why not change it?' asks Abby.

I take a deep breath, then exhale. 'It's not that simple.' How do I explain that it has taken the actions of a complete stranger to make me realise how much of my life is wrong? Or that I've become completely obsessed with finding her?

Abby senses my reticence and doesn't press me. 'Fair,' she says, turning to Sadie. 'How was practice tonight?'

'Crap,' I say, before Sadie can get a word in.

Abby laughs and raises her glass to me in a toast. 'Cheers to crap, then.'

I take a long drink, the cold beer sliding down my throat. Alcohol doesn't have all the answers, but there are times when it can definitely help you forget the questions. I place my glass back on the counter, when a thought occurs to me.

'So where was Tart Attack tonight?' I ask, turning to Sadie. 'We could have really used her out there.'

Sadie shakes her head. 'Dunno. She was here last week.'

'Actually, I was really hoping to have a word with her,' I say, keeping my tone as casual as possible. I hate to raise the spectre of an old flame in front of Sadie, but needs must. For a moment there's an awkward silence.

'You mean with Bex?' asks Abby. Both Sadie and I turn to her. I've never heard 44's real name and I'm pretty sure Sadie didn't know it either. Until now.

'Yeah,' I say, nodding. 'You don't happen to have her number, do you?' Out of the corner of my eye, I see Sadie draw a breath.

God, I'm such a rotter! What if Abby says yes?

'Sorry. That was two or three iPhones ago,' Abby says, shaking her head.

Sadie exhales, her relief almost palpable and I have to admit that I'm relieved for her. She quietly snakes her hand across to Abby and the two lock fingers.

'But I know where she works,' adds Abby brightly. 'If that's any help.'

I'd been meaning to get my hair cut for some time. Honestly. The back was bushy with split ends and the fringe was definitely too long. So the next day, when I find myself outside Hair Affair in Chelsea, it feels like an entirely justifiable visit. One that I definitely did *not* need to flag up in advance to a certain Met police detective, who made me promise not to interfere with an on-going criminal investigation.

I was surprised when I discovered that 44 worked as a hairstylist, much less at a posh salon in the most upmarket part of London. I'm not sure why. I guess I'd made a load of assumptions that, looking back on it, were totally unfounded. First, that because she consorted with criminals, she herself might not be legitimately or gainfully employed. Second, that because she was a top-notch athlete in an aggressive sport, she might not *also* have an occupation that was so creative. Or feminine. Or . . . safe. In all, I was dead wrong about 44. Or Bex, whose real name is Becky apparently, according to Abby.

I've made an appointment for a cut and blow dry. She must be good because when I first rang, the receptionist said she was fully booked for the next week, but a few minutes later the woman rang back with a cancellation. Now, here I am on the King's Road, which seems a continent away from Bermondsey. I pause just outside the salon – it's a swish-looking place sandwiched between a French baby clothing store with eye-wateringly expensive designer romper suits in the window, and a Danish espresso bar whose sign promises 'a splash of class and a dash of hygge' with every cup.

Inside the salon I can see gorgeous wood floors, a line of four black leather styling chairs down the left, and two sinks at the rear, next to a door leading off to some treatment rooms at the back. One wall is covered in mirrors and the other has been painted a striking blood orange. The latter is peppered with bold canvases covered in abstract black and white prints that look as if a group of toddlers was left unsupervised in an ink shop.

Apart from that, the entire room is white and spotlessly clean. There is a tall, thin receptionist behind a desk on the right with kohl-rimmed eyes and purple-black hair cropped asymmetrically in a style which is somewhere between provocative and bewildering. I peer at her, wondering if the haircut was intentional?

Two stylists, including Bex, are attending to female customers, with a third customer seated on an uber-modern grey wool sofa by the window listlessly thumbing through a magazine. Bex is on the far side of the room blow-drying the hair of a heavy-set woman in her late fifties. She looks completely different without her skate gear on, so much so that I'm not sure I would have recognised her. Her black hair (normally hidden under her helmet) is cut in a heavily angled bob that is sheered to no more than bristles at the back, but sweeps long and low across one side of her face in a perfect curtain. It's straight, shiny and gorgeous, the stuff of TV commercials, and I wonder why I never noticed it before. She's wearing tight black leather leggings and a dark purple and black striped tunic that falls to just above her knees and hangs stylishly off one naked pale brown shoulder. All in all, hairdresser Bex is lush! No wonder Abby had a thing with her.

As I push open the door and take my seat on the sofa, I see her grip the two sides of her customer's hair with an expert eye and scrutinise the length in the mirror. Then she picks up her scissors and trims an infinitesimal amount from one side, totally absorbed in the task. When she is finished, she smiles at the customer and whisks off the gown with a flourish. The older woman is obviously delighted, stroking the back of her hair gingerly, as if it was a tabby.

She crosses over to pay the receptionist while Bex disappears somewhere out the back, never once glancing in my direction. I wait nervously for her to reappear. Maybe coming to her place of work wasn't such a clever idea, after all. For one thing, it now seems too public (and much too genteel) for any sort of confrontation, and for another, I literally have no idea what to say to her. I glance around, wondering if it's too late to do a runner.

Before I can decide, Bex reappears from a door at the back and walks over to the receptionist. She looks down at the appointment ledger, then turns and crosses over to where I'm sitting, stopping short just in front of me.

'Hello,' she says in a neutral tone. 'You're here for a haircut?'

I nod, suddenly unable to speak. I peer at her furtively as she leads me over to the chair and hands me a gown. If she recognises me, she gives no indication, though surely she must?

'It's *Clemency,* isn't it?' she asks, our eyes meeting in the mirror. In that moment I understand she knows full well who I am. After all, she's the one who stole my driver's licence.

'Yes,' I say, as she coils a luxurious pebble grey towel around my neck, cinching it tightly, then tucking it into my gown. 'It's Clem, actually.' She nods.

'You've not been in before.'

It's not a question, merely a statement. I shake my head while her eyes drift down to my hair. She begins to paw at it in a proprietary sort of way, whisking the fringe forcefully over to the wrong side, then righting it just as quickly, then tilting my head forward and raking her fingers through the back of my hair, as if she's looking for hidden treasure in the roots, rather than dandruff or something even worse. My pulse has started to race at her touch. It had not occurred to me how tactile this would be, how *intimate*, and it throws me even further off kilter. I feel suddenly vulnerable, as if she's the one in control, when it was *my* idea to come here and confront her. Finally, she stops pawing me and I lift my head. Her eyes pinpoint me in the mirror.

'So,' she says, almost accusingly. 'What did you come for today?'

My stomach dips and I stare at her for a long moment, before I realise that she's talking about *my hair*. I swallow. 'Just a bit of a tidy up,' I stammer. She nods and picks up her scissors, wielding them like a weapon.

'Same again?' she asks.

She proceeds to give me the best haircut I've ever had. I'm not sure how. She does the same things, uses the same tools in exactly the same ways as all the other hairstylists I've ever been to, but somehow the end product is *miles* better. When she's finished, she picks up a hand mirror and shows me the back and sides, and I almost want to hug her with gratitude. My new haircut looks simple, stylish and fun. It looks confident, like I'm in complete control of not just my hair, but also my life. Which clearly I am not. It seems 44 is anxious to be rid of me, as before I can even thank her properly, she is ushering me out of the chair and towards the receptionist.

The haircut is eye-wateringly expensive – far more than I can afford. When the receptionist shows me the bill, I literally gape at her. It is a razor-sharp reminder of why I've come. I turn accusingly towards 44 but she has already disappeared out of sight into one of the back rooms. I stare down at the sum – do I even have this much in my account? Perhaps they'd consider a credit plan so I could pay in instalments? (By the time I'd finished, I'd definitely need a trim – a shining example of debt entrapment, if ever there was one.) I hand my card across and hope for the best. 'All good,' says the kohl-eyed receptionist a moment later when my account has no doubt been emptied. She hands me back the card and I manage a feeble smile in return.

I am now poorer but no wiser. As I put on my coat and leave the salon, I realise that my plan to confront 44 at her place of work was badly conceived on so many levels. The only good news is that I now look fabulous, a fact that appears to be lost on the surly young man behind the counter at a small café a few doors down. As I wait for my mozzarella panini to heat up, I stare out of the window and replay the encounter with Bex in my head, this time seizing control and demanding answers. Indeed, so busy am I with this fantasy that I nearly miss her hurrying past the café window heading towards the bus stop. She takes her place at the back of a small queue of passengers just as a bus draws up. I glance longingly at my panini, still warming in the machine behind the counter. The surly young man has disappeared somewhere into the kitchen at the rear. I probably don't have enough money to pay for it anyway, I think with dismay. Then I dash out of the door towards the bus.

Chapter Seventeen

Inside the bus, Bex takes a seat almost immediately on the right and I pull my hat down low over my face and skulk past her to the back row. I watch her from behind furtively as the bus lurches through traffic, picking up passengers and setting them down. We cross the Thames at Battersea Bridge and Bex never once looks up, so absorbed is she by her phone. I can't help but wonder what her preferred screen tipple is. *Candy Crush*? *Angry Birds*? Or maybe she's cruising on *Fem* or *Scissr*. I realise that I know almost nothing about her, apart from the fact that she's great on wheels and a whizz with scissors. As we approach Clapham Junction my phone rings and I see that it's my sister. I shut off the call, but when she rings twice more, I finally pick up, speaking as quietly as possible. 'Julia?'

'Clem! Thank God I got you. I need your help,' she says urgently.

'What is it?'

'Robby didn't come home last night.'

'Oh. Well, is that really surprising? I mean . . . it was bound to happen sooner or later. Given the circumstances. Wasn't it?' I say, as gently as possible. I am aware even as I say these words, that Julia and I have rarely, if ever, been in the position of me dispensing *her* advice, rather than the other way around.

'I need you to check his Instagram account and see if

he's posted anything in the last twenty-four hours,' she says tersely. As ever, Julia is all business – she does not appear to have heard a single consoling word I've said.

'About what?'

'About anything! But especially any new . . . activities.'

'He's not allowed to do new *activities*?'

'Yes. Of course he is. Just not . . . new ones. At least not yet.' I realise now that activities is a euphemism.

'Julia, aren't you two supposed to be disentangling your lives?'

'Yes. We're in the *process* of that, but for now we're still . . .' Once again, she hesitates.

'Still what?'

'Still emotionally conjoined.'

'What does that even mean?'

'My therapist says that our personalities still overlap; our marriage identity takes years to unravel, and we need to be careful. We mustn't rip it apart. We have to undo it slowly.'

'Or else what?'

'Or else it won't work. He and I both *agreed*.' She stresses this last word emphatically, but for the first time I can hear the strain behind her words. Julia is genuinely worried that her soon-to-be ex-husband may already be moving on. And even though this was the goal, it clearly pains her. I feel suddenly anxious for her. Although splitting up with Robby was her idea, I'm not sure she's prepared for the reality of life without him.

'All right, I'll take a look,' I say gently. 'When did he block you on social media?' I ask.

'Last week.'

Right. This is probably when he met someone new. No doubt Robby is less 'conjoined' than Julia. The bus wheezes to a stop beside Clapham Junction and I see Bex jump up.

'Julia, I gotta go. I'll call you later!'

I follow Bex off the bus and into the station. Seriously? More travel fares I can't afford? But she passes right through the crowded hall and out the other end, emerging onto the high street. Just like the first night I followed her, she moves at breakneck speed. I practically have to run to keep up. After two blocks she suddenly shoots off to the left down a side street and I scurry around the corner.

Only to run smack into her.

She's been waiting for me – that much is clear. Her arms are crossed belligerently and her jaw is set in an angry line. 'Why are you following me?' she demands.

'I'm not,' I stammer. Which is obviously untrue.

'Bollocks,' she says. She waits for me to reveal myself.

I take a deep breath. 'Why'd you steal my ID?' I say instead.

'I didn't.'

'Bollocks.'

We stare each other down for a long moment. She inhales deeply, purses her lips, looks around, then finally looks back at me. 'You got a sister?' she asks.

'Yes,' I say warily, thrown a little off guard.

'Older or younger?'

'Older,' I say. She nods.

'She look out for you when you were young?'

'She bossed me around, if that's what you mean.'

'But she had your back, right?'

I think of Julia walking me home from school when we were kids, clutching my hand so tightly at intersections that I would wince out loud with pain. 'I suppose so,' I say.

'Well, I'm just doing the same,' she says.

I consider this for a moment.

'Come on,' I say with a nod back towards the high street. She frowns.

'Where?'

'I'm gonna buy you a pint. And you're gonna tell me what this is all about.' She hesitates. 'Otherwise, I go to the police,' I add. She shrugs.

'Fair.'

We both turn and head back around the corner to a pub called the Ugly Duckling. Inside, it is reassuringly dark and nearly empty, apart from a pair of old geezers perched on stools at the bar. I do not mention that a) I have already informed the police or b) I can ill afford to buy drinks.

To my surprise, Bex orders a ginger shandy, so I do the same. We watch in awkward silence as the barman pulls the lager with thickly forested forearms, then tops it up with ginger beer. As soon as I've paid, we migrate towards the back of the pub and find a booth. Once seated, she takes a long draw of her shandy. She sets down the glass, nodding at it. 'Our nan used to give us these when we were kids,' she says. 'Told us it would put hair on our chests, just like the boys. We thought that was a *good* thing.' She gives a brief grim laugh, then shakes her head.

'You and your sister?' I ask.

She hesitates. 'Half-sister,' she corrects me. 'Different dads.'

'Right,' I nod. Unlike her sister, Bex and I look nothing alike.

'No surprises there,' she says. 'Mum was never the sort to hold back.'

I think of Julia and how little she and I have in common, despite the fact that we share the same blood, the same DNA, the same history. It all adds up to something, I guess.

'Where'd you grow up?' I ask.

'South-east London. Off the Old Kent Road. But we spent most of our time with our nan a few miles up the road. She's the one who really raised us. Taught us how to get by. Mum was in and out of trouble all the time. Still is.' She takes another drink from the shandy and I see the side of her jaw pulse slightly. How fiercely we hold onto the legacy of our parents, I think.

The estate. Her nan's flat.

'In Deptford?' I ask.

She eyes me a little warily, then nods. 'Yeah, that's right.' She doesn't ask me how I know where her nan lives.

'Tell me about your sister,' I say.

She gives a wan smile. 'She takes after Mum,' she says evenly. Her tone is shot through with a rainbow of emotion: frustration, resignation, obstinacy, pride.

'What's her name?' I ask.

She laughs.

'Mum named her after herself. They're both called Adele. I mean . . .who *does* that? The cheek of it.' She laughs.

'Men do it,' I say with a raised eyebrow. 'All the time.'

'True,' Bex admits.

I smile. *Adele*. In fact, it's every bit as exotic as I imagined.

'She looks like me,' Bex nods.

'You two could be twins. The first time I saw you in street gear outside the gym, I nearly fell over. It was weird.'

'I'm older,' I say. We both understand there's little point in pretence; she knows my age full well.

'Not enough to make a difference,' she says.

'No,' I agree. We sip our drinks in silence for a few moments. The atmosphere has eased. It could almost be companionable.

'How'd you get my ID?' I ask eventually.

'Wasn't difficult,' she says with a shrug.

'No, I expect not.'

'Your wallet fell out of your bag at practice,' she explains. 'I put it back in your locker for you.'

'Thanks,' I say with a smile.

'No worries,' she says cheekily.

'Just without the ID,' I offer.

She looks at me. 'It was only meant to be a safety net. In case she got nicked. Which she did, of course. Only like . . .a week later.' She rolls her eyes. 'I told her not to mess about with it. But she never listens to me.'

'Sisters, eh?' I say. I think of Julia and her frustration with me every time I turned a wayward corner in my life. We both take a long drink from our shandy. Bex holds up her now-empty glass.

'My round,' she offers.

'Cheers,' I say. 'I'm a little bit skint right now,' I add.

She laughs and picks up my glass, returning to the bar.

Over the second pint I learn more. Inevitably, Adele's downfall involves a man. Or two men, in fact. One a boyfriend, the tall man I saw her leaving the flat with the evening I went there: Anton, whom she is fiercely attached to. The other, a local gang kingpin whom Anton is more or less entailed to, like some sort of indentured servant, who goes by the street name of Popeye. No doubt Popeye answers to someone even higher up the food chain. A tenuous chain of power connects them all, stopping with Adele. And by extension, me.

Bex tells me that Adele Senior is currently serving seven years in HMP Bronzefield for benefit fraud, a specialty of hers over the decades. It was her mum's fourth conviction, but the first that had resulted in a custodial sentence, and the judge had made an example of her, hence the relatively long

167

bang-up, though Bex was pretty sure the sentence would be commuted in the end.

Adele had only been twenty when their mum was sent down, so Bex had decided to save on rent and move back into her mum's flat to look out for her. For a while, the two sisters had got along OK, until Adele had started seeing Anton and then it became a case of Bex constantly reining her in, as both Anton's and Popeye's influence over her grew. Eventually things came to a head and Adele moved out, and since then she'd bounced around between living with Anton, staying with mates, and living with their nan in Deptford.

'Sometimes I go whole weeks without speaking to her,' says Bex. 'Then I start to feel guilty. Like I'm one of those single mums who leaves the kids asleep and nips across the road for a quick pint.' She laughs. 'I tell you one thing: I am *never* having kids of my own. Too much aggro.'

I smile. Once again, I can't help but think of Julia.

'Um . . . there's something else,' I say tentatively. I've been waiting to tell her about the stolen passport, and when I do, her eyes widen with alarm. She shakes her head slowly.

'Stupid. Little. Shit.' The words come out in staccato bursts. I let her have a moment, can see her mind working furiously over this latest piece of news.

'So . . .' I say finally. 'What happens now?'

Bex takes a deep breath and lets it out.

'We go and get it back.'

Chapter Eighteen

'Where'd you learn to cut hair?' I ask Bex on our way to the Tube. We're heading towards the flat in Deptford, where she reckons Adele is staying at the moment.

'Prison,' she says.

'Right.' I keep my voice level, but in truth I'm a little stunned. She never said anything about her own criminal past.

Adele laughs and shakes her head. 'Night school, you plank.'

'Oh.' Instantly, I colour.

'Got the top marks in the class,' she says proudly. 'Plus, I was the only one who knew how to cut a fringe with a shank.'

'Really? You can do that?'

She laughs and shakes her head. 'God, you're such an easy mark. But I did come top of the class.'

'Well, you're bloody good at it,' I say.

'Thanks.'

'And you're also an awesome skater! Where'd you get *that* from?'

'Dunno. My dad maybe. He was a semi-pro footballer. Played for Welling United. Not that I ever met him. He and Mum split up when I was one.'

'How come you dropped out of derby for so long?'

She shrugs. 'Needed a break.'

'Right.' I hesitate. 'So it wasn't anything to do with . . . anyone?'

She stops and turns to me. 'Like who?' she asks.

I shrug. 'No one in particular. You know what squads are like,' I say, once again colouring. 'Personalities.'

She shakes her head. 'I just needed to sort my head out, that's all. Derby got a bit too . . . intense. Sometimes the timing just isn't right.'

And now I wonder what exactly she's referring to. Or more precisely, who? My mind flits briefly to Ethan. Maybe in a parallel universe, he and I would be together right now, sharing a cheese plate. Except there's no doorway to that universe, I remind myself. Not for me. And not for Bex.

When we reach the flat in Deptford, I hold my breath as Bex roots around in her handbag for the key. My stomach starts to churn, like I'm heading into an audition. I can't believe I'm about to meet my identity thief in the flesh.

'Damn,' mutters Bex under her breath. 'Can't find the frigging key.' Suddenly, the door opens and I see Adele staring out at us with laser eyes. Up close, seeing her is deeply unsettling – like I'm looking at a younger version of myself. She's wearing expensive dark blue leggings and an oversized, olive green jumper that hangs perfectly on her frame. She's far more attractive in the flesh than I imagined, and far more striking than me. I can't help but stare, drinking in every detail of her: the bits that are the same, as well as those that are different. We're about equal height and build, and her hair is almost the same colour and length as mine, but her lips are fuller and more sensuous, and her nose is slightly longer. She looks at me with eyes that are eerily familiar, and when I catch her scent, it is strangely intoxicating: vanilla and spice. I can't help but inhale sharply.

'What the hell, Bex?' she says quietly, her gaze darting between us. Her voice is deeper than mine: gravelly and alluring. It's the voice I've always wanted, I think now. I just didn't know it.

'Relax,' says Bex. She pushes past Adele into the room, leaving me alone on the doorstep. Adele glares at me, then opens the door a bit wider and gives a curt nod for me to enter. I step inside her nan's sitting room and it looks like a thousand others across the land: a worn dark brown sofa on one side of the room opposite a large but slightly outdated television on the other. In the corner sits an old creased beige leather recliner, and in front of it is a wooden coffee table stacked with magazines and a tabloid newspaper open to the puzzles page, covered top to bottom with blue ink. I stare down at it. Every single puzzle has been completed in full: sudoku, suguru, lexica, even the cryptic crossword.

Bex follows my eyes. 'Adele and Nan are fiendish at puzzles,' she explains.

'She does words. I do numbers,' Adele says evenly, as if she's challenging me to disagree. She raises an eyebrow and something passes between us like a baton. Recognition maybe. Or respect. Or something else altogether.

'Where's Nan?' Bex asks.

'Playing bridge,' says Adele, never once taking her eyes off me. Her gaze is fierce and I flush under it. There's a hot thread of energy radiating between us, and in the end, I force myself to sever it by turning away. My eyes travel around the room, aware that she's still watching me. I feel myself altering under her gaze, as if I've fallen down a rabbit hole and emerged as someone else. A thought suddenly occurs to me: she's not *my* doppelgänger any longer. I'm hers.

I move further away, deliberately putting more distance between us, and step towards some framed photos atop a small chest of drawers in the corner. In one, two little girls fly high on adjacent swings, their heads thrown back in laughter. And in the second, a strikingly pretty teenage girl with short dark hair gazes provocatively into the camera, her hands defiantly on her hips. Instantly, I realise this must be Adele Senior – she has the same bearing as her younger daughter. Out of the corner of my eye, I see Adele turn to Bex.

'What's all this about?' she says in a low voice.

'Not very clever, adding breaking and entering to your rap sheet,' Bex replies. 'Not to mention passport theft. What the hell were you thinking?'

I turn to watch them.

'No one broke into anything,' says Adele defiantly. 'I needed a clean passport.'

'Why?' Adele's eyes dart towards me.

'Anton's cousin has somewhere we could lie low for a bit. In Cyprus.'

Bex rolls her eyes. 'You need to give her back her stuff.' She motions to me, her tone low and forceful.

'I don't have it,' says Adele.

'Bollocks,' says Bex. Adele's eyes darken and the two sisters glare at each other for a moment, like warriors sizing each other up for battle. I freeze, afraid to breathe.

'Fine,' snaps Adele finally. She spins around and disappears down a hallway. Once she's gone, Bex turns back to me.

'That's Mum,' she says in a more relaxed voice, nodding at the photo of the young woman. 'Back in her rebel youth. Which never really ended, to be fair.' She laughs.

'Don't talk shit about Mum,' says Adele, coming back into the room a second later.

'Why not? She talks shit about us,' counters Bex.

Adele thrusts the driver's licence out to me. I reach for it, feeling bizarrely guilty for taking it back. 'Thanks,' I say, a little awkwardly.

'A pleasure,' she says, one eyebrow raised. Is she mocking me?

'Where's the passport?' demands Bex.

'I *told* you. I don't have it.'

'Who does?'

Adele purses her lips, refusing to speak, and Bex stamps her foot with exasperation.

'I gave it to Anton,' Adele snaps.

'For what?'

'I don't know.'

I peer at her, trying to discern whether she's telling the truth.

'You need to sort yourself out, Adele. You're gonna end up like Mum,' says Bex, shaking her head.

Adele doesn't say anything for a moment, but I see her nostrils flare, and something in her manner wavers, as if the veil of her bravado is fluttering briefly, revealing a glimpse of something else beneath. She draws a deep breath. 'I will *not* end up like Mum,' she says in a steely tone.

'Then quit.'

'I can't. Not yet.'

'Why not?'

'Anton—' She breaks off.

'*What* about Anton?'

Adele's mouth creases into a tight line. She gives a quick shake of her head. 'I need to put things right. With Popeye.'

'Oh Adele.' Bex's tone is newly tender. She takes a step towards her and lays a sisterly hand on her shoulder. 'What you got yourself into, baby? What's *he* got you into?'

Adele says nothing, only blinks rapidly a few times. Bex pulls her into a hug, wrapping her arms around her sister's shoulders protectively. I see Adele stiffen.

'I can fix it,' says Adele. 'I just gotta do one more thing.'

Bex pulls back and looks her in the eye. 'What sort of thing?'

'Just . . . a thing.' Adele takes a step backwards and shakes her head.

'And then?'

'And then we'll be clear,' she says.

Bex frowns uneasily. 'Adele. You've been lucky so far. But sooner or later, your luck is gonna run out.'

'If I do this one thing, then Anton and me . . . we can go somewhere else. Start over,' she says.

'Why can't *he* do it?' Bex demands.

Adele shakes her head. 'This one's gotta be me,' she says evasively, her eyes sliding over to me then back again.

Bex sighs with frustration. 'Adele!'

'What if it was someone who looked like you . . . in-stead,' I offer slowly.

Both women turn to me, their faces blurry with confusion.

'What are you saying?' asks Bex, frowning.

'Maybe . . . I could do this last thing . . . instead of her. You said it yourself – she and I could be twins. So I wear her gear. And no one will know.'

'Anton will know!' says Adele.

'Not if you don't tell him,' I say.

Adele stares at me, incredulous. 'You are one crazy bitch, you know that? Why the *hell* would you do that? And why the *hell* would I let you?' she demands.

The three of us stare at each other for a long moment, my mind buzzing.

Why indeed?

I'd blurted the idea out rashly, almost without thinking. But I have a strong premonition that Adele is heading into a firestorm. And that only I can save her.

'Because she's gonna bring in the cops,' says Bex then.

My eyes meet hers, and it's like she can see right through me. If the police knew in advance, they could be there waiting.

'Is that true?' asks Adele, turning to me with alarm.

I shrug, then nod. 'You're looking for an exit route. I'm offering you one.'

'I was looking for sunshine and a bleeding beach!' cries Adele. 'Not five years in the bang-up with Mum!'

'If we help the police catch Popeye, you could get immunity from prosecution,' I say.

'Adele, it's a good offer,' says Bex urgently. 'You're already a long way down that hole. And she's throwing you a rope.'

Adele takes a deep breath and exhales. 'Take your goddamn ID,' she says, nodding at the driver's licence. 'But no way am I gonna roll Anton over.'

'Were you serious?' asks Bex a few minutes later as we're walking back to the Tube.

'Dunno,' I say with a shrug. 'Maybe.' *Was I?*

'Have you got a death wish or something?' she asks.

I smile. 'Maybe I just want to catch the bad guys.'

'Nice try, Wonder Woman,' she says.

I laugh. 'Except I failed,' I say.

'Hey.' Bex pauses then and lays a hand on my arm, stopping me. 'Even so, it was much appreciated,' she says. And I can tell she means it.

The truth is I spoke on impulse. I don't know why I was willing to put myself in danger for Adele; even before today, I'd become obsessed with her. But meeting her in the flesh, I felt a bond so intense it was like I'd been drugged.

I knew I had to try to help her. That our fates are somehow linked.

★

The next morning, I text DC Meadows first thing to say I have some new information that might be of interest. I also suggest that it would be best to share this information in person, preferably somewhere outside the station. I figure he knows me too well to ignore my missives at this point, and sure enough, after half a minute I receive a terse reply: *Scattered Hare, 6.30 p.m.*

Result! The message is brief, even by his standards. But still. A drink in a pub. On Friday night! Could this possibly be our second non-date?

I hastily text back: *See you then.* And practically skip out the door to work.

'So, all ready for the big day?' asks June half an hour later, after we've opened up the shop and are unpacking a delivery of dry goods. I look at her askance. How on earth could she know about my meeting tonight with DC Meadows?

'Um . . .which would that be?' I ask cautiously. Apart from this evening, my weekend is not shaping up to be particularly memorable. Declan and I are minding the shop tomorrow, when the most exciting thing will likely be a large delivery of designer waxed paper bags. On Sunday my sister is coming to London for an all-day seminar on Rebuilding and Recovery, so I am meeting her for breakfast just before, the timing of which she has insisted upon, which means I will not get to lie in. More fool me.

'The lunar eclipse,' says June, her tone vaguely admonishing. 'Tomorrow night.'

'Ah right.'

Sliding doors. The secrets of the universe. How could I forget?

She slices open a large carton filled with spelt and rye crackers packaged in boxes so tiny you only have to glance at them and they're gone. (June has rightfully observed that the smaller the box, the better the product sales, perversely.)

'January is the Wolf Moon and full eclipses are blood-red because of the refraction,' she explains. 'So they're calling this the Super Blood Wolf Moon.' I smile.

Of course they are.

'And you'll be watching?' I ask, as she starts to hand me a stack of boxes. She halts mid-handover, one eyebrow cocked. Behind me, the bell on the shop's door tinkles, indicating the first customer of the day.

'It's the celestial event of the year,' says June earnestly. 'I wouldn't *dream* of missing it.'

'Missing what?' says an all-too-familiar voice. We both turn to see Marcus standing there, beaming at us.

'The lunar eclipse,' I explain.

'Oh yeah! The Blood Wolf Moon!' he says. 'I read about it on Space.com. It sounds amazing!'

June smiles and throws me a look that says: *See?*

'Where are you planning to watch it?' he asks eagerly.

'I'm not,' I say.

'Greenwich Park,' says June to Marcus. 'By far the best spot in South London. But get there early. It'll be crowded and the best place for visibility will be on the highest elevations.'

'Rightio,' he says, nodding emphatically.

'What are you after, Marcus?' I ask pointedly, indicating the cheese counter. After we split up, I had to ban Marcus from stopping in at Say Cheese unless he was there to make a *bonafide* purchase.

'Do you know, I've had this intense craving all week for Stichelton?' he says now, as if his cheese needs are also of celestial significance. I sigh and turn towards the privy to serve him, but June leaps up to beat me to it.

'Me too!' she says. 'I've got just the thing.'

*

Later that day, DC Angus Meadows slides into a booth opposite me in the Scattered Hare. Charlie Bucket and I came straight from work on the Tube, but not before I'd dashed upstairs, changed back into the swingy green dress, brushed my teeth and gargled, reapplied deodorant, and checked my make-up and hair. Once seated, he nods at the latter. 'Nice haircut,' he comments.

'Thanks,' I say, feeling extremely chuffed that he noticed. *Score!*

He nods at Charlie Bucket, who is sprawled beside the booth looking his usual shaggy self. 'Shame you didn't throw him in for a trim, as well.'

'Couldn't afford it. It was me or the dog.'

'Good call,' he says, fixing me with the same appraising look he used the other night when I opened the door to him at my flat. I feel my face slightly flush.

How does he do this to me with just a glance?

'So,' he says. 'What startling discovery do you have for me today?'

I reach for my bag, fumbling for a moment, then pull out the driver's licence, throwing it on the table. Gus leans right back in his seat, eyeing it.

'I am not even going to ask how you got that,' he says slowly.

'Good,' I reply. He picks up his pint glass, takes a long drink, then sets it down.

'How did you get that?'

'Let me assure you my actions were entirely legal.'

'Clemency.' His chocolate voice is newly stern.

God, he makes my name sound delicious!

'Yes, Angus?' I say sweetly.

'Did you steal it?'

'*Is* it stealing, really?' I ask. 'When it's yours to begin with?'

He snorts with exasperation. 'Seriously,' he says, leaning forward intently, all business now. 'You need to tell me.'

'Fine,' I sigh. 'She gave it to me, if you must know.'

'Why?' he demands.

I relate the story of Bex, the haircut, and our little trip to see Adele. After I finish, he shakes his head in disbelief. 'You offered to switch places with your identity thief? To do something illegal?'

'It was a good plan.'

'It was an incredibly stupid plan!'

'But we could have caught them red-handed. I was trying to help her *and* you at the same time!' I say defensively.

'Who exactly do you think is *them*?'

'She and Anton are mixed up with someone called Popeye, apparently. And he's into all sorts, according to Bex. Drugs, fraud, probably other stuff as well.'

Gus narrows his eyes as he takes in this information. 'Popeye,' he repeats.

'Yes. Do you know him?' I ask. He hesitates, then shakes his head. But I can see a tiny pulse throbbing in the side of his jaw.

'This isn't a game, Clemency,' he says intently. 'These people are dangerous. *Criminals* are dangerous.'

'But you would have been there as back-up! Or someone like you,' I stammer, not wanting to conjure up a rescue scene straight out of Mills & Boon, lest he get the wrong idea. 'Someone with a uniform. And a gun. And all that,' I mumble.

'It's not that simple,' he says, shaking his head. 'In fact,' he adds pointedly, 'protecting you is proving to be *surprisingly* difficult.'

He says this intently, and I see at once that he's genuinely worried. And maybe a little flustered, suddenly. We stare at each other for a long moment, then he picks up his pint glass and takes another long pull, before setting it back down. Then he splays his hands out on the table across from mine, as if he wants to stop the world for an instant and hold it in place.

'It's good of you to *want* to protect me,' I offer quietly. My left hand is only a few inches from his, and it would be the work of an instant to slide it over to his. I edge it a tiny bit closer to see if he will meet me halfway. He is staring right at me with eyes that are unreadable. I see him swallow.

Is this a thing, I wonder?

'It's my job,' he says then, his chocolate voice a little hoarse.

Right. I ease my hand back to where it was, and Gus sits back in the bench, moving his hands to his lap. And just like that, the moment is gone.

'So, what happens now?' I ask, trying to conceal my disappointment.

'Do you want to press charges?'

'Against Adele? No.'

'What about your passport?'

Ah yes. That is a bit of a sticking point. I really do not relish the idea of Anton and Popeye freewheeling around London with my passport. Who knows what they'll get up to? Still, it's not enough to justify sending Adele to prison. If I want my passport back, I'll have to get it without the help of the Met Police. I shrug.

'It's probably changed hands five or six times by now,' I say.

'You do realise we've still got a warrant out for her arrest,' he reminds me.

I shake my head. 'She's a troubled young woman who's been led astray. We need to *help* her. Not arrest her.'

'You don't have to rescue everyone, Clemency,' he says with a sigh. 'People lead difficult lives. And they make bad decisions. They get what's coming.'

'And you've never made a bad decision?' I ask. He pauses, drawing a long breath.

'I've made a few in my time,' he admits. I want to press him for details but decide against it.

'I can't just abandon her,' I say.

'Why? You don't even know her! And she stole from you!'

'Because . . .' I pause, searching for the right answer. I don't know why I need to help Adele, but I do, and I can't really explain why. 'Because our stars are crossed,' I say finally. Gus stares at me for an instant, then literally snorts with derision. I flush beet-red. It is quite possibly the stupidest thing I've ever said, I think with regret. June, at least, would be proud.

'Please tell me that you don't own crystals. Or tarot cards,' he says.

'Would it matter if I do?' I reply, my voice raised slightly in a challenge. After all, why should he care if I'm into mysticism? Unless our budding relationship is about more than just solving crimes? Gus eyes me for a long moment, gauging whether I am serious.

'Each to his own,' he says then.

And I am none the wiser.

Chapter Nineteen

'I can't believe you tracked her down without me. I thought we were a team!'

Bianca is hissing out of the side of her mouth. We're lying on our backs curled up like pill bugs, knees drawn to our chests, in the wind-relieving pose. Except that every fibre of my being is focused on *not* breaking wind in the crowded room of lithe, young *yogini*. None of whom appear to suffer from bloating and excess gas, as I do. I crane my head sideways and see that our instructor is frowning vaguely in our direction.

'You were busy!' I whisper. In fact, Bianca has been AWOL lately. I've not heard from her in days.

'Still. It was very disloyal,' she whispers.

'Fidelity being one of your top qualities,' I remind her.

Bianca snorts in reply. The instructor moves into something called Eye of the Needle, which basically means twisting your legs into a sort of pretzel, and Bianca and I attempt to follow, my thighs screaming in protest.

'Speaking of which, how goes it with the Willies?' I whisper.

'Fine,' she says abruptly. She is staring straight ahead and I wonder fleetingly if I've offended her, which seems extremely unlikely, given that it's Bianca. What is *more* likely is that she's withholding something.

I was surprised to get a text from her this afternoon

suggesting we meet for an early evening class. Saturday isn't usually one of our yoga days. Bianca is normally tied up on Saturday evenings, so I'm intrigued that she is free now.

'Just fine?' I ask.

She shrugs. 'Yep.'

'You're not seeing one of them later?'

Bianca shakes her head. 'Nope. Having a break this weekend.'

Bianca on a break? From men?

The instructor moves into a seated position and we follow, crossing our arms in front of our faces in a spiral called the Eagle Pose, which never fails to make me think of cheese straws. My stomach rumbles audibly.

'So, no plans to see *any* of them?'

'Your obsessive interest in my diary is bordering on stalkerish,' Bianca says with exasperation.

'Nothing new there,' I reply with a grin. 'Anyway, remember you're shagging for two.'

'Not at the moment,' she says.

I turn to her with amazement, but she shifts abruptly so that her body is facing slightly away, refusing to meet my eye. Evidently, she does not wish to discuss her love life any further. Which is literally a first.

After yoga we go for a quick bowl of noodles at an Asian canteen nearby. I refrain from grilling her about the Willies, sensing that for now at least, her private life is *verboten*. Anyway, Bianca is far more intent on the Adele question. 'So what do we do now?' she asks, once we're hunched over our bowls.

'Not sure. We left things a bit vague at the pub.'

Bianca rolls her eyes, slurping up her noodles.

In fact, what happened was that Gus ended our drink

rather abruptly, saying suddenly he had to dash. *To where? I'd thought with dismay.* Though obviously I had no right to enquire. It was Friday night, after all. His life was obviously more interesting than mine. But when I tried to ask what would happen to Adele, he cut me off.

'Clemency, just leave it with me, OK?' he'd said as he shrugged on his coat, a fading dark brown leather bomber jacket that looked like it had genuinely seen action on the front. It even had one of those shearling collars that nestled right up to his neck, just like a World War Two pilot.

Oh, to be a shearling collar, I'd thought wistfully.

'OK?' he'd repeated then, quite pointedly.

'Fine,' I'd shrugged. And then he'd gone, taking his little lamb collar with him.

Now Bianca sighs and pushes back her bowl. 'As usual, it's up to me to come up with a plan,' she says briskly.

'Hang on! Who tracked down my identity thief?' I cry.

'And who let her get away?' counters Bianca.

'I didn't let her get away. She's right where I left her!'

'About to commit another crime. In *your* name, probably.'

I frown. This is true. Apart from my concern over her welfare, I'm equally uneasy about the fact that Anton and Popeye still have my passport. 'But it's not *her* we need to catch,' I say with a sigh. 'She and Anton are just . . . minions.'

'So *who* then?' asks Bianca.

'Popeye,' I say. Whom we know next to nothing about. Other than his nickname, which according to Bex, stems from the fact that he used to be in the Merchant Navy. When I tell Bianca this, she raises a wary eyebrow.

'A sailor?' She shakes her head with distaste.

'What have you got against sailors?'

'Used to date one. He insisted on dragging me out on his boat every weekend. It was cold, wet and mind-numbingly dull. Half the time there was no wind and we'd be bobbing about like a giant cork. And the other half there'd be a screaming gale and we'd be on the verge of flipping. It was an appalling way to conduct a romance.'

'You'll be pleased to know he's not a sailor anymore. He's a criminal,' I say.

Bianca snorts. 'Far preferable.'

'Anyway, we're not looking to date him. We're looking to put him in jail.'

'Then we're going to need a little more to go on, besides the fact that he has a seafaring past.'

'True,' I agree. And Adele is hardly going to give us more information. I wonder fleetingly about Gus, whom I suspect knows more than he's letting on, but quickly decide he's probably the last person on earth who would give me the information we want. Especially after he explicitly warned me to leave the case alone.

'What about the sister?' says Bianca.

'Bex?'

'Wouldn't she know how to find him?'

'I don't know. Maybe.'

'Right,' she says, whipping out a small compact mirror from her handbag and flipping it open. She tousles her hair with her fingertips, eyeing it from various angles, like a jeweller appraising a diamond, before snapping it briskly shut. 'Time for a trim,' she says decisively.

'You do realise we could just ring her. I've got her number.'

Bianca cocks her head at me. 'Sweetie, where's the fun in that?' she asks. 'Besides, I'm multi-tasking.'

The next morning, I endeavour to rouse a sleeping Charlie Bucket in order to take him out before I'm due to meet my sister. He lies stretched across the foot of my bed like an enormous hairy log. Somehow, he knows that it's Sunday, our day of rest, and that he is well within his rights not to budge. When I pick up his lead and rattle it over his head, telling him it's time for a walk, he merely opens one dubious eye, as if to say: *A walk is entirely out of the question at this time.*

'Please, Charlie Bucket,' I say, in my most cajoling tone.

He sits up, yawns, then begins to diligently lick one of his front paws, which strikes me as a tactical ploy; Charlie Bucket rarely engages in grooming purely for the fun of it, so he is clearly making a point. I stamp my foot petulantly on the floor like a toddler. 'Charlie Bucket, outside NOW!' I say.

He lies back down, lowering his head with an oomph and shuts his eyes. Never have I felt more powerless. I am meant to be his master! I consider leaving him, but I will likely be away until lunchtime, and not even Charlie Bucket's massive bladder can withstand an entire morning without being emptied. Instead, I storm over to the kitchen and return with a large jar of peanut butter, which I open and shove beneath his sleeping nose. His eyes flick open instantly.

'Out,' I say sharply, nodding towards the door. Slowly he heaves his massive body off the bed and ambles to the front door, where he sits down and refuses to budge until I open the peanut butter, dip an index finger in, and let him lick it clean, an action which quickly leaps into my top three most disgusting acts of pet ownership. I attach his lead and drag him out onto the landing, where once again he collapses on his haunches.

'Seriously?' I ask. I dip my finger in the jar again. We make our way down the stairs in similar fashion, Charlie Bucket pausing every three or four steps for another sticky top-up. When we reach the bottom, he plants himself once again and suddenly I hear Carl's front door open and close, followed by his feet hurrying down the stairs. *Uh oh.* I hastily open the door out onto the street and tug on the lead, but Charlie Bucket refuses to budge. 'Come on!' I hiss, just as Carl barrels round the last bend and stops short. His eyes flick to the open jar in my hand.

'Are you *feeding* your dog in our common space?'

'I'm trying to get him outside!'

'Not hard enough!'

Charlie Bucket suddenly lunges at him and Carl leaps back up the stairs a few feet, his face blanching. I yank hard on the lead, nearly severing my arms from my shoulder sockets, and as I do the jar drops to the floor, smashing on the tiles and smattering peanut butter across a wide arc. Charlie Bucket instantly moves in on a recovery mission, while Carl, now horrified, hisses: 'The glass!'

'Yes, yes, I know,' I say, dropping quickly to my hands and knees to pick up all the remnants of glass. Though I suspect Charlie Bucket's cast-iron constitution could probably manage a few shards.

'Here,' snaps Carl. He hastily withdraws a plastic shopping bag from his coat pocket and holds it out to me.

'Thank you,' I say. While I gather up the glass and Charlie Bucket diligently cleans the floor tiles – *what a good boy!* – Carl quickly descends the stairs and slips past us out the door.

'I'll expect this hallway to be disinfected upon my return,' he snaps, while I glare at his retreating back.

Though I did not intend to take him with me to brunch, Charlie Bucket has other ideas. After we've done a few laps round our local square (and Charlie Bucket has filled two poo bags, lifted his leg against three tree trunks, two fences, one post box and even a parked bicycle whose owner swore at us), he stops at the front door of my building and refuses point-blank to go back inside.

'Fine, you win,' I say wearily. My sister will be thrilled.

We arrive a few minutes late at the venue: a café near Borough Market that Julia has chosen from some online list of hip London breakfast spots. I can instantly see it's going to be tricky with a behemoth in tow – the place is heaving with bearded types and trendy millennial parents with infants slung over their shoulders. Buggies and bags cram the narrow spaces between tables, and the waiters are forced to shimmy through in order to deliver food. I glance uneasily at Charlie Bucket, whose bulk will definitely not make him popular. I sidle up closer to the window and spy Julia at a tiny table for two against the far wall, and when she sees me, she waves enthusiastically. She half rises to her feet, but then her gaze alights on Charlie Bucket, and I see her face crease with concern. She glances around the crowded café, frowning, then threads her way through the tables to the doorway.

'Clem, what were you thinking?' she admonishes, nodding at him.

'Sorry. I promise he'll be good.'

She rolls her eyes. 'I'll speak to the waiter.'

Julia turns and searches for a waiter while I bend down and hiss into Charlie Bucket's ear.

'All right, *best* behaviour mate.'

After a minute Julia reappears holding her coat, latte and menu. 'He says we'll have to sit outside,' she says ruefully, indicating a small table on the pavement beside me. It is mid-January and the temperature is hovering a few degrees above freezing. *Whoops*.

'I'm so sorry,' I say as we sit down at the table. 'If we

188

were French, everyone inside would just bunch up.'

'But we're not French,' she says, flashing a joyless smile. 'And we never asked to be.'

True. Julia never wanted to be anything but herself. Though I often wonder why she doesn't seem to experience the same self-doubt as the rest of humanity. Is she missing some vital gene? We settle into our chairs, pulling our coats tightly round us for warmth.

'How *are* you?' I say, infusing my voice with as much concern and sympathy as I can muster.

'Fine,' she says too quickly, adopting her usual no-nonsense tone. 'Absolutely fine,' she reiterates after a moment, smoothing her paper menu out in front of her carefully. But she doesn't *look* fine. She looks drawn. And there are shadows under her eyes, as if she hasn't been sleeping. On top of that she looks cold. We are both bundled up in our parkas, and Julia has pulled up her hood, so that only the pale oval of her face is visible, surrounded by a halo of fake fur.

'Good for you,' I say half-heartedly. Who knows? Maybe denial is the best way forward in her situation.

'Why didn't you get back to me?' she asks then.

'About . . . what?' I say hesitantly.

Julia's eyes widen with alarm. 'There's something on the Instagram account, isn't there!' she says, nodding with certainty.

Shit. I completely forgot to check Robby's Instagram account, much less ring her back about it. 'No!' I say. 'Definitely not. Nothing. Just . . . the usual stuff.'

'Really?' she asks suspiciously.

'Really,' I say, nodding emphatically.

She inhales, considering this for a moment. 'You'd better show me,' she says, holding out her hand for my phone. 'You might miss something obvious.'

Uh oh. What if there's something bad on his account? Slowly, I retrieve my phone from my pocket and open Instagram. I type Robby's name into the search bar, holding my breath, and am simultaneously both relieved and offended a moment later when a notice informs me his account is now private. He's blocked me too! The rotter!

'It was fine the other day,' I stammer, which is only a teeny-weeny bit of a lie. I honestly can't remember the last time I looked at Robby's Instagram, which is generally full of a) pictures of bikes b) pictures of *him* on his bike and c) pictures of his mates on their bikes, living their best #blokesonbikes life. Yay #lycra! I hold the phone out to her and Julia frowns at the screen.

'He's definitely hiding something,' she says.

'He's building a new life, Julia. You both are. Isn't that the goal?'

She shakes her head. 'But the process is meant to be open. And honest,' she says earnestly. 'It's meant to be completely *transparent.*'

Really? Is transparency a good thing? Shouldn't they both have the privacy and space for reinvention?

'Maybe you should just ask him,' I suggest.

She looks at me aghast. 'Maybe he should just *tell* me!' she replies.

I frown. Suddenly it occurs to me that Julia isn't *really* looking to reinvent herself – it's her relationship she's struggling to rebuild. Ironically, she's trying to achieve that through the process of divorce. I peer at her – does she even realise that's what she's doing? I think back to when she first told me they were separating and the reasons why. She catalogued a host of issues, as if she was trying to persuade herself along with me: financial pressures, work-related stress, diverging interests, the fact that they each took the other for granted. The marriage had cruised along happily enough for the first few years, she'd said, but then it began to wobble every time they met an obstacle, like a dodgy fairground ride that begins to feel unstable halfway through. 'So, we decided maybe it was best to just . . . get off,' she'd said sadly. 'Before someone got hurt.'

The truth is Julia wasn't used to failure, and I think the prospect of it genuinely terrified her. And if she couldn't make a success of her marriage, then maybe she could make a success of her divorce. Which explains why she'd thrown herself at it with such gusto. But now, even that was spinning beyond her control.

The waiter appears with our food then: Eggs Benedict for her and a chorizo omelette for me. Charlie Bucket sits bolt upright, his enormous head looming beside the table. I see his pupils dilate as they fixate on my chorizo. 'Lie down!' I say quietly under my breath, planting my hand atop his head and pushing him down like he's a giant, recalcitrant Jack-In-The-Box. Eventually, he drops bodily onto the pavement with an audible groan.

'Can *you* ask him?' says Julia now, in a pleading tone. I look up at her with surprise.

'You mean . . . ask Robby if he's seeing someone?'

She nods.

'But you *live* with him,' I say. 'Can't you ask him?'

She shakes her head with distress.

'But what about the process? Wouldn't I be . . . interfering somehow?'

Julia frowns with genuine despair. She blinks several times. 'I think the process may be broken,' she admits.

My heart twists for her. I feel badly for my sister, I really do. But inserting myself into the middle of her divorce makes me uneasy. While I believe in the notion of blood ties (*do I really?*), family bonds only take you so far, and some things really ought to be off-limits. Your mum doesn't need to know how often you get cystitis, for example. And your dad doesn't need to know that the scented candles he gives you every year for Christmas make you sneeze. Still, before we part, Julia extracts a reluctant promise from me to ring Robby.

And find out if he's shagging someone else.

As Charlie Bucket and I walk home, I get a call from Bianca.

'Where *are* you?' she says accusingly.

'On Borough High Street. Where are you?'

'Outside your flat.'

'Why?'

'Thought we'd drive over to Chelsea.'

'Now? I'm not even sure the salon is open on Sunday!'

'It is. I checked.'

'Besides, Bex may not even be working. And if she is, she's probably booked out.'

'She's there. I called a few minutes ago,' says Bianca.

'Did you get a booking?' I ask.

'No.'

'So we're driving all the way to Chelsea for . . . what exactly?' I ask.

Bianca huffs. 'Sweetie, this wouldn't be the first time I blagged my way into a top salon at short notice.'

'Fine,' I sigh. Charlie Bucket and I can kiss our afternoon of Sunday relaxation goodbye.

'She'd better be as good a stylist as you say she is.'

'She's better. She's also eye-wateringly expensive.'

'So am I,' says Bianca. 'I'll pick you up in five minutes.'

When she pulls up in her Mini Cooper a few minutes later, she rolls down her window and pulls a face. 'Why didn't you tell me he was with you!' she says, nodding at Charlie Bucket.

'You didn't ask.'

'Will they even let him in?'

'If you can blag *your* way in, surely you can blag his way in.'

'Get in the car. He'd better not get hair on my upholstery.'

Easier said than done. Bianca's car is basically a two-seater with two tiny bucket seats behind that are only suitable for people with no legs. Charlie Bucket has to clamber over the gear shift just to get in, but he seems game enough. Once he's climbed inside the front seat, I position his face between the seats and give his enormous bum a hearty shove with my shoulder and he tumbles into the rear, turning around with some difficulty and finally managing to right himself, albeit slightly hunched over. Instantly, he starts to pant. Bianca and I climb in.

'What's that smell?' she says, wrinkling her nose.

'Peanut butter.'

'I'm not sure you should be entrusted with pet owner-ship,' she says.

'Why not? It's his favourite!'

We drive along the Embankment and it's a pleasant enough ride, in spite of the panting. 'So,' I venture after a minute. 'I thought you normally spent Sundays à deux?'

'We are à deux. À trois, actually.'

'Yes, but we're upright. Which isn't really your preferred position, is it?'

'You'd be surprised.'

'No, I definitely wouldn't.'

'Can't I spend Sunday with my best friend?' she says. 'And her faithful canine companion?' she adds, glancing in the rear-view mirror with obvious distaste.

'Seriously. What's up?'

'Nothing. I needed a break, that's all.'

Normally, when Bianca gets fed up with one guy, she merely substitutes another, like the manager of a football squad. So something has definitely changed.

'One of them has got to you,' I say. 'It's Willem, isn't it,' I add, because honestly, he's the only one worthy enough. She purses her lips, then takes a corner too fast and Charlie Bucket and I both pitch to one side. I hear his claws scrabbling on the side panels as he struggles to right himself. 'Whoever he is, he's not worth dying for,' I hasten to add.

'The Dutch are so infuriating!' she says through gritted teeth. 'With all their tulips and canals and cannabis. Who gave them the right to be so . . .' She breaks off distractedly, taking another corner too fast, and I brace myself with one hand against the dashboard.

'Tall?' I offer, eyeing the road with alarm. 'Attractive?'

'He's just so annoyingly . . . *frank*.' She spits out this last word like it's the ultimate shortcoming. Rather than a quality most people would welcome.

'Isn't honesty a good thing?'

'Not always,' she snaps. I wait for her to elaborate but she doesn't.

'So ditch him,' I say lightly, calling her bluff. 'Plenty of other guys called William out there. Ones who are perfectly capable of deception and fabrication and . . . obfuscation. I suspect you've only just scratched the surface of wayward Willies.'

Bianca scowls but says nothing more, and I know not to press her.

What are best friends for?

*

When we reach the salon, we park just around the corner, and Charlie Bucket manages to extract himself from the back seat like one of those clown acts from a circus car. At full height, he and the car are basically on an even par. He gives an enormous shake of his withers once he's back on the pavement, then turns to me expectantly, as if to say: '*Now what?*'

'Come on,' I say, attaching his lead. Bianca has already set off without us and when we round the corner, I see that she's gone inside and is working her magic on the receptionist. But as we push open the glass door, I see the latter shake her head quite definitively and indicate the crammed appointment ledger on the desk. In the next moment, the receptionist's eyes stray to Charlie Bucket and widen with alarm. I realise now that this was a really bad idea – the salon is abuzz with activity. All four chairs are full, there's a fifth customer having her hair washed at the rear and another waiting on the sofa. Bex is with a client at the far end of the room and when she sees me enter, she frowns slightly. I give a tiny wave to her, then cross over to Bianca, who is smiling sweetly at the receptionist.

'It really is an emergency,' she says. 'My friend and I would be so grateful.' She pauses then and lowers her tone slightly. 'It's my father's funeral tomorrow. And you know what mothers are like. Your best is never *quite* good enough, is it?'

'I'm sorry, madam, but there's nothing I can do. We are genuinely fully booked.'

'Bianca,' I murmur. 'Maybe we should go.' All the customers have now noticed us and are beginning to stare. Or at least, they're staring at Charlie Bucket. And me.

'I'm just trying to honour his memory,' she says to me. She turns back to the receptionist. 'You'd do the same, I'm sure.'

'Vicky, is there a problem?' We turn around and see Bex standing there, her eyebrows raised.

'I was just explaining you don't have any slots available for these ladies today,' says the receptionist. Bex turns to us, her eyes flicking between us.

'What is it you're after?' she asks politely.

'Just a quick consult, that's all. Five minutes,' says Bianca quickly.

'Fine,' says Bex. I see that the woman whose hair she was working on is now seated beneath one of those massive hair-dryers in the corner, and Bex's chair is empty. She motions us over to it, and Bianca crosses the room and sits down in the chair as if it were a throne, while I perch uneasily by the mirror in front of them, with Charlie Bucket at my feet.

'Right,' says Bex. 'What are we after today?' She raises another quizzical eyebrow at me. Everyone in the salon is surreptitiously watching us.

'We just need some advice,' says Bianca. 'Maybe a few . . . pointers?'

Bex hesitates, then takes up her position behind the chair and runs a practised hand through Bianca's hair.

'I'd say this style is a little heavy for you,' she says cautiously. 'The top and sides need thinning. And I'd build in some more layers at the back, too.'

I see a shadow of irritation pass across Bianca's face.

'Actually, I was thinking more of a retro look,' Bianca says then. 'Nineteen thirties maybe? Let me show you.' She pulls out her phone and types something in, then holds it up for Bex, who peers down. After an instant, the corners of her mouth twitch upwards. I crane forward to see that Bianca has googled a photo of Popeye's girlfriend, Olive Oyl.

Genius! I almost laugh out loud. Bex's gaze flicks up to mine.

'That's an unusual style,' she admits. If anything, this is an understatement. Even by cartoon standards, Olive Oyl's hair is truly outlandish. 'Not one I can help you with,' she adds.

'Too bad,' says Bianca cautiously.

Bex locks eyes with me. 'But I might know who can,' she says.

Ten minutes later we're stuffed back into Bianca's Mini, speeding east along the river the way we came. We're heading towards a pub in Rotherhithe called The Salty Dog. Apparently, Popeye makes it his unofficial base. Just as we were leaving the salon, Bex had grabbed my arm from behind and murmured a warning into my ear: 'Be careful,' she said. 'He's no clown. In spite of the name.' Our eyes had met, and instantly, I'd been reminded of Gus's warning: *Criminals are dangerous.* As we speed towards the pub, I consider texting to let him know where we're going, but I know he'd be furious with me. Besides, we've got Charlie Bucket with us for protection. Who'd be daft enough to argue with him?

It takes us a while to find the pub. It's not far from where I live, but it's in an area I don't come to very often. We keep turning down back streets only to find they don't go all the way through. But when we eventually do stumble upon it, we're both mildly surprised. I was expecting something run-down and shady, but I couldn't have been more wrong. The Salty Dog is adorable! Small and square and as traditional as they come, with ancient leaded glass windows, a tidy white plaster surround, a mansard roof with dormers to the front and three picnic tables lined up neatly along the pavement in front. The street is narrow and cobbled and sits right behind the Thames, and a sign by the door says it is one of the oldest pubs in London, dating to the middle of the sixteenth century.

Bianca stares at the upper windows with an approving eye. 'He may be a sailor, but he's got good taste,' she says.

We push our way inside, where it's warm and welcoming. The benches and long wooden bar are made of centuries-old dark oak, and tall white candles light each table. It's mid-afternoon now, past the lunch rush, so the place is only about half full with people lingering over the remains of half-drunk pints and Sunday roasts. As I look round, I feel the little tingle of excitement I always get in a place as old as this, where you can almost smell the history. I grab Bianca's arm with excitement and whisper in her ear: 'Shakespeare must have drunk a pint or two here! And Marlowe.'

'And loads of other chaps in tights,' she murmurs.

We approach the bar and perch on a couple of stools, looking around. Charlie Bucket seems perfectly at home, settling down at our feet, and no one seems to worry about his looming presence, which is another point in the pub's favour, as far as I'm concerned. The bartender is in his forties with a beard and shaggy hair and a small white bar towel slung over one shoulder. He's hunched over at the far end of the counter chatting idly to a customer, but when he sees us sit down, he immediately comes over.

'What can I get you?' he asks.

'Pint of ginger shandy,' I say, partly out of deference to Bex, and partly because we need to keep a cool head if we're going to be fighting crime.

'She means a Martini,' says Bianca to the barman. 'Make that two.'

'*Two* pints of ginger shandy,' I say to him, a little more forcefully. Bianca turns to me with a look of exasperation. I glare at her. She sighs and turns back to the barman, who is now leaning against the back of the bar, his arms crossed, with a look of bemusement on his face.

'What's it gonna be, ladies?' he asks.

Bianca sighs. 'Fine. Shandy it is,' she says with thinly concealed disgust.

We watch as he draws two half pints of lager then tops them up with ginger beer, sliding them across.

Bianca regards hers uncertainly. 'Feel like I'm back in lower sixth,' she grumbles. I watch as she takes a tentative sip and wrinkles her nose. 'Palatable. But only *just*,' she says.

'Glad you like it. Cause you're buying,' I say with a grin.

'No surprises there.' She withdraws a debit card from her phone and hands it across to the bartender, who rings through the sale. When he gives it back to her, I muster my courage, keeping my voice as casual as I can.

'You don't happen to know if Popeye's around, do you?' I ask.

The bartender regards us silently for a moment, wiping the counter with the cloth. 'He's downstairs,' he says. 'Who's asking?'

I hesitate. 'Olive Oyl,' says Bianca breezily with a smile. 'And Sweet Pea.'

She raises her glass in a toast to him, and he gives a grudging laugh before disappearing down the stairs. 'Cheers,' says Bianca to his retreating back.

We wait. I'm not sure if I have butterflies in my stomach, so much as a swarm of bees. *Maybe this was a bad idea?* I take another sip of shandy, but it slides down uneasily.

'So do you actually have a plan?' Bianca says under her breath. I can tell from her voice that she, too, is nervous. 'I mean, you can't just ask for your passport back.'

'Why not?'

'Because he'll refuse.'

'Not if he knows I'm onto him. Maybe he'll listen to reason,' I say.

Bianca snorts. 'Because criminals are always reasonable,' she mutters. She takes a long drink of shandy, then eyes her glass. 'I tell you one thing – he better have an anchor tattoo.'

'Got two, in fact,' says a male voice behind us. We turn and see that Popeye has come in through another doorway at the rear, surprising us. He pulls up the sleeve of his jumper and shows us a bulging forearm, where sure enough, there's a small, decorative anchor entwined with a rope. 'The other one's a little more private,' he explains, pulling his sleeve back down. 'But if you'd like me to get it out . . .' He raises an eyebrow.

'That won't be necessary,' I say quickly. 'We'll take your word for it.'

He turns to focus on me and I squirm a little under his gaze. We've never met but still he might recognise me. He's not bad-looking actually: short and completely bald, like his namesake, but his body looks fit and trim, as if he works out regularly, and he's got an appealing, slightly swarthy, complexion with large dark eyes and wide full lips. I reckon he's in his late thirties or early forties, one of those men who ages well and knows it. His eyes drift down to Charlie Bucket.

'Nice dog,' he says then, patting Charlie Bucket on the head.

'Thanks,' I reply. An animal lover!

'What's he called?' he asks.

'Bluto,' says Bianca, her voice taking on a slight edge. He laughs and fixes her with a look, before turning back to me.

'Do we know each other?' he asks. ''Cause you look really familiar.'

'Like Adele?' I say.

He narrows his eyes, regarding me. 'She tell you where to find me?' he asks.

I shake my head. 'She doesn't know we're here.'

'So how *did* you find me?'

'Spinach,' says Bianca. 'Lots of it.'

'What exactly can I do for you two *ladies*?' His tone is cordial but just this side of menacing. I raise my chin a little defiantly.

'You can start by giving me back my passport,' I say. 'And then you can release my *friend* . . . from any further obligations.' He tilts his head to one side and sucks in a deep breath.

'Right. Well, here's the thing: I don't have your passport. I never did. And if Adele told you otherwise, then she's lying. And as for her *obligations*, she can do whatever the hell she likes. I'm finished with her and that tool boyfriend of hers. In fact, I'd go so far as to hire Bluto here, before I hired them two again,' he says, indicating Charlie Bucket.

'Bluto's very expensive, actually,' says Bianca.

'You just can't get good help these days,' I add, shaking my head in mock dismay. 'We have the same problem in cheese.'

'I'm not really interested in your problems,' he says.

Rude! And now he really does sound menacing!

'You know who *is* interested in my problems?' I ask. 'The Met Police.'

He regards me stonily for a moment.

'I think we're done here,' he says coolly, and then he turns on his heel and disappears through the same door he came in. After he's gone, I heave a sigh of relief, and turn back to Bianca. I hadn't realised it, but my fists had been clenched tightly the whole time.

'Well?' I say to her. She raises an eyebrow.

'I take back everything I said about sailors,' she says. 'The man is anything but dull.' She picks up her pint and takes a drink. 'This is growing on me,' she says, indicating the glass. She signals to the bartender for a refill.

'What do you reckon about Adele?' I ask.

'Sweetie, I hate to break it to you, but I think your little friend may be telling tales.'

Chapter Twenty

Was Adele really lying? Later that night, I dither about whether to text Bex. Once again, she didn't turn up to roller derby this evening, so I couldn't confront her. Is it possible they're *both* playing me? (Note to future self: drinking two pints of ginger shandy before skating practice is a seriously bad idea if you do not want to spend the entire evening rolling back and forth between the rink and the toilets.) Eventually, I decide against texting Bex, and opt to fulfil my familial obligations instead, fortifying myself first with a stout glass of whisky.

When Robby answers the phone, he sounds genuinely pleased to hear from me. 'Clem! How goes it?' I smile when I hear his voice down the line. In all the hoo-ha over the divorce these last several months, I'd actually forgotten how much I *like* my brother-in-law. For all his bloke-ishness, he's still basically a good guy: kind, easy-going, tolerant even. (He'd have to be, to put up with Julia.) My sister's soon-to-be-ex will never set the world on fire, but he's no firebrand either, and isn't that a good thing?

We make small talk for a few minutes, during which time I manage to establish that a) Julia is nowhere within earshot and b) he has not clapped eyes on her since early this morning, when he waved to her on his way out of the door to meet some biking mates. I breathe a tiny bit easier at this. When I ask him how he's adjusting to single life, he sighs.

'You know, I thought I'd be anxious to get back out there on the dating scene. Especially with all these new apps and stuff. But so far, I haven't had much appetite for it,' he admits.

Excellent! I think, smiling. Job well done. Robby is clearly not bed-hopping.

'These things take time,' I offer sympathetically. 'You don't want to rush it.'

'I met someone terrific last week, though,' he adds. 'At the supermarket! Can you believe that?'

Seriously? He met someone at the supermarket? How annoying! I go to the supermarket every frigging week and never meet a single soul, apart from drifting pensioners, surly shelf-stackers and unruly toddlers with beleaguered mums in tow. I scowl into the phone. Only men have romantic encounters in supermarkets, I think crossly. Women never do.

'That's great,' I say half-heartedly. *Is that why you blocked us from Instagram? To hide pix of you and her fondling the root vegetables? Poor Julia!*

'She's married, unfortunately,' he says then, a bit wistfully.

'Oh,' I say. All is not lost! 'Too bad,' I add, just for form's sake.

'But then, so am I,' he adds, with an almost conspiratorial chuckle.

'Yes, you are,' I say emphatically. Because marriage is meant to be sacred! He really shouldn't be speaking of it so lightly.

'Anyway, time will tell,' he says.

Such an irritating phrase! What does he mean by this, anyway?

Then he tells me not to be a stranger and rings off, and I am none the wiser.

Maybe I don't really like him, after all.

*

The next morning, I drop Charlie Bucket off with June and go for my Monday morning skate. I need to reflect upon my next course of action. Do I go back to Nan's flat and confront Adele? Or call Bex? Or maybe I should ring Gus, who I am longing to speak to, if only to hear his voice, which is increasingly like aural catnip to me. Is it possible to develop an actual addiction to a sound?

I head east through the back streets of Southwark and past Pepys Park with its fabulous views across the river to Canary Wharf, then decide to carry on all the way to Greenwich Park, where there are excellent paved paths for skating. The hill there is a killer, but maybe the views from the Observatory will clear my mind.

I forgot how high the damn thing is, however. As I approach the park from the river, I can see the Great Equatorial Dome looming over the surrounding parkland like an enormous architectural turnip. I opt for the long, less steep path that winds up from the rear, but even so uphill skating is not for the faint of heart, and when I finally reach the line marking the Prime Meridian, I am huffing and puffing. I drink some water from a fountain before glancing down at my phone, which has been tucked into my waistband on silent.

Crikey! Three missed calls from Gus!

Surely this is a good sign? Clearly, while I was fantasising about him during my way over here, he must have been thinking about me, too. Should I ring him back now? Or play it cool and wait a little while? Maybe I should at least go home and shower and wash my hair first. What if he wants to meet up?

I then notice with vague unease two other missed calls from my boss, Philip, (highly unusual) followed by a terse text message from him. Really it is more like a directive: *Be at the shop at 12.*

No 'please'. No 'thank you'. No explanation. And on my day off, too! I know that I am still officially on probation, but really, there are limits to what an employer should require. What about worker's rights? It's already 11.15 so I set off back down the hill, silently fuming. I'll have to wait until I've seen Philip to ring Gus back.

When I reach the shop, I'm dismayed to see from the outside that Philip is already here, surveying the cheese privy, while June looks on. I glance down at my phone. He's six minutes early! And I skated so fast! Now I'm tired and sweaty and not very presentable but needs must. Poor June has always been incredibly nervous around Philip, so I really shouldn't delay – she flusters easily, and his manner isn't exactly user-friendly. When I push open the door, I see that Charlie Bucket is sprawled across the centre of the floor, as per usual. He raises his head and wags his tail when he sees me, and at the sound of the bell, Philip turns around.

'Ah, there you are,' he says peremptorily. He turns to June. 'Could you leave us alone for a few minutes?'

June freezes uncertainly. The shop is so small that there's really nowhere for her to go, except possibly to the toilet, which is about the size of an *actual* toilet, and not somewhere you would be expected to languish. Her panicked gaze drifts over to mine and I nod imperceptibly towards the front door.

'Absolutely,' she says then, recovering herself. 'I need to pop over to the newsagents anyway. We're out of . . .' she hesitates, her eyes frantically roaming the room, ' . . . sticky tape,' she says then.

'Thank you,' says Philip. We watch as June retrieves her coat and handbag and slips out of the door, whereupon Philip turns to me.

'Is something wrong?' I ask nervously.

'I thought I'd ask you the same,' he says, peering at me.

'Um. No. Everything is fine,' I reply carefully. *Sort of.*

'Are you quite sure?' he asks.

'Yes.'

'Because if there *is* something wrong, that you would like to share with me, now would be an opportune moment,' he declares pointedly.

I can only stare at him, mystified.

'*Before* the police arrive,' he adds, looking at his watch. 'Which will no doubt be soon.'

'Philip, I don't understand. What's happened?'

'You don't know?' he asks, his eyes narrowing suspiciously. I shake my head.

'Honestly. I've no idea why you're here.'

'So you're saying that it was *not* you who went to the shop's main bank branch this morning at 9 a.m. and requested a cashier's cheque for the full amount that was held in the account.'

Oh good Lord. Adele. The passport.

I stare at him speechless, my mind whirring.

'Clemency, I await your explanation. Which I trust will be forthcoming soon.'

'I think I can explain,' I start to stammer.

Can I though? I can certainly hazard a guess.

'You *think*? Or you *can*?' he asks. 'There's a difference.'

'I believe what's happened . . . well, really . . . it's a case of . . .' I hesitate, speaking slowly. Of *what*, I think?

'I believe the word you're looking for is *theft*,' he interjects.

'Philip. I promise, it's not what you think,' I say, shaking my head.

'Then perhaps you'll enlighten me.'

'Well, it *is* what you think, but it's not me who's

207

responsible. Well, maybe I'm a teeny-weeny bit responsible because I could have possibly prevented it. But I didn't actually *do* it . . . if you see what I mean. Someone else did it. Someone very . . . troubled. But they're not really to blame, either. At least, I don't think they are . . .' My voice trails off.

'So who is to blame?' he asks. I look up at him.

'I'm not entirely sure,' I say finally. He sighs, raising his thumb and two fingers to his forehead, as if it pains him. As if *I* pain him. He stares at the floor for a long moment, then looks back at me.

'Clemency, are you familiar with the concept of double jeopardy?' he asks. I frown.

'I think so. At least, I saw the movie,' I say. 'The original 1955 one, not the crap remake with Tommy Lee Jones,' I add. 'Which apparently was dreadful.'

'I think you should know that it does not apply here.'

I frown. 'What do you mean?'

'It means that there are no second chances. As far as I'm concerned, you *can* be tried twice for the same crime: in this instance, stealing from Say Cheese. And me.'

'Oh.'

'It also means that you're fired. As of . . .' He glances once again at his watch in a manner that can only be described as theatrical. 'Now.'

I stare at him. 'Now?' I ask. *Don't I even get a fair trial?*

'Yes. You are officially removed from your post.'

'But who will run the shop?' I ask, bewildered. Surely not him?

Just then the door chime tinkles and June enters, bearing a large roll of sticky tape. She pauses when she sees us and flourishes it.

'Got it,' she trills nervously. 'We can tape away!'

'Jane,' says Philip, turning back to me but nodding towards her. 'Jane will run the shop.'

I stare at him; open-mouthed.

'It's June, actually,' says June quietly behind us.

Five minutes later, I am standing in the shower, numb. Hot water streams over me. I stand directly beneath the shower head as if caught in a deluge and turn my face upwards, allowing it to cascade down upon me, filling my nose, my mouth and even my ears. Drowning me. Because honestly, I deserve it.

How could I be so stupid?

Of course Adele would go after the shop's money! How did I not realise it was at risk? I should have reported the theft of my documents to Philip immediately. He could have changed the shop's bank account with a single phone call.

Oh God, what will Gus say? Maybe he already knows?

I turn off the water quickly, realising that may be why he rang me. I grab my towel and start to dry myself off, when I hear my door buzzer ringing insistently. Someone is literally holding it down continuously, the harsh noise not far off that of a dentist's drill. I grab my dressing gown, a pale blue hooded affair with floppy dog ears that Julia gave me two Christmases ago and rush to the buzzer. 'Who is it?' I ask.

'DC Meadows,' says Gus. And even though my insides do a little happy dance at the sound of his voice, I can tell he's hopping mad. I press the buzzer and immediately hear his footsteps running up the stairs. I glance quickly around the flat. It's a tip, as usual – no time for damage control, on either it or me. When I open the door a moment later, Gus is standing there, a little breathless.

'Why didn't you answer my calls?' he demands, stepping inside the flat. I close the door behind him.

'I'm sorry, I didn't see them,' I stammer.

'What the hell is going on? You do realise there's a warrant out for your arrest right now? *Your* arrest. Not someone who looks like you!'

'I know. It wasn't me. Honest. It must have been Adele.' He stares down at me. God, he looks amazing! Seven days of stubble is truly perfection on him.

'I thought you told me she didn't have your passport,' he says.

'She may have been lying,' I admit, a little sheepishly.

He rolls his eyes. 'Oh, do you think?! Where have you been all morning, anyway?'

'I went for a long skate. To Greenwich.'

'Alone?' he asks.

I shrug. 'I always skate alone.'

'Great,' he says, running his hand through his hair with frustration. 'So no one can vouch for you.'

'Surely we're *both* suspects at this point? Not just me!' I say.

'Yes, of course you're both suspects. But your boss said you stole from him a few months ago. Is that true?'

He stares at me and for a long moment I genuinely cannot answer. I close my eyes, because I can't bear to see the look of hope mixed with dismay on his face.

You know when people have a near-death experience and see their whole life flash before them in a series of images? Well, that's what happens to me now, except that what I see is every mistake I've ever made unspool in my mind like a bad disaster movie: every crap decision, every oversight, every bit of deceit, every slip of the tongue, every error in judgement.

'Clemency?' I open my eyes and Gus is still staring at me.

'It was more of a short-term loan,' I say weakly.

'Oh God,' he says, with thinly concealed dismay.

'I was going to pay it back, I swear! And he was never meant to find out. I was broke because Adele was stealing from me and I didn't have enough money to cover my mortgage, and I just needed a couple of hundred quid to tide me over . . .' I stop speaking.

'You really are a mess, you know that?' he says quietly. I can hear the disappointment in his voice, as if he's only just realised. I nod, tears welling up in my eyes.

'Yes,' I whisper. *Because I do*. And evidently he does, too. He takes a deep breath and turns away.

'You believe me, don't you? About the loan?' I ask.

'I don't know why I should,' he says finally. He sounds tired. And finished.

'What happens now?' I ask.

'You'll be arrested. Again. Probably soon. I took a big risk coming over here to warn you. I should go.'

'What do I do?' I ask, feeling panic rise inside. Gus takes a deep breath and exhales. He walks over to me and looks me in the eye again, taking me by the shoulders.

'You need to tell them *everything* this time. Every . . . little . . . thing. Do you understand? Start at the very beginning.'

I nod. 'They won't put me in jail, will they?'

'I hope not.'

'You *hope* not?' I ask with alarm.

'Clemency, it's not up to me!' he says with exasperation.

'But . . . can't you vouch for me?' I ask desperately. 'I mean, we're friends, aren't we?'

He looks down at me and for a moment I almost think he's going to kiss me, then he drops his hands and takes a small step backwards.

And I realise the answer is no.

We were never friends – much less something more. Gus stands there frozen, his eyes full of regret. And I think how things might have turned out differently if our stars had been aligned. But I guess we both know this isn't our sliding doors moment.

The buzzer rings, startling us. I turn and press the button. 'Who is it?' I ask, though I'm pretty sure I already know.

'Met Police,' says a gruff voice. I turn back and see Gus's eyes flash with alarm.

'Damn,' he mutters, looking around.

'Quick!' I nod towards the kitchen. 'The fire escape.'

Chapter Twenty-One

They use handcuffs this time – and it hurts. I hadn't realised how bloody uncomfortable they are. The edges are squared off and dig into your wrists, even if they're loose. By the time we arrive at the station, my wrists are starting to chafe and I'm feeling weirdly claustrophobic, even though it's only my arms that are restrained. My chest feels tight and panic bubbles up inside me like overheated milk.

I can't help but remember all the miscarriages of justice I've heard about in the past. Wrongful conviction was a favourite conversational topic of Marcus (whose not-so-secret addiction to true crime lay behind his decision to go into the law). He even volunteered for a justice charity for a few years, corresponding with several prisoners who vigorously maintained their innocence, until one of his prison pen pals suggested they swap autoerotic asphyxiation scenarios. So I knew that even the best justice systems were capable of making mistakes.

What if I became one of them?

When we arrive at the station, the same world-weary sergeant is on duty. Doesn't he ever have time off? He clearly recognises me because as I'm escorted past, his eyebrows shoot up, as if to say: *We knew you'd be back!* Then I see his gaze drop to my feet, as if he expects Charlie Bucket to be right behind me, like some sort of canine accomplice.

Poor Charlie Bucket! Dogs are so empathetic. He seemed

to sense that this time, things were a little more serious; when they put the handcuffs on me and escorted me out, he jumped up from the sofa and tried to come along. I had to order him back inside using my sternest voice, and he looked back at me with such mournful eyes that it nearly broke my heart. 'I'll be back later,' I'd told him. Which I am really hoping is true. Otherwise, the carpet will be ruined.

Once again, I'm taken to a holding cell on the guilty side of the building, my new home away from home, where I wait for ages. (I've discovered that police time, just like hospital time, exists in a parallel universe, where minutes multiply as rapidly as breeding rabbits.) Finally, I hear voices outside in the corridor, although sadly, not the one I'm hoping for, and the duty sergeant unlocks the door and escorts me down the hall to an interrogation room. A moment later, DC Hill enters. *Hello!* A familiar face, I think with relief.

He doesn't look happy to see me. In fact, he looks grumpy, in spite of his recent holiday, and I instantly sit up straighter, as if my posture might somehow be taken into account.

'So,' he says with a sigh. 'We meet again.'

He sits down opposite me and tosses a manila folder onto the table between us. I note that it's fatter than the last time. A lot fatter. He quickly reads me my rights and turns on the tape recorder, reciting both our names and noting the time and date, then leans back in his chair expectantly. I'm not sure whether to wait for him to speak or try to win him over.

'I hope you had a nice holiday,' I venture hopefully. He raises an eyebrow.

'Benidorm. With my in-laws. Not my choice,' he says grimly.

Ah. No wonder he looks grumpy.

'*You've* been busy,' he indicates the folder.

'*She's* been busy,' I correct him.

'According to this, you've *both* been busy.'

He opens the folder and flicks through the pages, frowning down at them. I wonder fleetingly what Gus has told him. Then he crosses his arms and sits back in the chair, regarding me.

'You know what I think?' he asks. 'I think maybe you and she are a bit of a team.'

I stare at him open-mouthed.

A team? Me and Adele?

Actually, this is far worse than I expected.

'Definitely not,' I stammer.

'Why not? You *know* her, don't you,' he says.

I shake my head. 'No! Not really. I mean . . . I've *met* her. I hardly know her. There's a difference.'

'But you're friends with her sister. Teammates, even.'

I hesitate. I *am* friends with Bex. Sort of. And we are definitely teammates. 'Bex has nothing to do with this,' I say.

'Nothing?' he presses me. Once again, I hesitate. Bex *did* take my ID and give it to Adele. So I suppose that's something.

'Bex was only trying to help her sister stay out of trouble,' I say cautiously. 'I would do the same.'

'Really? You'd break the law to help your sister?'

'No! I'd *never* knowingly break the law,' I say emphatically, rolling my eyes.

'Never?' His tone is sceptical. He is staring at me expectantly.

Of course I've broken the law. More than once, actually.

Suddenly panic flares somewhere deep inside, and it is all blaring sirens and flashing lights. I really could be in proper trouble here, and I honestly do not know what to say at

215

this point, whether to try to explain, or keep silent and get legal advice. I wish now that I'd exercised my rights to a phone call. Perhaps Marcus would have been able to help? But then I hear Gus whispering in my ear, like some sort of guardian angel: *Tell them everything,* he'd said.

So I do.

In the end, I do not have to spend the night in jail. *Thank heavens.*

DC Hill listens patiently while I relate the events of the last several months, only once or twice rolling his eyes over the stupidity of my actions (which strikes me as fair). And then he tells me that I'm free to go, provided I do not break any more laws, nor hamper the course of justice.

Although he puts it more succinctly: *Stay out of trouble,* he growls, as I'm leaving. *And out of our way.*

When I arrive home at a little past midnight, Charlie Bucket launches himself at me like a giant furry missile, literally knocking me to the floor. I lie back on the carpet and let him have his way – I'm too tired to resist and anyway a part of me welcomes the attention. There is no love more unreserved than that of a dog for its owner. Especially when they have not been given their dinner.

I feed us both, shower, then pour myself a stiff whisky and climb into bed. Charlie Bucket seems to sense that I am downcast; rather than settle at my feet as usual, he plants himself alongside me like a fallen tree trunk. I cuddle up to him and it helps, in spite of the fact that he snores.

I lie awake for some time, listening to him. So now I am broke and unemployed. *Well done me.* But at least I can apply myself full time to finding Adele. Because if I'm ever going to get Philip's money back and clear my name, Adele is the key: Adele, who lied to me. Who I felt sympathy for, and felt connected to. Were our stars really aligned? Or have I been a complete fool?

No wonder Gus has washed his hands of me.

Charlie Bucket and I sleep the sleep of the dead, and when I eventually awake, his head is on the pillow right next to mine, and it is already past nine. I give him a grateful pat (and silently praise his enormous bladder) then reach over to check my phone. Maybe Gus has had second thoughts, I think hopefully. But there are no texts, no emails, no missed calls. Only a notification from my mobile phone provider that they have been unable to take payment, owing to insufficient funds. *Good morning!*

After tea and toast, Charlie Bucket and I head out. We pause outside the shop and wave to June through the plate glass window. She comes to the door and opens it.

'Are you OK?' she asks, her forehead creased with worry. Charlie Bucket rushes up to nuzzle her and she reaches down to fondle him.

'I'm fine.'

'This doesn't feel right.' She nods at us. 'With me in here and you two out there.'

'You'll manage fine, I'm sure. And you've got Declan to help.'

'Declan nearly quit yesterday out of solidarity,' she says. 'Except he needs the job. So do I,' she adds, a little sheepishly. 'I hope you don't mind.'

'Of course not.'

'But we both think Philip's a tosser.'

I smile. Philip *is* a bit of a tosser. But I still deserved to be sacked.

'What will you do?' asks June. 'For work?'

I hesitate.

Gosh. I have literally no idea.

I'd been so focused on finding Adele that I haven't yet considered how I will pay my mortgage. Much less keep myself stocked in Cheesy Wotsits. I have skills, but what job could possibly accommodate both Charlie Bucket and me? He isn't the sort of dog that can be left on his own all day. Nor is he one to fit in easily to doggy day care, even if I could afford it (which I definitely cannot). I glance down at him, and suddenly I see him for what he is: a gigantic, hairy liability. Another massive error of judgement, to add to the rapidly growing list of my recent infractions. In spite of it all, I reach down to pat his head. For better or worse, I can't imagine life without Charlie Bucket. Even if it lands us both on the bread-line. 'Oh, we'll manage, won't we, mate?' I say breezily.

June frowns. As usual, she can see right through me.

DC Hill made me promise not to interfere. But I did not promise to desist entirely. I take this vow seriously – I need to be careful that my own investigations do not somehow impede his, but it doesn't mean I can't search for Adele myself. So after Charlie Bucket has finished his morning constitutional in the park, we head over to Deptford on the Tube. Over the past few weeks, Charlie Bucket seems to have got over his fear of the London Underground; this time he manages the escalator with ease, and when we reach the bottom he strolls onto the platform like an old pro, swinging his tail casually and glancing around with pride, as if he should be awarded a medal for canine bravery. But a few minutes later, when the train comes screeching around the corner, he flattens his entire body against my side, nearly pitching me over. I reach down to give him a reassuring pat – still a coward at heart.

When we reach Nan's block of flats it is late morning, and I silently pray that we don't meet the tabby. I wait beside the outside door, but no one comes in or goes out for a full ten minutes, by which time Charlie Bucket is lying beside me with his head resting on his paws with boredom. Eventually, I sidle up to the door panel and press all eight buzzers, holding my breath. A couple of scratchy voices enquire who's there, but sure enough, someone buzzes me in without waiting for an answer. I redouble my hold on Charlie Bucket's lead and climb the stairs to Nan's flat, where we knock on the door. After a moment I hear signs from inside, and then the door opens to reveal a plump older woman about my height with thick glasses and wispy grey hair piled high atop her head. She wears hot pink flared tracksuit bottoms and a bright orange cardigan with large pink flowers embroidered on it. When she sees me, she blinks with surprise.

'You're early,' she says.

I hesitate uncertainly. 'I wasn't expecting you before teatime,' she adds.

'Sorry,' I stammer. 'I was just . . . passing.'

'Where's Jerry?' she asks. 'It's him who usually comes.'

I stare at her. *Who does she think I am?*

'He's tied up,' I say cautiously. She nods, then her eyes drift down to Charlie Bucket sitting patiently at my side.

'Council lets you bring dogs out?' she asks with surprise.

I nod. 'For security,' I say.

She shrugs. 'Guess you can't be too careful. Hope he's house-trained.' She opens the door wide and nods for us to enter. 'Toilet's down the hall,' she informs me with a nod.

Once again I hesitate. Is she being polite?

'Oh really, I'm fine—,' I start to say, but she is already shuffling off down the corridor. I glance around quickly before I follow her. There's no sign of Adele anywhere.

'It started last night,' Nan is saying over her shoulder. 'Noise nearly drove me mad. I'm a light sleeper. A moth could fly past and I'd wake.'

We arrive at the bathroom: white linoleum floor and a matching peach bath suite that must be circa 1980. There's a pale peach shaggy bath mat and a turquoise shower curtain with bright orange goldfish splashed across it. She points to the toilet – it's the old-fashioned sort with a handle rather than a button on top and it is running continuously. 'Been doing this non-stop,' she says. 'I've tried everything I can think of.'

Uh oh.

I know precisely nothing about plumbing. I stare down at it, frowning.

'These old loos have mostly been retired by now,' I say, trying to sound authoritative. She is watching me expectantly, so I step forward and jiggle the handle a few times, to no effect, then cautiously lift the lid and peer inside, where I see a ball and pipes and water overspilling in a continuous fountain. I do not have a clue what to do – I might as well be asked to perform an appendectomy.

'Good to see a lady plumber,' she remarks. 'Didn't you bring any tools?'

'Um . . . they're in the van,' I say, over my shoulder. She sniffs, apparently satisfied. I replace the lid, turning back to her. 'I might need to order some parts,' I say tentatively, remembering the stock phrase invoked by every single plumber on every single plumbing job, since time immemorial. Nan sighs.

'Can we use it in the meantime?' she asks.

I shrug. 'Sure,' I say. *Who knows?*

'For everything?' she asks, pointedly.

'Um.' I hesitate uncertainly.

Nan lowers her voice a little conspiratorially. 'It's just . . .

I've been trying to hold off all morning,' she explains.

Poor woman!

'Are you here on your own?' I ask.

She shakes her head. 'Normally there's two of us. But my granddaughter's away working for a few days. Just as well, I guess.' I frown. If Adele holds down a normal job, this is the first I've heard of it.

'Does she work nearby?' I ask. We leave the bathroom and she shuffles back down the hallway towards the front room.

'She moves about. Sales, apparently. Though what they're selling, I don't want to know.' She flicks her hand, as if she can swat away the notion.

'Will she be home anytime soon?'

'Lord knows. That boss of hers has got her working all hours. He picked her up yesterday morning first thing and she said she'd be back in a few days. He drives a flashy red Camaro. I told her right then: *no one up to any good drives a car like that.*' She pauses and turns, scrutinising me. 'Your car's not red, is it?'

'It's white,' I say, nodding towards my non-existent van parked outside. *Doesn't every plumber drive a white van?*

She nods, apparently satisfied, then turns to open the front door to let us out.

'I've never warmed to him. Doesn't even use a proper name,' she adds. 'What sort of man calls himself after a cartoon character?'

It's a rhetorical question; she clearly doesn't expect an answer, but it takes me a moment to realise who she's talking about.

Popeye lied to me! They *both* lied to me! He said he was finished with Adele, but clearly he hasn't.

'Then the police come by, asking about Adele. Two

221

uniforms showed up yesterday afternoon, and a third this morning. That's how I know they're up to no good.' She shakes her head. 'Adele needs to find herself a proper job.'

'The police were here this morning?' I ask. She nods.

'One turned up just before you did. Said he was a detective. No uniform, but he flashed a badge, and it looked real enough. Asking all sorts of questions about Adele. But wouldn't tell me anything.' She frowns, looking genuinely distressed. 'If Adele's in trouble, it'll be the end of me,' she says sadly.

'I'm sure she'll be all right,' I stammer.

Am I?

'He told me to ring him if she turned up. As if I'd turn my own granddaughter in.' She shakes her head. 'Nice-looking though. Could have been on the telly, that one.' I stare at her, frowning. DC Hill is not a natural candidate for television.

Gus was here.

'They didn't make coppers like that in my day,' Nan says with a wistful smile.

Charlie Bucket and I turn to go, and Nan takes off her glasses to wipe at the lenses with a tissue which she removes from her sleeve, before neatly tucking it back in. She replaces her glasses and peers at me as we stand in the doorway. 'You look *just* like her, you know,' she remarks, as if she's only just realised. 'Just like my Adele.'

'Do I?' I ask.

She nods, then cocks an appraising eye at me.

'Afraid she's got the edge on you looks-wise,' she adds with a smile. 'Apart from that, you could be twins.' She gives a little wave, then closes the flat door, leaving Charlie Bucket and I standing there.

Cheers, Nan.

Chapter Twenty-Two

On our way home, Charlie Bucket and I stop at the police station. I know DC Hill told me not to interfere, but the knowledge that Adele is with Popeye is surely important? But when we push our way through the double doors inside, my heart sinks. The station is heaving and once again, the smell of cannabis is cloying.

Crikey. Crime never stops, does it?

People of all sorts cram the waiting area: every age, size, gender and hue is represented. A young black guy is seated in the corner holding an ice pack to his bleeding lip, and on the far side of the room, an angry blonde woman with hair falling past her waist is shouting insults at a beleaguered young PC, threatening to sue. As I look around at the range of humanity on display, I can't help but think that Samuel Pepys is up there somewhere in heaven, saying: *I told you so.*

When the duty sergeant spies us, he flashes me a caustic look. 'Maybe you should get a room,' he says, his voice laced with sarcasm. 'That way we could charge you rent.'

'I'm here on police business,' I inform him coolly.

'Surprisingly enough, so is everyone else,' he says, indicating the room full of waiting people.

'I'd like to see DC Hill.'

'So would everyone else,' he repeats. 'You'll have to wait. It could be some time.'

'I'll deal with this, Trevor,' says a familiar voice behind

me. I turn around to see Gus standing there, arms folded across his chest, one eyebrow cocked in what I am almost certain is disapproval. My insides clench nervously, but another part of me leaps with joy at the sight of him. I give a little sheepish wave.

'Hello,' I say cautiously.

'You'd better come through,' he says, spinning on his heel and leading me back to the interrogation rooms. I follow him with a lump halfway between hope and dread lodged in my gullet. I'm not sure I can bear it if Gus tells me off again; I was planning to slope in and out of here quickly without seeing him. When we reach the interrogation room he stands in the doorway and nods for me to enter.

'Wait here,' he says tersely, then disappears. I sink down onto a chair and pull Charlie Bucket between my legs for comfort. Evidently Gus does not intend to chastise me, but where's he going? After a minute, DC Hill pokes his head into the room and throws me a look. 'Seriously?' he says.

'I'll be quick. I promise,' I say. He steps into the room and sits down heavily opposite me.

'What is it now?'

'Adele is working for Popeye. He came and picked her up in his car early yesterday morning.'

He widens his eyes with exasperation. 'We *know* that.'

'So maybe he forced her to do it!' I say.

He frowns at me sceptically.

'I think she's quite capable of committing a crime *all by herself*,' he says. I shake my head.

'He's got some sort of hold over her. She wouldn't have done it unless . . .'

'Unless what?'

'Unless she *had* to,' I say.

'What makes you think that?' he asks.

I hesitate. I *know* I'm right – I can feel it in my gut. But my instincts are unlikely to win DC Hill round.

'Look, Adele's not stupid,' I say. 'She knows she'll be top of the list of suspects.'

'Well, actually she shares that honour with you,' he reminds me.

'It doesn't add up. She must have been desperate.'

Just then, Gus sticks his head through the doorway, interrupting us.

'Sorry,' he says, nodding to DC Hill. 'You're needed downstairs.'

DC Hill sighs and rises to his feet. He crosses to the door, before turning back to me.

'People commit crimes for all sorts of reasons,' he says. 'It doesn't make them blameless.'

Once he's gone, Gus steps into the room and sits down in the chair opposite me. Charlie Bucket heaves himself off the floor and crosses over to him, wagging his tail and burrowing his nose into his lap. Gus fondles him for a moment, then looks up at me.

'So?' he says. I bite my lip, uncertain what to tell him.

'I think Adele's in trouble,' I say.

'Adele *is* in trouble,' he replies.

I shake my head. 'No. I mean with Popeye. She told me she was finished with him.'

'Clemency, she *lied* to you. More than once.'

'What about Popeye then?' I ask. 'She was with him yesterday morning. He's *definitely* involved.'

'We're on it,' he says pointedly. 'You need to trust me.'

I hesitate, trying unsuccessfully to read his mood. He no longer seems angry with me, nor disappointed. But apart from that it's hard to fathom what he thinks.

'I think you should go home now,' he says.

'And do *nothing*?' I ask.

'Exactly,' he says. 'I know how difficult that is for you. But think of it as a test,' he adds pointedly. My eyes narrow at him.

'A test of *what*?' I say, a little affronted.

'I'll let you work that out,' he says, standing up and indicating that I should go. I rise to my feet, frowning. What exactly is he testing? My judgement? Whether I am worthy of his trust? Or whether I can simply follow the most basic of instructions? I'm not sure I want to sit his test, I think stubbornly!

'Will you ring me later?' I ask.

He turns back to face me and raises an eyebrow. 'Do you want me to?'

He is staring at me pointedly, and his tone is vaguely suggestive, as if he's really asking something more. Is this another test, I wonder? I stare at him and my insides start to whirl.

Yes, I think! Whatever he's asking, the answer is yes!

Instead, I play it cool and give a guarded nod. 'Yes, please.'

'Fine,' he says, a shade too complacently. 'I'll ring you later.'

Reluctantly, Charlie Bucket and I head back to my flat, where I make us both a snack: bone-shaped dog biscuits dipped in peanut butter for him, artisan Welsh Cheddar on toast for me. As I bite into the glorious mound of melted deliciousness, I cannot help but feel a pang of regret. No doubt I will be forced to exist on supermarket cheese going forward, a thought which makes me shudder. After lunch, we flop down on the sofa and I stare at the ceiling. One hour of unemployed idleness, and I am already going out of my mind with boredom. I should be scouring the job ads. For what, though? Adele has probably done me a favour with respect to Say Cheese, but I've no idea what I want to do with my post-cheese life. In the meantime, all I can think about is her.

There must be *something* I can do to find her. I try ringing Bex but she doesn't pick up, another worrying sign. Maybe they're together? Or maybe the route to Adele is through Popeye. In the end, I text Bianca.

Hey. What you up to?

Sitting at my desk pretending to work.

Can you get off early?

What for?

Subterfuge! And possibly peril, I add after a moment's hesitation, figuring that I should probably come clean. Just as I suspected, Bianca is not the slightest bit put off.

Can I be ginger?

I was thinking maybe olive, I write back. There's a brief pause while she contemplates my meaning, but then I see the telltale line of jumping dots as Bianca begins to type her response.

So we're back hunting seafarers?

Yep.

Better bring that mutt of yours along.

For protection?

Better than nothing.

I glance over at Charlie Bucket. This last point is debatable. After the morning's exertions, he has now fallen into the deepest of slumbers and is snoring loudly beside me on the sofa. He's not used to putting in even half a day's work, and truthfully, at the moment he looks like he's the last animal on earth who could protect us. Carl's cat would be a better prospect.

He's not unwilling, I type. Though he probably will be, when I try to rouse him.

Can I wear my sailor cap? Bianca asks.

If you must.

And sing sea shanties?

Definitely not.

Killjoy.

This is a serious mission.

I can be serious!

Fine. Pick me up at 4. I toss the phone onto the floor and try not to think about what Gus would say. One thing seems patently clear.

I am definitely going to fail his test.

Bianca arrives only a few minutes past four, which for her is exceptionally punctual. We lure Charlie Bucket down the stairs and into the back seat of the Mini by tossing in a few dog biscuits, and then set off in the direction of The Salty Dog.

'What did you tell Lionel?' I ask as we drive off. Bianca has only been in her current job six weeks, long enough to establish that her new boss, Lionel, is entirely unworthy of respect. She shrugs.

'He wasn't around. Too busy rogering the company accountant, I expect. Or the marketing assistant. Or the . . . pencil sharpener.'

'Really?' I ask.

She nods. 'Serial shagger.'

'Has he tried it on with you?' I ask.

She guffaws. 'God, no. He's terrified of me.'

I sigh. 'I miss office gossip,' I say.

'No, you don't.'

'Yes, I do. It was never the same in the cheese shop. Nothing exciting ever happened. Unless you count the weird recurring rash on Declan's toes. Or that time June rescued a baby hedgehog in her garden.'

Bianca pulls a face. 'Think I'd prefer the rash,' she says. 'Anyway, you won't have *that* problem anymore, will you?'

'I suppose not.'

'And you're about to catch a bonafide criminal.'

'True.'

'Which is the very definition of excitement. So cheer up, sweetie.'

We stop the car around the corner from the pub and I can't help noticing a red Camaro parked on a side street a short distance away. 'Look,' I say, pointing excitedly. 'He's definitely here. That's his car.'

Bianca frowns at it. 'Figures,' she says in a disparaging tone.

I indicate the Mini. 'Hang on! Have you ever stopped to think about what your car says about *you*?' I ask.

'I'll have you know that every single one of the Beatles owned a Mini Cooper,' she says defiantly. 'So did Madonna. Plus, this car inspired the invention of the mini skirt,' she adds. 'Or at the very least, the naming of it.'

'So it says *what* about you, exactly?' I ask.

Bianca considers this for a moment, then shrugs. 'That I can drive.'

We climb out of the car and I turn to Charlie Bucket. 'Come on. Time to get out.' Bianca has laid an old plaid blanket across the back seat and Charlie Bucket has fashioned a sort of nest out of it. He is now wedged in quite comfortably, and the look on his face says that he'd really rather not.

'OUT!' I order. He groans and struggles to his feet, then steps across the gearshift and lands heavily on the pavement.

'You're working, mate,' says Bianca to him.

Charlie Bucket looks up at her with alarm.

His pace becomes more sprightly when he realises where we're headed, however. The prospect of dropped crisps is enough to ensure that pubs have earned a special place in his heart for ever. When we enter, we see at once the place is empty – the same bearded bartender is behind the bar drying glasses. He clearly recognises us and gives a nod as we approach.

'Afternoon, ladies,' he says. 'What'll it be? Ginger shandy? Or Martini?' He gives a cheeky wink to Bianca. She starts to speak.

'Neither,' I say, quickly cutting her off. 'We're here to see Popeye.' The bartender shrugs, plucking another glass from the sink.

'He's not around,' he says casually.

I frown, turning to Bianca. 'Do I look gullible?' I ask. 'Because everyone around here keeps lying to me.'

'Don't take it personally, sweetie,' says Bianca. We both turn to stare at him expectantly. The bartender sighs and sets down the glass.

'I'll see if I can find him,' he says grudgingly, and leaves the room.

'One drink wouldn't have hurt,' grumbles Bianca after he's gone.

'We need to hang onto our wits.'

'Speak for yourself,' she says. 'I've got plenty to spare.'

Charlie Bucket is busy casing the room for crumbs, nose to the floor, barging aside stools and table legs in the process. After a minute the bartender returns and motions to a door leading to a stairway.

'Downstairs,' he says with a nod. Any pretence at politeness is now gone.

Bianca raises an eyebrow at me as she crosses to the door. I grab Charlie Bucket's lead and follow. We descend a steep wooden staircase where the plastered ceiling is so low, I could almost reach up and touch it. It opens out into a cool cellar at the bottom with whitewashed cement walls. On the far side, a line of kegs sits tidily in a row on a metal frame, rubber hoses leading up to the ceiling, with a small refrigeration unit on the floor and a wall-mounted fan. The air is thick with the slightly sweet smell of hops. The bartender crosses the room to a door on the far side and nods for us to follow. He knocks briefly then opens the door, standing aside for us to enter.

The interior room is a small office of sorts. There's a metal desk covered in papers and a couple of shelves filled with file folders. Popeye sits behind the desk leaning right back in a chair, his feet propped up on top of it. I can't help noticing his shoes, which are expensive leather two-tone lace-ups in cobalt blue and dark brown. *Snazzy.*

'Look what the dog dragged in,' he says. He lowers his feet as we step into the room. I turn and spy Adele and her boyfriend seated together on a black plastic sofa opposite the desk. Anton is leaning back against a cushion with a makeshift ice pack held over a badly swollen eye. Below that I can see a nasty cut on his cheekbone and a split lip. His breathing looks labored too, like something else hurts. Adele doesn't look much better; she sits too close to him, gripping his arm tightly. There are dark circles under her eyes and her face is set in a grim mask. I draw a breath and pull Charlie Bucket into the room closer to me, glad suddenly for his bulk.

'So here we all are. Almost like a reunion,' says Popeye, smiling. 'You've met Adele. And this is her greezy gem of a boyfriend. Who likes to think he's a bit of a chief.'

I nod at Adele. 'You OK?' I ask her.

She purses her lips, her eyes darting to Popeye.

'She will be. By this time tomorrow,' he says. 'Won't you sweetheart?' He turns back to us. 'Couldn't stay away, could you, Blondie?' he says to Bianca.

I roll my eyes. *What is it about men and blondes?* Bianca snorts down her nose at him, but I can tell she's on edge.

'You stole my money,' I say to him.

He frowns at me. 'First, of all, I believe it was your *boss's* money,' he says carefully. 'And second, it wasn't me who took it.' His eyes swivel over to Adele, who looks down uncomfortably.

'But who knew cheese could be so profitable?' says Popeye. 'Clearly, we've been in the wrong line of work.'

'We just finished Christmas trading,' I inform him hotly. 'It's our busiest season, and we have massive suppliers' bills to pay at the end of January.'

'Well, that explains it then,' he says. 'Anyway, it was more than I expected. And certainly enough to pay off these two's debts,' he adds, nodding towards Adele and Anton.

'I got fired,' I say.

He frowns. 'You seem pretty resourceful. I'm sure you'll find something. I'll let you know if we have any openings on the bar.'

'What about the money?' I ask.

He shrugs. 'What about it? Your boss drives a BMW and takes his holidays in the Seychelles. I think he'll get by.'

True.

'The police will go after Adele, you know.'

'Maybe. Or maybe they'll go after you,' he counters. Either way, Popeye is clearly not concerned that he'll be implicated. Why?

'I thought you were finished with these two,' I say, nodding towards the sofa.

'That was before I found out that knobhead here,' he

nods at Anton, 'was skimming from me. So yesterday's errand was payback. And now Adele has one more little job to do before Anton's debt is clear. Don't you, Adele.' He does not look at her when he says this, and it is not a question.

My eyes stray over to Adele and I see her draw a deep breath. Our gaze locks for an instant before she looks away.

'And then they're clear?' I ask.

'And then they're clear,' he says.

'Why should I believe you?'

'Why should I care if you don't?' he counters.

Also true.

I am rapidly running out of cards here, and Popeye knows it.

'Hey Blondie, you got a boyfriend?' he says, swivelling around to face Bianca.

'She's got three,' I inform him coldly.

'Then there's room for one more,' he replies. 'Except I don't really like to share.'

'In fact, it's only one,' says Bianca coolly. 'And his dick's a whole lot bigger than yours.'

Popeye's eyebrows shoot up. He places his hands on the desk and rises to his feet, where I can just see the top of a small pistol tucked into his waistband.

'You know what, Blondie? I'm already a little tired of you. I think it's time for you two to go.'

'What makes you think we won't head straight to the police?' I ask.

'For the same reason Adele won't.'

I glance over at Adele and once again, our eyes lock. This time there's a fierce urgency in her gaze. The look is half pleading and half threatening.

Whatever he's got on them, it must be big.

Chapter Twenty-Three

'So we go straight to the police, right?' says Bianca, once we're back in the car.

I frown. 'I'm not sure.'

'You can't be serious!'

'Look, Adele's in trouble. And whatever it is, she's in so deep that he's certain she won't finger him.'

'But surely she's going to prison either way?'

'Yeah, maybe. But we need to work out what he's got on her.'

'How do you propose to do that?' Bianca asks.

I ponder this, running through our options, which admittedly, seem limited. Or maybe even non-existent.

A text comes in on my phone just then – it's my mobile phone provider informing me that I will now be paying 4 per cent more for exactly the same service this year. *Happy New Year!* Just beneath it are three texts I've sent to Bex over the past forty-eight hours, asking her to get in touch. I frown down at them. There must be a reason why she's not returning my calls. I look over at Bianca.

'Fancy a little more subterfuge?'

'Can I wear my wig this time?'

'If you like,' I say. 'But we're heading back to the salon.'

She pulls a face. 'I never get to wear the wig!'

'By the way, since when has it only been one?' I ask.

'One which?'

'One Willy.'

'Oh,' she says, colouring. She takes a deep breath then lets it out. 'I may or may not have agreed to an arrangement,' she adds, a little cryptically.

'What sort of arrangement?'

'It's not binding,' she emphasises.

'*What's* not binding?'

'It's really just a trial run.'

'For God's sake, what are you talking about?' I ask.

She sighs. 'I may have agreed to a trial period of . . . exclusivity,' she says, slurring this last word, like it's some sort of cosmetic surgery she's ashamed to own up to.

'No!' I say, both shocked and delighted. 'With Willem?' I ask.

She shrugs. 'He got me in a weak moment,' says Bianca. I smile.

'New year, new you!' I say. Bianca scowls.

'Invoking the world's worst marketing slogan will not endear you to me.'

When we reach the salon, it's nearly closing time. Bex is at the back sweeping up and another stylist is finishing up blow-drying a customer. When the receptionist sees us enter, her eyes narrow. 'We're closing,' she informs us quickly.

'We just need a quick word with Bex,' says Bianca, flashing her most winning smile. At the sound of our voices, Bex turns around, then crosses over to us, broom in hand.

'It's fine,' she tells the receptionist. The phone rings and the receptionist eyes us suspiciously before turning away to answer it.

'What is it?' says Bex to me quietly.

'Can we talk?' I ask. She takes a deep breath, then shakes her head.

'Not here.'

'Where?'

She hesitates. 'There's a pub round the corner called the Drunken Duck. Meet me there in five minutes.'

'Fine,' I say, wondering if she'll really turn up.

We've no choice but to trust her, so we head round the corner. Both Bianca and Charlie Bucket seem pleased at the prospect of another pub. 'It's half past six,' says Bianca with an arch smile. 'The witching hour.'

When we enter, she looks around and gives an approving nod – we're in Chelsea, after all, and the pubs here are a notch above average. Instead of dank swirly carpeting and wooden stools, this one has polished oak floors and old velvet sofas. '*Definitely* time for a drink,' she announces, approaching the bar.

'We're working,' I remind her.

'*You're* working. I'm driving.'

'Precisely why you shouldn't be drinking.'

'Martini please,' Bianca says to the bartender, who is now approaching. She's a short, heavy-set woman in her mid-forties with a sandy bob and a no-nonsense expression.

'Single or double?' she asks.

'Double,' says Bianca.

'Single,' I say at the exact same moment. The bartender raises an eyebrow and Bianca turns to glare at me.

'Single,' she says grumpily, turning back to the bartender. 'The dirtier the better,' she adds.

'Pint of ginger shandy for me, please,' I say.

Just then my phone rings and I see that it's Gus.

Uh oh. I did ask him to call. I cautiously press the answer button and try to sound cheery. 'Hello.'

'Where are you?' Even without a greeting, his voice is utterly delectable. It also sounds slightly suspicious.

'Um. At home,' I say casually. I hear him take a deep breath and exhale.

'Clemency, I'm outside your flat,' he informs me.

'Oh.' *Damn!* I do not even have time to reflect on what might have occurred if I'd stayed at home tonight and not engaged in subterfuge.

'Shall we try again?' he asks. I can tell his patience is wafer-thin.

'I'm at the pub with my friend Bianca,' I say. This is not a lie, but I still feel guilty. He hesitates.

'Which pub?'

'The Drunken Duck.'

'I'll come and meet you. Where is it?'

'Um. In Chelsea,' I admit. Which is to say: *miles* away.

'Right,' he says then. 'Just thought I'd let you know where we'd got to on the case.' In that instant I spy Bex come through the pub's front door – my eyes lock with hers as she walks towards me.

'Could I ring you back later?' I ask quickly.

'Sure,' he says. Though he does not sound sure. Not at all. 'I wouldn't want to interfere with your evening,' he adds tersely. In fact, he sounds gloriously angry. And then he hangs up.

Bex approaches the bar and sits down on the stool next to mine.

'Ginger shandy?' I ask.

She shakes her head. 'Whisky,' she says. 'Make it a double.'

We signal to the bartender and Bianca orders. I turn back to Bex.

'I'm sorry to come to the salon,' I say. 'But we really need to talk.' She takes a deep breath and exhales.

'I think we both know who needs to apologise here,' she says.

*

Once her drink arrives, we move to a booth at the back of the pub. For the next several minutes I quiz Bex about Adele's recent activities, and she answers my questions cautiously. Yes, she knows that Adele and Anton are still embroiled with Popeye. Yes, she knows that Anton has been stealing from Popeye, and owes him a large sum of money. And yes, she knows about the raid on the shop's bank account, she admits. 'But only *after* she'd done it,' says Bex, shaking her head.

Adele had gone to Bex the previous evening in desperation. She was tired and hungry and knew the police were after her, but needed somewhere to lay low for the night, as the police were watching both Nan's and Anton's flats. She told Bex she had one more job to do for Popeye and promised to leave before dawn. When Bex woke up in the morning, Adele was already gone.

'Look, I know Adele's done some really stupid shit,' says Bex. 'But this thing yesterday? She didn't have a choice. Popeye would have killed Anton.'

I frown. 'Couldn't she have gone to the police?' I ask.

Bex rolls her eyes. 'And say what? Anton's been running Class A drugs for Popeye for more than five years. And he's got a string of priors. He gets caught now? They'll lock him up for good. Adele didn't want that.'

'But Adele's the one who will go to prison,' I say. 'Doesn't she care?'

Bex inhales deeply, pursing her lips. 'Not if they disappear,' she says.

'Disappear *how*?' I ask. It's not that easy to disappear! Bex's eyes flick over to Bianca and they exchange a glance.

'Sweetie,' Bianca reminds me carefully, 'she's still got your passport.'

*

An hour later, Bianca drops Charlie Bucket and me off at home. I climb the stairs to the flat, lamenting the fact that I can no longer pilfer cheese from the shop for my supper. Just as I'm about to put the key in the lock, Carl leans out over the upstairs banister and calls down, 'Clemency, the police are here. I let them in.'

In the next second, my front door opens to reveal Gus standing there. I stare at him.

'Clemency?' Carl's voice floats down again from above.

'Thanks, Carl,' I call up the stairwell.

'Hello,' Gus says. I raise an eyebrow, looking past him to see if he's alone.

'*Them*?' I ask.

'Well, just me,' he admits.

'Are you here on *official* business?' I ask.

He considers this, then shrugs. 'After a fashion.'

'Do you have a warrant?' I ask.

'No.'

'Is there some reason you needed access to my flat?'

He frowns. 'It was more comfortable than the stairwell?'

'So you're not planning to arrest me?'

'Not this time.'

'Fine.'

I step past him inside and close the door behind us, while Charlie Bucket noses Gus's crotch. 'Sorry, he's hungry,' I say, a little embarrassed. I drag Charlie Bucket away by the collar. 'I mean . . . not *that* sort of hungry. Dog food hungry.'

'That's reassuring,' he says.

I hang up my coat and cross to the kitchen, where I fill Charlie Bucket's bowl and put it down on the floor. I am so nervous my hands tremble slightly. Gus follows, pausing in the doorway.

'So how was the pub?' he asks. I turn around to eye him. He's leaning against the door frame casually, his arms crossed over his chest, but there's a glint of scepticism in his eye.

'Fine,' I say. 'You don't believe me, do you? That's why you stayed. To make sure,' I add.

He regards me silently. 'I didn't say that.'

'No, but you thought it. I *was* at the pub. With my friend Bianca. I swear.'

'OK,' he nods. 'I believe you.'

The silence stretches out between us, and somewhere deep inside it I hear a chorus of possibilities – there are so many different outcomes to this story. I take a deep breath.

'In fact, I went to *two* pubs,' I say slowly. 'And I saw Bex. And Adele,' I admit.

Gus stares at me, his eyes dark, his face a complete mask, although I see the slow rise of his chest as he inhales. I stop breathing, my heart in my mouth; I am absolutely terrified he will be furious with me, but I cannot lie to him any longer, this lovely man whom the stars – and my doppelgänger – have thrown into my path.

He takes a few steps towards me, stopping only a foot or so away. I wait for him to speak but he says nothing, which is worse than unbearable.

'Are you mad?' I finally ask.

'Should I be?' His voice unfurls across the space between us, quiet and meltingly soft – he does not sound angry. He sounds dangerous. And resolute, as if he's already made up his mind. He takes another step forward, until he is practically on top of me.

'Probably,' I say, nodding a little nervously up at him. 'Or at the very least . . . disappointed,' I add, my voice barely above a whisper.

'Disappointed,' he repeats.

I nod again, unable to speak.

He is so close that I can feel the warmth of him, together with the heat rising up in me, threatening to consume me from within. Gus reaches down and with a single finger beneath my chin, lifts my face towards his.

'I'll let you know,' he murmurs, just before his lips touch mine.

Chapter Twenty-Four

Evidently, he is *not* disappointed. Not by a mile. I know this because he does not let me leave my bedroom for the next twelve hours, apart from two quick trips to the toilet, and one foray to the kitchen to stock up on rations around mid-night, once we have both worked up a fearsome appetite.

Nor am I. If anything, my own expectations of making love to a delectable copper are exceeded a thousand times over. Gus is tender and delicious and passionate in all the right places. And while I'm lamentably out of practice, I decide afterwards that lovemaking is really just like dental hygiene: even if you mislay your toothbrush for a while, you never forget how to use it. Or more importantly, where it goes. When I tell Gus this, he laughs and rolls over on top of me, nudging my knees apart and suggesting that after all this time, my teeth probably need another round of polishing.

Though his hands are nowhere near my mouth.

Just before eight the next morning, we are lying in bed half dozing when his phone pings with a text. Gus rolls over and stretches across the floor beside the bed to reach for his phone, while I admire the sight of his naked bum. When he's retrieved it, he peers down at the screen, while I prop myself up on one elbow and walk my fingers across his chest, which has just the optimal amount of hair. It is short and sparse and ever so slightly curly. Neither mole nor baboon, but something nicely furry in between; a piglet, perhaps. I decide not to share this with him. After a moment he frowns.

'What's up, DC Meadows?' I ask.

'Hill says we've picked up some new intel overnight. Apparently, there's a big drop happening later over in Thamesmead. He thinks it's linked to Popeye.' He grunts and rolls out of bed, bending over to retrieve his clothes.

Adele! Though I do not say this out loud.

I've still not told Gus everything that transpired yesterday, partly because we were overtaken by events last night, and partly because I wasn't sure exactly how much to divulge. Specifically, I have not told him that Adele has one more job to do for Popeye. But I *have* told him that she was forced to steal the shop's money to pay off Anton's debt.

More importantly, I have not revealed that I saw Popeye yesterday. I eye Gus silently as he hurriedly begins to pull on his trousers.

Is it too late to tell him now?

And if I do, will he be furious? I lie there watching him get dressed, my heart beginning to race, my mouth suddenly dry. I am genuinely torn over the best course of action: tell him now and risk his wrath, or hold off and see if I can fix things myself. He finishes tying his shoes and stands up, turning to me.

'Sorry, I gotta go,' he says with a rueful smile. He leans forward and gives me a kiss on the lips – it is only brief, but when our lips meet he holds them there for a moment. *God, his lips are amazing!* Unbearably soft and warm and the kiss feels so real, like he really means it. He pulls away and looks down at me. 'Will I see you later?' he asks.

I nod, a lump rising in my throat. He turns to go and I watch through the open doorway as he ruffles Charlie

Bucket on the head and lets himself out of the flat. Then I lie back against the pillows and contemplate the weight of what I've done.

Or more accurately, what I've *not* done.

A moment later Charlie Bucket, who has been relegated to the living-room sofa for the past twelve hours, shuffles into my bedroom and hurls himself onto my bed. He sinks down beside me and looks straight into my eyes, and I swear the look in them is sadly accusing. But then he takes a deep breath and lays his chin right across my arm, as if he has already forgiven me.

I rise and shower and eat some breakfast, though my stomach is in knots. Charlie Bucket needs his morning constitutional, so I take him out and we do several laps around our local square, my mind turning over the options all the while. If Adele carries out the drop and the police know about it, she'll take an even bigger fall – she could end up in prison for years. But if I alert her, then I'm perverting the course of justice, not to mention the course of my own love life. Gus would never forgive me, if he somehow found out, and Popeye would never be brought to justice. And who knows what would happen to Anton?

But what if I could alert her without the police or Gus knowing? She would not commit an even bigger crime than she already has and might not end up in prison. But then Popeye would remain free, and once again Anton's fate would be uncertain. Would Popeye release him? Or would he and Adele still be in debt? After nearly an hour of endless circuits, my mind is no clearer. Finally, Charlie Bucket stops short and refuses to walk any further.

He looks up at me balefully, as if to say: *Are we there yet?*

'OK, come on big fella,' I say, taking pity on him. We

head back to the flat and when we get inside, the memory of Gus is so strong it hits me like a powerful wave. I close my eyes for a moment. I can almost feel the warmth of him, can taste his scent and hear the murmur of his voice in my ear. A part of me wants to sink down and lose myself in the swirling currents of last night. But another part of me is agitated – Adele is out there somewhere, about to commit another crime. And if anyone is going to stop her, it will have to be me.

I go to the wardrobe and grab my skates, together with the blonde wig, stuffing it into my coat pocket. Charlie Bucket, who is lying on his sofa, instantly raises his head with alarm, as if to say: *Are you leaving?* I pause and frown at him.

'You can't come with me,' I tell him, shaking my head. He continues to watch me anxiously as I pull on my coat and find my keys, as if I am somehow going to disappear for ever. I turn to him with exasperation: when I want to take him out, he refuses; and when I want to leave him behind, he becomes a barrel of neediness. Obstinacy, thy name is dog.

Perhaps June would have him? Philip banned me from the shop, but he didn't ban Charlie Bucket. So I grab the lead off the shelf and instantly he leaps off the sofa and heads to the door, wagging his tail expectantly. We head downstairs and outside and Charlie Bucket goes eagerly to the shop door. June comes to the glass and he almost shivers with delight when he spies her, barking once or twice excitedly, tail wagging in overdrive. Of course he misses her! June opens the door and reaches down to pat him. 'I miss you too, Charlie Bucket,' she says, a little woefully. She sees the skates on my feet and looks up at me.

'I don't suppose you'd watch him for me, would you?' I ask hopefully.

'Sure,' she says. 'We'd be delighted.'

We? I look past her to see Marcus perched on a tall stool at the counter. Funnily enough, I've not heard from him in several days – a length of time which has to be some sort of non-contact record. Right now he waves at me and I wave back.

'How was the eclipse?' I ask.

June casts a quick glance over her shoulder. 'Oh,' she says, lowering her voice slightly. 'We missed it, in the end.'

'Really? What happened? Was it cloudy?'

'No. Conditions were perfect. Marcus and I met up before for a glass of wine and got talking and . . . never quite made it.' Again she tosses a glance in Marcus's direction, and almost in unison, they both smirk.

OMG! Marcus and June are an item!

I pause for a moment, taking this in. Now that I think about it, their union makes perfect sense. Why had it not occurred to me earlier? I should have set them up years ago!

'I guess if you've seen one lunar eclipse, you've seen them all,' I say.

She smiles a little shyly. 'You can always count on the moon,' she says.

I head off on my usual route, skating through the streets round the back of Bermondsey Spa Gardens and over to Southwark Park, where I do a fast loop around the outer path, before heading east to Canada Water. The modern stone plaza here is perfect skating terrain. At weekends it is full of boarders trying out fancy moves, but right now it is relatively quiet. I keep moving east and cut along the path by the canal at Garter Way up towards the basin at Surrey Water, and then hop across to Rotherhithe Street.

I know exactly where I'm heading. The Salty Dog is only

about a quarter of a mile away, and as I draw near, I slow right down, contemplating a plan of action. The truth is I still have no idea what to do, but something has propelled me here, and now that I'm so close, I'm not going to leave without trying to see Adele. I find a bench around the corner and sit down for a moment, pulling the blonde wig out of my coat pocket and putting it on. One of my skates is giving me grief; today should have been laundry day and I grabbed my last clean pair of socks, which also happen to be the least suitable for skating. I bend down to untie the lace and pull it back up, but just as I do, a red Camaro turns the corner from Rotherhithe Street and cruises past me. As I straighten up, I see Adele and Popeye fly right past me in the car.

Damn! I've missed her!

I quickly retie the skate and jump up, but by the time I get going again, the Camaro is more than a block away, turning onto the main road. I set off after it, skating as fast as I can, adrenaline spurring me on. When I reach the high street, I see they are stopped at a set of lights a few hundred yards ahead, so I slow my pace and bend low like a speed skater, hovering behind a line of cars. When the light changes, I follow at a distance over the roundabout and onto Jamaica Road, before turning right onto Bermondsey Street a few blocks north of Say Cheese.

Thank goodness for London traffic. I'm able to follow them easily enough as the Camaro turns onto Tooley Street, and only then does it become clear where they're going. A minute later the car pulls over in a layby next to London Bridge Station and Adele jumps out, hoisting a small black duffel bag over her shoulder. She glances around, nods once at Popeye, then turns and hurries into the station. After a moment, the Camaro pulls away.

Quickly I skate across to the station entrance, drawing

frowns from several commuters as I whizz past. Fortunately, the rush hour is not yet fully underway, but it still takes me a minute to spy her in the distance, standing beneath a small destination monitor, her face tilted upwards. She's wearing the same dark blue pea coat and violet beanie, and I linger against the far wall of the station behind a newspaper seller, watching her.

Where's she heading? And more importantly, what's in the duffel bag? Just then my phone buzzes. I glance down and see that it's Gus ringing.

Whoops. He has an uncanny knack for sensing when I'm heading into trouble. I hesitate, watching his name flash on the screen, then reluctantly truncate the call. Just then Adele spins round, heading rapidly towards the platforms at the far end of the concourse. I follow cautiously, skating as slowly as I can and hugging the wall. She passes through the gates and onto the platform, walking down past the first several carriages and then climbing onto the train. But when I try to follow, the guard stops me. He's middle-aged and bald, with one of those droopy moustaches that looks like a hairy horseshoe hanging upside-down beneath his nose. When he speaks, the entire moustache vibrates ever so slightly.

'Tickets please,' he says.

'Can I buy one on the train?' I ask quickly.

'No.'

'How long before it departs?'

'Two minutes.'

'Where's it going?' I ask.

He raises an eyebrow and the moustache twitches. 'Where do you *want* to go?' he asks suspiciously.

'Um . . . don't really mind?' I say, flashing a winning smile.

'Dartford,' he replies.

'Great.' I spin round, speed-skate over to a bank of machines nearby and shove my debit card inside, punching in the buttons for Dartford. When the machine spits out the ticket, I grab it and skate back, braking just short of him and flourishing the ticket.

'No skates on the platform,' he says in a bored tone, as if skaters boarding trains are an everyday occurrence.

'You could have told me that earlier!' I say.

He shrugs, a big expansive movement of his shoulders. The droopy moustache seems to shrug with him.

'I'm telling you now.'

'Fine.' I drop to the station floor right at his feet and tear at the laces, literally ripping the skates off my feet, before jumping up again and thrusting my ticket out.

'No bare feet either.'

'They're not bare!'

He looks down at my socks. They are novelty socks I got a few years ago as a Secret Santa present: flesh-coloured with five painted toes and a purple strap across the top, like mock flip-flops. There is even a mock ankle bracelet on the right one.

'Funny lady,' he says, though he does not look amused.

The tannoy announces the train's departure just then.

'Please?' I say in my most pleading voice.

He sighs and nods for me to pass. I dash through the gate just as the departure whistle blows and hurl myself into the nearest carriage as the doors slam shut behind me, collapsing onto a seat with a sigh. My phone buzzes again.

'Hello?'

'Avoiding me already?' says Gus in a playful tone. *Oh God!* His voice is even more sexy now that I know what it sounds like beneath the bedcovers.

'Sorry, I was on the Tube,' I say, wincing. *Almost true?*

'Where you heading?' he asks casually. I hesitate uncertainly. I really do not want to lie to him again.

'Dartford,' I say. *True!*

'Oh. How come?'

'To see an old friend. Lives out that way.' *Not quite true.*

'Be careful. It's a crime hotspot.' *True!*

'What's happened with the drop?' I ask.

'Hill's on it. Meant to happen soon.' *Also true.*

'You're not involved?' I ask.

'No, why? Do you *want* me to be?' He sounds bemused.

'Just curious,' I say. *Definitely true.*

'I'm working on some other stuff. Plus, I've got a hot date later,' he adds a little suggestively.

'Oh yeah?' I smile. 'How hot?'

'Smoking.'

'Sounds risky.'

'I have high hopes. What time are you back from Dartford?'

I hesitate. *I have absolutely no idea.*

'Can I text you?' I ask.

After he hangs up, I practically swoon in my seat. I may be broke, unemployed, and about to mix with dangerous drug dealers, but my new boyfriend is a velvet-voiced cop who thinks I'm smoking hot.

True!

I remove the blonde wig and stuff it back into my pocket, then lace my skates back on and roll slowly through the car, holding onto the seat backs to steady myself as the train wobbles along the track. A few people give me odd looks as I pass, but most are absorbed in their phones, books or newspapers. I pass through the first and second carriages, and when I reach the third, I spy the back of Adele's violet beanie in the last row. She's at a table by the window facing the other way, and as I draw near, I see that she's wearing earphones. The duffel bag is clutched tightly across her lap like a newborn. Her head rests against the window and her eyes are closed. A man in his mid-thirties with thinning hair and a rather tragic goatee is seated opposite her at a diagonal beside the aisle. He's scrolling through his phone as I roll slowly towards him. I come to a halt right by his side. He sees my turquoise skates first, then raises his head to blink at me.

'Excuse me,' I say quietly, nodding towards the seat beside him opposite Adele. 'Is this seat taken?' Adele's eyes are closed and her music is turned up loud enough that I can hear the tinny vibrations of Stormzy telling someone to shut up. Goatee Guy frowns, then glances around at the multitude of empty seats around us. 'I'd like to sit with my sister,' I explain, indicating Adele.

He sighs and nods, grabbing his satchel, then moves to a seat a few rows back across the aisle, without saying a word. I manoeuvre myself round the table (not easy on skates) and drop heavily into the seat opposite.

Adele opens her eyes with alarm. She looks at me with blurry confusion and I lean forward across the table. 'Surprise,' I whisper. She yanks her earphones out and glares at me.

'What are you *doing*?' she hisses, scanning the carriage anxiously.

'Just thought I'd come along for the ride.'

'Are you insane? You shouldn't be here!' She speaks in a furious whisper, trying not to draw the attention of those around us. I look around and Goatee Guy is looking a bit miffed. He reaches in his pocket and pulls out AirPods, which he shoves in his ears, then fiddles with his phone. Evidently, we're annoying him.

'It's *you* who shouldn't be here,' I whisper back. 'They *know*.'

'Who knows?' she replies. I lower my voice even more.

'The police,' I mouth.

'You told them?' Her voice is louder now and I shake my head.

'It wasn't me. They've got other sources.'

Her eyes darken. 'Who then?'

'Does it matter? The point is: they're waiting for you.'

'Christ! I knew it was a mistake to get involved with you!' she says.

'Me?! What did I do?'

'Bring me crap luck!' she cries. I stare at her aghast, then lean across the table.

'Can I remind you that *you* stole from me? And got me fired to boot?'

She shakes her head slowly. 'Everything in my life has gone to hell since Bex gave me that ID! *Everything*. You're like some kind of . . . bad jinx.'

'You didn't need *my* help to screw up your life. You were doing just fine all by yourself,' I whisper.

'You have *no* idea about my life,' she says, practically spitting out the words.

We face each other, breathing hard, and her words land like blows. For all my fantasies of our connection, she and I are just two women on a train who barely know each other. My hopes of helping her seem ludicrous. Adele doesn't want me or my help. She leans forward intently, speaking low.

'I bet you grew up with two parents, not one,' she says. 'And lived in a nice house, where you could actually *breathe*, instead of a mouldy flat in a tower block where you used to lie in bed at night and imagine that the patches on the ceiling were gonna swallow you while you slept!'

I stare at her, abruptly silenced.

'And I bet you went to one school, instead of five because your mum got kicked out of all the others. Either because she had too many ciders at the school fair or stole from the tombola. Or just . . . forgot to collect you one day.'

I swallow uneasily. My parents may have been flighty, and my upbringing a bit slipshod, but it was never dangerous or frightening. Behind us, Goatee Guy senses that things are amiss. He is surreptitiously watching us from his seat. I shoot a dark glance at him over her shoulder, and he looks away.

'How could you *possibly* understand what it's like to be me?' Adele continues through clenched teeth. 'You work in a goddamn *cheese* shop.' As if luxury dairy products are the ultimate proof of privilege. Which I suppose they are.

'Not any longer,' I mumble.

She rolls her eyes. 'Then welcome to the real world. Where the rest of us live.'

We stare at each other for a long moment, the atmosphere between us churning. She takes a deep breath, checks her phone, then shakes her head slowly. 'Christ. What the fuck am I gonna do now?'

'You can't do the drop,' I say.

'No kidding,' she says hotly. Her eyes dart around the crowded carriage in panic. I can see her mind working furiously, scrolling through the possible scenarios – none of them are good.

'I'm out of here,' she says finally, starting to rise.

'Wait.' I lurch forward, grabbing her wrist hard enough that she winces and forcing her to sit back down. She lands heavily, her nostrils flaring with anger. Her eyes fall to my hand, still clamped tight around her wrist, as if my touch is like an electric current, and only then do I release her. We face each other, both breathing hard. After everything that has passed between us, I still feel compelled to save her, though I'm not sure why. I can't walk away from Adele or her problems – any more than I can escape my own.

'I have an idea,' I say cautiously.

She swallows uneasily, eyeing me. 'Why should I trust you?' she whispers, her tone low and menacing.

'You *need* me,' I say. 'And I need you,' I add.

She frowns, slowly shaking her head. She rubs her wrist with the other hand. 'What is it you want from me?'

'Listen to me,' I say urgently. 'We swap clothes in the toilet and I do the drop. So the police will go after me, not you. You get on the next train back to London.'

She rolls her eyes. 'So *you* go to jail? How's *that* work?'

'That's my problem. The drop will be done, so you'll be holding up your end of the deal with Popeye. And Anton will go free.'

'It's not a drop, it's an *exchange*,' she hisses. I stare at her. *Oh.*

'So you're collecting . . . ?' I allow my voice to trail off in a question.

She widens her eyes. 'Kittens!' she says in an exasperated tone. 'What do you *think* I'm collecting?'

I take a deep breath and exhale slowly, trying to stay calm. 'Right. OK. Fine,' I say. 'Whatever it is, I'll manage.'

Really, I think?

'And take it back to Popeye,' she says.

'And take it back to Popeye,' I say, nodding. This is far more than I'd bargained on, but I've come this far, I can't give up now.

'What happens then?' she demands.

Truthfully, I haven't quite worked out that part of the plan. But it will almost certainly involve the Met Police. And a very angry Gus.

'Leave Popeye to me,' I say. She stares at me a long moment, her jaw pulsing anxiously.

'Make *damn* well sure they get him,' she says then.

I swallow, then nod. 'I will.'

We both know what's at stake here if I fail.

Have you ever been in a toilet on a Southeastern Rail train? They are cramped and smelly and somewhat less than salubrious – not exactly somewhere you'd like to hang out, much less use as a dressing room, especially if there are two of you crowded inside. Fortunately, Adele is wearing tight black leggings which just about fit me, though once I've got them on, I'm not sure I'll ever get them off again. In contrast, my own jeans hang loosely off her slender frame. *Oh to be young again*, I think wistfully, as she frowns at the sight of herself in the mirror.

'Not my style,' she mutters.

'Ditto,' I say, pulling her black and purple argyle sweater over my head, which looks fabulous on her and hulking on me. I feel like a garish lumberjack.

How can that even be possible, when we look so alike?

I sigh. 'What size shoe are you?' I ask, frowning down at her brown leather boots.

'Seven,' she says.

'Ah.' So our feet, at least, are not identical – I'm a size five. Size seven boots will feel like clown shoes on me. And anyway, Adele is now staring down at my roller skates with something akin to disgust.

'No effing way am I wearing those,' she says with a nod.

'Fine. We keep our own shoes,' I reply. I'm faster on skates anyway. 'Give me your coat and hat.'

Adele scowls and hands over the blue wool pea coat and violet beanie.

At last! I think gleefully, pulling them both on. When we're finished, we stand side by side, looking at our reflection in the mirror.

'Damn,' she mutters.

I nod. At a quick glance, or if you didn't know us well, we could genuinely pass for each other. I feel like we've stepped out of a *trompe l'oeil* painting. Adele takes a deep breath and lets it out, then turns to me.

'This bloody well better work,' she says.

'It will.'

There are only a few minutes left before we're due to reach Abbey Wood, the station right by Thamesmead. Adele quickly briefs me on the details: she is meeting two Algerian men in a park by the river who will hand over a similar-looking bag in exchange for the duffel bag.

'How come Popeye is using you for the exchange?' I ask. 'Why doesn't he do it himself?'

'Because he doesn't trust the Algerians. If they have a leak, or make an error, or something else goes wrong, like a tip-off to the cops, then he doesn't want to be involved.'

'So someone else takes the fall.'

'Popeye's not stupid. He always stays one step away from the action.'

'Not this time,' I say.

For the first time today, Adele smiles at me – a big, broad grin.

'One more thing,' I say. 'I'm gonna need your phone.'

'No way am I swapping phones!' she says, shaking her head.

'I didn't say swap.'

She stares at me for a moment, and I can see her mind turning this over. If there's a last-minute hiccup or change, then Popeye may try to get hold of her, and I'll need to answer. 'I'll give it back after,' I say.

'What am I meant to do with no phone in the meantime?' she says, handing it over.

'You'll survive. What's the pin?' I ask.

She hesitates, frowning.

'Twenty-two, twenty-two,' she says.

I look up at her, stunned.

'Did you steal that from me, too?'

As I get off the train, I do not even want to *think* about how creepy it is that my doppelgänger and I have chosen the exact same pin code for our mobile phones, even if it is an obvious one. We've agreed that Adele will get off at the next station and catch the first train back towards London. She's desperate to free Anton but I persuade her to wait until Popeye is in custody, so she agrees to lay low for a few hours at Bex's flat until I've rung Bex and given the all-clear.

The first thing I do when I'm on my own is ring the station and ask to be put through to DC Hill. The duty sergeant tells me that Hill is unavailable. 'That's because he's in Thamesmead,' I say. 'About to bust a drug deal. And I need to speak to him.'

'Who is this?' the sergeant demands.

'Tell him that if he wants the Algerians, then he needs to ring me back *now*.'

I hang up and wait, and sure enough, less than sixty seconds later my phone lights up. 'I thought that would get your attention,' I say when I answer.

'Clemency, what the hell do you think you're doing?' says Gus sharply.

Uh oh.

'I can explain.'

'Start now,' he says tersely.

'I've swapped clothes with Adele and I'm about to do the drop,' I say quickly. There's a moment's pause while he takes this in.

'Are you insane?'

'Hill needs to tell his men to grab the Algerians, but not me. They need to let me get away.'

'Absolutely not!'

'I promise. I'll lead them straight back to Popeye.'

'Clemency, you're out of your mind if you think I'm going to let you do this.'

'Gus, you don't have a choice. I'm already nearly there.'

He hesitates. 'In Thamesmead?'

'Yes.'

There's a beat while he contemplates this.

'So you lied to me,' he says.

'No. I said I was on a train to Dartford. I am.'

'You said you were going to visit a friend.'

'Adele may not be my friend, but she needs me.'

I hear him sigh heavily down the phone.

'This isn't a game, Clem. You could get killed.'

'So could she,' I counter. 'How is that any better?'

He hesitates, breathing hard down the phone.

'Look, they don't know it's me,' I say. 'I look just like her. It'll be fine.'

'You cannot know that.'

'Just promise me you'll tell him. We need to get Popeye.'

He hesitates for a long moment. 'Fine,' he says. And then he hangs up the phone. Just like that.

Without even a *fare-thee-well*.

Chapter Twenty-Five

The station at Abbey Wood is bigger and more modern than I expected, with an arched ribbed wooden ceiling that looks like the underside of a boat. As I pass through the concourse, I see signs advertising Crossrail, the long-delayed east–west transport project that has been burrowing beneath London for so long that most of us now regard it as urban myth.

Outside it's a typical London winter day, grey and blustery, and as I exit the station, I see a small parade of run-down shops and a few pubs, with a vast housing estate looming in the distance. The area proves to be a bleak mixture of sixties Brutalist architecture and suburban brick dotted with shabby green spaces. Few people are about and altogether it feels grim and dehumanising. No wonder crime thrives here. What else is there to do?

Adele was told to look for four concrete tower blocks perched beside a small inland lake, and it isn't long before I spy them in the distance standing like four sentinels among a clutch of others. I skate slowly towards them, taking in my surroundings and occasionally moving between the pavement and the road. When I enter the estate itself, I see that it is far bigger than I realised. There must be a dozen tower blocks in all, interspersed with low-rise buildings, all linked up by elevated concrete walkways with vast car parking areas at the ground level. There is not a blade of grass, nor a single tree, in sight.

I head towards the row of four towers, the lake just visible beyond. In the distance I can make out the vast grey ribbon of the Thames – the river is incredibly wide here, the far shore barely visible. This really is the fag end of London, I think. Adele told me the Albanians would be driving a black Astra hatchback and they would park beside the lake by the farthest tower block. I have texted this information to Gus to pass on to DC Hill, so while I am scouting for the Astra, I'm also looking around for evidence of Hill and his men. Surely they'll be here somewhere? Though so far, I haven't spotted them.

I've fastened the duffel bag securely onto my back by its long shoulder strap. It's made of cheap black plastic fabric in a capsule shape – the sort of bag you see in every outdoor street market across London – and is heavy enough to slightly affect my balance. I've got the cash (Lord only knows how much). And Adele says they'll exchange a similar bag filled with *gear*. What sort of gear, Adele didn't tell me and I didn't ask. 'Am I meant to check what's inside?' I'd asked her nervously. She'd shaken her head.

'No way would they cross Popeye,' she'd said, a little ominously.

Right, I'd thought. Adele and I are about to do something so dangerous, that even Albanian criminals wouldn't consider doing it.

Fabulous.

My nerves grow jittery as I approach the tower blocks. A trio of young boys fool around on BMX bikes popping wheelies, and when I glide past they regard me with open hostility, their eyes dipping suspiciously to my roller skates, like I'm some sort of alien life form. I move past them and see a skinny young mum wheeling a toddler in a pushchair along the concrete path by the lake. She's talking on her mobile, smoking a cigarette and pointing out a clutch of ducks to the toddler all at the same time, and I have to admire her ability to multi-task.

Apparently, the Albanians have been shown a photo of Adele, so the plan is for them to find me, rather than the other way around. She was told to park herself on a bench by the lake, placing the black duffel bag on the ground by her feet, and then wait until they make contact. When I move past the towers to the walkway by the lake, I see a series of benches about a hundred yards away and slowly skate towards them, though the black Astra is nowhere around. I park myself on the closest one and place the bag on the ground just as instructed, then take out both phones. No calls or messages on either, which I take as a good sign.

I'm not sure what I was expecting from Gus, anyway. He's not an angry emoji kind of guy. I suspect the silent treatment is more his style. *Oh God*. What if I never hear from him again? I cannot bear to think about it, so I push him out of my mind and concentrate on the job ahead.

A Deliveroo guy with a shiny black helmet passes in front of me on a bike, his boxy canvas bag wobbling on his back, making him look like a giant overloaded beetle. When he reaches the row of tower blocks, he pauses and glances down at his phone, then stares up at them with obvious confusion. On the far side of the lake a council worker in a dark green uniform and bright yellow hazard vest slowly sweeps up debris, dumping it into a wheeled container by his side. And a young black woman wearing maroon leggings and a pale blue hoodie is jogging circuits around the lake. Apart from this, it all seems pretty quiet. Maybe I'm too early?

I hear an ice-cream van pull up and stop at the far end of the car park behind me, its music tinkling. It's not really ice-cream weather, but I guess even ice-cream vendors have to pay the rent in winter. Or maybe he's under cover? Within moments the BMX boys are buzzing past me on their cycles like flies to a carcass, jostling to be the first at the window, their bikes discarded on the ground. There are a handful of other empty cars scattered around the car park, but none looks suspicious. I take out my phone again. Should I text Gus an apology? Or would that just seem hypocritical?

Suddenly, I hear a car pull up about a hundred feet directly behind me and park. I don't want to risk turning around, but annoyingly I can't see who it is. How obnoxious if it *is* the Albanians – they must know that I can't see them from this angle! Instead, I hold up my phone as if I'm photographing the lake and flip the screen. It takes me a moment to get the angle right, but sure enough, I can see a black hatchback with two men inside. I store my phone back in my pocket and wait anxiously for them to approach.

I know virtually nothing about Albania. *Where is it, exactly?* Somewhere near Croatia. Or Macedonia. Or maybe Italy? Presumably they speak Albanian. And hopefully English. So far, I haven't even heard a car door open yet, so what the hell are they doing? Don't they want to get this over with? I don't think I have ever felt as self-conscious in my life, as I do right now. I feel like there's a giant arrow in the sky pointing straight down at me: the ultimate wallflower at the school disco, standing alone by the side of the gym, except instead of waiting for a pimply-faced adolescent with unforgiveable hair to sidle up to me, I'm waiting for a ruthless foreign drug dealer.

A few minutes tick by. The longer they make me wait, the more irritated I grow, until I am practically fuming. Why is it that women are always forced to wait for men anyway, I wonder crossly? Women have agency, too! We can be the instigators and the askers, or the ones who are late. We can even be the criminals, if we want to be! Though I guess the latter is not something I should really aspire to. Or maybe I already *am* one?

Suddenly, out of nowhere, a dark-haired man materialises beside me, shattering my reverie. He slides noiselessly onto the bench like an oversized python, deftly dropping a black duffel bag at his feet without a sound. Honestly, where did he come from? I never heard a thing! I steal a glance out of the side of my eye and see that he is early thirties, dark-haired, rough-shaven, lean and not very tall. More of a wiry build, though I'm trying not to look at him directly. He is staring straight ahead at the lake and pulls out a pack of cigarettes and calmly takes one out, putting it in his mouth, then removes a lighter from his pocket and lights it, inhaling deeply. What happens now, I think? Am I supposed to say something? Or do I wait for him to speak? He inhales again deeply, and out of the corner of my eye, I see him lift his head and blow three perfect smoke rings up into the air.

Damn. They're rather beautiful.

I'm not a smoker, but if I could blow smoke rings like that, I'd probably take it up. I am so busy admiring the smoke rings drift across the water that I almost do not see him make the switch, which he does with his feet, hooking my bag with one ankle, and nudging his duffel bag with the other ever so slightly towards me. In the next instant, he takes one more drag of his cigarette, flicks it expertly in a high arc towards the water, reaches down and collects my bag and then stands, shouldering it and walking back towards the black Astra. Not a single word has been exchanged between us.

Who knew drug deals could be so easy?

A moment later I hear three things simultaneously: the gunning of the Astra engine, the sudden wail of a siren, and a woman's voice shout: 'Armed police! Stay where you are!'

I look in the direction of the voice and see that the young female jogger is fifty paces away, crouched low behind a parked car, a pistol pointed expertly at the Astra. Suddenly the Deliveroo guy is racing towards the Astra at top speed on his bike, having ditched his meal bag, and so is the council dustman, who has chucked his broom and is running full pelt towards us.

OMG they're all coppers!

I turn around to check the ice-cream van and see the elderly seller staring at the Astra in open-mouthed amazement. At least someone around here besides me isn't law enforcement! In the next instant I see three shiny black 4×4s come flying around the corner and screech to a halt in the car park, blocking both exits, their red lights flashing. The two Albanian men abandon the Astra and start running in the only direction available to them, away from the lake, and I too jump to my feet, sling the duffel bag over my back and take off. But instead of following them, I skate straight towards the dustman who is running in my direction. At a hundred paces, confusion smears his face – he clearly has no idea what I'm doing. He also doesn't know I'm a jammer.

The one thing we jammers know how to do is evade the opposition. So I wait until he is ten paces away and then use a classic derby technique: I fake right then juke around him, lunging hard to one side with my left leg and my right shoulder out in front, and then shoot right past, leaving him to stop short and spin around in bewilderment. Once past, I can't help glancing over my shoulder – the look on his face is priceless, and I feel the same familiar zing of triumph that I get on the track.

Score!

Now I'm skating flat out, heading towards the estate on

the far side of the lake, bending low and lengthening my stride to get as much speed up as I can. In the distance I hear the policewoman shout another warning at the Albanians and then I hear two shots ring out far behind me, but I'm concentrating too hard to look behind to see what's happened. When I reach the other side of the lake, I skate between another pair of tower blocks and up a long ramp giving access to a maze of walkways. I feel like a lab rat – walkways lead everywhere and there's a dizzying array of choices, but I pick one heading vaguely in the direction of the train station and carry on. I'm so short that if I bend as low as possible, I am barely visible above the tops of the concrete sides of the walkway, though anyone looking down on me from the surrounding towers will be surprised to see me rolling like a marble through the concrete passages of the estate.

I reach the edge of the estate and shoot out onto the main road, heading in the direction of the station, moving as fast as I can in the traffic. The station is less than half a mile away and I am travelling at more than 20 mph, so I should be there in a few minutes. I fly around a roundabout and carry on straight when suddenly I hear another siren. After a moment, I spot another police car heading straight towards me from the opposite direction, its lights blazing. Instinctively I start to slow, my heart accelerating, but a moment later the car flies right past me on the opposite side of the road, clearly in pursuit of the Albanians rather than me.

When I reach the station a few minutes later, I shove my return ticket into the gates just as I hear a train for London Bridge announced on the tannoy. In the distance I hear more sirens and I race inside, lunging up the stairs in my skates, taking two at a time. When I reach the platform, the train is just pulling in and I quickly jump on board, flinging myself onto the nearest seat, exhausted and exhilarated. The sirens grow louder and louder, and then suddenly grind to a halt nearby.

Gosh, they sound close.

The train whistle blows and the doors shut, but the train lingers on the platform for a long, agonising moment. I crane my neck to see out of the window towards the stairs. Could it be *me* the police are after? Surely not? Didn't Gus explain to DC Hill?

After another few moments the train slowly pulls away and I sit back in my seat, breathing more easily. Perhaps I only imagined the sirens were nearby. I lean my head against the window and gaze out at the retreating platform. I am one step closer to my goal of helping Adele, but who knows what I have sacrificed in the meantime? Gus will no doubt be furious with me. Perhaps he'll wash his hands of me entirely. Maybe I'll never see him again.

Just then I see a gaggle of people burst onto the platform at the station, half of them wearing police uniforms. I crane my neck to watch, pressing my cheek right up against the glass, as they mill around for a few moments, then start to disperse, until only one man remains behind. He's wearing plain clothes, his arms crossed over his chest, and is staring in the direction of the retreating train. And even though he is now a long way off, I'd recognise that shearling collar anywhere.

Chapter Twenty-Six

'You lied to me,' I say hotly, when Gus answers his phone a moment later.

'That's entirely possible,' he replies. 'Clemency, you need to get off that train!' He must be still on the platform. I can hear the wind blustering and the blare of a tannoy in the background.

'I can't,' I say grumpily. 'It's moving. Quite fast, actually.' I stare out the window as the countryside whips past. 'You told me you weren't involved in today's drop!' I say.

'I'm afraid you involved me when you confessed that you were about to commit a crime!'

'I did not commit a crime!' I say. 'I *intercepted* one. There's a difference.' An older black woman sitting across from me pauses for a moment in her knitting and frowns, trying unsuccessfully to avert her eyes.

'I'm not sure a judge would see it that way,' says Gus.

'It will never go before a judge! Unless you turn me in!' I cry. At this point the elderly woman hastily gathers up her knitting bag and moves hurriedly away, passing into the next carriage. I frown at her retreating back.

Was it something I said?

'Clemency, I don't *need* to turn you in! Eight different drug enforcement officials witnessed your exchange this afternoon. They took photographs!'

Eight? I only saw three. Where were the others? Hiding in the bins?

'Did you get the Albanians?' I ask.

'Yes, we got the Albanians,' he sighs wearily.

'So it worked! Just like I knew it would. But we still need to get Popeye.'

'Clemency, you do *not* need to get Popeye,' he says sternly.

'Yes, I do.'

'Why?'

'Because I promised Adele I would.'

'We've been over this. You do not owe Adele *anything*.'

'I do.'

'What? What exactly do you owe her?' he demands.

I hesitate, biting my lip. On every rational level, he is right. Really, I do not owe the woman who stole my identity anything. But on a completely different level – on another plane of understanding altogether, where the stars and the universe and the heart collide like asteroids (and yes, I realise that this level is probably an irrational one) – I owe her everything. Because she's altered the course of my life forever. If it hadn't been for her, I'd still be mired in my old existence, doing a job I didn't really like, for an employer who didn't trust me, dodging dates with my ex-boyfriend and subconsciously lusting after married film producers.

'Clemency, I'm listening,' says Gus sternly. I can't help but smile a little into the phone. Even when he's angry and impatient and brusque – even when he's *patronising* – his glorious voice still makes me smile.

'Because if it hadn't been for Adele,' I say finally, 'then I never would have met you.' Then I hang up. Before he has a chance to reply.

*

I need a new plan. If the police aren't going to help me catch Popeye, I'm going to have to figure out how to do it on my own. I really don't have a choice. If Adele (or someone looking like Adele) doesn't turn up at London Bridge Station with a duffel bag full of gear sometime in the next hour, then I do not even want to think about what will happen to Anton. Much less Adele, once he gets his hands on her. And possibly me. So I'm going to have to go through with the rendezvous and deliver the drugs to him myself, without the support of DC Hill and his team. Or Gus, apparently. Which will *definitely* make me a criminal – or at the very least, an accessory to a crime.

I reckon Adele's clothes will fool Popeye for approximately three seconds. Five, if I keep my face lowered and don't say a word. I now have twenty-seven minutes until the train arrives at London Bridge. I've already texted him from Adele's phone to say when I'm due in, as instructed, and he has replied with a big thumbs up. Not sure what I was expecting, but isn't it funny that criminals use all the same emojis as we do? Next, I ring Bianca.

'What are you doing?' I ask.

'Trying to flog a new brand of water. Which, as it's literally just water, is more difficult than it sounds.'

'I need your help.'

'Sorry, I have a deadline.'

'Can you get out of it?'

'No. I have a very expensive lifestyle to maintain.'

'What if *my* life depended on it?'

'Your *actual* life? Or your fantasy life.'

'My actual life. And by the way, if you're referring to my love life, it's *not* a fantasy. At least, it wasn't last night, when a very handsome policeman turned up in my bed. Though it might be, going forward,' I add.

'What's happened?' she asks eagerly.

'Help me out and I'll tell you all the details.'

'Sweetie, I don't really want all the details.'

'Look, I need you to meet me at London Bridge in twenty-five minutes!' I cry desperately. 'Please?'

'Fine,' she sighs.

'And bring me some shoes.'

'What kind of shoes?'

'Ones without wheels.'

I give Bianca the time of the train's arrival and the platform number but sidestep her questions about the exact nature of our mission. I think even *she* might draw the line at aiding and abetting a drug drop. She thinks we're catching criminals, which I really hope we are, ultimately. But as soon as I hang up, my phone lights up again.

'Bex?' I ask.

'It's Adele. What's happening?'

'I've got the gear and I'm on my way back,' I say quietly. 'I've texted Popeye.'

'What about the cops?' She sounds worried.

'They know I'm coming.' Which is true.

'So they're going to be there?'

'Yes.' Possibly to arrest me, though Adele doesn't need to know that.

'OK. You'll call me on this line as soon as you've got him?'

'Yes.' Or even if we don't, I think. *Definitely* if we don't.

Adele hangs up and as soon as she does, my phone pings with a text. Suddenly I'm so popular! Is this what it's like to be a drug dealer, I wonder? The text is from June.

Are you back soon?

Uh oh. I'd forgotten all about Charlie Bucket. It's already past closing time at the shop.

Could you hang onto him a bit longer? I text back.

Sorry. I've got chromatherapy tonight.

Ah. Of course. June has been studying for a diploma in colour healing for the past year. Apparently, colour energy can be used to treat all sorts of afflictions: green is good for ulcers and blue for high blood pressure. Though my favourite is yellow, which June says is used to treat impotence. Colour therapists recommend eating bananas to those who can't get it up, apparently.

Carl has a key to my flat, I type.

Tried that. He's not home.

Damn. Of course he's not. The one time I need him.

Could you maybe drop CB off at London Bridge on your way to class? I'll be there in fifteen minutes.

There's a long pause while June considers this. It occurs to me that, as she is no longer my employee, there really is no imperative for her to do my bidding. A moment later her reply appears.

Marcus will bring him to London Bridge.

I hesitate. Marcus? Really? Things always seem to go awry when Marcus gets involved. But I have no choice.

Fine, I text back.

So now I just have to get to London Bridge, evade the police (who I suspect will be waiting for me), deliver the drugs to Popeye and then make sure he gets caught. *Easy peasy!* After a few minutes the train rolls into Lewisham Station, the penultimate stop before London Bridge. I sink low in my seat, keeping my head down, but not before I see two uniformed cops arrive on the platform, looking around. They position themselves right by the exit and scrutinise everyone getting off the train, which does not bode well for my arrival at London Bridge.

Clearly, it's time for more subterfuge. Quickly I unlace both my skates and remove them. I glance at the duffel bag – it's already quite full and really isn't big enough to hold them, even if I *was* prepared to open it and look inside (which I'm definitely not). And if I carry the skates, I might as well also sport a banner advertising my presence. I could leave them on the train, but I really can't bear to part with them, so in the end I tie the ends of the laces together and hang them around my neck tucked inside Adele's black and purple sweater, one skate dangling a little awkwardly under each breast.

Now for the wig. I duck down to the floor, remove the violet beanie, stuff it in my pocket and position the blonde wig firmly on my head. Then I take off the dark blue pea coat, lay it out on the seat beside me and roll the black duffel bag up inside it, then stuff the whole thing like a sausage under my arm. I've done as much as I can for now; without the skates, hat, duffel bag and coat, and wearing the blonde wig, I might just evade detection. I frown down at my socks, which are bound to draw attention, so I hope Bianca makes it in time with my shoes. I cast my eyes around the carriage. A silver-haired man wearing a green anorak several rows away is staring at me suspiciously. I smile brightly at him and he looks away.

As we approach London Bridge, I watch anxiously for the platform to come into view. A few dozen commuters are milling around waiting for the train to arrive, but Bianca is not among them. I spy another pair of police officers at the far end of the platform by the escalators. Gus must have made sure every station was covered. The rotter! The train pulls in and comes to a halt, and several people in my carriages get up to disembark. I linger until I'm the very last person off the train, scouring the platform through the window, but still no sign of Bianca.

A little reluctantly, I step down onto the concrete platform in my fake sandal socks and walk briskly towards the escalator, the skates bouncing around like pendulous teats beneath my jumper, and the bundled duffel bag clenched tight beneath my armpit. The two police are waiting by the exit, casting their eyes around. They're not looking for a blonde, fortunately, and they don't seem to notice that I'm not wearing shoes, so I walk right past them, holding my breath, and step onto the escalator. When I am halfway up, I spy Bianca just getting on at the top. I try waving to her, but she doesn't recognise me, not until she is almost abreast of me, at which point I am hissing to her over the barrier, trying not to draw attention to myself.

'Bianca!' I say.

She clocks me, then rolls her eyes. 'You didn't tell me I was meant to wear my wig!' she hisses.

'It's subterfuge! What did you expect?' I whisper back over the middle barrier. By now she's sailed right past and when I reach the top, I turn around to see her get off at the bottom, smile politely at the pair of police officers, then step back onto the up escalator. I hover around the top waiting for her, glancing around nervously.

The same transport guard with the horseshoe moustache is still by the ticket gate. I see his gaze travel from my wig all the way down to my white socks and then I see him raise an eyebrow. In the next instant, he lifts his walkie-talkie and speaks a few words into it. I glance down anxiously at Bianca, who is now about halfway up the escalator, and motion for her to hurry up. One of the pair of police officers at the bottom pulls out his walkie-talkie, then after a brief exchange, swivels around to look upwards. I duck back out of view.

Bianca reaches me a moment later and I grab her arm. 'The shoes!' I say quickly and she reaches into a plastic carrier bag and pulls out a pair of flat leather moccasins, complete with little beaded tassles. I look up at her and roll my eyes. 'Who am I? Pocahontas?' I ask.

'They were on sale!' she says. 'You know I can't resist a bargain.'

'I can't think why,' I reply, hurriedly shoving them onto my feet. 'Here, take these,' I say, shoving the skates into the bag and giving it back to her.

We turn and rush to the barrier, but the droopy moustache guard blocks our way. 'Could I see your ticket please, madam?' he asks.

'Fine,' I say, feeling around in my pocket and eventually producing a ticket. Just then I hear a familiar voice call my name in the distance.

'Clemency!' I turn to see Marcus being dragged through the station at warp speed by Charlie Bucket, who gallops the last fifty feet when he sees me and practically bowls me over, with Marcus arriving flushed and panting in tow.

'*Loving* the blonde wig!' he says, pointing to my hair and handing me the lead. The guard steps forward with a frown.

'Excuse me, sir, can you please remove the animal and step aside?' he says curtly.

'Why? What's going on?' asks Marcus, suddenly alert.

'Nothing,' I say to him.

'Madam, I'm going to need to ask you some questions,' says the guard to me.

'Why? Has she done something wrong?' demands Bianca, stepping forward and using her most imperious voice.

274

'We have a right to detain any passenger,' says the guard, turning to her.

'I'm sorry,' says Marcus officiously. 'But if she's being detained, then *we* have a right to know why.'

'It's just routine questioning,' says the guard, though he is undoubtedly wrong-footed by both of them, and he is still eyeing Charlie Bucket warily.

'The law stipulates that you need reasonable grounds to detain someone,' says Marcus staunchly. I have to stifle a smile. When we were going out together, his lawyerly affectations used to drive me mad, but right now I could almost kiss him. Almost.

'We're just making routine checks,' says the guard. He steps forward and takes hold of my elbow, and at this, Charlie Bucket suddenly lunges forward, snarling at him. The guard leaps back as if he's been scorched.

'He hates moustaches,' I say apologetically. 'I think it's genetic. Please don't take it personally. Yours is *lovely*.'

'Get him away from me,' says the guard in a panicked voice. I can tell he's genuinely terrified. Funny how some people are frightened of dogs, even tiny ones. Which admittedly, Charlie Bucket is not.

Charlie Bucket lunges and snarls again and the guard retreats another few paces. 'Control your animal!' he bellows.

'We're leaving now, you needn't worry,' says Bianca forcefully. She steps forward, taking my arm and nods to Marcus, who does the same on the other side, and the pair of them escort me away between them.

I can't believe it: Marcus and Bianca, working together at last.

Like guardian angels.

Chapter Twenty-Seven

Once outside the station, I pull the pair of them into a corner behind a billboard and pull off the wig, then I unwrap the duffel bag and put the blue coat back on, stuffing the wig in the pocket.

'What's going on?' says Marcus excitedly.

'We're catching criminals,' Bianca tells him.

'Excellent!' he says.

'It's a little more complicated than that,' I say nervously. 'First we have to commit a crime. And then we get to catch the criminal.'

'What do you mean *commit a crime*?' asks Bianca suspiciously.

'We have to make the drop,' I say, indicating the duffel bag.

'What drop?' says Marcus. He and Bianca both stare at me, alarmed. 'What's in the duffel bag?'

'I'm not sure,' I say evasively. 'But whatever it is, it cost a lot of money.'

'You don't know what you're carrying?' asks Bianca, clearly shocked.

'I don't *want* to know!' I say. 'I know that it's illegal. That's enough.'

Bianca raises her eyes to Marcus, then both of them turn to me.

'Open the bag,' demands Bianca.

'No!'

'We need to see what's inside,' says Marcus eagerly. The two of them grab the bag off my shoulder and unzip it, and all three of us peer inside. Bianca reaches in, gingerly pawing the contents, revealing a series of tightly sealed plastic bags containing white powder, bundled in neat rows.

'I told you,' I say, peering at the bags uncertainly. 'It's obviously . . . contraband of some sort.' I know next-to-nothing about illicit drugs, though I'm a big fan of licit ones.

'But *what* sort?' says Bianca suspiciously. She picks up a bag and examines it closely. 'I'll tell you one thing: it's not cocaine,' she says authoritatively.

'It doesn't look like heroin, either,' says Marcus, frowning at it. I look at him askance.

'How would *you* know?' I ask.

He shrugs. 'Police videos,' he replies.

'Let's open one,' says Bianca eagerly.

'No!' I cry.

'Good idea,' says Marcus. He opens a bag and gingerly sniffs it, then holds it up to Bianca, who licks a finger, dips it inside and then puts it in her mouth. She hesitates, then pulls a face.

'It's salt,' she pronounces.

'What?' I exclaim.

'Ordinary table salt. Not even the good stuff,' she says with a sniff.

'Ha!' exclaims Marcus. They both turn to me accusingly.

'Don't look at me! I'm just the messenger! It must have been the Algerians!' I say.

'You didn't even *think* to check the goods you were collecting?' asks Marcus.

'Sweetie, you are such rubbish at this,' says Bianca, shaking her head.

'Adele told me not to! She told me they wouldn't dare double-cross Popeye.'

'Let's face it, she's pretty rubbish at this, too,' says Bianca.

'Oh God,' I say. 'Now what? How do we catch Popeye in the act, if he's only taking delivery of table salt?' Marcus and Bianca frown at each other.

'But he doesn't *know* it's table salt,' says Marcus slowly. 'I say you still go through with the drop,' he adds. He quickly reseals the bag and replaces it, then zips up the duffel bag, handing it back to me.

'Yes,' says Bianca, nodding her head vigorously. 'He's right. You need to do the drop!'

'But he'll notice! Probably straight away! And then he'll be angry.'

'Exactly. So we just need a tape recording of his reaction when he finds out,' says Marcus. 'And that should be enough for a conviction.'

'But what if he gets angry with *me*? Or violent?'

'You just tell him what you told us: that you never looked inside the bag,' says Bianca.

'But what if he doesn't believe me?' I cry.

'Sweetie, you have a very gullible face,' says Bianca. 'He'll totally believe you.'

'Besides, we'll be right there to support you,' says Marcus.

'Right where?' I ask.

'Close by. Watching. We promise,' says Marcus.

'How close?'

'In the meantime, we'll alert the police,' says Bianca.

'Good idea,' says Marcus, looking up at her.

'But the police want to arrest *me*!' I say.

'Then it's the best way to clear your name,' says Marcus pointedly.

Bianca steps forward and grips my shoulders in both

hands, giving them a little shake. 'Sweetie, you've got this,' she says urgently.

'No, I really don't.' I shake my head.

'You do,' says Marcus. He and Bianca both nod at me emphatically.

'For the sake of justice,' he says earnestly. 'If not your own.'

Two minutes later I am standing beside the same layby on Tooley Street where Adele got dropped off earlier this afternoon. Behind me is the station, and behind the station the Shard rises up majestically like a giant silver thorn skewering the sky. Marcus has positioned my iPhone upside down at the top of my waistband with the microphone sticking out and the recording function switched on. He and Charlie Bucket are stationed about fifty yards away behind a giant billboard, and Bianca has been sent to find the police. It's rush hour and there's a steady stream of traffic along Tooley Street; I search anxiously for the red Camaro. Suddenly I hear an unfamiliar ring tone and realise it's Adele's phone. I take it out of my coat pocket and see the message *Unknown Caller* flash up on the screen.

'Hello?' I answer cautiously.

'Where the hell are you?' says Popeye angrily.

'Tooley Street, where you left me,' I say, trying my hardest to mimic Adele's South London accent.

'You were meant to meet me on the other side! By the Shard. Outside the Shangri-La!'

'Coming,' I say quickly and hang up. Adele must have forgotten that bit. She really is crap at this! I scurry over to where Marcus and Charlie Bucket are hiding behind the billboard.

'What's happening?' says Marcus.

279

'I'm at the wrong exit! He's on the other side. Outside the Shangri-La. Call Bianca!' We run along the road, dodging commuters, with Charlie Bucket trailing behind us on the lead, and Marcus frantically trying to ring Bianca. The station is massive and it takes ages to get there, even though the Shard looks so close it feels like I could reach out and touch it. I see the sign for the Shangri-La before I spy the red Camaro pulled over in the drop-off area outside, its engine running. Around it several black cabs are parked up waiting for hotel fares. Marcus hangs back behind a pillar and I approach, slowing down to a walk, but as I draw near, Adele steps out from behind another pillar, grabs my arm, and pulls me back with her.

'What are you doing here?' I say with alarm.

'I forgot to tell you about the meeting point!'

'No kidding! Why didn't you just ring me?'

''Cause Bex took her phone to work!' Adele rolls her eyes. She nods at the duffel bag. 'Is that it?'

'Sort of,' I say uneasily.

'What do you mean *sort of*?'

'The Albanians double-crossed us. It's table salt.'

Adele literally blanches at this news. 'What are we gonna do?' she says anxiously.

'Don't worry. I have a plan.'

'What sort of plan? And where are the cops? You said the cops would be here!'

'Just trust me. I got this,' I say.

Do I? Do I really?

Adele hesitates. 'I don't have much choice,' she says.

I pull away from her and keep walking towards the Camaro. When I reach it, I see Popeye glaring at me from inside, but I don't even hesitate. I climb right into the passenger seat and close the door behind me, then hand the duffel bag over, meeting his eye. It's dark and he frowns slightly as he takes the bag.

'You're fucking late,' he says, focusing on the duffel bag.

Oh my God. He doesn't know it's me!

I shrug, saying nothing. He unzips the bag and paws through the contents, counting the bags and weighing them in his hands for several moments. Then he frowns down at it.

'It's short,' he says finally. 'They fucking shorted me! The pricks!' He shakes his head and looks out the window for a moment, thinking. I hold my breath. Does he really not know it's worse than that? And have I got enough on tape yet to incriminate him? I'm just about to open the door and run, when suddenly he whips around to face me.

'Unless it was *you*,' he says accusingly.

Uh oh.

I stare at him. 'No,' I shake my head. 'Honest. I didn't even look inside. I swear!' He peers at me more closely, his face twisting into a bewildered grimace.

'Fucking hell! Where's Adele?!'

I reach for the door handle and try to open it, but he's locked it from his side. Then his hand darts out like a cobra and grips my throat in a vice-like hold, pinning me back hard against the headrest. I start to flail but he presses down hard on my throat and suddenly I cannot breathe.

'What the hell's going on?' he snarls.

I try to speak but he's choking me. I'm flailing at him with my hands, but he is stronger than me and out of the corner of my eye I'm frantically looking outside for help. Where are Marcus and Bianca, or even Adele? Aren't they supposed to rescue me? I've got one hand on his face trying to push him away and with the other I reach up and grab the rear-view mirror, snap it off, and smack him as hard as I can across the forehead with it.

'Ow!' he shouts and releases me for an instant, his hands moving to clutch his head, where I can already see blood beginning to ooze. I gasp for air, struggling to regain my breath.

'You idiot!' I shout, coughing. 'The Albanians didn't short you! They conned you!' He stares up at me through his hands, blood slowly beginning to trickle down his arm.

'What are you talking about?'

'It's table salt!' I say, nodding at the duffel bag.

'Fucking hell,' he mutters. He opens the glove box and grabs a box of tissues, pressing a wad to his head. 'The two of you. You're like some kind of bad dream. Ever since I got involved with you two . . .' He breaks off and shakes his head. I realise that he's referring to me and Adele.

'It's not our fault if you chose shoddy business partners! Adele and I had nothing to do with this!'

Just then I hear someone rapping on the window and look up to see Bianca standing there. She motions for me to roll down the window, then jerks a thumb behind her, where a fresh-faced young policewoman now steps forward. She has chubby cheeks, strawberry-blonde hair pulled back in a ponytail, and looks about fourteen. It would not surprise me in the slightest if, when she opens her mouth, she has braces on her teeth.

'This is PC Griffiths,' says Bianca, smiling down at us. 'She's here to make an arrest.'

Chapter Twenty-Eight

In spite of her youthful appearance, PC Griffiths behaves just like a real law-enforcement official. She asks us both to step out of the car and when she sees the duffel bag full of white powder, she immediately calls for back-up. When Popeye explains that it's only table salt, she shrugs. 'That'll be for the lab to decide,' she says firmly. She peers at his head injury, frowning. 'That wound looks nasty. I think you'll need to get that looked at,' she says, her eyes swivelling towards me accusingly.

'I was defending myself,' I cry, outraged. 'He could have killed me!'

'Is that true, sir?' she asks, turning back to him. Popeye is still holding the wad of tissues to his head. He scowls at me.

'She's a liar,' he cries. 'It was an unprovoked attack! She lost her temper and hit me out of the blue.'

'Hang on! *He's* the liar!' I reply. 'And what about the duffel bag? It may be table salt, but it's packaged like drugs. He's clearly a drug dealer!'

'The bag is hers,' says Popeye. 'She was carrying it when she got in the car! Every taxi driver around here saw her.' He points to the taxis lined up outside the hotel. PC Griffiths sighs.

'Right. We're going to need to take you both in. Can you please turn around?' She pulls out two pairs of handcuffs and swiftly clips them to our wrists.

Seriously? Again?

Popeye is eyeing me malevolently. A moment later a squad car comes racing around the corner and screeches to a halt, red lights flashing. 'Are we being arrested?' asks Popeye, incredulous. 'For table salt?'

'Yes sir,' she says officiously.

Popeye glares at me as we're both loaded into the back of the police car. Marcus and Charlie Bucket have now joined Bianca on the pavement outside the hotel. 'Don't worry. We'll look after Charlie Bucket,' calls Bianca. Marcus nods vigorously by her side, giving me the thumbs up.

By now it's early evening and as we drive to the station, I'm hoping Gus will be off duty.

Maybe he won't find out?

Then again, I'm meant to be meeting him later tonight for our hot date. If we still *have* a hot date. Which is doubtful. Maybe I should ask PC Griffiths how long this is likely to take.

When we enter the station and are escorted through the reception, we pass my old friend, the duty sergeant. His gaze swivels from me to Popeye's head injury, then back to me. 'Honestly, you're like a bad rash,' he says to me quietly as I am led past the front desk.

'I was defending myself,' I mutter back. Popeye turns and gives him a quizzical look.

'You know her?' he asks the duty sergeant.

'Know her? We can't get rid of her,' mutters the duty sergeant.

'Join the club,' says Popeye. And the two men exchange a sort of blokey virtual high five with their eyebrows. I scowl at them. Surely that's against some sort of professional code of conduct?

We're taken straight to the holding cells on the naughty

side of the building and I'm a little miffed when they assign Popeye my usual one and lead me to the one next door. They've confiscated our possessions, but when I first got out of the car, I'd quickly embraced Bianca and had slipped Adele's phone into her pocket, together with the information that Adele was across the road watching us. I didn't want the police to get hold of it – Adele's in enough trouble as it is.

Now I'm wondering if Adele has gone to get Anton. I really hope so. This might be the only window of time to free him, while Popeye is being questioned by the police. I really hope they have a plan for how to disappear. Even if it *does* involve my passport. After only a few minutes, the fresh-faced officer who arrested me returns and leads me to an interrogation room, where DC Hill is already waiting for me. He sits down at the table, and motions for me to sit opposite. Then he sits back in his chair and folds his arms.

'Well, well, well,' he says. 'You certainly led my officers on a merry dance this afternoon.'

'They were supposed to let me get away!'

'They did. Though not intentionally.' He flashes me a mirthless grin.

'I was helping your investigation.'

'Let me be very clear – you were *obstructing* our investigation. There's a thin line between serving the public interest and breaking the law. And today you crossed it.'

'Are you saying I broke the law?'

'Intentionally obstructing an enforcement agent is a criminal offence.'

'But I was trying to help you!'

'Ah,' he says in a patronising tone. 'Here's the thing. We neither asked for, nor wanted, your help. I believe DC Meadows was fairly explicit with you on that particular point, was he not?'

I figure this is a rhetorical question, so I do not answer.

'So are you arresting me?' I ask glumly.

'For possession of table salt? No.'

'What about obstruction?'

'Tempting,' he says in a sardonic tone. 'But no.'

'And Popeye?' I ask. 'He really *was* expecting a delivery of Class A drugs. You recovered the cash from the Albanians, right?'

'Yes,' he says.

'So?'

'So we'll do our best to secure a conviction,' he says. 'But if we don't have enough evidence, it's more likely he'll be bailed and released. It would certainly help if your friend Adele would come forward at this stage,' he adds.

I frown. This is unlikely. DC Hill knows this as well as me.

'You can't release him,' I say. 'He could come after me!'

'Then you might want to lay low for the time being. Maybe get out of town.'

Get out of town? Where? And with what? I'm broke!

'Right now, he's being treated by the nurse for a nasty head wound,' says DC Hill in an accusing tone.

'He was choking me! I could have been killed!'

'All the more reason you need to stop larking about,' he says, his voice now sharp. He stands, signalling the interview is over. The young PC who arrested me pokes her head in through the doorway. She's holding a plastic bag of my possessions and now hands them to me.

'Am I free to go?' I ask.

'Yes. But if you interfere again, we'll lock you up,' he says sternly. He starts to leave and I stand up, but he pauses in the doorway. 'Not so fast. I believe DC Meadows would like a quick word.'

Uh oh.

I watch DC Hill go and I sit heavily back down in the chair, my nerves flaring. Suddenly I really do feel like I'm in the dock, waiting for sentencing. The clock on the wall ticks silently by over the next few minutes, during which time, Bianca texts me.

We're outside in reception! Are they holding you?

No.

Can you leave?

Not yet.

Do you need a lawyer?

I hope not.

Don't say anything that might incriminate!

Too late.

Just then I hear footsteps in the corridor and Gus enters. I hurriedly stuff my phone in my pocket as he sits down opposite me, grim-faced. I wait for him to speak, but he says nothing for a long moment. 'Are you hurt?' he finally asks. His voice is distant and tightly controlled, cool even.

'I'm OK,' I say.

He nods, just once. 'You're being formally cautioned for obstruction of justice. Do you understand what that means?'

'Yes,' I answer. *Do I?*

'The caution will go on your record and remain there for six years. It may be used against you in future in a court of law,' he continues.

Gosh.

'I understand,' I say, my voice barely above a whisper. Actually, I didn't *really* understand: I now have a police record. I guess I really am a criminal, after all.

'You're free to go,' he says then, standing up briskly and turning away.

'Is that it?' I ask quickly.

Gus pauses in the doorway and turns back to me.

'I mean . . . is that all you want to say?' I ask, my voice a little desperate. Our eyes lock and he stares at me for a long moment, his face rigid.

Surely that can't be it?

'That's all,' he says. And then he disappears.

Without even a *fare-thee-well*.

I stand there for a long moment, then stumble out into the corridor. I make my way down the hallway, my eyes blurry with tears. My heart feels like it's slowly being crushed from within. It's almost worse than when Popeye was choking me; at the very least, it feels just as painful. Gus clearly wants nothing more to do with me. And the idea that I may never see him again, much less hear his voice, or feel him in my arms, is gutting. I've just forsaken the best thing that has happened in my life for ages.

I walk down the now-familiar hallway and push through the door into the crowded reception area, looking around through teary eyes. From across the room Charlie Bucket woofs, breaking free from where Bianca and Marcus are holding him. He sprints across the room and hurls himself into my arms, literally bowling me over. I collapse in a heap on the floor and grip his fur fiercely. His entire body wags with relief, and he is licking me all over my face and neck. I feel a warm rush of affection.

It's not quite the love of a good man. But for now, it will have to do.

Bianca and Marcus rush forward and help me to my feet. 'Are you OK?' Bianca asks with a worried face. I nod, suddenly unable to speak. She locks her arm in mine and nods to Marcus, who takes the other.

'Let's get you home,' she says then.

Chapter Twenty-Nine

They take me back to the flat. Once there, Bianca marches me off to the shower, where I stand under a stream of steamy water, endeavouring to banish the events of the day. When I close my eyes, two images flash before me relentlessly: Popeye's face twisted with anger, his hand tight upon my throat. And the look in Gus's eyes when he realised he could never trust me again. After several minutes I finally emerge, quickly towel-dry my hair and pull on my warmest track suit. Bianca is waiting for me in the kitchen with a large glass of red wine that she has pilfered from my pantry, while Marcus has rustled up a mushroom and gruyère omelette from the remnants of my fridge. They sit me down at the table and order me to eat. I fork up a mouthful, suddenly ravenous – the omelette might be the best thing I've ever eaten.

'Aren't you guys hungry?' I ask, feeling guilty suddenly.

'No sweetie,' says Bianca. 'We just want to make sure you're fed and watered before we go.'

I look from one to the other. Clearly, both are keen to be away; they must have other plans. Bianca hasn't even taken off her coat.

'You guys go. I'm fine,' I say, waving them away.

'Are you sure?' asks Marcus. He, too, is obviously eager to be off. June is probably finished with her chromatherapy class by now.

How adorable is that?

'Totally sure. You guys were amazing today. I can't thank you enough,' I say.

'What are friends for?' says Marcus, grabbing his coat.

Indeed.

I finish the omelette and watch as Charlie Bucket licks the plate spotlessly clean, if not exactly hygienic. I can't help wondering what Gus is doing right now. It's almost nine o'clock, which is to say, past the starting time for most dates, even hot ones. Had I been in any doubt about the status of ours this evening (I hadn't), it seems patently clear that it's not happening. I wonder if I should text him to apologise? Though truthfully, I'm not sure what I'd say.

I'm not sorry that I intervened to save Adele from prison. But I do regret losing Gus in the process.

I sigh and pour myself another glass of wine. I've double-locked the front door to the flat and checked the lock on the kitchen window three times. I've no reason to think Popeye will come after me – what would he possibly gain by doing so? But DC Hill's words keep rolling around in my mind like loose marbles.

Best lay low for a while. Maybe get out of town.

How long exactly is a while, I wonder? A few days? A week? A lifetime?

Maybe I should go and visit my sister in the Midlands, which is about the only option I can afford at the moment. It isn't so bad staying with her; she and Robby share a spacious condo with all the mod cons. She's not very keen on letting Charlie Bucket lounge on her sofas, but when she and Robby go to work, we usually have the run of the place.

Once I've finished clearing up the dishes, I decide to telephone her. It takes about a dozen rings before she picks up, and even then, she sounds a little breathless. 'Hey, it's me,' I say.

'Clem! Gosh. You're calling late,' she remarks.

'Am I?' I glance over at the clock with a frown. It's 9.10 p.m. *Julia time*.

'How's it going?' I ask.

She hesitates for a beat. 'Um . . . fine. Well, better than fine, I guess. Good. Quite good, actually,' she adds, a little haltingly. She doesn't elaborate, nor does she reciprocate the question, and for a moment there's an awkward pause.

'So I was thinking of maybe coming to visit,' I say tentatively.

'Visit *me*?' Julia asks, sounding totally thrown off guard.

'Yeah. You know . . . just for a few days. Or maybe . . . a week.'

'A week! When?' Now she sounds positively alarmed.

'I don't know. I was thinking maybe soon. I could use a change of scene, you know? I could even catch a train up there tomorrow?'

'Oh wow. Clem,' she stammers. 'As much as I'd love to see you, I don't think I could manage a visit this week. Or next. Work is pretty crazy right now. What about we pencil in . . . Easter?' she suggests.

'Easter,' I repeat. Easter is more than two months away.

'Or May Bank Holiday,' she says. 'The weather's always better around then, isn't it honey.' Just then I hear a man's voice concurring in the background.

'Definitely,' says the voice. 'Tell Clem I said hi,' I hear the voice say.

'Is that Robby?' I ask, a little confused.

'Here,' says Julia, obviously speaking to him, rather than me. '*You* speak to her. I'm getting refills.' I hear her get up and then there's a rustle of something – bedclothes maybe?

'Hello Clem,' says Robby cheerily a moment later.

'Hi Robby. So, um . . . you and Julia. What's going on?'

'I know,' he chuckles. 'Who would have thought? After all this time. Just goes to show you!'

'Wow,' I say.

What, exactly, does it go to show? That they've both behaved like idiots?

'Really pleased I didn't chainsaw the sofa,' says Robby.

'I'll bet,' I say.

'You should totally come up for May Bank Holiday! I'll take you mountain biking.'

'Great,' I say, trying to stifle my enthusiasm. Mountains and bikes? Who ever thought this was a good combination? 'Well, I guess I'll let you guys get back to your refills,' I say.

'Cheers Clem. And thanks for the pep talk the other night. It really helped.'

'Did it?' I ask, mystified.

'You totally got me thinking,' he says. 'Anyway, see you soon.'

Which bit of it was the peppy part?

I can't quite remember. Though I guess I'm happy to take credit.

I'll be fine, I decide, hanging up the phone. And frankly, crashing Julia and Robby's newly feathered love nest would be unbearable. Quite possibly worse than tangling with vicious London drug dealers. Besides, I've got Charlie Bucket here to protect me. What could possibly go wrong?

Twenty minutes later he and I are curled up in bed together watching *Bake Off* when my flat buzzer rings. *Oh my God!* Maybe Gus has come, after all! I leap out of bed and run to the intercom, though I can't help clocking my appearance in the mirror on the way. Disaster! My hair is still damp and my face looks blotchy. Also, it may be my imagination, but I think I'm developing an enormous bruise on my neck – it looks like a hippopotamus gave me a hickey. The buzzer rings again and I press the button.

'Who is it?' I ask, my heart hammering in my chest.

'It's Adele,' says a woman's voice urgently.

'Adele! What's happened?'

'Can I come up?'

I buzz her in and hear footsteps rushing up the stairs. *Now what?* I don't even have time to consider how disappointed I am that it's not Gus. Instead, I move to the door and yank it open, only to see Popeye standing there with a pistol jammed in Adele's back. He shoves her inside and follows, then closes the door behind him with his foot.

'Nice of you to answer,' he sneers.

'What are you doing?' I ask, trying to keep the fear from my voice. Charlie Bucket, who had been sound asleep on my bed when the buzzer first rang, now comes lolloping into the room. He trots over to Popeye, wagging his tail affectionately. Popeye reaches down to fondle him, and Charlie Bucket sniffs at the pistol with interest, while I can only watch in despair.

Seriously?

'Give me your phone,' Popeye orders. I throw an uneasy glance at Adele, who nods, then I turn on my heel and go into the bedroom, retrieving my phone from the bedside table. I return and hand it to him.

'Sit, both of you,' he orders, motioning towards the sofa. Adele and I sit down next to each other. Charlie Bucket seems to take offence at the fact that we're on his sofa and jumps up next to me, even though there isn't enough space. We have to bunch up to accommodate him, and he is partially sprawled across my lap, panting with excitement.

'Time to talk about my money,' Popeye says, levelling the gun at us. 'And how you two are gonna get it back for me.'

He has a plan to recover the cash, which he proceeds to outline hastily. He intends to hold *me* for ransom in exchange for its return, but use Adele as a decoy to make the switch, to ensure that he still gets away with me as hostage for security. By the time the police realise they've recovered Adele and not me, we'll be well on our way – to where, he doesn't say.

'Why not release us both?' I ask. 'I'll just slow you down. I have really short legs.'

'Rumour has it you're faster on wheels than any of us,' he says.

True.

'You're my insurance,' he says then. 'Until *I'm* safe and sound, you won't be either. If both of you behave, then no one gets hurt, and you go free,' he says to me. 'I'm only trying to recover what's mine.'

'What about Anton?' asks Adele anxiously. Popeye swivels around to eye her.

'Anton is unlucky,' he says tersely. Adele blanches.

Oh God. What does that mean?

Apart from the bit about Anton, his plan is not a bad one. Popeye is clearly smarter than his namesake. 'Right now, I need you to ring your copper boyfriend,' he says to me. Adele frowns and turns to face me.

'You're seeing a cop?' she says accusingly, like I've somehow just betrayed her.

I shrug. 'Not any more,' I say. 'It was just a . . . thing.'

'Christ,' she says, shaking her head. 'I knew you were bad news!'

'You're *both* bad news, as far as I'm concerned,' grunts Popeye.

I glare at him. *How did he know about me and Gus anyway?*

'Go on, get him on the line,' he says, handing me my phone. 'Make sure he knows it's you.'

I hesitate, then take it. 'Um . . . just so you know, he might not pick up,' I say a little hesitantly. I find Gus's number and press the call button. 'He's not actually speaking to me at the moment,' I add, a little sheepishly.

'Put it on speaker,' orders Popeye. The three of us listen while, sure enough, the phone rings several times, then finally goes through to voice mail. I look up at him uncertainly.

'See?' I say. He rolls his eyes.

'Leave it to you to fuck that up, too,' he says, holding out his hand for the phone. I pass it over. 'Let's see if this helps.' He quickly types in something and presses send. A moment later the phone rings. He holds it up in front of me. I can see Gus's name flash up on the screen.

'Answer him. Just so he knows it's you,' says Popeye.

'Gus?' I say tentatively.

'Clem! What's going on?' says Gus urgently. Just hearing his voice floods me with relief, even though he sounds really worried. Popeye snatches the phone back off me.

'Detective Meadows,' he says brightly. 'We have a little proposal for you.'

Gus is all business during the call. His voice sounds tense, guarded and utterly professional. He asks a few specific questions to clarify the terms of the exchange, but otherwise does not attempt to negotiate, threaten or stall. In total, the call lasts less than a minute, and as soon as Popeye hangs up, he stands up.

'Time to go,' he says, motioning with the gun for us to stand. He throws me Adele's coat, which is hanging on a hook by the door and I put it on.

'Both of you – hands behind your backs,' he says. He quickly secures both our wrists with zip ties, then he nudges us forward and we move to the door. Instantly Charlie Bucket leaps off the sofa and is at my side, tail wagging eagerly. 'Forget it,' says Popeye.

'Go lie down,' I tell Charlie Bucket sternly. 'I'll be back soon,' I say more gently. Charlie Bucket looks at me beseechingly, then goes and climbs onto his sofa, watching us anxiously. We shuffle out into the hallway and just as Popeye is about to close the door, Charlie Bucket leaps off the sofa again and moves to the door, barking loudly in his deep bass. Popeye slams the door with a scowl and grabs Adele's arm with one hand, while shoving the gun into my back with the other. 'Move it!' he growls. We hurry down the stairs, with Charlie Bucket barking behind us.

We spill out onto the street where a black Audi is parked illegally right in front of the cheese shop. Popeye shoves us both into the back seat and climbs into the driver's seat and starts the car. As we pull away from the curb, I can still hear the faint sound of Charlie Bucket barking.

Good boy!

Maybe Carl will notice the commotion, though he's more likely to file a noise complaint than raise the alarm. I press my nose forlornly up against the window, looking back at my flat as we drive away, wondering if I will ever see Charlie Bucket again. He has been the best and most faithful of companions. I wish now that I'd fed him on premium dog food, rather than the generic stuff.

And that is when I see Gus step out from the shadow of a nearby doorway and dash across the road to his car. He must have been right outside my flat the whole time. Maybe our hot date wasn't cancelled, after all.

Chapter Thirty

It takes all my self-control *not* to turn around to make sure that Gus is following, but I don't want to alert Popeye to his presence. Adele didn't seem to notice him, either. We head east through Bermondsey and once or twice I glance behind us, but all I can see is glare from multiple sets of headlights. Popeye makes a couple of terse phone calls with one hand while driving with the other, occasionally swearing at traffic under his breath. We are heading back along the river, and Adele is turned away from me in her seat, hunched over, no longer my ally since the disclosure about Gus.

Gosh, she sure holds a grudge.

Though in fairness, she must be worried sick about Anton. If we're going to get out of this, Adele and I are going to have to work together, so I slowly lean over towards her and gently bump her shoulder with mine. I am half expecting her to flinch or pull away and am surprised when she doesn't. Instead, she straightens and turns a little towards me. Our eyes meet in the darkness and once again I feel a little jolt of connection. I flash her a little smile of reassurance, and she gives the tiniest ghost of a nod in reply.

We are heading towards Thames Barrier Park just south of London City Airport. The swap will be done there at the children's playground right beside the water. Popeye told Gus to leave the duffel bag with the money at the bottom of the climbing frame. I will fetch it and take it back to him, so that

Gus can see I'm alive, though Popeye has ordered him to re-treat and watch me collect the money from a distance. Once Popeye has the money safely in his hands, he'll release me.

Except it's not me he's planning to release. It's Adele.

I have no idea what happens next. There is no way Gus will be able to tell from a distance that it's Adele and not me who is coming towards him in the dark, and by the time she reaches him, Popeye and I will be gone. But at least Gus knows that Adele is with us. He would have seen her get into the car. Anyway, I've no idea if he'll adhere to Popeye's instructions not to bring back-up. Gus may not be prepared to take any chances, as it's my safety in the balance, as well as Adele's. How much is he prepared to risk?

The route out to the Thames Barrier is much quicker than I expected. We take two tunnels, the first beneath the Thames at Rotherhithe and a few minutes later, when we're on the north side of the river, another tunnel under Lime-house by the docks. When we finally emerge, we're on a fast, elevated road and I can see the towers of Canary Wharf whizzing by on our right. The area is scruffy and industrial and only half developed; it's a vast building site, with almost more giant cranes than buildings. By the time we exit the fast road we're nearly there. The Thames is visible only a short distance away, with the enormous, silver flood barriers rising up like giant, gleaming shark's teeth in the distance. Popeye drives to the far end of the park and pulls over in a tiny dead-end car park beside a housing development.

'Right. Both of you. Out,' he says to us, motioning with the gun.

Adele and I exchange a wary glance, then slowly climb out of the car. He instructs us to head along a narrow path leading between two buildings towards the park. When we reach the gates, I see that they're locked, but he tells us to climb around the perimeter of the fence where it meets a line of bushes. There is just enough room to squeeze past, and then we drop down onto the grass on the other side.

Not surprisingly on a cold January night, the place is utterly deserted. The river is about fifty yards to our left, and I can tell at once that it's high tide. The wind is up and the dark water churns and slaps against the path that edges the park, making ominous sounds. Just seeing it makes me shiver. I'm not a fan of large bodies of water at the best of times – anything much bigger than a bathtub scares the wits out of me – but they especially frighten me at night. In darkness, I've always thought water takes on an unfathomable, almost malevolent quality. The sooner we are away from here the better.

Popeye grabs hold of my right arm with one hand, and with the pistol in the other, he orders Adele to walk along beside us. We move through a picnic area on the edge of the park, cross behind a large memorial pavilion, pausing only when we reach a sunken ornamental garden full of eccentrically landscaped box plants undulating in rows like long waves. He orders us down into it and we thread our way through the maze of hedges, pausing deep inside, where we are almost totally obscured by the hedge itself. I see him check the time on his phone. It can't be long before the appointed hour now. He orders Adele down on the ground in between two hedges and secures her ankles with zip ties and her mouth with a wide strip of tape. 'Don't even think about it,' he says to her ominously.

Then he motions for me to follow him to a bank of grass a short distance away. We lie flat on the ground, and I can just make out the playground a few hundred yards away. 'Let's hope your boyfriend can follow instructions better than you two,' he whispers in the darkness.

Will he, I wonder?

I glance around us. The park is eerily quiet, almost ghost-ly. We wait in silence for a few minutes, peering out into the darkness, until Popeye suddenly stiffens. I follow his gaze and see a dark figure at the far end of the park moving quickly towards the playground. Sure enough, he appears to be carrying something slung over his shoulder and my heart begins to race. It must be Gus!

'Not a peep,' Popeye says into my ear, nudging me with the tip of the gun.

We watch in silence as Gus drops the bag at the bottom of a small slide attached to the climbing frame, then glances around him. He hesitates only for a split second, then heads back the way he came towards the far end of the park. When he is nearly out of sight, Popeye spins me around, taking out a knife from his jacket pocket and quickly undoing the zip tie that binds my wrists.

'Your turn,' he murmurs into my ear. 'And no funny stuff, or I might not be so nice to your friend back there.' He motions with the gun towards where Adele is lying some fifty feet behind us. I nod and set off towards the playground. By now I can no longer see Gus, though I'm sure he's out there, watching from a distance. No doubt he's taken cover somewhere, just like we have. I walk briskly towards the climbing frame and as I draw near, I see the black duffel bag right where he left it.

Thank God.

But as I reach for it, I hear a sound behind me, and turn to see Gus crouched inside a small children's play tunnel. He raises a finger to his lips and I freeze. He must have been hiding there all along, and someone else must have dropped the money. Which means he's got back-up. I don't know if I feel worried or reassured by this, as it could all go horribly wrong, but I grab the bag and shoulder it, then turn and walk quickly back the way I came, trying not to look at Gus. When I reach the sunken garden and jump down into it, Popeye grabs the bag and quickly opens it, pawing through the contents. Once he's satisfied, he kneels down and cuts the ties on Adele's feet and hands and orders her to stand.

'Right,' he says, nodding towards me. 'Swap coats.' We hesitate for an instant and then both remove our jackets and swap them. I pull my own coat on, already lamenting the loss of Adele's lovely dark blue pea coat. Then Popeye turns to her and motions towards the playground. 'Get going,' he orders.

Adele hesitates, her eyes darting quickly to mine, then shakes her head.

'No,' she says staunchly. 'I'm not leaving without her.'

Popeye's face darkens. 'What the fuck!' he says angrily.

'You've got what you came for,' says Adele fiercely. 'You can shoot us both right here. Or you can let us go.' She is standing squarely facing him, her chin raised slightly. If she's frightened, she doesn't show it. No way is she going to play by his rules.

What a badass! Honestly, in that moment I could kiss her!

Popeye glares at her for a long moment, his jaw twitching furiously. And then suddenly he whips the butt of his gun hard against the side of her head, knocking her flying. I jump on him, trying to grab the pistol, and we both go down in the dirt. He raises his other hand to punch me, but I duck and somehow the punch misses, and the pistol goes flying out of his hand deep into the hedge. We both lunge for it in the darkness but the hedge is thick and neither of us can see where it landed, much less reach it. I can hear Adele moaning on the ground behind me. Popeye punches me hard, his fist landing square on my cheekbone, and I fall backward, once again seeing stars. He jumps to his feet, grabs the bag and starts to run towards the river. Before I can even think what I'm doing, I leap up and follow, but not before I see Adele out of the corner of my eye on her hands and knees, one hand clutching her head. Popeye races towards the river and I run as fast as I can after him, though I quickly fall behind. He reaches the river several seconds ahead of me and when he does, he throws the bag right over the edge into the water, then jumps in himself.

What the hell?! Is he going to swim away?

And then I hear an outboard engine turning over, and his head appears, together with his arms reaching for the rope that holds the boat fast to a metal ladder on the shore. He's tugging at the rope, which seems to have got snarled, and in the next instant I reach the edge and leap right into the boat beside him, landing in a heap on the floor with a jolt. It's a small inflatable RIB, the sort that tool up and down the Thames in summer with tourists, and it wobbles crazily with my weight. He snarls and turns towards me in fury, and in the next instant I spy the duffel bag on the floor beside me, grab it and chuck it hard over the side into the water. Popeye cries out as the bag hits the swirling waters with a smack and starts to sink. He gives a fierce shout, halfway between a scream of agony and a war cry, and lunges at it with both arms, trying desperately to grab it, but he misses, and in the next instant we both watch the bag disappear beneath the current.

Maybe he doesn't fancy night swimming either.

Popeye spins around to face me with a look on his face that says I am well and truly screwed. I start to back away, but the RIB is only about eight feet long and so there's nowhere to go. The boat is now bobbing furiously in the waves and I am thinking I have only two options: the water or the shore, which is a few feet above my head. Even if I stretch, I'm not sure I can make it to the ladder.

And then I hear a voice behind us shout *'Police! Stay where you are!'*

And it's exactly the voice I've been waiting for.

Chapter Thirty-One

And oh-my-God is there back-up! Gus is the first on the scene, but within a few seconds of his arrival, another dozen police descend upon us in full force like a swarm of hornets, some in full SWAT gear. Popeye's face goes from fury to shock to swift and total comprehension of how much shit he is in.

'Don't move! Show me your hands,' shouts Gus as he edges towards us. His gun and his concentration is focused solely and squarely on Popeye, who slowly raises his hands in the air. Two other officers rush forward and one grabs the rope pulling the boat tighter into the shore.

'Get her out of here,' orders Gus in a hoarse voice and the second officer extends a hand to me. He hauls me up onto land and a third policewoman rushes forward and quickly pulls me away to safety some distance away.

Not once does Gus even look at me.

The policewoman asks if I'm hurt and I shake my head, though my cheek is throbbing from where Popeye punched me. She leads me out of the park to a side road some distance away where I see four black SUVs, their red lights flashing silently, as well as a police van. She opens the rear door to one of the SUVs and suggests I wait inside, but I turn to her.

'My friend's still out there. In the sunken garden. She's hurt,' I say urgently, gesturing towards the park. 'I'll show you,' I start to offer.

She shakes her head and gently but forcefully pushes me

into the back seat of the car. 'No, madam, that won't be necessary. We'll find her,' she says a little brusquely. 'Was anyone helping the man who abducted you?' she asks. I shake my head.

'No, I don't think so. He drove us here on his own.'

'Fine.' She hands me a recovery blanket, which feels a little like tin foil, and a packet of biscuits and a juice box, like I'm in primary school, and orders me to stay put, then closes the door with a decisive thunk. For the next several minutes I watch from the back of the car as they conduct a search of the park, their torch beams criss-crossing eerily in the darkness. I wait anxiously for any sight of Gus or Adele, but neither appear. Eventually two more officers arrive, escorting Popeye, handcuffed, between them. They load him into the police van and one climbs in after him, while the other stands guard outside. But there's still no sign of Gus or Adele. Finally, when I can stand it no longer, I climb out of the car and walk over to where the policeman is standing beside the van. He's speaking into a walkie-talkie. Once he's finished, I step forward.

'Excuse me, could I speak to DC Meadows?' I ask.

'I'm sorry, but he's not available.'

Of course he isn't. Not to me, at least.

'Did you find my friend?'

He shakes his head. 'No, ma'am. We haven't found anyone yet,' he says. 'Though we just recovered a gun in the bushes.'

I stare at him. Adele must have made her own way out of the park somehow after the police arrived. In all the commotion, under cover of darkness, I guess it wouldn't have been too difficult to slip away. I can't really blame her. Besides, she stuck around when it really counted. I hope her head is OK.

305

The bossy policewoman appears suddenly from nowhere and not-so-gently steers me back to the police car. Once I've been reinstalled in the back seat, she and her partner both climb into the front seat and start the engine.

'Where are we going?' I ask anxiously.

'Back to the station,' she says. 'We'll need to take a statement from you.'

'What about the others?' I ask.

'They're still searching the area, madam.'

She turns away and picks up a clipboard, indicating that our Q & A is over, but there's still no sign of Gus. He never even came to check on me.

Or wish me *fare-thee-well*.

DC Hill debriefs me in person, and he does not look happy to be working late. He plunks a tape recorder on the table between us, plants himself in the chair opposite me, then orders me to tell him everything that happened from the time I left the station earlier today, until now. I relate every detail of the evening's events as best I can, and when I get to the part about throwing the money in the Thames, he draws a sharp intake of breath and leans forward, stopping the tape recorder. 'Hang on,' he says. 'You threw the money in the Thames?'

'Yes,' I say. *Surely he knew that?*

'Half a million quid?' His voice is utterly incredulous. Apparently, he did *not* know that.

'Yes,' I say, a little confused. 'Didn't Gus see me? He was right behind me. I mean, he turned up like . . . three seconds later!'

DC Hill places his fingertips on the table and slowly shakes his head from side to side.

'We did not know that. What do you think my guys are

back there searching for right now?' he says in a stern voice. 'They're turning that park inside out!'

I stare at him, stunned. *Whoops.*

'Did it not occur to you to tell someone?' He is practically shouting at me now.

Gosh, he's cross!

I shake my head. 'No one ever asked,' I say, in as apologetic a tone as I can. And I assume Popeye was not exactly going to volunteer this information. He stands up abruptly, shoving his chair back roughly in the process.

'Wait here,' he barks, then quickly leaves the room. Once he's gone, I look around the room with dismay.

Where exactly am I going to go?

It is nearly 2 a.m. when we finish, and I am so tired that all the ceiling lights in the hallway radiate with little halos on them. A policeman is detailed to drive me home, and once there, I realise that I do not have any keys, so we are forced to wake Carl, who is seriously ornery, though he backs down when he sees that I have a police escort.

Charlie Bucket, on the other hand, is over the moon when I unlock the door, as if we have been reunited after a months-long separation, rather than a matter of hours. Once I've rinsed away the evening's events under a hot shower, I crawl into bed and tumble into unconsciousness, my canine partner by my side.

Chapter Thirty-Two

I wake late the next morning and the first thing I see is Charlie Bucket's enormous shaggy head on the pillow next to mine. *Groan*. Only two days ago it was Gus in that spot. How quickly things change! I close my eyes and try to conjure his memory, but after everything that has happened in the interim, it eludes me. Maybe I dreamed the whole thing. I sit up and immediately feel a tender heat rise in my cheek where Popeye hit me. I cross to the bathroom mirror and, sure enough, the side of my face is swollen, the skin mottled and bruised like a Victoria plum.

Smashing.

The police recovered my phone last night, but then promptly confiscated it as evidence, so I am well and truly on my own this morning. Even if I wanted to contact Gus, I have no means of doing so – and I'm not sure what I'd say if I did. He was definitely outside my flat last night when Popeye rang him, so what does that mean? Had he forgiven me? If so, why didn't he speak to me last night after they captured Popeye?

I'm also worried about Adele. Without my phone, there's no way to find out what's happened to her. As I eat my porridge and stare out of the window, I try to put myself in her shoes. Where would she have gone when she left the park last night? Anton would have been top of the list, surely. So she would have made her way straight to The Salty Dog to try to free him. But what if it had taken her too long to get there? After all, she was on foot with no phone. What if the pub had been closed and locked already? She'd have been forced to wait until morning. I quickly open my laptop and check the pub's hours of operation. The Salty Dog is due to open in half an hour. I might just make it if I go now.

Charlie Bucket leaps up as soon as I put my coat on, his tail wagging a little desperately. There's a slightly manic look in his eye, as if he cannot bear to be left alone yet again. Also, I remember with dismay that he's yet to have his morning constitutional. I frown. I reckon it would take us forty minutes to walk there on the lead. Adele might have come and gone by then. So that means we'll have to skate. It's not an enticing prospect. The last time I took Charlie Bucket out on skates, he spotted a black cat on the opposite side of the road and we both nearly met an untimely end. Now I hold up the lead in front of his face. 'Do you promise to behave?' I ask sternly. Before he can reply, I stuff some trainers in a backpack and attach the lead to his collar and open the door. We don't have much time.

Anyway, Charlie Bucket has been known to break his promises in the past.

Once we get outside, he takes care of his business immediately and after that he's surprisingly compliant. He trots along happily by my side, with me on the road and him on the pavement, the lead stretched between us. We garner a few odd looks from passers-by, and even a wolf whistle from a trio of scaffolders, though I'm pretty sure it's Charlie Bucket they fancy rather than me. When we eventually reach The Salty Dog we are five minutes before opening and Charlie Bucket is panting hard.

It's the most exercise he's had in a long time, possibly ever, and I am just bending down to pat his head, when a familiar voice startles me from behind. 'Did he pull you here? Or you him?'

Oh God. I'd know that voice anywhere.

'It was a joint effort,' I say, turning around. Gus is standing a few feet away. Clearly, he had the same idea as me this morning. His expression darkens suddenly when he sees my cheek. He steps forward, nodding at it.

'Are you OK? They told me you weren't hurt last night,' he asks with concern.

'It's nothing,' I say quickly.

'I'm sorry. I didn't realise.'

'It's just a bruise. I'm more worried about Adele,' I say. 'She took a far worse hit than me. That's why I'm here.'

He nods, and glances up at the pub. 'Me too,' he says.

I hesitate. 'But you're here to arrest her. And I'm here to *help* her,' I say, a little desperately.

'No. We're *both* here to help her, Clemency,' he says, stepping forward again. 'We want the same things. The same outcome.'

'Do we?' I ask.

Gus is staring at me intently and my heart is pounding, my stomach flopping around like a just-hooked fish. What exactly are we talking about here? Adele? Or us?

Just then the same bearded barman unlocks the pub door from the inside and props it open. He frowns a little when he sees us. Gus turns back to me. 'Could I please handle this one?' he asks pointedly. 'Alone?'

'Fine,' I say with a sigh.

I sit down on the picnic bench and pull Charlie Bucket between my legs, while Gus walks up to the door of the pub, removing his ID from his jacket pocket, and disappears inside. He's gone for nearly ten minutes, and when he eventually returns, he drops down beside me on the bench.

'They're both gone. Someone jimmied the back door lock last night.'

'Did you search the cellar?' I ask.

He sighs. 'Yes, Clem, I searched the entire place.'

'You know he's working for Popeye, right?' I say, with a nod towards the pub.

'Yes, we know that.'

'What are you planning to do next?'

'I haven't decided yet.'

'Is Popeye still in custody?'

He nods. 'He won't be bailed at this point. Not after what happened last night.'

'Good,' I say. That's one load of worry off my mind.

'And I'm sure you'll be relieved to know that we recovered the money this morning,' he adds. I glance over at him and the corners of his mouth twitch upwards slightly. 'Though what prompted you to throw half a million pounds into a swiftly flowing tidal river, I'll never know.'

'I was trying to stop him fleeing!'

'There were better ways.'

'It worked, didn't it?'

'Miraculously, yes.'

He turns to look at me and I feel myself blush. His face is so close to mine, his lips only inches from my own. I would so love to lean forward and kiss him right now. But something stops me, and Gus does not move either. I find him impossible to read right now. For all I know, I'm still in the doghouse.

He does offer me a lift home in his car, which is something, at least. Charlie Bucket is only too happy to accept, leaping into the back seat as if he belongs there. As I climb into the passenger seat, Gus reaches into his coat pocket. 'Oh,

I almost forgot,' he says, pulling out my phone in a sealed plastic evidence bag. He hands it to me, but I hesitate, looking at him with surprise.

'Did you *steal* that?' I ask.

'No!' He looks at me askance.

'I thought they needed it for evidence,' I say.

'And I told them you needed it more,' he explains. 'Besides, they got what they needed.'

'Oh. OK, thanks,' I say, a little embarrassed.

'Not all of us are thieves,' he says, rolling his eyes and starting the car.

Ouch.

It's only a ten-minute drive back to mine and we ride along in awkward silence. Once again, I find him utterly inscrutable. Should I invite him in for a cup of tea when we get there? Or would that seem presumptuous? I haven't even asked him why he was outside my flat last night! But somehow I can't bring myself to form the question.

Eventually we reach Say Cheese and he pulls over in front of the shop. He puts the car in neutral and switches off the engine. 'Thanks for the lift,' I say, a little awkwardly.

'A pleasure,' he says.

I peer at him. *Is it really?* Or is he just being polite? I put my hand on the door handle, then pause. 'About Adele,' I say cautiously. 'What will you do now?'

'Carry on looking for her. We need her evidence to convict Popeye. She's too important.'

I nod, mulling this over.

'Could she and Anton cut a deal?' I ask.

He shrugs. 'I'm not the final word. But yes, I think they're in a very strong position, if they work with us. Especially after the abduction.' I stare at him, frowning.

Abduction. It sounds ridiculous, but it hadn't really

312

occurred to me that we'd been abducted until just now. First, I'm a criminal. And now I'm an abductee. An unemployed abductee, but still . . .

'So if you were me,' Gus says slowly, 'where would you look next for her?'

My eyebrows shoot up with surprise.

'Are you asking for my help with an investigation, Officer Meadows?' I ask, unable to stifle a grin.

Gus fixes me with an admonishing look.

'It's Detective Meadows,' he corrects me. 'And yes. I am,' he adds in a slightly more conciliatory tone.

I hesitate. I've already been turning this question over in my mind. If I was working on my own, I would probably head to Chelsea next, to find Bex. Where else would Adele and Anton go? I look over at Gus uncertainly.

Can I trust him? Do we really want the same thing?

'Can we come with you?' I ask then. He frowns a little, glancing over his shoulder into the back seat.

'*Both* of you?'

I lift my chin a little stubbornly. Because Charlie Bucket and I are a package deal. 'Yes.'

Gus shrugs and turns the car back on. 'OK.'

I direct him to the salon in Chelsea, and on the way, the atmosphere between us lightens a little. We chat a bit more easily, and Gus asks me about my plans for work. 'I haven't had a lot of time to think about it,' I say truthfully.

'Fair,' he says.

I stare out of the window. The prospect of job-hunting makes me feel vaguely ill. I have absolutely no idea what I will do.

'You like all this, don't you,' he adds a moment later. 'Helping people. Catching the bad guys.' He smiles over at

313

me, but I can tell from his tone that he's serious.

'Yeah, I do,' I admit.

A lot, actually. For the past few weeks, tracking down Adele, I've felt more alive than I have in years.

'And you're good at it,' he says then. I glance over at him. He's watching the road so I can't tell what he's thinking, but that sounded suspiciously like a compliment.

'Thanks,' I reply. I look out of the window so he can't see my grin, but inside I'm cartwheel-happy.

'What'd you study at university?' he asks.

'Psychology,' I say.

He nods. 'You should look into forensic psychology. One of my colleagues did an MSc in it a few years ago. She said the programme was excellent.'

I turn to look at him, a little surprised that he'd suggest this for me, after all we've been through. Maybe he doesn't think I'm irresponsible after all. Or untrustworthy. Or rash.

'I will,' I say, a little flustered.

A part of me is dead pleased that he thinks enough of me to propose this, but the other part is thinking – how on earth would I fund another degree? Gus has no idea how bad my financial situation is. And I would really hate for him to find out. The sick feeling returns to my stomach.

When we reach the salon, we pull up just outside and at once I can see through the window that Bex isn't on the shop floor. Gus stays in the car and I go inside to quiz the purple-black haired receptionist, who seems a little peeved when I ask about Bex. 'She called in sick this morning,' she informs me coldly. 'I had to cancel all her appointments.' She looks at me accusingly, as if Bex's absence is somehow *my* fault.

'You couldn't give me her address, could you?'

'Definitely not.'

'What if it was the police asking?' I say.

Her eyebrows shoot up in response.

It's surprising how much you can achieve with the force of the law behind you. It turns out that Bex lives nearby, in a council flat on the border between Battersea and Clapham, just over the river. It takes us less than fifteen minutes to get there. We drive over Chelsea Bridge and skirt around the outside of Battersea Park, pulling up to the estate about five minutes later. When we arrive, Gus parks and switches off the engine. I turn to him a little nervously.

'Could I please handle this one?' I ask. 'Alone?'

I'm not joking and Gus knows it. I need time with Adele to persuade her to come forward. If he comes with me, it will just scare her off. He looks at me for a long moment, and I can tell that he is sifting through the possible outcomes in his head. He can either trust me to bring in Adele on my own, and risk losing her if I screw up or she panics and flees, or do it himself, and risk the same.

'Okay,' he says cautiously. 'I'll give you ten minutes. But if you're not out by then, I'm coming in after you.'

'Deal,' I say, and climb out of the car. The estate is a mix of concrete high and low rises that probably dates to the fifties. Bex lives on the third floor of one of the lower buildings and it takes me a few minutes to find the right block and entrance. When I do, I press the buzzer for her flat and for a long moment no one answers. Finally, when I have almost given up, I hear her voice come through cautiously. 'Yes?'

'Bex, it's me. Clemency. I need to talk to Adele,' I say urgently.

Once again there's a long silence, and then I hear the door buzzer going. I race up to the third floor and find her

315

flat door, but before I can knock, it opens to reveal Bex standing there. She looks behind me down the hallway. 'Are you alone?' she asks.

'Yes.' She motions for me to come in and closes the door. I step into a tiny entranceway and see a small kitchenette off to the right and a sitting room directly ahead, with plate glass windows and a concrete balcony looking out onto the middle of a grassy quad. I take a step inside and see Adele standing just out of view. She has a nasty cut on her temple, and there are dark circles under her eyes. I cross over to her.

'Are you OK?' I ask anxiously.

She nods. 'Head hurts,' she says with a weak smile. 'But I'll live.'

'And Anton?' I ask.

She hesitates, then nods towards the bedroom. 'Asleep. They roughed him up pretty bad, but he's OK.'

I nod, relieved.

'Popeye's in custody,' I tell her. 'They told me he wouldn't be bailed.'

She closes her eyes for an instant, clearly relieved. 'Hope they lock him up for good,' she says. 'Man's a menace.'

Behind me, Bex gives a little cough. I turn to her and our eyes meet. 'Hey,' she says to Adele. 'We're out of milk. I'm gonna nip down to the shops, OK?' It's like she can read my mind because I really want to talk to Adele alone. She grabs her coat and slips out, and once she's gone, I turn back to Adele, who sinks down onto the sofa. I sit down beside her.

'Adele, what you did last night was incredibly brave,' I say.

'Nah.' She shakes her head, then looks away.

'Really. You're a badass,' I say with a smile.

She laughs a little, then grimaces from the pain to her head.

'Seriously. He could have killed you,' I add earnestly.

She shrugs. 'I just called his bluff,' she says. 'No way was I gonna leave you there. I reckoned I owed you that much.' She looks away then, a little embarrassed.

'Thank you,' I say. I grab her hand and give it a little squeeze. She purses her lips and nods.

'Sorry I did a runner when the police came,' she says. 'I figured you didn't need my help by then.'

I smile. 'They got there just in time,' I say. 'I was lucky.'

'We both were. For once,' she adds. She shakes her head then and smiles. We sit in silence.

'Before I met you, I thought you had this fantastic life,' she says, after a moment. 'Good job, great flat. When Bex found your ID, I thought maybe I could just *be* her. Everything about your life seemed better than mine. That's why I went to all those places you hang out in. I was like . . . trying it on, you know?'

'Now you know better,' I say jokingly.

She turns to me earnestly. 'No,' she says. 'I don't.'

'You can still have that life, Adele. The one you want. It's not too late.'

She rolls her eyes and shakes her head, then nods towards the bedroom. 'Look at us. Bashed up, hiding out here, wanted by the cops. There's nothing out there for us,' she says, indicating the world outside.

'It's not true,' I say urgently. 'You guys are young. You can still make a go of things.'

She shakes her head. I can see she's not convinced.

'Look, the police need your help to convict Popeye. Both of you. If you guys come forward now, you can cut a deal. They'll protect you, and you can start over somewhere else, completely clean. You can get away from all this.'

A pained look crosses her face, as if my words are little arrows. She shakes her head and I see tears start to well in her eyes. She turns away, swipes at them with the heel of her hand. 'It's too late for all that,' she says. 'Me and Anton. We done too much bad stuff. That shit sticks.'

'No. It's not too late. You need to trust me,' I say. 'They're waiting for you to come forward.'

Suddenly we both hear a noise outside. A moment later, there's a knock at the door. Adele's face immediately creases with fear. She looks at me anxiously.

'I thought you said you were alone,' she whispers. I take a deep breath.

'Someone gave me a lift here,' I admit. 'He was waiting downstairs.'

There's a loud bang on the door, much more urgent this time, and then we hear Gus's voice. 'Police! Open up!'

Adele panics and leaps up. 'Oh my God! It's that cop boyfriend of yours, isn't it?' she hisses. 'Popeye was right!'

She looks around in a panic. I take her by the shoulders.

'Please, Adele! You need to trust me,' I say urgently. 'He can help you. I swear!'

Gus bangs again over and over, and this time he calls out my name loudly. I can hear the utter panic in his voice – he's clearly terrified, and so is Adele. She starts to back away from me, like a trapped animal.

'Go into the bedroom,' I tell her quickly, and she nods and rushes down the corridor, disappearing. I hear the bedroom door open and close, and I turn and cross to the flat door. When I open it, Gus grabs me, pulling me into a clench so tight that I can barely breathe.

'Clem!' he utters with relief.

'I'm OK,' I say quickly into his neck.

'Christ, that was a stupid plan!' he mutters into my hair.

He is breathing so hard, and I can feel his heart pounding inside his chest. 'I thought I'd lost you again,' he says. I pull back and look up at him.

'It's not that easy,' I say.

He smiles, in spite of himself. 'I get that.' He heaves a huge sigh of relief, then indicates the room behind me. 'Are they here?' he asks quietly.

I nod. 'She's terrified, Gus. We have to help her. We have to help them both. They're just kids.'

He nods, swallowing. 'OK,' he agrees.

'You promise?' I ask.

'I promise.'

I look up at him and I can't help it any longer. I lean forward and bring my lips to his and his arms pull me in close. He kisses me hard, and for a moment I lose myself completely, forget where we are, my lips melting into his.

Suddenly there's a noise behind us.

'Seriously?' says Bex. We both spin round, embarrassed.

Bex is standing a few feet away in the hallway holding a pint of milk and her keys. She looks from me to him, then back at me again.

'You gonna introduce us, or what?' she says.

'Bex, this is Gus,' I say awkwardly. 'He's um . . . my friend. He's also a cop,' I add, a little reluctantly.

Her eyes widen and she slowly shakes her head.

'Well,' she says. 'Aren't you just *full* of surprises.'

We're lucky Bex is there. It takes a little time, but between the three of us, we persuade Adele and Anton to turn themselves in. Gus calls for a squad car to come to collect them and take them back to the station, where DC Hill is waiting to debrief them, once they've been seen by the nurse for their injuries. Gus escorts them downstairs to the waiting car and I stay behind to speak to Bex alone, promising to join him in a minute.

Once they've gone, she turns back to me. 'Damn, woman,' she says, shaking her head and smiling. 'Shit doesn't half happen to you.'

I laugh. 'It's been a crazy year so far,' I agree.

'I owe you one,' she says. 'Or a hundred,' she adds.

I shake my head. 'We're even. Adele saved my life last night. She was amazing.'

Bex smiles. 'She's a good kid. She deserves another chance.'

'I'll make sure she gets it. And so will Gus. I promise.'

Bex nods, forcing back tears. She wipes at her eyes with the back of her hand. She indicates the direction the others just left.

'Seems nice,' she says with a shrug. 'For a bloke. And a cop,' she adds grudgingly. 'Where'd you find him?'

'In a café,' I say.

'No shit.' She laughs.

'I stole a sandwich,' I add.

She rolls her eyes. 'Figures.'

Epilogue

Hurrah for victim's compensation! Not only did my boss and I get reimbursed for the money we lost, but Adele and I both received a lump sum on top, *for injuries sustained while taking an exceptional risk to prevent a crime.*

When DC Hill presented me with the cheque, I thought he was joking.

'What's this for?' I'd asked with genuine amazement, staring down at it.

'The Criminal Injuries Compensation Authority would like to thank you for your outstanding contribution towards making Britain a safer place,' he'd said, his tone more than a teeny bit glib.

'Are you serious?'

'I wish I wasn't. But yes, it's all yours. They usually come in the post,' he admits. 'But I arranged to have it sent here. Wanted to see the look on your face.'

I was so excited I leapt up and hugged him. Which definitely wasn't appropriate. He literally peeled my arms from around his neck and physically removed me, repositioning me at a safe distance a few feet away.

'A simple thank you will suffice,' he said.

Later that night Gus gave me a very different kind of reward, which was no less gratifying. In fact, he insisted on giving it to me more than once, and who was I to argue? Since the abduction, he has been spending most nights here with Charlie Bucket and me. He says it's because he doesn't trust me to stay out of trouble on my own. But really I think he likes waking up to nearly 200 pounds of canine affection every day. He's been training Charlie Bucket to go jogging with him before work each morning, and I've been training them both to bring me coffee and a croissant from my favourite bakery on the way home.

It's taking time, but they're both learning.

The reward from the compensation scheme has paid off my parent's debts to HMRC, and if I'm careful, it will even be enough to cover the first year of my master's degree. That's assuming I get in, which I'll find out in a few weeks. I had an interview for the programme last Friday. The woman interviewing me was in her early sixties and was surprisingly matronly; I think I was expecting Gillian Anderson, but what I got was closer to Dame Edna. When she asked me why I wanted to pursue a career in forensic psychology, I told her that I thought working with criminals would be more rewarding than working with cheese. She'd frowned at me over her cat's eye glasses.

'That depends on the criminal,' she'd said in a deadpan voice. 'And also the cheese.'

Adele and Anton did cut a deal in exchange for agreeing to testify against Popeye, who's in prison awaiting trial. In the meantime, Anton has been placed in a Jamie Oliver-style former offender's scheme that trains up top-notch chefs for restaurants. And Adele is applying to the fire service! She's having to jump through some extra hoops owing to her record, but DC Hill has written her a glowing recommendation, and I helped her fill out the application. Bex and I couldn't be prouder of her. She'll make a badass firefighter some day!

I told her I might have to commit arson, just to see her in action.

The other night she and I met up for a drink. It was the first time we'd been out together, and when we walked into Dolly's, the young bartender who'd served us did a double take. I hooked my arm in Adele's and pulled her towards the bar, while he eyed us suspiciously.

'One of you owes me money,' he said a little nervously, as we sat down at the counter. 'And I'm not serving you until I get it,' he added gruffly, his face a little flushed. Adele and I grinned at each other.

'It was her,' we both said, in the exact same moment.

Then we burst out laughing.

Tonight is Valentine's Day, and it's the first time in years that I've had someone to celebrate with who does not have dew claws and a tail. I take extra care with my hair and make-up, and after trying on virtually everything in my wardrobe, I settle for the swingy green A-line dress, as it hasn't failed me in the past. I've made a booking for us at the Italian place off Shad Thames that Ethan took me to, and when we arrive, they seat us at the very same table by the window. This would have been fine, but not two minutes later, Ethan arrives with his glamorous French wife, which feels a little close to the bone. He spies me at once and immediately comes over, insisting on introducing her, while I squirm a little uncomfortably in my seat. She is every bit as gorgeous as I'd imagined, and every bit as French, which is to say perfectly coiffed and immaculately dressed – and razor-thin to boot.

Ethan informs us happily that Cecile now lives in London full time, and that they'll be moving to a cottage in the country soon.

'Commuter belt,' he says with a grin. 'In Surrey. Who'd have thought?'

'With a garden and a fireplace?' I ask.

'Two, in fact,' he says proudly.

'I'm happy for you,' I tell him. And I genuinely am.

Once they're gone, Gus reaches for my hand. 'Old flame of yours?' he asks.

'Just a customer,' I say, with a shrug.

'He didn't *act* like a customer,' says Gus.

I smile. 'Are you jealous, DC Meadows?'

'Not at all. What about you? Are you envious?'

'Of her? God no!' I say. 'Far too much work being French. Looking effortlessly fabulous all the time. Plus, I'd struggle with the accent,' I add.

'I meant of their plans,' he says.

'Oh. Well, I wouldn't say no to the fireplace. Or the garden, come to think of it. Or her amazing figure, as long as I didn't have to work at it. But apart from that, not really. Why?'

'No reason,' he says. He takes a sip from his wine. 'You know, I have a working fireplace,' he adds then.

'Do you?' I ask.

He nods. 'And a garden too, actually.' I frown at him.

'Why have you kept this from me?' I say suspiciously.

He shrugs. 'You never asked.'

'Do you have herbaceous borders?' I ask. Julia is obsessed with herbaceous borders, though I have no idea even what they are.

He hesitates, frowning. 'Is that a trick question?'

'It might be,' I say.

'Then I'd rather not answer.'

'I thought you lived in Walthamstow.'

'I do.'

'So it's not a cottage. In Surrey.'

'No. It's a small terraced house. On a nice road, with many others,' he says.

I consider this for a moment, frowning. 'What are your neighbours like?'

'Perfectly congenial,' he says. 'Elderly mostly. A few young families. All sorts, really.'

'How do they feel about giant breeds?'

'I have no idea. Maybe you can ask them.'

'Can we go there this weekend?'

'I don't see why not,' he says.

'All three of us?' I press him.

'All three of us,' he says, in a reassuring tone.

I nod, a little relieved.

'Did you hear that, Charlie Bucket?' I whisper loudly, pulling the white tablecloth to one side. 'If you play your cards right, you might have a real garden to pee in soon.'

Under the table, Charlie Bucket hears his name and lashes his tail violently back and forth, almost causing our wine glasses to topple.

'Steady on,' says Gus, grabbing his glass.

I smile over at him.

Because me and Charlie Bucket are a package deal.

Acknowledgements

Huge thanks to my chief critic and reader Cody Sands. These books would not be written without her unerring eye and constant whip-cracking over my head.

Thanks as well to Nora Schlatte for advice and inspiration on all things roller derby, and Hugo Sands for guided tours of South London.

As ever, I remain indebted to my clever and steadfast agents: Felicity Rubinstein, Sarah Lutyens, Francesca Davies and Hana Grisenthwaite, together with the outstanding editorial team at Orion whose expertise hugely improved this book: Charlotte Mursell, Olivia Barber and Sanah Ahmed.

Lashings of gratitude to the faithful squad at Ink@84 Bookshop whose hard work and love of all things bookish allows me the scope to sneak off and write: Tessa, Maud, Daisy, Kitty, Maya and Margaret; and the crack canine-wranglers downstairs who do the same: Jill Crawford and Darran Anderson.

Finally, I remain indebted to the good women and men of London Metropolitan Police, who remain hard at work safeguarding our identity.

Credits

Natalie Cox and Orion Fiction would like to thank everyone at Orion who worked on the publication of *It Takes Two* in the UK.

Editorial
Charlotte Mursell
Olivia Barber
Sanah Ahmed

Editorial Management
Charlie Panayiotou
Jane Hughes
Alice Davis

Copy editor
Clare Wallis

Finance
Jasdip Nandra
Afeera Ahmed

Proof reader
Laetitia Grant

Elizabeth Beaumont
Sue Baker

Audio
Paul Stark

Production
Ruth Sharvell

Contracts
Anne Goddard

Marketing
Tanjiah Islam

Design
Rabab Adams
Joanna Ridley
Nick May

Operations
Jo Jacobs
Sharon Willis
Lisa Pryde

Sales
Jen Wilson
Esther Waters
Victoria Laws
Rachael Hum
Ellie Kyrke-Smith
Frances Doyle
Georgina Cutler

Publicity
Ellen Turner

If you loved *It Takes Two*, you will love Natalie Cox's debut novel, *Not Just for Christmas*

Charlie hates the holidays, and this year is shaping up to be her worst yuletide ever. Her boyfriend has left her for his personal trainer, her flat is out of bounds after a gas leak, and her mother has gone to spend Christmas in Melbourne with her fifth husband. Finding herself single, mildly concussed and temporarily homeless, Charlie hesitantly agrees to dust off her wellies and spend the festive season in Devon, looking after Cosy Canine Cottages, her cousin Jez's dog-care centre.

However, her plans for a quiet rural Christmas with only the four-legged friends for company are dashed as soon as she meets Malcolm the deaf Great Dane, Hugo, his gorgeous (but engaged) owner, and Cal, the undeniably attractive but unbearably haughty and patronising local vet . . .